David Donachie was born in Edinburgh in 1944, his conception entirely due to an Air Chief Marshal's love of fresh salmon. Educated (poorly) at Holy Cross Academy, he left at fourteen to work in his father's business. Since that unhappy experience, he has had more jobs than birthdays, selling everything from business machines to soap. His longest period of employment was working backstage in various West End theatres. He now lives in Deal with his wife and two children, Thomas and Charlotte.

Also by David Donachie in Pan Books

THE DYING TRADE

David Donachie

THE DEVIL'S OWN LUCK

PAN BOOKS
In association with
MACMILLAN LONDON

First published 1991 by Macmillan London Limited

This edition published 1993 by Pan Books Limited
a division of Pan Macmillan Publishers Limited
Cavaye Place London SW10 9PG
and Basingstoke
in association with Macmillan London Limited

Associated companies throughout the world

ISBN 0 330 31846 2

1 3 5 7 9 8 6 4 2

A CIP catalogue record for this book is available from
the British Library

Phototypeset by Intype, London
Printed by Clays Ltd, St Ives plc

To Vince and Tommy

Harry Ludlow should have run as soon as he spotted the frigate's topsails on the horizon, and got on with his proper business, the taking of French merchantmen for profit. Warships could be left to the Navy.

Now hull-up, she had been speedily identified as the *Verite*, a twenty-eight-gun frigate. Speedily identified because half the sailors aboard the *Medusa* were ex-Royal Navy, including Harry himself. Mind, they could not be sure that in a fit of revolutionary fervour the French had not re-named her. It was no great surprise to find the *Verite* in these waters. Given the recent activities of the *Medusa*, it was remarkable that they had not encountered something like her sooner. War had been declared two months before. Harry, working double tides, had got to sea before the fleet, cruising between the approaches to Brest, La Rochelle, and the Gironde estuary. He had taken a number of well-laden Frenchmen, and was already in profit from the enterprise.

Perhaps that was why he had decided to bait the *Verite*. He could outsail her in most instances. The *Medusa* was a fast-sailing schooner of graceful lines. Perhaps the Frenchman could best him in a really heavy sea. But given that as an exception, the *Verite* would have to catch him completely unawares to have a chance of taking or destroying him. Yet here he was, playing with her, deliberately not sailing at his best, drawing her on after him. And very likely, this was no chance encounter. The merchants of the coastal towns from Bordeaux to Brest would have complained loudly about their losses in ships and valuable cargo. Many voices would have been raised, insisting that something be done to rid them of this pest.

The proper course of action for a privateer was to get as far away as possible from such a potential threat. Harry had quite deliberately chosen to do the opposite. He was now the object of much curiosity, since he hadn't bothered to explain what he was about.

His brother James had been the first to air his doubts, using the privilege of being both family and a shareholder in the *Medusa* to question the captain's decision.

'A little sport?'

'We're not out here for sport, Harry,' said James, putting aside his sketch pad.

Harry just smiled, not the normal reaction of a captain whose orders have been questioned.

'I'm not sure that it is entirely sport.' His brother's question had taken him slightly unawares, forcing him to examine motives which, till that moment, had been instinctive.

'Then what is it?' There was no rancour in the question. James was no sailor and he readily acknowledged it. He would defer to his elder brother in all matters nautical. But he was no fool, and he was curious.

'I think she came out looking for us.'

'All the more reason to avoid her. If she gets within range she'll blow us out of the water. Even I know that.'

'She won't get within range.'

'She's gaining on us now.'

Harry gave his brother an amused look, aware that even someone as inexperienced as James knew that the *Medusa* was not sailing at her best. Rigged as she was the *Medusa* could sail very close to the wind. Heading north, with a steady west-nor'-west breeze, she had more than an edge on the *Verite*. James had watched the crew ease the braces to loosen the mainmast sails so that they would not draw their best. Eased just enough to look, from a distance, as though the *Medusa* was really trying to get away. He had also done a quick sketch of the crew putting the kedge over the side, four barrels lashed together, with just enough ballast to keep them below the surface. This, acting as a drag on the ship, further reduced her rate of sailing. James, using the excuse of his inexperience at sea, was determined to make his brother explain. And not only for himself. He was the only one who dared ask, and it was plain from the looks Harry was getting that James was not the only one who had doubts.

'I confess that I'm an ignorant lubber, Harry. But I can smoke a risk as quick as the next man. And since you're the one who's always harping on about taking no chances at sea, it being such an unforgiving element, it seems a strange way to be going on.'

Much nodding of heads greeted this remark. The crew, especially after their recent successes, had a lot of faith in their captain. They knew him to be a 'proper seaman', equally at home on the quarter-deck of a hundred-gun ship as on a minnow like the *Medusa*. A man who had been at sea since before he was breeched, and who'd had charge of all classes of ship in all manner of weather. A man who'd survived the terrible carnage of a proper sea battle, for Harry, as a junior lieutenant, had taken part in the Battle of the Saintes. Their captain had spent more time afloat than he had on land. He was the type to be careful of his ship and his crew, and given that nothing could be sure at sea, they felt safe in his hands. A few reassuring words and all would be well. There was only one problem. He didn't know what to tell them. Was his behaviour a hang-over from his Navy days, an ingrained desire to do battle with the enemy? Or was it the streak of unpredictability in his nature which had caused him so much trouble in the past, trouble which had placed him here, aboard the *Medusa*, rather than on the quarter-deck of a man-of-war?

James deserved an answer. Yet how to describe something made up from so many strands of experience? Harry was, quite literally, at home on water. He knew the elements, all his senses tuned to pick up the constant variations in the weather and the state of the sea. And he knew, just by looking at the *Verite*, a whole mass of things which would take for ever to explain. He knew that the plan he had yet to fully form had a reasonable chance of success. He had observed the way the frigate was handled. How to distil that into a simple reply?

'If she came out looking for us, we must find a way to discourage her.'

'Surely the fact that she cannot catch us will suffice for that?'

'Not so, James. How we must have hurt the French trade. Our name and activities here, I think, stung them into sending out a warship to either take us, or chase us away. I suppose we should take that as a compliment.'

'That still doesn't explain why we are not doing everything in our power to avoid them.' James gave Harry a look that made it plain that he was not going to be fobbed off.

'I am not obliged to explain my actions, even to you, brother.' Harry said this quietly, with a smile. Not always a gentle man, he still felt the need to treat James with respect. How different his brother looked from the gaunt creature who had come aboard at the beginning of their voyage.

'You're ready enough to explain everything else we do, why not this?' James picked up his sketch pad again, and with quick strokes started to draw Harry, an action which had one purpose. It allowed him to remain silent.

Harry's smile grew even broader.

'I have obviously not explained fully, that aboard ship a captain's word is law.'

'What about a brother's word?'

'Such distinctions do not exist at sea.' Harry indicated the *Verite*. 'But since I have brought you out to sea to make a sailor of you, I see no harm in continuing your education.'

'You're wasting your time, brother, I'm only fit to haul on a rope. If Father was still alive, he would disown me.'

The idea of James, even now dressed in a smart buff coat, hauling on ropes, was absurd. Harry, yes. They were similar in appearance, if you excluded girth. Both handsome men with fair hair, Harry was broad and his face weatherbeaten. His clothes, no matter what the quality, rarely made him look like a gentleman. James was pale, slim, and elegant, his movements refined. His natural milieu was the drawing-room of a grand

4

house, not the quarter-deck of a ship. He behaved in a manner that befitted a rising artist, someone whose commissions were shown in the salons where the rich and influential gathered, a man who'd been proposed as a member of the Royal Academy.

When Harry was a boy, their father had been a senior naval captain. While the family was comfortable, they were not wealthy. He'd entered his eldest son on the books of his ship as soon as he could, committing him to following in his father's footsteps. By the time James came along, their father had become an admiral. By the proper exercise of influence, he had secured for himself a three-year term of command in the West Indies, retiring from that with a substantial fortune. Admiral Ludlow then did the proper thing; bought a country estate, including a couple of parliamentary seats, and set himself up as a landed gentleman. His younger son had, quite properly, been kept away from a life at sea. For him, it had been tutors, school, and university. Gilded youth, some said. Had the recent scandal destroyed all that?

'If you look closely, James,' Harry continued, his glass trained on the frigate, 'you will observe that the man who is in command of the Frenchman is lacking in sea-going experience. His crew are not much better. And he seems to have put to sea in something of a hurry.'

'How so?' James put aside his pad and raised his telescope to look at the frigate.

'First, his ship is not properly trimmed. He's stowed his holds badly. She seems to be down at the head. The way he has rigged her sails is making this worse. It is a common mistake to assume that the more sails you set, the faster you will go through the water.'

James had a noncommittal look on his face. He knew that Harry, ten years his senior, would want him to say something intelligent, something that would demonstrate that Harry's lengthy explanations, these last weeks, were having some effect. But for the life of him he could think of no observation that would please his elder brother.

'Observe how his bowsprit dips into the sea. He is overpressing her,' said Harry patiently. 'That is, pushing her head down even more, increasing the drag on the bows, slowing himself quite considerably.'

'Perhaps he is playing with us.'

'Now that would be an interesting game!' Harry's eyes lit up at the prospect.

'Which takes us back to my original question. You have yet to explain the purpose of the game.'

'The purpose?' said Harry, with feigned surprise. 'Why, I intend that she should be taken or destroyed.'

'Then you had better pray for some assistance.' James indicated the guns on the deck. They were not enough to take or destroy a frigate.

'You know me, brother. I'm not much given to prayer. I'm happier with a fine calculation of chances.'

'A fine private calculation?'

Harry laughed out loud.

'James. You are incorrigible. Father was right to educate you. You would never have made a King's officer.'

'You mean I would actually be able to uphold a family tradition. Now that would be unusual.' This time they both laughed. Few people could make a joke of Harry's dismissal from the service. James was one of them.

They were more like friends than brothers. Perhaps it was the difference in age which had kept them from mutual jealousy. Harry, away at sea most of the time, had always been a hero to James. As a small boy, nothing pleased him more than his elder brother's homecoming. Harry, perhaps because of the long separations, loved James, and was open in his affections. Naturally, as James grew older, his awe and hero worship had been replaced by insolence until he had reached an age where, despite the ten-year gap, they could behave as equals.

Equals with different skills. Harry had spent his life at sea, first in the Navy, and then, after his dismissal from the service, in the running of fast cargoes from the Indies. James, with his better formal education, could show away in Latin and Greek, and discourse wisely on philosophy. But his first love was art. He had studied under Reynolds, taking a basic ability to draw and turning it into a sought-after gift for painting.

Harry was as lost in a drawing-room as his brother was on a quarter-deck. Even his sister, Anne, who adored both her brothers, would blush for shame at some of Harry's more blatant gaucheries. But home was in the country, and Harry compensated for the occasional *faux pas* with his daredevil attitudes. He rode harder to hounds than any of their neighbours, played effective, if unstylish, cricket, and always entered for the more physical competitions at the local fair.

Both had sadly neglected the duties that fell upon them as heirs to a great deal of land, wealth, and influence, leaving that task, after their father's death, to their sister Anne's husband. Arthur, Lord Drumdryan was a man with a title, but no money of his own. Their brother-in-law had happily taken it upon himself to ensure that neither their wealth nor their influence were in any way diminished by their frequent absence. He appointed the two members who sat for the parliamentary seats that Harry controlled, and corresponded regularly and fluently with whoever was in power. For this Arthur was rewarded with a life of luxury that he could otherwise never have attained. It was one of the few points of friction that existed between Harry and James. Affable Harry liked Arthur well enough. James, seeing instead a stiff pedant, couldn't abide him.

Harry reflected that, given the gossip that was current in town, James had chosen to accompany him on his voyage as the lesser of two evils. That he had to leave London was plain. The thought of facing their brother-in-law in such a situation would, for James, be intolerable. And in this respect Arthur was just as much at fault. For a man who prided himself on the quality of his manners, he showed a singular lack of restraint when it came to what he saw as James' failings.

Country or sea air, it seemed to have had a positive effect. James had been drinking to excess just a few weeks before, seeking to drown his sorrows. Now he was, again, the rational, urbane man that Harry remembered. The cause had never been mentioned. James might have had the words to eloquently describe his difficulties, but his brother certainly lacked the verbal skills to effect a cure. And given his own chequered past, Harry was not humbug enough to remonstrate with James.

7

Arthur would not have been able to contain himself, which would have led to another family row, another demand from James that their brother-in-law took too much upon himself.

Yet where would Harry be without him. Certainly not here, in the Bay of Biscay. It was Arthur, who, hounding the Admiralty, had arranged Harry's Letters of Marque, permitting him to sail as a privateer, plus the exemptions needed to crew the *Medusa* in time of war, when the nation was chronically short of proper sailors.

'You still haven't told me what you intend. I'm beginning to suspect that you don't know yourself.'

That had been true when James had first asked, but now Harry, as usual thinking while he was talking, had ordered his thoughts, putting aside the nagging suspicion that he was behaving impetuously.

'If she's come out looking for us, then giving her the slip won't stop her. In fact, it will tell her more about us than I'd want her to know. If we stay in these waters we are bound to run into her again. First she would try to catch us out, like being upwind of us at first light and close enough to get off a couple of broadsides before we could get out of range.'

'And if that fails?'

'There are lots of other possibilities. But if we continued to evade her, it would only be a matter of time before she came after us with a couple of consorts.'

'Can the French muster three frigates just to chase us?'

'They wouldn't have to be frigates, James. Even a couple of ships smaller than the *Medusa* would answer. As long as they could slow us down enough for her to come up and finish us. Right now, what she needs to know is how fast we sail, and how the *Medusa* handles.'

'Can she really learn that much from this distance?'

'Why yes! You can tell a great deal from just observing the way a ship sails. About her crew, and her captain.'

'That explains her actions, Harry, not ours.'

'So we turn the tables on her. I want to draw her on, into exactly the kind of situation that I suspect she would be forced to use on us. With this wind it's the best chance we've got.

Somewhere over the horizon are the frigates of the squadron blockading Brest. We must interest one of them in the *Verite*.'

'But won't she turn and run if she spies a British warship?'

'I expect so. But then it will be our job to slow her down, and let our ship come up to engage. A neat reversal, wouldn't you say?'

'Harry. You're mad.'

'Am I, James?' Again that nagging suspicion that his brother might be right. 'If I am going to have to fight this fellow, I would rather fight her in company than alone. And I think I can keep us out of harm's way for long enough to make that happen.'

'And in this fine calculation of chances, how long have you allowed?'

'Till nightfall. If we haven't come across one of our warships by then, we'll slip the kedge and outrun her in the dark. That way she will not see our rate of sailing.'

James pulled a gold hunter from his waistcoat pocket.

'We have about ten hours,' said Harry.

'The whole plan is ingenious.' There was a twinkle in James' eye.

'I think so,' said Harry.

'Especially considering you have only just thought it up.'

Harry tried to look stern and uncomprehending, but the smile forced its way through.

'I have to have some pleasure in life, brother, and besides, as you have often remarked, I have the devil's own luck.'

They sailed on through the morning, the *Verite* slowly gaining on the *Medusa*. Harry kept a strict naval routine on the ship, echoing the Navy in the way he split the watches and messed the men. The *Medusa*, fully manned, was a crowded ship, again just like a man-of-war. Fast, and armed with twelve nine-pounders, her job was to capture merchantmen, not destroy them. For that she needed men to form boarding parties and to provide prize crews after a successful action. That they could also handle the guns with speed and accuracy was a commendable bonus, one that Harry had insisted on. Most of his fellow privateersmen would not have bothered to expend the money on powder and shot necessary to make their crew proficient in that area. Harry, perhaps more prescient, knew that if he stayed at sea long enough he was bound to encounter an enemy warship. Good gunnery could mean the difference between escape or capture.

The lookout in the tops gave the cry of 'sail ho' at about two o'clock, just as the watch was changing. Everyone stayed on deck as the sail was identified as a British seventy-four-gun ship.

'I'd have preferred a frigate,' said Harry, raising his glass to his eye. 'Though with this fellow, it may not make a great deal of difference.' He indicated the Frenchman.

'Let me know the minute you make her number,' he shouted to the lookout. Harry reached into a locker and came out with an official naval signal book.

'As part of your nautical education, James, I shall give you the honour of supervising the raising of the signals.'

'Ay, ay, Captain,' said James, touching his forelock and assuming a gruff lower-deck voice. 'Would ye care to be a-telling me which one?'

'I think we could start with "Enemy in sight". He should deduce from that we are being chased. Then our name, letter by letter, and the signal for a Letter of Marque. He should be able to tell from that who we are.'

'Might he not also deduce that he is being tricked?' James was already leafing through the signal book, looking for the flags required.

'He'll come and have a look. Once he's seen the *Verite* he'll give chase. Even together we represent no threat to a seventy-four.'

'How can you be so sure of all this?'

Again Harry looked mildly surprised.

'I mean, how can you assume that this fellow will understand your intentions. Can you be sure that he will try to attack the enemy?'

'He won't be in command long if he fails to! They shot Admiral Byng for failure in that quarter.'

'All right, but how can you then be so sure that he will do what you want him to?'

'He doesn't have to do what I want him to. He just has to do the right thing.' Harry said this so emphatically that further questioning seemed superfluous. Yet James was as aware as anyone of the gap that existed between an officer's duty and his actions.

'What we have to hope is that she is not one of the Forty Thieves, because if she is, we might as well abandon the whole thing.'

Harry was referring to a class of ship, seventy-four gunners, that, in an age noted for its corruption, were notorious for the poor quality of their build. They were slow, slab-sided tubs made of green timber that leaked in any kind of sea. It was one of the great burdens of the Navy that, being so numerous, they formed the backbone of the fleet. That they were also known as 'widow makers' testified to the number that had been lost in storms.

'Will that make it difficult?'

'It will probably make it impossible. I can only seriously delay that Frenchman for so long without endangering our ship. Eventually we are bound to sustain some damage. And if he does manage to get a clear shot at us . . .' Harry shrugged his shoulders, but the meaning was plain.

'I don't suppose that anyone will persuade you to drop the whole idea?' Harry looked sharply at his brother. 'And it is not fear that makes me say that.'

'I can't stand the suspense,' said Harry, glancing aloft. 'I shall have to go and have a look myself.' They both knew he was ducking the question.

Harry tucked his telescope into his belt, and headed for the shrouds. These ran, like an ever-decreasing rope ladder, from the side of the ship up into the top. Harry climbed up the mainmast shrouds, then on to the topmast shrouds. He climbed up to the crosstrees, slinging his leg over the topmast yard and allowing his body to roll with the action of the ship. He nodded to the lookout, and raised his glass to his eye.

The seventy-four, just a sail on the horizon to the naked eye, leapt into plain view. His heart gave a little flip as he recognized the *Magnanime*. He had sailed in her as a lad when his father

II

was captain. He knew her to be a flyer despite her age. She had been captured from the French by Anson. Many ships since built by British yards had been broken up, but the *Magnanime* sailed on. Built from timber cut on the site, put together under cover instead of being allowed to rot in the open, she was visible proof of the ability of the French to design and build better ships than the British.

If her bottom was clean and her timbers still sound she could manage twelve knots in this wind. That might explain her position, out here on the edge of the area patrolled by the blockading squadrons, a role normally reserved for the frigates. He watched her for a while, noting the way she was sailing and remembering his days aboard her as a young, and mischievous, midshipman. Captain Ludlow had seen his eldest son stretched across a gun many times, stoically receiving a beating for some escapade or other.

Harry turned his glass back to look at the *Verite*. The way she was being handled, the *Magnanime* might even have the legs of her. It all depended on the seventy-four's captain. He didn't know who had her now, but from the mere knowledge that it was such a fine, fast sailing ship, he could finalize the details of his plan.

Handing his glass to the lookout, he slid down a backstay to the deck and snapped out the orders to stand by. Orders that would cast off the kedge, trim the sails, and man the guns. James tried to stay out of the way as this operation was carried out. The deck was suddenly still, everyone in their place, ready for the moment when the *Verite* sighted the *Magnanime*.

II

The cry of 'sail ho' did not interrupt the punishment taking place on the deck of the *Magnanime*. Very few of the crew, brought aft to witness the punishment, turned their heads from the bloody scene before them. The grating was rigged, and the bos'n, sweating freely, was finishing his two dozen with the cat. The man had long since passed the point where he could feel any pain. He hung limp, the ropes binding him to the grating cutting into his wrists, the blood running freely down his torn back and staining his grimy duck trousers at the waistband. He was the third member of the crew to receive a flogging on this occasion and the deck leading from the grating to the stairwell was already liberally spotted with dark red stains. The canvas at the man's feet, laid down to catch the blood, was swimming with the rapidly blackening gore, as it mixed with the sea water which had been thrown over the gaping wounds of the previous 'offenders'.

As soon as the punishments ended, hands would be set to swabbing and holystoning the deck. More flogging would follow if it was not returned to its previous snow-white condition. No one would speak out at this, for it only took a malignant officer to imagine that he overheard any dissent to make a case which could have a man hanging from the yard-arm for mutiny. Thus men whose daily lot was back-breaking work, on a diet of poor food and often foul water, with constant exposure to disease, death, and injury, said nothing, refusing even to glance at their commander, lest he see the look of hate in their eyes.

Oliver Carter, himself looking at the deck, did not even raise his eyes to the lacerated back as the cry came, and since he didn't move, neither did anyone else. They were not entirely still. Bentley, the First Lieutenant, his eyes fixed steadily on the man hanging limp on the grating, was swaying perceptibly, an action which had little to do with the motion of the ship.

The other officers stood in various poses, seemingly indifferent to the scene. They had observed much of this in their life, too much on this commission, and it would never do to be seen to be moved by it. The marines, lined up on the poop, muskets in their hands, looked out over everyone's head towards the bows. Only their officer, Mr Turnbull, evinced any interest in the scene taking place beneath their noses. The parson, Mr Crevitt, stood Bible in hand, silently mouthing a prayer. He too gazed at the victim's back, but he seemed to do it from a sense of duty, a feeling that he could not offer comfort if he had not observed the pain. The bucket of salt water was thrown over the man's back as the bos'n put the blood-stained cat back into its red baize sack.

Outhwaite, the surgeon, ran forward as they cut him down. He examined the man quickly, and ordered the waiting seamen to take their messmate below. He stood, looking at his captain, who seemed to be in some kind of trance. Carter suddenly realized that Outhwaite was looking at him. It seemed to bring him back to the present. Bentley, too, seemed to awake from his dreamlike state.

'Punishment completed, sir,' he said, looking around, as if unsure that what he said was correct.

Carter stood beside Bentley, with the look of a man waiting for something on his face. The other officers deliberately turned their heads away, wishing neither to assist their first lieutenant, nor to risk the wrath of their unpredictable commander by acknowledging that the second-in-command had failed to behave correctly. Bentley was rescued by the lookout, who chose to complete the message.

'Schooner fine on the weather bow.'

'Permission to dismiss the men, sir,' said Bentley.

'Carry on, Mr Bentley,' said Carter coldly. Even in the lofty tone normally used by a captain when issuing orders, his lack of regard for Bentley was manifest.

The orders were given. The men dispersed slowly, their feelings for what they had just witnessed plain in their gait. At this point the captain would normally have left the deck, but he stayed, waiting to hear details of the other ship.

'Sail has hoisted a signal,' cried the lookout.

'Get the hands about their duties, Mr Craddock,' snapped Bentley, turning to the second lieutenant, an elderly red-faced man. Aware that Carter was staring at him, Bentley pulled himself erect and sent a midshipman aloft with a telescope. The midshipman called down the number of the flags. Another young gentleman leafed through the signal book.

'The sail is signalling "Enemy in sight" sir.'

Silence followed this shout. Bentley was shaking his head, as if to clear it.

'Ask her to make her number, Mr Bentley,' said Carter, plainly angry.

'She hoisted a fresh signal, sir,' said the voice from above. Shout followed shout as the signal midshipman on the quarterdeck deciphered the message.

'She's the *Medusa*, sir,' said the young man finally. Then after a pause to read the last few flags, 'Privateer.'

'Privateer,' shouted Carter, his face going red. 'What the devil is a privateer doing flying naval signals?'

'Why, I imagine he is trying to tell us something, sir.' Bentley made no attempt to mitigate the sarcastic tone in his voice. Even though they were accustomed to Bentley's insolent air with the Captain, the other officers registered embarrassment. Carter flushed bright red.

'He has no right to tell us anything in that manner, Mr Bentley. And neither have you.'

'Ay, ay, sir,' said Bentley quickly, but there was a trace of a smile on his lips. He walked up to his captain and spoke quietly in his ear.

15

'If I'm not mistaken the *Medusa* is owned by Harry Ludlow.'

Carter said nothing, but the look of anger turned to one of shock.

'Another sail, same bearing,' cried the midshipman that Bentley had sent aloft.

'He's giving me orders, damn him,' snapped Carter.

'She's flying French colours, sir.' Then almost without a pause: 'She's let fly her sheets. *Medusa* has worn. She's signalling, sir. "General chase".'

Bentley, coming to life, started to rap out a series of orders that would bring all hands on deck and send men up into the tops to set more sail.

'Mr Bentley,' screamed Carter. 'Belay!'

Everyone stopped where they were. Was this the long-awaited confrontation? No one knew why such a hard horse captain allowed Bentley such liberties. They had waited a long time for the moment when Carter would haul him up with a round turn.

'Belay, sir?' said Bentley quietly. Again that smile.

'Are you obeying the instructions of a bloody privateer, man?'

Carter's shouted question ignored the presence of everyone else. Yet they were left to wonder why a captain was brought to discussing his orders, publicly, on his own quarter-deck.

'I am seeking to profit from the news she is giving us. If the *Medusa* is running, she can only be running from a superior enemy. That would imply that the chase is French. Perhaps a warship?'

Carter's face froze. Bentley was talking to him in the most outrageous manner, completely ignoring the courtesies required when addressing a superior officer. He also had the right of it, and no one would really understand Carter's hesitation.

'Permission to make more sail, sir,' said Bentley.

'Carry on, Mr Bentley.' It was hissed rather than spoken. Carter turned his back on Bentley, wanting no one to see the expression on his face.

Harry rapped out his orders as the *Verite*, having sighted the *Magnanime*, shot up into the wind, her sails flapping. The cable holding the kedge was cut, and the parties manning the falls let go of the sails. The man at the wheel spun it quickly and the *Medusa* wore round. Another command had the men hauling again, this time bowsing the sails tight. The *Medusa* was round, with the wind abaft the beam, and heading quickly for the *Verite* before the Frenchman, having missed stays in his attempt to tack, had got any way on him.

Harry, having had James standing by, added the signal 'General chase' to the one already flying. He knew that he risked causing offence. No naval officer would take kindly to any sort of command from a mere privateer. But he could think of no other clear way to signal his intentions, other than the use of the Navy's own signal book. He left the signal flying long enough to ensure that it had been read, before hauling it down and replacing it with 'Am engaging'.

The seventy-four was cracking on. Harry saw sails flashing in and out as the captain looked for his best point of sailing. The *Magnanime* heeled over under the press of sail, her lower larboard ports under water as she shot along, her bowsprit sending up great cascades of water. Harry himself was gaining fast on the *Verite*. His first task was to outreach her and get ahead so that the *Medusa* could interfere with her attempts at flight. But before that he must sting her in the tail, sting her so hard that she would turn to deal with him while the gap between her and the *Magnanime* was still wide enough to ensure escape.

The guns were run out to starboard. He could not run out his larboard guns. The heel of the ship was too great to allow that. But they had been run out, loaded, run back in, and bowsed tight inboard. They were ready to fire the minute the *Medusa* shortened sail and the deck became level again. Right now it was like a pitched roof.

Harry stood there, his arm looped round a backstay as he watched the relative positions of the three ships. He was gaining fast on the *Verite*. He raised his glass to watch the Frenchman's quarter-deck. At all costs he must ensure that they didn't best him by turning to fight him before he had got into position. Again he noticed how the French captain was overpressing her, pushing her head down by carrying too many upper sails, more

17

obvious now with the wind pushing him forcefully. That, and what he had seen of her attempt to bear up and get away, underlined his earlier feeling that it was not only the captain who lacked experience, but the entire crew.

The whole scene seemed to freeze. Men stood still, and to an untrained eye so did the ships. The gain seemed barely noticeable, and James, exhilarated in spite of his doubts, felt the first pangs of impatience begin to invade his excitement. His drawing materials had been put aside.

'How long before we catch him?' he shouted to his brother.

'Within the hour,' said Harry, as though that meant immediately.

They raced on, with only the position of the *Medusa* seeming to alter, as she slowly increased the distance between herself and the seventy-four, and drew closer to the *Verite*. Yet the seventy-four was gaining. Harry could see the French officers plainly now, gathered at the taffrail, their glasses concentrated on the *Magnanime*. They would be content, sure that if need be they could deal with him and still get away. He was looking forward to surprising them.

Harry steered the *Medusa* until she was sitting in the Frenchman's wake. There was a flash from the stern and he saw the ball fired by the stern chaser fly overhead to land harmlessly in his wake. They would keep shooting at him, hoping that they would wound a spar, or even better the mast, and thus reduce his speed.

'Is there nothing we can do in reply, Harry?' shouted James, as the second ball sent up a plume of water on the starboard side.

'Not for a while. We could only use the starboard chaser, and on this deck I would think we would just be wasting powder and shot. But when we pay them back, it will be more than in kind.'

Ball followed ball, one better aimed than the rest going clean through the maincourse, leaving a neat round hole. But they missed the wood, their prime target if they were to achieve anything. Harry gave orders to stand by. Men ran along the steeply sloping deck to take up their various stations. Harry knew that his guns were pitifully light for an action against even the smallest frigate, but his attack would be delivered against the unprotected stern. Any ball that could penetrate the deadlights, which had been shipped to cover the frigate's stern windows, would run the whole length of the lower deck. The potential for damage to wood was minimal. But flesh and blood could not withstand it. His aim, anyway, was to make him turn, and seek to rid himself of this pest.

Harry yelled the command and the way came of the *Medusa*, as the quarter-master swung the wheel. She came round, her starboard guns facing the stern of the *Verite*. Harry did not fire a broadside, but instead instructed each gun to fire as it bore. One by one the guns went off, smashing into the heavy wooden shutters. He could hear the sound of breaking glass as one shot followed through the hole made by the previous round. He shouted again, and those men set to look after the sails hauled on their ropes to bring the yards round. The *Medusa* caught the wind, and as the guns were reloaded she set off again in pursuit of the quarry.

Three times Harry carried out this manoeuvre, but instead of firing into the stern of the *Verite* he set his guns at maximum elevation, firing on the up-roll, both trying to hit a spar, as well as unnerving those directing the battle from the quarter-deck of the frigate. The actual damage he caused was minimal, but the French captain could not let the *Medusa* just continue, since she was bound to inflict some serious damage eventually.

Harry, gaining speed in the wake of the *Verite* after his fourth sally, saw the French crew rushing to man the sheets. These ropes, once loosened, would allow the yards to swing, taking the pressure off the sails. The helmsman could then use the rudder and the remaining forward movement of the ship to swing her broadside on to the *Medusa*, bringing her guns to bear on the smaller ship that would, if properly aimed, inflict terrible damage.

But this was just what Harry had set out to do. First to get the *Verite* to confront him, thus slowing her down. Then to use the superior sailing qualities of the *Medusa* to get past the Frenchman. Placed in front of her, the task of slowing her down would be simpler. The question was, which way would the *Verite* turn? Would she tack or wear?

Harry had all his men in place. He watched the rudder, hanging from the great sternpost, waiting. He wanted to pass her stern close to, and fire a full broadside into it as he did so. He saw the sails flap as the yards were released. The rudder started to swing the *Verite* to starboard. He set the wheel and trimmed the *Medusa*'s yards to take her to larboard. It was a dangerous manoeuvre. If the Frenchman came round quickly, she would get a broadside off at him before he could get out of the way. Harry was entirely reliant upon their lack of skill.

The side of the *Verite* started to show, the row of open gun-ports coming into view. He could see the men on the guns trying to lever them round so that they could fire on the *Medusa* as soon as possible. The *Verite*, coming up into the wind, was trying to use that to check her way. Harry needed the same wind to escape. It was kinder to him than it was to the French-man, whose sails were simply not coming in quick enough for a speedy manoeuvre. Harry, at the wheel himself, had the wind perfectly placed abaft the beam. Still, it was a narrow scrape. The *Verite*'s side disappeared in a cloud of smoke. One shot smashed the stern lantern, but the rest fell harmlessly, churning up the sea behind him.

'Back the fore topsail,' he yelled as he came across her stern. The *Medusa*'s speed was slightly checked, and as she drifted by the *Verite* his gunners, now firing from a steady platform, poured a telling broadside into the Frenchman at point-blank range.

'Man the braces,' he shouted. 'Haul away!' The foretopsail was hauled tight again and the *Medusa* sailed past the French-man. Harry let her pay off to keep his ship out of the arc of the enemy's guns. He saw that they were setting sail again. But now he was ahead of them, and he could see that the last manoeuvre had cost the *Verite* a good mile. The *Magnanime* was coming up hand over fist.

Now the most dangerous part of the game had to be played. He had to slow his opponent down when she had the weather gage. Up until then he had held the advantage of the wind. He loaded his guns with grape. His guns were too light to cause any serious damage to the mainmasts of a warship at this range, but a steady diet of grapeshot across her deck would make them shear away, slowing their progress. As long as they did not take the wind out of his sails he would be able to manoeuvre. If it should happen that the *Verite* got between him and the wind, he would be at the Frenchman's mercy, and that, even with poor gunnery, could only have one result.

He darted in and out firing his guns from a position on her larboard quarter, then turning away and using his speed to get out of harm's way. And his plan was working. The *Verite*, faced with his assaults, could not maintain her best rate of sailing, constantly having to shear away to avoid his thrusts. The *Magnanime* was closing. Four times he stood in towards her quarter and fired his deadly grapeshot. The screams could be clearly heard across the intervening sea. The *Verite* replied with as many of her forward guns as could be brought to bear, but these were few, and wildly aimed.

The critical moment was approaching, the time when he would have to actually take station across the bows of the *Verite*, a time when she would have to turn to meet the bigger enemy bearing down on her. At that moment she would be doomed, for the *Magnanime* would do as much damage to the *Verite* as the *Verite* could do to the *Medusa*.

'Bar shot,' he called to the gun captains. He was going in much closer on this attack. So now he would aim at the sails, using two ingots linked by chain to slice through some of his opponent's rigging. If she was busy splicing ropes, she would have fewer men free to man the guns on both sides. Harry turned to his brother, who stood at the taffrail, sketching madly, as he tried to record the scene for a future series of paintings.

'We come to the high point of the action, James,' he shouted. 'You will observe the *Magnanime* will soon be shortening sail, reducing to topsails only. She will turn to face our foe, and seek to rake the *Verite*. If the French captain is wise, he will fire a broadside for the sake of his honour, then strike his flag. I fear I must leave the Navy to take the man's sword, but I will try to get you over there in time to record the ceremony.'

James just smiled and waved, then carried on drawing.

Harry gave the orders that brought the *Medusa* round yet again. The French captain might be inexperienced, but he was no fool. He knew what was coming, and the action of the *Medusa* had ceased to interest him. He had manned his starboard guns and was turning to face the *Magnanime*, himself shortening sail to avoid the risk of fire.

'Aim high,' shouted Harry. 'He'll be down to topsails soon.' The *Medusa* was practically stationary, Harry having reduced sail, just like the *Verite* which lay broadside on to her, her larboard guns unmanned. He could see the topsails of the *Magnanime* through the enemy rigging. He gave the command and the *Medusa*'s guns spoke. He heard the whistle of the bar shot as it sliced its way towards his now vulnerable foe. He was in high spirits, his face flushed; he knew that success was assured.

At that moment his face froze. The *Magnanime* should have come on, ready to turn and pour a broadside into the Frenchman. Instead he saw the bigger ship back its topsail and lose what little forward speed it still maintained. It was heaving to, out of range of the enemy's guns, leaving him at the mercy of the *Verite*. There was a period in which no one moved, except his brother, who was still drawing furiously, unaware of the danger. He saw the gunners on the *Verite* rush to the larboard side. Their guns were already loaded and run out. His, aimed at the rigging and reloaded with bar shot, were useless.

He just had time to turn round and shout to his brother to get down, when the side of the *Verite* erupted in smoke. The world exploded around him, guns were dismounted, the side was smashed and the deadly splinters took their toll. He started to give commands that would get his ship under way, removing her from this arc of certain destruction, but hearing the cracking sound of wood splitting, he looked up to see the mainmast breaking above the cap. There was a tearing and crashing sound as it ripped apart the rigging. Blocks were falling and men were running as the great length of timber crashed to the deck. Harry opened his mouth to shout as something hit him. He staggered then collapsed on deck, blood streaming from his head. He tried to rise. Surprised to see James still standing with a shocked look on his face. Then there was blackness.

III

The bright blue sky hurt his eyes as he tried to open them. He was aware of the light, the pain in his head, and a powerful smell of bad breath as a silhouetted head came between him and the sky. Another dark shape obscured some of the sky.

'Back, sir, I pray. Let him breathe some air.' The other head pulled back and Harry heard his brother's voice.

'Will he survive?'

'Too early to say, sir. Too early to say.'

In the background Harry could hear shouted commands. Men were moving about, blocks were creaking and ropes straining. He judged by the motion of the deck that he was still aboard ship. But which ship? He struggled to sit upright. The sharp pain in his head made him fall back again.

'Easy now, sir,' said the man above him. Any comfort intended from the words was entirely washed away by the foul blast of air. Harry lay back, the memory of the action with the *Verite* filling his mind. Something had gone wrong, and he could not think what it was. Why had the *Magnanime* hove to at the critical moment?

'Mr Outhwaite. I would be obliged if you could move your patient below. We are about to commence firing.'

The voice cut through Harry's pain. At first he refused to believe that he had heard right. But Outhwaite's reply laid any doubt.

'A few moments more, Captain Carter, if you please. No good will be served by killing a man for the sake of a minute.'

'Waste not a minute,' said Harry.

'You remember, Ludlow.' Another shadow stood over him.

Harry lifted his head again. This time he ignored the pain. He started to get up from the deck. Hands grabbed him to help him up. He stood swaying, trying both to remain standing and to focus on the man before him.

'Harry?' James' voice was full of concern.

'A fine calculation, James. Is that not what I said?'

'You must come below, sir,' said Outhwaite.

'I calculated everything, James. Everything except the fact that this man would be captain of the *Magnanime*.'

Harry tried to point at Carter. But he was too weak to raise his arm.

Oliver Carter was not as tall as Harry remembered. Or was it the fact that he had grown fat that made him seem small? But the face, round though it now was, carried the same expression. And the smile, utterly without warmth, was very familiar. The hatred in the eyes was unmistakable.

'I'm glad you are up and about, Ludlow. You are just about to see me remove a serious hazard to shipping.'

Harry looked past Carter to where the *Medusa* rocked on the ocean swell. Nearly all of her rigging was over the side. Her masts were reduced to stumps, jagged where they had broken off. Boats which had been alongside his ship were pulling furiously away. He shrugged off the arms supporting him and staggered towards the bulwark.

'Stand by to commence firing, Mr Bentley.'

Harry looked at his ship. The damage to the *Medusa* was great, but her hull was sound. Given his crew and a little assistance from Carter, she could be jury rigged and sailed home. He fell forward against the side of the ship, struggling hard to avoid passing out again. With a great effort he turned to face Carter. As he opened his mouth to ask the man he hated for help, Carter, looking straight at him, shouted: 'Fire!'

Harry did speak, but his words were drowned out by the roar of the guns. He spun round to see the damage inflicted.

The *Magnanime* was a floating gun battery of enormous

power. Yet the *Medusa* should have withstood her broadside for longer. But his poor ship simply blew apart after the first round had been fired. The last thought that Harry held before he passed into oblivion was that Carter had lined the deck of his ship with gunpowder barrels. The *Medusa* did not sink. She disintegrated.

Hatred was not an emotion with which Harry Ludlow felt comfortable, sensing that somehow it caused him more suffering than the person it was directed against. So while as capable as the next man of holding a strong dislike, his affable nature and abundant optimism tended to hide this. Few people could, by their mere existence, upset him.

As he lay in the cot, he thought back to their first meeting. Harry seemed to remember a degree of friendliness. Carter had been the premier of Admiral Hood's flagship, the *Barfleur*, a three-decker of a hundred guns. Hood, having held the command in the West Indies, was superseded by Rodney, who commanded a combined fleet of thirty-four ships of the line. A few months later, in March 1782, these two gentlemen were to fight a most decisive battle. Rodney, breaking the French line in defiance of the Admiralty's Fighting Instructions, changed the whole nature of naval warfare. Harry had joined Hood's ship in January of that year as fourth lieutenant.

It would be hard to describe the gulf that separated a fourth lieutenant from the first lieutenant, especially aboard a flagship. Yet the icy reserve, so common in such a situation, was wholly lacking. On meeting the other members of the wardroom, he had been left in no doubt that Carter was a hard man to mess under. For him, nothing could have been further from the facts. Carter, on deck, seemed to go out of his way to praise his abilities. The premier also encouraged Harry to air his opinions at table. Young men find such attention from their superiors flattering. Harry was no exception. If the others in the wardroom had noticed that he was being favoured, they had chosen to ignore it.

*

The curtain of his cot was pulled back. Harry kept his eyes shut. Even in the dark of the screened-off cabin, the faint light from the lantern hurt his head. He knew that the man who had tended him on deck was leaning over him by the blast of foul breath that hit his nostrils.

'Still out cold by the look of him.' The voice was deep and rasping, the kind of voice that denotes the heavy drinker.

'It is to be hoped that the Lord will see fit to spare him.' Another voice, also deep, but much clearer in tone.

'If'n there be such a thing. It would be a kindness if he were spared your ministrations. After the damage your lord and master has done, a dose of your supplications could see him off.'

'Captain Carter has merely done his duty.' Quite a sharp response. Defiant.

'His duty, you say.'

'I had the honour to assist him in the writing of the dispatch.'

'Then I hope you did not imperil your soul.'

'I shall leave medical matters to you, sir. I would suggest you leave the state of my soul to me.'

'All I'm asking is that you leave this one, body and soul, in peace.'

'There is a proper function for prayer. The vital spirit is succoured by it. You cannot contend that the power to heal is merely a physical thing.'

'True. But being spiritual has the power to kill, usually through boredom. Snuff, Parson?'

Harry heard just one sniff, so he assumed that the parson had declined. He could also tell that the other man had been careless in his distribution, for some of the mixture was tickling his own nostrils. He tried in vain to contain himself, but to no avail. A huge sneeze rent the air, jerking him off the bed and sending a searing pain through his head. He fell back on the bed with his eyes open.

'Bless my soul,' said the parson. 'It looks as though he's come round. Praise the Lord.'

'As a man of science I'd rather praise the snuff.'

'Can we not look to a higher authority for this provision?'

'Only someone as indoctrinated as you could look for divine

inspiration in my spilling a little snuff. I have the unsteadiest hand in the fleet.'

'A fine boast for a surgeon.' There was no Christian charity in that remark. 'You must be hungry, sir. Some soup, perhaps?'

The man with the bad breath leant over him again.

Harry blinked, and with a convincing stab at the air of a man just waking up, he said, 'Where am I?'

'He appears to have lost his wits,' said the parson, leaning over the surgeon's shoulder to look at him.

'What a fine example of dogma,' said the bad-breathed man with more than a trace of asperity. 'He asks a perfectly natural question, and you doubt his sanity before you even answer it. You, sir, are aboard the *Magnanime*.'

Harry said nothing. He looked past the surgeon, taking in quickly the details of the cabin. Fixed wooden bulkheads told him he was below the gun-decks. The deep shelves were filled with a variety of instruments and an array of apothecary's bottles, each labelled in Latin to denote its contents. No daylight, or fresh air, pierced this section of the ship. The smell of the bilges, and of packed humanity, was all-pervasive. But the lanterns did show that at least the cabin was dry. Very likely the surgeon's own quarters.

'Do you recall the action with the Frenchman?'

'Yes. And I also recall the sinking of my ship. How long have I been like this?'

'All last evening and through the night. You've taken a nasty blow on your head, Mr Ludlow. I've stitched you back together again. You didn't budge throughout. Some of the hands claimed you was dead. Taking wagers they were.'

'We all prayed for your eventual recovery,' said the parson sonorously.

The other man gave an eloquent grunt. The surgeon put his arms under Harry's back and lifted him to a sitting position on the cot.

'Bear a hand, Mr Crevitt.'

The parson quickly pushed a bolster behind Harry's back. His eyes were now in focus, and in the dim light he could see the faces of his two attendants. The one who had helped him up had a ruddy vinous complexion and a purple swollen nose. Watery and bloodshot eyes stared out from under an untidy, unpowdered scrub wig. His leather waistcoat was stained and dirty. His companion, tall and thin, was dressed in clerical black, relieved only by the white swallow tail of the parson's collar round his neck. A large hooked nose dominated the bony face. His complexion was sallow, in contrast to his sharp black eyebrows. He stood stooped because of his height, his gaunt face anxious and concerned.

'We should inform the Captain,' he intoned.

'Not yet. Soup first.' The vinous face smiled, displaying few teeth, all black.

'Outhwaite,' he said. He had too few teeth for such a name. 'And this be the parson, Mr Crevitt.' The parson gave the briefest nod of acknowledgement.

'I'll fetch the soup.' He pulled back the canvas curtain and left. Harry's head hurt abominably. He put his hand up and felt the bandage round his crown.

'Does it hurt?' Harry nodded very slowly. Reaching under the cot Outhwaite produced a bottle. He pulled the cork out and offered it to his patient. Harry took a sip, stifling a cough as the rough brandy hit the back of his throat. The surgeon took the bottle off him, and unfolding several chins as he threw back his head, gave himself a generous mouthful, with no discernible effect on his throat.

'The parson is not one for strong liquor,' snorted Outhwaite, wiping the back of his hand across his unshaven chin. 'He believes in the healing power of prayer. Damn fool I say.' He took another generous mouthful and re-corking the bottle he replaced it under the cot. Just in time. Crevitt came through the screen with a bowl of steaming soup.

'I have sent to tell the Captain,' he said with a defiant look at Outhwaite.

'What an honest fellow you are, Parson.'

'He left instructions. I heard them if you did not. "The very minute," he said.'

'Well I dare say that if you spend half your life on your knees to something you can't see, it comes natural to crawl to something you can.'

'Crawl!' Crevitt nearly spilt the soup.

'And bein' dependent on that bastard for your living don't assist.'

'God give me the strength,' said Crevitt, closing his eyes and raising his nose to heaven, his long thin face taking on a look of silent prayer.

'If'n you don't give Mr Ludlow that there soup . . .'

The screen was pulled back sharply. A small boy stood there. He was thin enough, but his midshipman's uniform, several sizes too big, made him look emaciated.

'Captain's compliments,' he piped in a high unbroken voice, as he whipped off his hat. 'And would Mr Ludlow report to him right away.'

'He will not,' said Outhwaite without turning round. Crevitt's face registered shock. 'He is not fit to report to anyone.'

Was it the parson's expression that so angered the surgeon? For he addressed him directly.

'And since when did civilians 'report'. I seem to recall that the proper form was to request the pleasure of someone's company.' Outhwaite now spun round to face the door. 'Well even if he does request, he still can't see him. If the Captain wants to see Mr Ludlow he can damn well come down here an' do it. An' seeing him is all that will be allowed. He is not yet fit to talk to anyone.'

'It is a direct order,' said Crevitt. This fuelled Outhwaite's anger even further.

'Well I look forward to the day he orders you to jump overboard. 'Cause you being so wedded to orders, holy or otherwise, you'll do it.' He turned back to the boy in the doorway. 'Compliments to the Captain, Mr Prentice. The patient is not fit to be moved. I will inform him the minute that he is. Mind you say the minute, lad. Carter is very keen on the minute.'

The young face went through several contortions. Harry could not tell if he was silently rehearsing the message to try and memorize it, or was there a trace of fear, a reluctance to carry such a negative response to a man like Carter? Outhwaite had no doubt.

'Just carry the message, boy,' he said kindly. 'His bile will be aimed at me, not you.'

'Perhaps you're right,' said Crevitt primly, looking at Harry's pale face. 'Perhaps he is not yet ready for an interview with the Captain.'

'Good God, Parson,' cried Outhwaite with a loud laugh. 'You'll be denying transubstantiation next.'

The boy dropped the canvas screen. Outhwaite stood up and moved aside to let Crevitt sit down on the edge of the cot. Silently he fed Harry the soup, which though thin, tasted marvellous to a man who had not eaten for over twenty-four hours.

As he swallowed the soup he thought of the events of those last twenty-four hours. Images crossed his mind. He heard the screams of wounded men. The face of his brother James, looking towards him with sudden shock.

'Casualties. There must have been casualties. My brother?'

'Your brother is fine, Mr Ludlow,' said Outhwaite. 'It was he who brought you aboard.'

'But what about the men?'

'A heavy bill there, Mr Ludlow,' said Crevitt.

Outhwaite's hand landed sharply on the parson's shoulder.

'Just feed him the soup, Mr Crevitt.'

Crevitt continued the silent feeding. Harry could not keep his eyes open. He was asleep before the bowl was empty.

He awoke with a clear head. James sat in a chair by the cot, a lantern above his head, reading a book. Harry lifted his head from the pillow, and immediately realized that movement only exaggerated the pain.

'James.' His brother looked round, dropping the book.

'You're awake. How do you feel?'

'How long have I been out this time?'

'Only a couple of hours. Outhwaite reckons you were just having a good sleep.'

Harry pulled himself up, his anger at being helpless outweighing the pain in his head.

'He also was most insistent that you rest.'

'Damn Outhwaite,' snapped Harry, wincing with pain.

'He said you would have a sore head.'

'He strikes me as a man who knows a great deal about sore heads.'

'Well, he has been careful with his bottle while tending you,' said James with a laugh. 'I threatened him with all manner of punishments if you died.' James stood up as Harry swung his legs over the side of the cot. 'Though I think that the offer of a purse full of gold has kept him sober rather than any threats I made.'

Harry decided not to mention the bottle under the cot.

'I asked about the hands, but they wouldn't say.'

'Ten dead outright,' said James sadly. 'And some shocking wounds. Few of those will survive. The *Verite* lacks even an Outhwaite.'

'The *Verite*?'

'Carter shipped them all off in the Frenchman as a prize crew. Bound for Plymouth. He wanted me to go too, but I refused to leave you. Harry, this is the man you fought?'

'Oliver Carter. Yes. I'm surprised he didn't ship me off as well.'

'That wasn't even suggested. I dare say he didn't relish the thought of you aboard a warship with your own crew.'

Harry allowed himself a slight smile at the thought.

'He stood off deliberately, didn't he?'

'Where are we headed?' Harry did not want to discuss the sinking of the *Medusa*, at least not until he had seen Carter.

'The *Magnanime* is bound for the Mediterranean. He intends to land us at Gibraltar.'

The screen was pulled back and Crevitt stood in the doorway.

'Mr Ludlow. Quite recovered I see. Thank the Lord.' He smiled, making his thin lips even thinner, and dropped the screen back in place.

'He's been looking in here every ten minutes,' said James.

'And now he's gone to tell Carter I'm up and about.'

The screen was pulled back again and Outhwaite shuffled in. Harry did not feel well, but he hoped that he looked in better condition than the ship's surgeon. Outhwaite was pale and shaking. His unshaven face was quite grey.

'Thank God you're awake,' he said, subjecting Harry to a

quick examination. Satisfied, Outhwaite reached under the cot and grabbed the brandy bottle. He took a large swig, and stood for a moment, head up and eyes closed, as the spirit assuaged whatever ache he had. Harry watched with fascination as the man seemed slowly to stop shaking, like someone coming out of a fit. It was a steady hand that held out the bottle a minute later.

'This is cause for celebration, gentlemen.' They both declined the offer, so Outhwaite helped himself to another swig. 'If you will forgive me, Mr James, I must tend your brother's wound.'

'Of course.' James made to leave.

'James. Did you manage to rescue any of my kit?' Harry was looking at the dirty and bloodstained clothes he had worn since being brought aboard.

'Oh yes, Harry. We had all the time in the world to clear the ship.' There was a trace of bitterness in James' voice. 'We even had time to bury the dead. Our stores are in the hold, along with the stuff he took out of the *Verite*. Then he had our hands shift a goodly amount of powder on to the decks.'

'James. Later.' Harry looked at his brother, knowing that for him to apologize was unnecessary.

'Of course. I've got your sea-chest in my berth. It's just across the way. Hurriedly packed I'm afraid. I did it myself. I also put in the contents of your desk.' Harry nodded, knowing that James was alluding to a small chest full of gold, plus the ship's log. 'You'll want some clean clothes.'

'The very best, James, the very best.'

Harry stood before the cracked mirror examining the growth on his chin. Carter had sent for him within minutes. Poor Prentice, the midshipman, was sent back with a stinging rebuke to the effect that Mr Ludlow would wait upon the Captain when he was dressed, and not before.

Warm water was fetched from the galley, and Harry set to, trying to make himself presentable. Outhwaite sat at a desk made up of two sea-chests, attending to his ledgers. Given the size of the accommodation, there was precious little room to move about.

'I dare say that I'm the talk of the ship,' said Harry, stripping off his bloodstained shirt.

'What makes you say that?' The surgeon looked suspiciously at him.

'Come, Mr Outhwaite. If you've spent any time in the Navy, you'll know well what a small world it is. My previous problems with your captain must be common knowledge by now.'

'It's no secret that you served under him when he was First Lieutenant of the *Barfleur*. You were Fourth, I believe.'

Harry hid a smile. Outhwaite was trying to be both honest and disingenuous at the same time. If he knew that, then he knew it all.

'Quite friends, I'm told, at one time.'

'Never friends.' Harry spoke more sharply than intended. But the surgeon had a point. An observer could have called his relationship with Carter friendly. Yet for Harry it had not been truly so. He had found it hard to warm to Carter, despite the older man's attention. They were from different worlds. Harry had been reared to the Navy, safe in the knowledge that with his father's connections he would be a post captain as soon as it was humanly possible, and barring death, in time he would climb the captain's list to become an admiral.

Carter was the son of a poor country vicar, with precious few of the naval or political connections so necessary to the advancement of a career. It was a matter of some pride to him that through a combination of tenacity and sheer ability he had reached his present position. The first lieutenant of a flagship could expect to have a very good chance of promotion.

Such a thing could never come quickly enough for any sailor. They were all very conscious of it. But with Carter it was an obsession. He saw what was in fact bad luck as some kind of conspiracy to do him down. His talk was peppered with references to 'luck' elevating fools to command. Having no money himself, he claimed to despise wealth, which he saw as the main cause of 'corrupt influence', which advanced the careers of less worthy men.

'Do you know the Captain well?' Harry asked.

'Odd that you should ask me that,' said the surgeon, without looking up. He was not to be so easily drawn.

'He and the parson seem cut out of the same mould.'

'Mould,' said Outhwaite, ruminating over the word. 'That's more'n a touch likely, seein' as how they grew up together.'

'Indeed? I dare say that the parson, like Carter, will welcome the money from the *Verite*.'

Outhwaite coughed loudly. His thoughts wandered too easily in that direction for him to be comfortable with the subject.

'Or has your captain been fortunate since I last saw him?'

'Chances of prize money don't come that easy, Mr Ludlow, as you well know. And there's been precious few for anyone these last ten years. And it's true to say that the *Magnanime* was not favoured on our last commission. Three years on the Leeward Islands, and nowt to show.'

The West Indies again. He cast his mind back to the *Barfleur*'s wardroom, with Carter, as usual, at the head of the table. He could hear the bitter tone in the man's voice as if it were yesterday, as the premier harped on about slights, real or imagined. Harry should not have aired his opinions quite so freely, pointing out that most people only called influence 'corrupt' when it was operating on someone else's behalf, quite prepared to accept it as their just reward when it favoured them. Perhaps Carter had drunk more than was proper that night. Whatever the reason, the man was at his most venomous. The way he put Harry in his place went beyond the bounds of good manners.

And matters had not improved, despite an apology the following day. At first it seemed as though their relationship would return to its former level. But over the following weeks Carter's attitude changed. Dinner, never a great pleasure with him at the head of the table, now became a trial as he repeatedly referred to the things he found objectionable in the younger man. Gone were the days when he encouraged Harry to speak. Now his every utterance was torn apart. Worse than that, it seemed he was no longer trusted to watch the ship. The premier now made a point of being on deck to countermand his orders.

To combat this, Harry had assumed an air of studied indifference. This seemed to enrage the older man even more. The insults started to assume a more personal dimension. Before long, every opportunity was taken to make some unpleasant, and public, reference to Harry's height, indolent manner, lack of abilities, and not least the glittering prospects that awaited him despite all this. Easy going, Harry Ludlow might be. But he could not sit still for ever, to be insulted with impunity. And Carter was such a tempting target.

In service, on a ship at sea, this created problems. But they were not insurmountable ones. Plenty of people sharing the wardroom were not close friends. But the naval tradition of good manners, plus the need to 'live and let live' when you could be cooped up with the same people for months on end, usually kept such feelings in check. He and Carter had failed to observe the conventions. It was to land them both in trouble, and Harry on the beach. And the pity was that they had just thumped the French fleet under Admiral de Grasse. Promotions were being handed out all round. Carter, like Harry the object of a court-martial, was passed over. He could only blame one person. Harry Ludlow.

'This should be an interesting interview, Mr Outhwaite.'

'Now don't you go overtaxing yourself, Mr Ludlow,' said Outhwaite. He stood up to check Harry's bandage for the tenth time, fussing like a mother hen. 'You must remain calm, sir. Or you'll be back in that cot, for sure.'

Harry could not smile as he peered into the surgeon's tiny mirror. The cabin was filthy, with various rusty and bloodcaked surgical instruments lying around. The mirror was no exception. Outhwaite had abandoned his ledger work. Trying to turn the subject away from Carter, he prattled on about the ship while Harry shaved. From the little the man said that was of any use, Harry gleaned that the *Magnanime* had endured a dull time, with worse to follow. Returning to Spithead at the end of a three-year commission, they had been hurriedly revictualled for the Mediterranean.

'No shore leave, sir, no, not never. And no wives or sweethearts. Gunports shut tight, marine sentries, and guard boats rowing round at all hours. The men weren't too happy afore that, but they was mad as hell when they found they wasn't getting ashore. Three years' pay, and not a penny paid out. And the stuff they've put aboard, Mr Ludlow. Some of that beef has been in casks ten years since, by the smell of it. Leastways the water and biscuit is fresh.

'There's a war on, says they. Bugger the war, says I. And the French, for that matter. Jacobins the lot of them. Some of our lads need Greenwich Hospital. They're beyond my care. Not that I'm idle, mark you. Beats me how with all them guards I'm still findin' myself with a dozen cases of the pox to tend. And it's not the hands that we took aboard at Spithead either, though they have a fine set of diseases of their own. I say to you, Mr Ludlow, and no mistake, if the Frenchies were women, our lads would have them over in a trice. Never known the like. It would be petticoats up and peace in two minutes flat.'

This was followed by a wheezing laugh. 'Now that might be the way to fight a war. Mind you, it could be that it's the Portsmouth doxies who are the sharp ones. Maybe we should set them on the French.'

Harry remained silent throughout, concentrating on the act of shaving, lest in the poor light he give Outhwaite more work to do. The surgeon obviously mistook the reason for his silence.

'Perhaps a drop of brandy to raise your spirits,' said Outhwaite hopefully. He was looking for an excuse for a swig himself, though usually being alone was reason enough.

'I think a clear head would be better, Mr Outhwaite,' he said, turning towards him.

'I have often heard people refer to sobriety and a clear head as though they be directly related. I, myself, have never found it so. Quite the opposite. I have often noticed how a drop of spirits, particularly of a morning, clears the mind of the smaller things, and allows contemplation of nobler ideals . . .'

Harry turned. Outhwaite stopped as he looked into his patient's eyes. He was babbling, and he could not say why.

'I know of your quarrel, Mr Ludlow,' he said quietly. Harry raised his eyebrows questioningly. 'As you observed not a minute ago, it's a small world. A couple of hands on the ship served with you and Mr Carter before.'

Harry knew that to gain redress for what Carter had done he desperately needed allies. He longed to know what orders had been given on the quarter-deck when the seventy-four hove to. Was it too soon to commit himself?

'You're not fond of the Captain, are you?'

'I never said any such thing.'

'You don't have to.' It would serve no purpose to embarrass the man by saying that he overheard him talking to Crevitt. Outhwaite creased his brow, trying to think what could have given his opinions away.

'I have been known to say that Captain Carter is a strange fellow, Mr Ludlow. And I question his methods, him bein' a real hard horse commander. And a bloody flogger to boot.'

'I remember him as a taut disciplinarian, but not exceptional with the lash.'

'He's more than that now. We was in the middle of a floggin' when we spied your ship. And that's been a near daily occurrence these last few months. We did have a spot of trouble. The hands got a mite upset. So there's many who will say he's right. That you need discipline. And that's what drives him to flog the men. That's as maybe. The premier, Mr Bentley, pushes him to it. And him, it is almost as if he enjoys it. They are a strange pair. They don't see eye to eye, and the hands suffer for it. Not that there's anything new about that, but with those two it's different. Mr Bentley seems to bring out the worst in Carter.'

'What are you saying, Mr Outhwaite?'

'I'm sayin' that drink hasn't so addled my brain that I don't know what you're up against. I'm sayin' you mind how you go, 'cause he'd clap you in irons if he could find an excuse to do so.'

'Perhaps, after I have seen Captain Carter, we can talk again.'

From being open and outspoken, the surgeon suddenly seemed to withdraw into himself, as if he'd remembered his obligations.

'I'll tend your wound, Mr Ludlow, for that is my duty.' His watery bloodshot eyes were steady for once. 'I cannot promise to tend your business.'

'I think you will find, Mr Outhwaite, that I am very capable of tending my own business.'

37

Harry was annoyed with himself. He had been too direct. Yet surely Outhwaite's earlier remarks, let alone what he'd overheard, showed a hint of sympathy. Would they all be like the surgeon? Common sense told him that he could not look for any real support from the commissioned officers of the *Magnanime*. They might know what Carter had done. They might even be ashamed. But he was a stranger, and this was their ship. Unless Carter was a much worse captain than Harry had heard so far, they would do nothing, individually or collectively. They would examine the events in the light of their own careers and act accordingly.

That was even more true of the standing officers, those who were appointed to the ship by warrant from the various Boards of the Admiralty: pursers, carpenters, and the like, as well as the surgeon. Commissioned officers came and went, but the warrant officers could spend their entire sea-going career in one vessel. To them, Carter was just a passing phase. The name of their ship meant more than any one man's reputation. Besides, as yet, there was no saying whether the man's reputation was about to be dented or enhanced.

Nor, regardless of what Outhwaite had just said, could he look with any confidence for assistance from the hands. Never mind their lowly status, which would probably debar their testimony. Sense would tell them to say nothing. They depended on the captain for everything. 'A captain is a god on his own quarter-deck' was a well-known expression. And it was true. A certain amount of care had to be taken with the officers, since a means of redress existed for them, should they feel that their captain was going too far. Not so the hands. How could a man on the lower deck go against him, when he alone decided what was a punishable offence, and the level of pain that offence deserved? He couldn't hang them without a court-martial, but short of that, he could do what he liked. Many a man had expired at the grating, to be entered in the ship's log as having died while receiving punishment.

IV

Harry was not surprised that Carter kept him waiting. He paced back and forth on the quarter-deck before the entrance to the great cabin, in plain view of a fair proportion of the crew. The Captain would want everyone to know how little he cared for the comfort of Harry Ludlow. In another man, Harry might have been amused, laughing at the need for such behaviour. Not Carter. He fought to keep his temper in check. To occupy his mind, he looked around the ship, seeing familiar things, in spite of the years. Eventually the signal came, the marine sentry opened the door, and he was ushered in.

Sitting down, behind a polished table covered with papers, it was even more noticeable that the man had grown fat in the eleven years since Harry had last seen him. Then he had been slight and wiry, like whipcord, his face pinched with a permanent expression of dissatisfaction. Now his face and body showed the effects of command, and the sedentary existence that that brought. But the look of utter disdain was still there, not lessened by a fuller face. He was five years older than Harry but looked twenty. His small fat body seemed stuffed into his uniform. His belly, once so flat, was now a great bulge straining his waistcoat. The dust from his newly powdered wig had settled on his shoulders, taking the gloss off his epaulettes. He did not stand up as Harry entered. At his side stood Crevitt, a Bible very obvious in his hand. A young marine officer stood off to one side by the door of one of the Captain's other cabins.

Harry took in the details of the great cabin at a glance. With the ship on a southerly course, the room was in shadow. How shabby it looked compared to the same room when his father had occupied it. Then it had boasted fine carpets from the East; mirrors, paintings and polished furniture; silver had gleamed on the table, even when, as now, it was being used as a desk.

Carter must still despise wealth by the look of the place now. Chequered canvas covered the planking on the floor. The decor was sparse in the extreme, and the lack of furniture emphasized the emptiness of the cabin. No cabinets or silver ornaments. No pictures. Just the polished bulkheads that separated his sleeping cabin from this room. The lockers which formed seats below the stern windows were covered in worn velvet. The chairs to match the dining table were ranked along the walls. No one, it seemed, was to be invited to sit in the Captain's presence.

'I am curious to know by what right you dare to give commands to a King's officer, Ludlow?' No preamble, no pleasantries, however false. The years dropped away, and Harry could hear that same voice hurling insults at him from the head of the *Barfleur*'s wardroom table. 'I refer, of course, to your flying of Navy signals in the most outrageous manner.'

'They were more in the nature of a request.'

'I did not see any request in your signals.' Carter's lips were pursed together in disapproval.

'Admiral Kempenfelt, when he laid down the present signals, quite rightly assumed that no officer would need to be requested to attack an enemy warship.'

'You have no right to fly signals from that book at all.'

'I think every Englishman has the right to confound the King's enemies, just as every officer has a duty to do so.'

'You dare to remind me of my duty, sir?' The Captain's studied demeanour slipped a bit. He was fussy about his duty.

'I do. Since you obviously require to be reminded. By your actions.'

Carter thumped the desk with his fist. 'I will not have you questioning my actions in my own cabin.'

Harry longed to challenge him, to force him into another confrontation with weapons. As if Carter read his mind, he rubbed his shoulder at the point where Harry's bullet had pierced it. Harry fought to control himself. Only a fool would challenge a captain aboard his own ship. Carter would indeed clap him in irons. The only reason that Crevitt and the marine were there was in the hope that they would witness such an event.

'I require an explanation from you, for your failure to support me.'

'Require!' shouted Carter, his face going red. 'Who are you to require an explanation of me?'

'You knew that I commanded the *Medusa*?'

Carter sat back in his chair. He smiled to himself. The smile chilled the atmosphere rather than warming it.

'Did I? I must consult the ship's log, for I have no recollection of knowing who commanded the *Medusa*, or indeed the name of your ship before I had to sink her.'

'I know that you are no coward, Carter . . .'

'Captain Carter, Ludlow,' he said sharply.

'Yet you deliberately stood off and allowed my ship to be bombarded.'

'I think my superiors will approve of my actions.' He picked up a paper from the table and looked at it with exaggerated attention. When he spoke his voice had changed. Carter was all softness now. 'Have I not captured a fine frigate with the minimum of damage, either to myself or the prize?'

'And the *Medusa*?'

'Ah! The *Medusa*. A ship entirely unknown to me, flying signals it had no right to raise. A ship apparently attacking a superior enemy force.'

'Apparently!' Now it was Harry's turn to shout. Carter leant forward, hoping that Harry's outburst would continue. Harry checked himself again. Carter sat back, masking his disappointment with that same cold smile.

'Exercising due caution, I hove to, to ensure that my ship was not being lured into some trap. Having established this, I then proceeded to take possession of the *Verite* without sustaining any damage.'

'And my ship?' Harry's voice conveyed the strain he was under.

'I am sure that you are aware of the dangers that attend the operations of a Letter of Marque, Ludlow, and of the low esteem your profession commands. I really could not endanger a King's ship for the sake of a privateer.'

'I had thought that the danger was from our enemy.'

'Our enemy?' he said, throwing back his head and laughing. 'There are many dangers at sea, Ludlow. You have no right to this, but you may, in the presence of Mr Crevitt here, study the ship's log. You may even read a copy of the dispatch that I sent to the Admiralty.'

Carter threw the paper in his hand across the table. Harry ignored it. 'No, thank you.'

'A pity. For it reads well. It will be seen as a most economical action. And if the capture of a French frigate was insufficient to commend me to their lordships, I have added that I was able to crew my prize from your ship, which, no longer being afloat, had nullified the validity of the crew's exceptions. As I say, Ludlow, a most economical affair.'

'And all I say is that it is a proper subject for others to enquire into.'

Carter sat forward sharply. He knew that Harry was rich, well connected, and influential, just as he knew that in the end his superiors would support him. 'Are you threatening me?'

'I do not intend to let the matter rest, if that is what you are asking. I shall require more of an explanation than you have so far provided.'

'There you go "requiring" again,' said Carter, sitting back in his chair once more. 'It really is unbearable to be talked to in such a fashion. I have a mind to throw you out.'

'But you won't, Carter.'

'Won't I indeed?'

'No. You are enjoying this too much. You would not deny yourself the pleasure of observing my discomfort.'

'Anyone overhearing would think that I bore you some ill-will.' Carter's look became one of injured innocence, a look mainly directed at the silent Crevitt. 'You flatter yourself,

Ludlow. But then you always did carry a high opinion of your own merits. An opinion not shared by many.'

'I look forward to the day when we meet ashore, Carter.'

'Captain Carter!' Crevitt nearly jumped out of his shoes as the man screamed at Harry. 'Show some damned respect, sir.'

'If you want to know how much I respect you, Carter,' said Harry softly, 'the last time I had the misfortune to meet something like you, I had to use a boot scraper to rid myself of it.'

Carter went purple and shot forward across his desk. The young marine seemed to clutch the hat under his arm more tightly, trying to suppress a laugh. Crevitt's cry of 'gentlemen' was wasted as Harry left the cabin, slamming the door behind him.

A seventy-four-gun ship was a large vessel. But it was not so large that some of the crew, particularly the officers on the quarter-deck, were unable to hear the shouted exchanges from the captain's cabin, even with the skylight shut. Not everything of course, giving the matters the tantalizing edge of any half-heard conversation. In this case it was in no way difficult to deduce what the row had been about. Each man had his own thoughts on the sinking of the *Medusa*, just as each man also had his eye on the likely benefits which might flow from the taking of the *Verite*.

The ship having been in commission at the outbreak of war, the crew were volunteer sailors. Likewise, the hands that had been taken on at Spithead had come from the first rush of those eager for employment at the outbreak of war. The ship had a near full complement. Young or old, they tended to be proper seamen. By the time that Outhwaite had laid the last stitch in Harry's wound, the whole lower deck, through the good offices of those who had served aboard the *Barfleur* at the time, were apprised of the bad blood that existed between the two men.

The officers were not far behind. Sailors, like any other profession, talked about their occupation extensively. They talked of battles, of near-battles, of success or failure at any number of things, mostly promotion. It took no great feat of memory for them to dust off the details of that well-known quarrel in which Harry Ludlow had put a bullet in Oliver Carter just after the Battle of the Saintes. Nor was it difficult to remember the furore that their duel had caused.

It was expressly forbidden by Royal Command for naval officers to duel. Flouting this rule was considered particularly serious when a junior officer challenged his senior to fight. It took no great sense to see the advisability of this attitude. In a service where almost everyone was concerned with advancing their careers, no one wanted ships to be commanded by men whose only qualification was their ability to shoot straight.

It was also common knowledge that, at the court martial following their duel, Lieutenant Harry Ludlow, given the possibility of saving his career with an apology to Carter through the court, had declined to do so. Indeed, he had defied them by going so far as to state that he was sorry he had missed. This left them with no alternative but to dismiss him from the service. Carter, technically in the right, since he had been challenged by a junior officer, was nevertheless reprimanded. More hurtful, he had been passed over in the general promotions that followed the defeat of De Grasse. He'd had to wait another five years for his step to post rank.

It was a scandalous affair, made more interesting by the fact that the accused was the son of an admiral. People's curiosity was further aroused by the fact that he had not, at any time, sought the intercession of those powerful friends of his father, who, exerting pressure on his behalf, would ensure his reinstatement in the service. Getting one's commission back, after dismissal, was fairly common, given influence and money, both of which Harry's father had in abundance. Why, even one of the *Bounty* mutineers was now serving as an officer in the Navy, and he had been condemned to hang. Putting a bullet in a superior officer was small beer by comparison.

As Harry emerged on to the quarter-deck, the officers, having given the most perfunctory nod, looked the other way. He walked over to the windward side and drew deeply from the fresh westerly breeze that was pushing the *Magnanime* along at a steady eight knots. Somewhere to leeward lay the coast of France. The watch on deck, less constrained by good manners than the officers, were staring at him openly, curious to get a good look at the man who was fully expected to cleave their captain in two at the first opportunity. Typical of the lower deck, the recounting of the argument between Harry and Carter had grown until it had become a Titanic struggle. Harry was now known to have a terrible and uncontrollable temper, given to such fits of rage that ten burly marines would be insufficient to restrain him. That he had emerged from the great cabin with not a speck of Carter's blood on his clothes had come as a great disappointment. There being no hue and cry, they had to assume that he had not chucked the bastard out of the stern windows either. Those with their rum ration on him doing Carter in made the excuse of his wound, obvious by the thick bandage round his head. Those who had taken their bets, seeing this tyro in the flesh, were content to wait to collect their reward.

James came on deck at that point, carrying a sketch pad, followed by a ship's servant with a canvas chair. Given his brother's dress and bearing, Harry would not have been surprised to see another servant in his wake, liveried and bearing a silver tray with a bottle and a crystal glass. He walked over to where Harry stood, his hair flying in the breeze.

'I can't set up here, Harry, it's too windy.'

'You can't set up here at all, James. This is where the Captain takes his leisure. As soon as Carter comes on deck, everyone vacates the windward side so that he can walk undisturbed.'

'Where can I go?' The man with the chair stood silently, waiting for a signal.

'Almost anywhere, James. But courtesy demands that you ask the officer of the watch.'

'Since I expect you to join me, perhaps you would be good enough to ask him.'

No fool, James, thought Harry. They had to talk. James would be curious about his interview with Carter, as well as what action he intended to take. But there were precious few places on the ship where they could guarantee not to be overheard. Voices, even whispers, could carry through the canvas screens which separated most of the accommodation. To be seen seeking somewhere to be alone below decks would only excite comment and encourage the more resourceful to eavesdrop. Here on the deck, with James sketching Harry, they could keep those wishing to overhear at a distance, and failing that, stop talking if they came too near.

Harry walked over to the officer of the watch. The man was grey haired and old compared to him. He turned, raising his hat as he did so. His thinning hair, and the thick whiskers that reached down his cheeks, flapped in the breeze. His face had a blank, non-committal expression.

'Forgive me, sir,' said Harry. 'I have yet to be introduced to the officers.'

'Craddock, Mr Ludlow. Second Lieutenant, at your service.' Very formal and stiff, neither friendly nor unfriendly. He made no attempt to introduce the midshipman standing by him.

'My brother wishes to try his hand at a few sketches, Mr Craddock. He has not been on this ship since he was a nipper. My father had her once, back in '75, and the prospect of executing some drawings excites him. I would request that you direct us to a part of the deck that will occasion you the least inconvenience.'

'Why, anywhere you choose, Mr Ludlow,' said Craddock eagerly, his expression, like the look in his pale blue eyes, softening visibly. Now his round weatherbeaten face took on a smile, the grey eyebrows were mobile instead of firmly set. He seemed relieved. He'd probably expected his first encounter with Harry to be the one in which he was required to explain the events of yesterday. He pointed his hat to where James still stood with the servant, patiently waiting. 'Though I would be obliged if you could vacate the windward side of the quarter-deck.'

'I wouldn't dream of occupying that space. I have just explained to my brother the unsuitability of such a notion. Son of an admiral he might be, Mr Craddock, but he is also, I'm afraid, an incorrigible lubber.'

Harry smiled, as much at his own forced bluff and hearty manner, as at the sustained look of relief on Craddock's face.

'Could you also oblige me with our position?' asked Harry.

'Most readily, sir.' Craddock clapped his hat back over the thinning grey hair and pointed towards the binnacle. 'But you would be just as well to cast your eye over the slate.'

Harry turned and looked at the slate hanging by the binnacle. It gave the ship's position as of noon the day before, with the changes of course listed and the speed of the ship as they had been recorded. They were making a steady eight knots from the spot where they had sunk his ship. If this wind held, not impossible at the time of year, they would easily raise the Rock of Gibraltar within four to five days.

'Most obliged, Mr Craddock.' Harry turned, and collecting James he made his way to the leeward side, still on the quarter-deck, just aft of the gangway. The wardroom servant followed, setting out James' chair before returning to his duties. Harry stood by the mainmast shrouds, looking over the waist of the ship to the hands working on the forecastle. James sat facing the bowsprit. No one could approach them without being seen.

'I'm glad to see you in one piece, Harry. I half suspected that you might try to kill each other.'

'I feel I shall kill him, James. The first chance I get. He knew that I commanded the *Medusa* though he denies it. He had prepared the most interesting dispatch. He's so proud of it that he even offered to let me read it.' James raised a quizzical eyebrow. 'I declined his invitation.'

'Unwise?'

'Not really, since he took great pains to inform me of its contents. It states that he took what action he felt proper to avoid the possibility of a trap.'

'A trap!' Heads turned towards them and James dropped his voice. 'Will he be believed?'

'Few will believe him. Especially when I am finished disseminating the truth.'

'So we will gain redress.' The pad was on James' lap. He flicked at it casually with his charcoal.

'Not as things stand. At least not from the Navy. They might not believe him, but they will support him. Has he not taken a fine prize at no cost to himself or the Exchequer? To repudiate him would mean compensating us for the *Medusa*.'

'So?' James was now sketching away.

'We would require some evidence that he was motivated by personal spite rather than professional caution. Only the ship's officers would be in a position to confirm that.'

'And if we could get them to say so?'

'Then the case is entirely altered.'

'I almost venture to say that such a thing makes things straightforward. Your face, however, tells me that would not be true.'

'How have you found the officers behaving towards you?'

'That depends on which one. We had the most appalling dinner in the wardroom last night, and it wasn't just the food, though Heaven knows that was bad enough. Bentley, who is the first lieutenant, was drunk. Worse than that, he was damned unpleasant to everyone. Quite ignored me, mind you, for which I was extremely grateful. I was relieved to hear we'd raise the Rock in four days.'

'What about the other officers?'

'Polite. Sympathetic in a way. Except the marine. He seems cast from the Bentley mould. Drunk as a lord. Captain's nephew, I'm told.'

'The rest. Friendly?'

'No. Not friendly.' James looked at Harry's face, as his brother stared intently over the side. 'Should they be friendly? After all, we are strangers. And didn't you advise me yourself of the innate dislike naval officers have for privateers?'

'That's true, and being ex-Navy myself, I cannot find it in my heart to blame them. They suffer all sorts of constraints in their profession, while we have none. It gives them no pleasure to see us taking prizes, and money, from under their noses. Their only hope of wealth is in prize-taking, unless they reach flag rank. To the average officer, a poor man usually, what we do is robbery. Stealing the bread, or should it be the prospect of cake, from their mouths.'

'It seems superfluous then, to even think they'd be friendly.'

'I speak of extreme cases. Not all officers are so single minded about chasing prizes. Besides, nothing brings out the best in a sailor more than another's misfortune. The sea is such an unforgiving element, so full of surprises, that each man knows he is a whisker away from such a fate himself. It is almost a superstition, as though they were warding off the evil eye with a show of kindness.'

'The gods are not mocked by a mere show.'

'I used the wrong word.' Harry turned and smiled. 'Observe that none of the officers seek out our company. No one enquires after our welfare.'

'Perhaps they fear to displease their captain.' James held up his thumb, measuring some object.

'I think they fear more that I may say something about their captain. About his recent behaviour.'

'And theirs, Harry.'

'I can't blame the officers for Carter's actions.' He turned to gaze out over the gentle swell of the sea.

'True. But if you have observed correctly, then by their reticence they are condoning what he has done.'

'They have a difficult choice to make.'

'It seems a simple choice to me.'

'Choices are always simple when you're not the one who has to make them.' From habit, Harry was scanning the horizon.

'You seem to be going out of your way to defend them, Harry.' James raised his voice as he continued. 'Carter has used this ship and everyone aboard it to settle a personal vendetta. If what he did was not criminal, then it ought to be. So the choice is very simple. Stark in fact. Anyone condoning a crime, is himself engaging in a criminal act.'

'Then it is a pity that what he did was not truly a crime,' said Harry quietly.

'You seem very sure of this, which I ascribe to your cloistered nautical upbringing. I, for one, am not so sure. I shall certainly consult an attorney, even if you don't.'

Harry laughed, glad that he was facing away from the quarter-deck. James was quite incensed. He had raised his voice enough for it to be heard on the quarter-deck, causing all there to turn and look out to windward.

'Well, brother. If they were not friendly before, they certainly won't be now. Why you are practically threatening to have them slung into the Marshalsea.'

'In irons,' said James with a quiet smile. 'At least overhearing that part of our conversation will give some of them food for thought.'

'Which is why you made sure that they did.'

'I would not want anyone to assume that we merely intend to let the matter rest. And how can you laugh at a time like this?'

'In truth, James, I can think of nothing better to do. Consult your attorney by all means, only make sure he is one who practises in the Admiralty courts, otherwise you may get some fool to take your case and spend a great deal of our money before realizing that he is wasting his time.'

'You are very certain that it is a waste of time.'

'It is. Unless we have more than half the ship's officers in court, willing to swear on oath that Carter knew I was aboard the *Medusa*, and that one fact directed all his subsequent actions.'

'So you don't intend to try?' James seemed to be concentrating on drawing, but Harry guessed that was just for show. He turned to face his brother, leaning against the bulwark.

'I'll most certainly try. But we will be in Gibraltar within the week if this wind remains steady. Not much time to persuade a group of complete strangers to risk their careers. And their verbal disapproval of Carter will not be enough. We need signed affidavits, sworn before a notary on the Rock. After that we must go to England while they sail on into the Mediterranean. And who is to say that they will stay together? They may be killed or dispersed to a number of ships, all going to different destinations. Calculate how long it may be before they are all ashore in England at the same time. It could be years.'

James looked beyond Harry. 'I think this young man is waiting to address us.'

Harry turned. The same small midshipman, the one he had snapped at this morning, stood to attention a little way off. His pale face was pinched, but he still had a lively expression. As Harry turned, he whipped off his hat and spoke in his high unbroken voice.

'Captain's compliments, sir. It is the Captain's intention to give a dinner this afternoon to celebrate the taking of the *Verite* to which end he has invited the French captain and all of those officers not required to watch the ship.'

'Surely he does not intend to extend an invitation to us?' asked James, jerking forward and dropping his pad. His usual sang-froid had entirely deserted him at the prospect of such a slight.

'The Captain has sent me to extend an invitation with the knowledge that, given Mr Ludlow's wound, you may not wish to attend.'

The boy was looking at the sky, his eyes tightly shut, as he waited for the blast of anger that was bound to follow his message.

'Damn . . .' cried James, beginning to confirm the lad's worst fears.

'Please inform the Captain,' said Harry, his upheld hand silencing his brother, 'that we will be delighted to attend his dinner.'

The boy's face dropped and he opened his eyes to look in astonishment at Harry.

'You may further say that no wound, short of a mortal one, would keep me from such an event.'

The boy's mouth worked silently as he sought some response. No words came. Instead he clapped his hat back on his head, turned and fled towards the poop.

'Harry. You are not seriously suggesting that we attend a dinner to celebrate the sinking of our ship?'

'I am.'

'In God's name why?'

'Because he does not want us to attend. That invitation was meant as an insult, and we were meant to react by an angry refusal. Pity that poor child for having to deliver it. But he has miscalculated. We shall most certainly attend his dinner. And just as certainly, the sight of me happily consuming his food is likely to bring on an apoplexy. At the very least it will entirely spoil the enjoyment of his meal.'

'It is more likely that the food will be ours,' sighed James gloomily. 'He stripped our stores out of the *Medusa* before he sank her.'

V

Harry and James, having checked with the quarter-deck that it would not be an imposition, had a look round the ship. To James it was rediscovering something that he had seen as a child, a dim recollection. It had seemed enormous to a child's eye. Now it seemed small and rather cramped. The smell was that of any ship, made up of salt, tar, wood, and numerous unwashed bodies. They had descended from the quarter-deck to the upper deck, a long clear space full of working parties with its rows of twenty-four-pounder guns bowsed tightly against the top of the gunports. They walked the length of the deck, from the wardroom door to galley stove and larder under the forecastle, then they made their way down to the gun-deck.

Harry, paying great attention to the massive thirty-two-pounder guns, was reliving part of his past. The sights, the sounds and the smells were all familiar, yet so very different to a man who had spent the last few years in flush-deck ships. To him it all seemed very spacious. That is, until you counted the number of people aboard. Above, men were working at various tasks, under the direction of petty officers. Here on the gun-deck the mess tables were down for the watch off duty. Home to five hundred men, the hammocks were now stowed in the netting along the ship's side and the deck was clear from one end to the other. How different it would be at night.

Regulations allowed fourteen inches for each man to sling his hammock. In truth, this was usually twenty-eight inches, as there was always a watch on deck, but that still made for a cramped mass of humanity in the available space. Normally a fairly noisy place, the gun-deck seemed quiet. There seemed to be a listless quality about these men who were, after all, at their leisure. Already, having observed the other hands at work, Harry had remarked that the *Magnanime* was not a happy ship. The dull behaviour of these men below decks only served to confirm that view.

'I am aware that you are familiar with the ship. But can you say that with certainty after such a short acquaintance with the crew?'

'This is my world, James. Or was,' replied Harry. 'I am sure that you can walk into a drawing-room full of strangers, and within minutes you will have noticed the atmosphere. A ship is no different.'

'I don't doubt you in any way. As I remarked to you earlier, dinner yesterday was a very unpleasant affair. If the hands are as glum as the officers at table, then this will indeed be an unhappy ship.'

'No skylarking. The midshipmen and the ship's boys. On a happy ship, however taut the discipline, the boys have fun. And the hands. The men don't joke here.' Harry stopped and looked at the deck behind one of the great guns. They were beside a mess table, and though he looked at the hands sitting there and smiled, the men did not respond. They walked on.

'I have been told that flogging is very common. Almost a daily occurrence. Odd that. I don't remember Carter being over fond of flogging when he was a premier.' Harry was speaking absent-mindedly. He was looking everywhere, absorbing a mass of detail. The deck was spotless, the ropes and the countless instruments needed to work the guns all slung in proper fashion. From forrard they heard the bleat, and the smell, of his own sheep in the manger.

'The debilitating effects of power. I remember Father first telling me how much power a captain had. He was quite sanguine about it. The effect, I mean. I must say it horrified me.'

53

'Perhaps it's Bentley,' said Harry. 'That is the premier's name?'

'It is. Swarthy looking cove with small eyes.'

'That can be a very powerful post. Depends on the captain, mark you. Outhwaite hinted as much. The first lieutenant really runs the ship. If he wants a man punished badly enough, there is little a captain can do to stand in his way. See that man there—' Harry indicated with his head. 'Over by the capstan. See how he moves. Very stiff.'

'A recent victim?'

Harry nodded. 'And not the only one I've noticed.'

'Yet it is generally agreed that flogging achieves nothing. That it makes a good man bad, and a bad man worse.'

'Easily said in the comfort of a salon, James. But if you are at sea, with an inexperienced crew, and half of them pressed men or the scourings of the gaols, how do you keep them in check?'

'Some captains manage.'

'A few. Not many. Can't say that it's something I'd want to use, but I can envisage many a situation in which I wouldn't want to be without it.'

'I wonder what you would have been like as a commander.' James smiled. 'Hang 'em high, I shouldn't wonder.'

Harry looked wistfully about the gun-deck. It could have been his, all this. 'Let's go and get some air,' he said, heading for the stairwell.

As they came on to the quarter-deck they could hear a raised voice.

'Bentley,' said James.

'The deck looks like a whore's bedroom, sir. Your want of ability is plain to a landsman's eye.'

Harry looked along the deck. It seemed fine to him, and he knew himself to be a stickler about such things. One thing had struck his eye. He noticed that the great guns, bowsed tight against the ship's side, were rarely used. The deck behind them was as smooth as all the other planking. If the crews had been given regular training on the guns, there would be grooves in the deck where they had been run in and out.

That was how it had been on the deck of the *Medusa*, with constant dumb shows, as well as the real thing. Firing guns was an expensive business, easier perhaps for him than for Carter, who had to account for his expenditure of powder and shot to the Admiralty. There were those in the higher reaches of the service who could see the sense in having well-trained gun crews. But they were in the minority, outnumbered by those who saw it as a waste of time, not to mention the clerks of the Ordinance Board, who saw only a waste of money.

To Harry it was false economy. Why eschew gunnery and engage yard-arm to yard-arm, when you could stand off, and using the greater sailing experience of your crew pound your adversary from a distance? Carter was obviously one of the old school, who preferred to rely on the bulldog tenacity of their crews in an engagement. The voice was raised again.

'And now you tell me that you alone are responsible, sir, that the hands have not been slacking in their duty. I say that either you are blind or incompetent, sir. Or perhaps you are avoiding the truth.'

Everyone was still, the officers, the midshipmen, and the hands. Yet there was no surprise on their faces to see one officer's public humiliation of another, in full view and hearing of the entire ship's company. To call a man a liar in such circumstances was coming it very high.

'What I said, sir,' replied the other officer in a tense voice, 'was that if anyone has been slacking, and I have not observed it, then I bear sole responsibility.'

'You also have a responsibility for the maintenance of discipline,' shouted Bentley. 'You will make it your duty to find out who the culprits are, and report them to me for punishment.'

'With respect, sir, I doubt I could do that.'

'Respect!' Bentley was purple with rage. The other officer flinched as he was hit by the spittle flying from the first lieutenant's mouth. 'You speak to me of respect in the same sentence that you refuse to carry out a direct order. Find them, Mr Mangold, or I will be obliged to do it for you.'

Bentley turned to look round the ship. That they were afraid of him was obvious. Suddenly everyone was very busy. His eye caught the two brothers standing observing the scene.

'I must protest, sir,' said Mangold. 'And in the strongest possible terms.'

'Protest, Mr Mangold. Do so by all means. And if you wish to see an example of the consequences of such a protest, just cast your eye towards the gangway.'

Harry, direct in the man's gaze, smiled. He was about to speak, but James beat him to it.

'And if you require an example of bad manners, sir, I suggest that you find yourself a mirror.'

Bentley was unused to people talking back to him. His response was therefore lame.

'I would remind you, sir, that you are guests on this ship.'

'It has been my experience that guests are normally the recipients of an invitation,' said James, adopting a foppish air. 'We are not, Mr Bentley. And should I ever be the object of an invitation from you, sir, I would take great care to decline it.'

Harry burst out laughing. No one else did. No doubt they were thinking that they would pay the price for James' barbs. Bentley was speechless, but he was trying to pull his features into the same unconcerned expression as James.

'It really is too tedious, Harry.' James addressed his brother in the same languid tone. 'And to think I believed you when you said that the Navy was recruiting a better class of officer.'

Bentley rushed from the quarter-deck, and down into the waist of the ship before James could insult him any more. But still no one laughed, and, even more remarkable, no one produced even a guarded smile. With good reason, because they must have known what was coming.

Bentley, still red-faced from ill temper, ran at a group of men laying out a sail on the upper deck. He grabbed the first one he came to and spun him round.

'Lazy swine!' he cried, and struck the man around the ears. 'Marines. Seize him!' The man, wholly innocent in Harry's eyes, staggered back as two marines came forward to take his arms.

'Leave him be,' shouted one of his mates, stepping in front of the victim. 'You murderous bugger. Weren't Larkin enough for you?'

Bentley froze at this. Then he seemed to go berserk. Seizing a marine's musket, he swiped the offending speaker in the groin. The man doubled over and fell to his knees. Bentley raised the gun over his head, obviously intending to crush the man's skull.

'Mr Bentley,' screamed Turnbull, the marine officer. His expression, like Mangold's, was one of fear. Perhaps not for himself, but for his superior, who was in the act of committing murder. The gun reached the top of its arc and stopped. The man on his knees looked up into Bentley's face, not with fear, but with defiance. The premier brought the weapon down at speed, stopping it just above the man's face. He then tapped him painfully on the cheek.

'We'll see how long that look is maintained when you are at the grating.' Bentley had his back to them, but Harry would have sworn that he was smiling.

Punctuality was highly prized in the Navy, and so all those who were invited to Carter's dinner were ready well before the appointed hour. Judging by the number assembled, he had indeed invited everyone on board bar the officers of the watch. Most stood in small groups talking quietly. The formality of the occasion was highlighted by everyone being in dress uniform. Dark blue broad-cloth alternated with silver facings and newly powdered wigs. The exception was Bentley, who had not troubled to change out of his everyday clothes. By his demeanour, let alone the state of his dress, it was plain that he was already in drink. He was showing away to Craddock and Turnbull in a loud voice. The contrast between the elegant, redcoated marine and the dishevelled premier was stark, despite the fact that neither had bothered to don their wigs.

Harry with his bandage, and James, bareheaded also, stood talking with the captain of the *Verite*. In contrast to the officers of the *Magnanime* he had taken the first opportunity to commiserate with them on the loss of the *Medusa*. They discussed the action between the three ships without rancour, the French captain striking his head in a theatrical way as Harry explained to him about the kedge that had so slowed the *Medusa*. He had been a mere master's mate before the Revolution, from which position he had never dreamed of command. His promotion to his present rank had been because of his abilities, rather than any revolutionary fervour. Most of his superiors, being well born, had fled France to avoid the 'Terror'. People with enough experience to sail a ship, let alone command, were in very short supply.

Inevitably their discussion came to the point at which the *Magnanime* had failed to support the *Medusa*. Suddenly the Frenchman's friendly air, and his fluency, seemed to evaporate, to be replaced by an inability to properly express himself in either English or his native tongue. He mumbled haltingly about the need for the larger ship to avoid a trap, but it was plain that he was merely trotting out what he had been told rather than something he believed. He was saved from further embarrassment by the announcement that the time had come to take their places for dinner.

'Today, at least, we can anticipate a good dinner, a meal liberated from the enemy,' barked Bentley, looking across to where they stood. 'Add to that the fact that it is free, and it promises to be a capital affair.' It was not plain if he was addressing the Ludlows or their companion.

'Remember,' said Harry, 'be hearty. We won't spoil Carter's feast by being glum.' Harry had said this to James several times, each mention producing a very glum response. How could James explain to his brother that he thought being 'hearty' the height of bad manners.

On entering the cabin they split up. The table which Carter had used as a desk now had the extra leaves fitted, and was set across the whole width of the cabin. James was directed to sit at one end of the table next to Bentley. Harry was off to the side, out of Carter's line of sight, seated between Crevitt and the young midshipman Prentice. Craddock sat opposite him, but he immediately engaged a large florid man on his right, well dressed and well fed, in deep conversation. It would never do to be seen talking to a Ludlow at the Captain's dinner. Harry looked down the table to see Bentley talking across James to the young marine officer. His brother's eyes were looking at the oak beams above his head, his face a picture of utter boredom. He declined to show any interest as the soup was placed before him.

Harry turned to the midshipman, wondering if Carter disliked the boy. He seemed to make a point of giving the lad unpleasant messages to deliver, and now he had placed him next to Harry, which could not be construed as a mark of favour.

Prentice sat stiffly, not looking right or left. Harry could not know that the tales of his temper, so avidly spread by the lower deck, had caused an even greater stir in the midshipmen's berth. Prentice, convinced that he was a sacrificial offering on the part of the ship, was terrified, fully expecting to be dead before he had finished his soup.

'Well,' said Harry quietly, trying to put the boy at his ease. 'How kind of the Captain to put me next to a sailor. I shall have someone to talk to.' Harry dropped his voice to a whisper, indicating with his eyes the parson busily engaged in talking to an officer on his left. 'I fear I won't have much in common with a parson.'

Prentice merely blinked, but Harry's pleasant manner had served to blunt his fear.

'The gentleman opposite, talking to Mr Craddock. Would he be the purser?'

The boy's head jerked forward once.

'You can always tell a purser. Best-fed man aboard.' A smile nearly showed on the midshipman's face. For people like midshipmen, who were always hungry, a fat man was a source of some jealous speculation.

'Now, you must tell me how long you have been at sea,' Harry continued. 'And then we can compare notes on the differences between your mid's berth nowadays, and what it was like in my day.'

Prentice turned and looked at Harry strangely. He could not conceive that this fully grown man had once been like him.

'I served aboard the *Magnanime* once. May well have had the same berth as you. I dare say, like me, you'll never forget the first day you came aboard a ship. The first thing I remember is the smell. How about you?'

'Yes, the smell,' croaked the boy.

'It seemed to get worse as you went down in the ship. Mind, the one I joined was fully commissioned and had just come back from a cruise. And the hands had been paid, so they were having a high old time on the gun-deck. Bodies everywhere, and no sense of shame in the women or the men. Bit of a shock that. To me anyway. A ship is nothing like home.'

Harry had struck the right chord. Like most of the boys who joined the Navy, Prentice had come from a warm domestic atmosphere to the floating maelstrom of a fighting ship. Prentice vividly remembered the shock of joining the *Magnanime*. How different it had been from the thoughts he had entertained, and the home he had left.

'It seemed to me like I was walking into hell.'

The boy nearly smiled. Crevitt on the other side, having leaned back to allow a manservant to fill his soup plate, responded to the word.

'Do I hear you lecturing young Mr Prentice on the evils of the midshipmen's berth, Mr Ludlow?' Harry turned to face him. There was little warmth in his look, but that did not deter the parson. 'I sincerely hope so; for if we cannot turn the young away from vice, then what chance do we have with fully grown men?'

To Harry, Crevitt was Carter's man, body and probably soul. He felt no reason to be polite. His soup was poured from a ladle as he replied.

'In my experience, Mr Crevitt, attempts to deny men their passions merely excited their ingenuity. Where there's a will . . .'

'Indeed.' Crevitt's soup spoon stopped half-way to his mouth, his face closing. The thought, be it passion or ingenuity, obviously displeased him.

'Why, some men cloak themselves in all manner of garb,' continued Harry, 'adopt a high moral tone, and condemn others, while themselves indulging in the very acts that they seek to bar to their fellow man. That is probably the best example of ingenuity.'

'Perhaps hypocrisy would be a better word.'

'Perhaps. Yet I dare say in your time you have occasioned across the odd parson whose behaviour has concerned you. Not all men of the cloth are upright and honest?'

'Ordination is one thing, Mr Ludlow. Salvation is quite another. None of us are free from sin. But as a general rule, men of the cloth are better at avoidance than your average tar.'

Crevitt was looking at Harry in a very direct manner. He was clearly not a man to take an insult lying down. Harry beamed at him over his spoon.

'Why, Mr Crevitt. I fear you have taken me in entirely the wrong manner. But I shan't worry, you being in the business of forgiving.'

'It is God who is in that business, Mr Ludlow. I am merely his servant.' His air of superiority goaded Harry.

'It has been my experience that servants often know more than their masters.'

'That is bordering on blasphemy, sir.'

'I speak in the terrestrial sense, of course. Looking around this collection of sinners, who would you say is a candidate for divine favour? Or more interesting, who here is destined for the fires of damnation?'

There was a loud crash and everyone at the table looked over to see Bentley being helped to his feet. His wine had spilled across the white cloth, and a servant was busy mopping it up.

'Damn chair,' snapped Bentley. 'Went from under me.'

He sat down and held out his empty glass to be refilled. Harry leant forward and looked over towards Carter. The Captain was the only one at the table not looking at his first lieutenant. He was staring at his soup plate, his face perfectly blank. Yet his struggle to control himself was obvious. After a few seconds he lifted his head, and with a false smile turned to engage his neighbours in conversation. As if on cue, everyone else followed suit.

Strange, thought Harry. Can Carter really ignore the fact that his second in command has turned up drunk and improperly dressed?

'I fear Mr Bentley is beyond your ministrations, Mr Crevitt, though you can't fault his timing. But such saintly behaviour on the part of the Captain. Such restraint. Surely that must excite divine admiration?'

'If not yours?'

'I have little experience of Mr Carter restraining himself, unless you referred to the events of yesterday.'

The spoon stopped half-way to the mouth. 'From the little Captain Carter has told me about you, restraint is not a virtue you would be able to advise him about.'

'*Touché*, Mr Crevitt.'

'It is my impression that you have a wholly wrong view of Captain Carter.' The spoon was now pointing at Harry.

'Perhaps. My view is coloured by his continual insults and his deliberate endangering of my life. I will not mention the cost of replacing my ship.'

'Such things are the effect of your quarrel. It would be more advantageous to examine the cause.' Crevitt put his spoon in the plate, since Harry's look left him in little doubt that he disliked being addressed so.

'You are addressing the wrong person, Mr Crevitt,' said Harry sharply. The parson opened his mouth to speak, but an angry voice from across the room made them both turn their heads.

'You, sir, are a drunken oaf.'

James' voice, raised in anger, cut across the buzz of conversation. Every head turned and silence fell. James was on his feet, his napkin in his hand. Bentley, his chair tipped back, was leering at him with a drunken smile.

'I intended it as a compliment, sir.'

'You are a disgrace to the uniform you wear.'

'Mr Ludlow,' Carter said. 'I would remind you of your manners.'

'You!' spat James, going red in the face. Harry had never seen this side of his urbane brother before. He looked as though he was about to burst a blood vessel. 'You have no right to remind me of anything. And as for this specimen here—' James indicated the still smiling Bentley.

'What a sensitive crew they are, these Ludlows.' Bentley leant on the table and looked bleary-eyed at Carter. 'Not like us, Captain Carter.'

'I would not wish to have to remind you of your manners too, Mr Bentley.'

'Neither would I.' There was a discernible pause before he added *sir*. Bentley's face had changed. The smile had vanished to be replaced by a challenging look. Harry, like everyone else, waited for Carter to check his first lieutenant. No one could doubt the insolence in the man's look and manner.

Carter said nothing.

'And as for you, sir,' said Bentley, turning back to James, 'perhaps you are accustomed to a more refined society, where allusions to the attractions of the fair sex are more guarded. But you are aboard a man-of-war now. And we address such things differently.'

James was staring at Carter. Plainly he too could not believe that he was allowing Bentley to behave this way. He turned back to the seated premier.

'I would not have a sodden lecher like you make any allusion to a woman in my company, let alone my sister.'

'All women are someone's sister, sir. But I never bother to enquire after their brother's health when I bed them.'

'Mr Bentley,' said Harry sharply. 'I have served in the King's ships, yet I cannot recall such a lack of manners in someone so close to being the host.'

'Manners?' sneered Bentley. 'Ah yes. Was not this denizen of the drawing-room telling me about mine today?'

'James,' snapped Harry. 'Sit down.'

His brother looked set to argue, but when he saw Harry turn towards Carter, his face drawn with repressed anger, he obliged.

'It's hardly surprising you chose not to engage the *Verite*. With such a person on your quarter-deck, perhaps it was too hazardous.'

'Damn you, sir,' said Bentley. Wine spilled out of his glass as he jerked his arm in anger.

'He seems however to enjoy a degree of freedom that I cannot remember from my days as a serving officer. Perhaps others at the table will tell me I am wrong.'

No one else was talking. There was something close to shame on the faces of the other officers present. Prentice, with youthful

63

curiosity, was the only one whose head was up. The others, like Carter, tried to concentrate on their food. But Harry's stare made the Captain look up. Had James smoked what his brother was about – for if he intervened now, he could ruin everything. The dinner could not continue with both the Ludlows and Bentley present. Carter would have to ask one or the other to leave. To pick on Harry and James, given the state of his subordinate, would be grossly unfair. The man had behaved abominably. Harry could not even begin to guess what it was that allowed Bentley such latitude. But now he had manoeuvred Carter into a position where he really had to check his first lieutenant, for if he didn't, he would be advertising to all that as a commander he was a mere cipher.

'Mr Bentley. You are unwell. I suggest that you retire.'

'Me, retire? For these upstarts?' Bentley leaned across the table, half out of his seat. 'From what I hear, they are not above a bit of unlicensed rogering themselves!'

James stiffened visibly, as Bentley turned towards him. 'That is, if the whore of their dreams is high born enough. Never mind that she be someone else's wife.'

'Stop him, Carter!' cried James. It sounded like pain.

'Perhaps when we have finished this commission you will introduce me to the fair Lady Farrar. Oh yes, Mr High-and-Mighty Ludlow. You were the talk of the town before we sailed. Stealing another man's wife is about the mark of your family. And what did you do when he sent to take her back. Her honour meant less than keepin' your skin. Perhaps you was never man enough for the lady, for I hear she went meekly enough. I shall make a point of seeking her out next time I'm ashore. I'm the stallion of all the world, I do assure you. I can certainly guarantee her a memorable gallop.'

'Shut your mouth!' yelled James. 'You are not fit to mention her name!'

'Am I not? I suppose you think you're the only one who's bedded her. If she'd stoop to dallying with the likes of you, I dare say she's pretty free with her favours. No better than a whore, most like.' Bentley roared with laughter.

James' slap knocked Bentley over his chair. Carter and Harry stood up together. Harry moved quickly round the other diners. James smashed a decanter, and was about to lunge at the prostrate Bentley. Turnbull, moving at surprising speed, pinned his arms, giving Harry enough time to get between his brother and the premier. James wriggled free, dropping the jagged remains of glass from his hand.

'Until now, Carter,' shouted James, his face red with anger again, 'I never quite knew what a scrub you are. Not only do you man your ship with dregs for officers, but you are incapable of discipline. Your behaviour yesterday was wholly in character. Should my brother not oblige with a bullet, then I most certainly will!'

'I will not be talked to like this!' yelled Carter.

'You will be addressed as you deserve,' said James. 'You are the scum of the earth. You deliberately stood off yesterday and allowed an enemy to rake our ship. And that to settle a private feud. Tonight you have done the same: stood aside where it was your responsibility to intervene. And you have allowed this drunken swine to sully the name of a woman that I hold in the highest esteem. You may think that your carefully worded dispatch will save you from censure, but I will make it my task to see you stripped of your commission. And if I fail in that, rest assured that I shall bend all my efforts to ensuring that you spend the rest of your life on the beach. You are not fit to command a herring buss, let alone a King's ship!'

Carter looked as though it was he who had been slapped. Bentley, having hauled himself up, was leaning against the bulkhead, blood seeping from the corner of his mouth. Suddenly he lunged at James. Harry made to intervene, but it was unnecessary. James nimbly side-stepped, and Bentley slewed across the table, sending dishes and glasses flying. James grabbed him and turned him over on his back.

'I would kill you if I thought you were worth it, you piece of dung!'

'Get out of my cabin!' screamed Carter.

'With pleasure, Captain,' said James, all urbanity again. 'Your dinner has been attended by the success it deserves.'

*

'I have to remark that's not quite what I had in mind when I asked you to be hearty,' said Harry. 'I never knew you had such a temper.'

'I feel a sense of shame at having displayed it, and that in front of people like Carter. And I don't suppose I have aided our cause a great deal.'

'Let's not fret about that, James. What is done . . .'

They paced the deck, using the windward side almost in a sense of defiance. James' calm behaviour was only skin deep. Harry knew that underneath he was still seething from the way Bentley had talked about Caroline Farrar.

'I cannot comprehend why Carter lets Bentley carry on in such a vile manner.'

'I think I have already said that I find it wholly in character.'

'But it isn't, James. I served with Carter when he was premier, and he would never have countenanced such behaviour in our wardroom. Bentley was openly challenging his superior to check him. You did not see the insolence in Bentley's look. Yet he did nothing.'

'Men change, Harry. I have often heard you talk of the odd behaviour of naval captains.'

'This is different. A wholly sane ship's captain is hard to find, given the isolation they suffer and the authority they wield. But to let your premier talk in that manner destroys all discipline. Did you see the looks on the faces of the others?'

'I did not. If you recall I was rather preoccupied.' Memory restored the angry tone.

'They were ashamed.'

'And well they might be.'

'Ashamed of their captain.'

James stopped. 'And Bentley, I would hope.'

'No,' said Harry turning to face him, 'I would say that they are frightened of him.'

'The man is a wreck. Judging by his complexion he is drinking himself to death.'

'Why doesn't Carter relieve him of his duties?'

James started pacing again. 'I would have thought that was perfectly obvious, Harry. You say the other ship's officers are afraid of Bentley. I say that Carter is afraid of him too.'

'It was unwise to challenge him so openly, James.'

'I will not accept such a rebuke from you,' said James, again showing a flash of temper. Harry was quite taken aback.

'Tactless of me. But your other threat was more telling. Without his rank, Carter would be nothing. I would hazard that he is more frightened of that than the prospect of death. Which makes the case of Bentley all the more strange.'

'All I know is that I must be kept apart from him. For if he dares to mention Caroline again, I shall not answer for my actions.'

'A man like that is a danger to the ship,' Harry carried on, trying to change the subject without seeming obvious. 'I admit there is no shortage of drunkards at sea, quite a few of them captains. But it is unwise for a sober person to leave any authority vested in a drunk like Bentley. Say something happened. Something that could be directly attributed to Bentley's condition. Any court martial would pillory Carter. I would hold out little hope for the officers of the *Magnanime* to speak out on our behalf, but in a situation which I just alluded to, they would sing mightily, and for the same reason.'

'That tribe? I've never seen people so supine.'

Harry had hoped that conversation would calm James down, but it seemed to be having precisely the opposite effect.

'They would be reluctant witnesses for us since it may adversely affect their careers. They would give willing testimony against Carter in such a setting for exactly the same reason.'

'Yet they too are frightened of Bentley?' James could not keep out of his voice the low esteem in which he held such an attitude.

Harry raised a finger. 'Is that because of the power he has over Carter?'

'This is all getting rather byzantine,' said James wearily. 'And I really cannot bring myself to care.'

'You were the one who said that Carter was frightened of the man.'

'He is. I saw it in his eyes.'

'Then whatever hold Bentley has over Carter must be damning.'

'I suppose it would do us no harm to find out?' This was said without much enthusiasm.

'I think we owe it to Carter, don't you?' said Harry gaily.

'Most certainly, brother, most certainly.'

Harry laughed loudly and distinctively. James nearly smiled at the thought that it was probably the only sound of gaiety to penetrate the now silent wardroom. But he could not. Instead he stopped and leaned against a bulkhead, trying to compose his face, so that Harry would not see the hurt.

'I wish I could help, James,' he said softly, putting his hand on his brother's shoulder. 'I don't have the words.'

'There are no "words", Harry. At least none that would lessen the burden. There are plenty for a swine like Bentley to use.' The anger came boiling up again at the mention of the premier's name.

'Keep me away from them all, Harry. For if one of them dares to speak her name again, I will kill them.' He screamed, loud enough to be heard all over the ship: 'Do you *hear*!'

Harry slapped James hard, then threw his arms around him, and pulled him into an embrace. James struggled free.

'Just leave me be, Harry.' His shoulders had slumped. He looked exhausted.

'Sleep, James,' he said, remembering how his brother had sat over him the night before. 'Sleep will help.'

'Would that were true, Harry.'

'Damn. I could kill them myself for bringing you to this.'

He took his brother's arm, and led him gently to his berth.

VI

James had been berthed in the steward's cabin. They talked for some time, Harry trying to repair the damage, trying to bring his brother back to the mood he had been in before dinner, to divert his mind from the doomed affair with Caroline Farrar. He felt that he had managed a partial success. But at a price. His head was throbbing as he left James' berth.

Harry had not been allocated any quarters, so he presumed upon the surgeon and returned to Outhwaite's cabin. It would have been polite to ask the man's permission but a quick glance into the surgeon's dispensary showed that Outhwaite was out cold, an empty bottle clasped to his breast. Since no other casualty seemed to occupy the space in his berth, and since a reasonably calm sea made the prospect of a sudden fall unlikely, Harry bedded down gratefully in the same cot. He had done little to warrant it, but he was tired from the exertions of the day. The pain he felt reminded him of his wound.

It was some time before the commotion going on outside his door roused him. He heard muffled oaths, the sounds of a struggle, a thud as someone fell. Then a sort of drumming sound. Painfully he raised his head from the pillow. He listened for a few seconds, but no sound followed. He swung his feet to the floor. Whatever it was, it was surely none of his concern, but he knew that he would be obliged to have a look. Curiosity would rob him of the power of sleep.

He pulled back the canvas screen, hearing a distant shout as he did so. James knelt in the open space between the cabins, a tallow candle in one hand and a knife in the other. The body lay crumpled up, the face hidden, but the officer's coat was plain even in the dim light. Other people were coming, their feet sounding on the wooden planking. The lanterns they carried began to illuminate the scene.

'Harry,' said James standing up, a curious expression on his face. He held out the knife. Harry did not look at the knife, his eyes were locked on to his brother's. He wanted to speak, but could think of no words to say.

'Seize him.' Carter's voice, loud and sharp.

'I found it.' James was looking at him with doubt plain in his face. He suddenly seemed to realize that other people were there. His face went blank as two seamen rushed forward and grabbed his arms. Carter came into the arc of light, followed by several other men. He knelt beside the body.

'Get the surgeon, man.' He pushed the raised shoulder of the man lying on the planking. The body rolled on to its back. Bentley's eyes were wide open. The front and side of his chest were covered in blood. He had not been stabbed so much as ripped open.

Outhwaite stumbled into several people before reaching the centre of the assembled group. He was soaking wet. No doubt he had been aroused from his drunken slumber by the liberal quantity of water the hands had poured over him. He knelt by the body, his shaking hand touching a point under the neck.

'Dead,' he slurred. 'Stone dead.'

Carter, who had not taken his eyes off the body since he knelt down, slowly looked up at James. His eyes went to the knife still in his hand. It was covered in blood. He turned to look at Harry, his eyes registering triumph, before he turned back to James.

'Well, Mr Ludlow?' he said quietly. It was plain which one he was addressing. Carter stood, and leaning forward took the knife from James' hand.

'Mr Carter . . .' said Harry.

'You will oblige me by staying quiet, Ludlow, or I will have you removed. I require an explanation from your brother, not from you.'

70

James looked at Harry. There was a question in the look, one that he could not ask.

'I have nothing to say.' James turned back and looked directly at Carter.

'Indeed. Speech would seem superfluous. And to think that you accused me of being a scrub. You, who claim good breeding. Was this a continuation of your quarrel, or did you just take the opportunity to kill him in cold blood?'

'I told you, Carter, I have nothing to say.'

'The judge who tries you will have something to say. And so will the hangman. I pray that I am available to see it and hear it.'

'Carter.' Harry's face was as white as the bandage round his head. He looked as though he was going to faint. Carter just stared at him.

'Master-at-Arms. Clap this man in irons and put him in the cable tier.'

Harry paced the moonlit deck, one thought chasing another as he tried to comprehend what had happened. He had left James apparently calm. Had he been only calm on the surface, and really still seething underneath? Harry had always thought of his brother as a totally rational man, seeing himself as the impetuous one. Yet recently James had thrown both caution and good sense to the winds for a woman, and when the whole affair came crashing about his head, the pain that it caused him was not hidden. He'd known then there was more emotion in James than he had realized. Perhaps that unpredictability was a family trait, shared by both. If so, it looked as though, this time, it would prove fatal.

He then damned himself for thinking like that. How could he condemn a man he loved so readily! His mind swung violently from one opinion to the other. James could not have killed Bentley. He simply did not have it in him to do so in that manner. And James would have admitted it straight away if he had. It was all a terrible mistake. Harry ran the scene through his head. Had James, hearing the same sounds that he had heard, reacted more quickly? Had he pulled the knife from the body just as Harry had emerged from the sick bay?

'But why didn't he say something?' Harry realized that he had spoken out loud. Again that vision of James' anger at the dinner. Harry loved his sister, but Anne was more than that to James, having practically raised him after their mother died. He would brook no comments on a woman he held to be as near a saint as it was possible to be. Even Harry had to tread carefully on that score. That partly explained his dislike of Arthur, Anne's husband. To James, no one was good enough for his older sister.

But that was nothing compared to the way he thought about Caroline Farrar, and Harry realized that James, by displaying the possibility of being discomfited by references to Anne, had merely encouraged Bentley, who was still smarting from the treatment that James had meted out to him earlier.

If Bentley had set out to upset James, then he could have chosen no better barb. Harry had never seen his brother react like that, always assuming that his demeanour was one of studied indifference in the face of praise or criticism. He could not recollect a time when he had seen him strike anyone. James was a man who relied on carefully delivered insults. Again Harry had to remind himself that he was not the only impetuous member of the family. There had been real power and venom in the blow he had given the drunken premier. And he had publicly threatened him. Now the man was dead.

Yet any number of people would have wanted to kill Bentley. That was plain by the attitude of all the officers aboard the ship in their reaction to the man's behaviour. Even Carter could have done it, after the way Bentley embarrassed him at dinner. For a moment Harry brightened at the thought, before dismissing it. You don't kill your premier for that. You relieve him and call a court martial. And what about that sailor who had called him 'murderous bugger'. A name had been mentioned, but Harry could not recall it. Perhaps someone had died at the grating, under Bentley's relentless flogging.

How well did he really know James? They had spent so much time apart. While that had made it possible for them to be friends, it had in some way clouded their opinion of each other. Harry knew that James saw him as a devil-may-care character, a man who loved a risk and revelled in a fight. A man who would be sadly bored in a domestic setting. Out of place in a well-furnished drawing-room.

That was a persona that Harry cultivated. Yet he, like other men, had deep longings which remained unspoken. He would never admit, even to James, how much he missed being a King's officer, how much he longed to follow in their father's footsteps and rise to surpass his vice-admiral's rank. To be sure, there was excitement in privateering. But there was no glory in it. In the same way he could not articulate his desire to have sons of his own. To take to sea, to teach, to watch, to chastise and praise, and turn into men that he could be proud of. And that would require a woman. She could not merely be a vehicle for him to sire children. She too must be special, an individual, spirited and independent. All these things were hidden. Private.

Was James the same, hiding his violent nature under a veneer of sophistication? Was he really a mass of seething passion barely kept in control? The look he had given his brother had tried to convey something, but Harry could not deduce what. But the evidence of his eyes kept coming up before him. Of his brother kneeling over the body with the knife in his hands. Of the violence of the blow he had struck Bentley earlier, and the look of hate and contempt in his eyes as he did so.

He shook his head, ignoring the pain. He must assume James innocent. Any other view was disloyal. And if he assumed him innocent, then it was axiomatic that someone else was guilty. If James had wanted to kill Bentley he would have done so in the open, issuing a proper challenge. So James was not guilty. That was what he was trying to convey in that look. So he must take steps to prove him so.

Harry's mind was racing, examining and discarding theories until there were only two left. One, that Bentley had attacked James and had been accidentally killed in the struggle. Or James had discovered the body, and pulled out the knife as the first step to aiding the victim. He would need to talk to his brother. That would require permission from Carter. He disliked the thought of asking Carter for anything, but it would have to be. He could hardly refuse. Not even a man as spiteful as he could deny Harry access. But that would not be possible until morning. His brain raced as he thought of the things he could do in the mean time. Sleep was out of the question. They would raise the Rock of Gibraltar in a few days. There was little time. One fact stood out amongst the mass of thoughts chasing each other round his brain. The second possibility put someone else in that gangway less than a minute before he himself looked out. Again the thought pressed on his brain. If James was innocent, then someone else was guilty. And the best way to clear his brother was to find that person, and either force a confession or accumulate enough evidence to establish his guilt.

Harry set himself the task of clearing his mind and ordering his thoughts. He could go into action against an enemy with a clear head, making a thousand rapid calculations and issuing instructions without hesitation. He wanted to apply that same attitude of mind to this problem. He knew that success would attend his efforts only if he did that.

Outhwaite, woken for the second time, was not pleased.

'Bentley's body. I need to look at it.'

'God give me some peace to sleep.'

'There's no time for that. I need to look at the body, and I want you to look at it with me.'

'He's laid out in his quarters. And if you think I'm going to rouse myself to look at him, you've got another think coming. A corpse might interest you, Mr Ludlow, but I for one have seen too many. I might consider it in the mornin'.'

Outhwaite made to turn over. Harry grabbed him roughly and hauled him up by his dirty stock.

'Now, Surgeon. Or someone will be examining you.'

'Unhand me, Mr Ludlow!' There was fear in his eyes, and his chins quivered. After all, one brother had just knifed the premier. Who knew what madness ran in this family?

'Get up, fetch your bag, and come with me.'

'I'm not sure this is proper, sir.'

'Proper be damned. Just get a move on.'

They came out of the dispensary. It was twenty feet away from the spot where Bentley's body had been found. A party had gathered with buckets, ready to swab the bloodstained planking. Harry stopped suddenly, causing the shuffling Outhwaite to bump into him.

'Belay there,' he said to the petty officer in charge of the party.

Harry took the lantern off the surgeon, and placed it, and his own lantern, so that the area where the body had fallen was well lit. This would be the best that could ever be achieved, since daylight never penetrated these parts of the ship. The blood had soaked into the planking, leaving a dark and copious bloodstain. Casting around, Harry noticed another stain some way from the main one. It was small and quite round. In the centre of the stain there was an indentation in the deck planking, a cut; even, and about a quarter of an inch long. Harry ran his finger over it. He fetched his lantern for a closer look. Outhwaite watched him fascinated. The hands pretended indifference, but they too were dying to know what he was about.

'I don't suppose you have a knife in that bag, Mr Outhwaite?' he asked.

'There are any number of knives, sir. Help yourself.' Outhwaite put the bag down beside him.

Harry opened it and sorted through the rusty instruments. He did not have much hope that the surgeon would be carrying the kind of knife he was looking for. Yet there it was, an officer's dirk. The knife was long and thin, but the blade was flat. Harry looked at Outhwaite questioningly.

'Very handy for removing musket balls,' said Outhwaite.

Harry put the tip of the knife into the cut in the floor. It didn't quite fit, seeming to reach the base of the cut without filling the sides. He then stood up, checked the point of the knife to see if it was sharp, then raised his arm. He let the knife drop. It stuck in the planking with a thud, swinging to and fro. He pulled it out of the wood and looked down at the mark. It was nowhere near as deep as the other.

Harry then dipped the knife into one of the water butts that the sailors had for swabbing the deck. He stuck it, with some force, into the planking. Water ran off the blade and formed a small pool around it. They were all watching him closely now. They looked at his face, but that gave nothing away. Harry took the lantern and began to search the area. Outhwaite stood looking aggrieved.

'Perhaps you would be better employed in assisting me, Mr Outhwaite.'

'I might. If I had the foggiest notion of what you were about.'

'I am looking for something, Mr Outhwaite.'

'What, pray?'

'I don't know.'

'I'd be pushed to know how you'll recognize it when you see it.'

'It will be something that should not be here. There was quite a struggle. I heard the sound and I would guess that Bentley did not die easily. He fought his attacker.' Harry looked at the surgeon, almost daring him to speak the words which were plainly on his lips: *Your brother*.

'Look here. Now this is strange.'

'What's that?' Outhwaite edged forward, his curiosity overcoming his fear. So did the hands.

'Powder. White powder.' Harry rubbed some of the powder which was spread on the deck between his finger and thumb. 'Dusting powder. I don't recall Mr Bentley wearing a wig?'

'He rarely did of late, in fact he rarely dressed up at all.'

'The other officers are more correct in that matter, I noticed.'

'Only when they are bein' formal, sir. I myself dust my wig when I'm dressed up.' Harry could imagine where most of the dust went.

'As you were for the Captain's dinner?'

'As everyone was for the Captain's dinner.'

'Quite. Everyone except Bentley, my brother, and I. James says it's no longer fashionable.'

'I've heard Mr Turnbull use that reason. He was bareheaded tonight, as he usually is these days.' Outhwaite leaned over to look at the planking. 'I don't see that a bit of dust signifies anything.'

'You may be right. But I would like you to record the fact that it is here.'

'Whatever for?'

'So that you may swear it to a jury, Surgeon. I would also bring your attention to this small stain. See the cut in the middle of it? I would say that is a mite deep if it was made by a knife being dropped. Look at where I stuck your knife in the planking. A bit nearer the depth, wouldn't you say?'

'Aye.' Outhwaite, kneeling now and examining the three marks, could not keep the wonder out of his voice. 'That stain is blood!'

'Which means that the knife that killed the premier was not dropped by whoever used it, but was deliberately stuck in the deck.' Again Outhwaite looked at Harry with that mute statement on his lips. 'Would you agree?'

'It seems likely.'

'See the other cut I made by dropping your knife. It's not the same size at all.'

'I don't see what you are drivin' at, Mr Ludlow.'

'My brother had the knife in his hand when he was put under restraint. That means that he picked it out of the floor, where it had been long enough for a quantity of blood to run off and make this stain. And not dropped either. Does he stab Bentley, stick the knife in the floor, then pull it out again in order to be discovered holding it? A strange thing to do if you have just killed a man.'

'I'm not sure I would know what was the proper thing to do.' There was a slight tone of irony in the surgeon's voice.

'The proper thing to do, Outhwaite, is to get away as quickly as possible. Unless you are determined to hang.' Harry stood up, and, dropping the dirk into the surgeon's bag, he picked it up and handed it to him.

'Now for a look at the body,' he said.

Harry made for the stairwell that led up to the gun-deck. Outhwaite followed, his slippers slapping noisily on the steps. Harry, shading his lantern and bidding the surgeon to do likewise, motioned him to be quiet as they came on to the gun-deck. In the glim light from the tallow wads burning in the sconces, they could see the outline of the hammocks swinging with the ship's roll.

The hands were tight-packed and seemed noisily asleep as they made their way down the alley between the hammocks and the guns. Harry knew that not all the hammocks would be occupied. Some would have slung something into theirs, to make it look as though they were full. These men would be off in the darker recesses of the ship, doing all those things expressly forbidden in the Articles of War. Those articles were so comprehensive that no ship could ever sail without breaching them. So it was not surprising how often they were quietly ignored.

Along the upper deck, they entered the silent wardroom. This room was the same size as Carter's quarters directly above. Paper and some sheet music were strewn across the large table which ran up the centre of the room. It seemed a much smaller space than the room above. The doors to the cabins which lined both sides were shut. A coffee pot steamed on the stove in the pantry, and the aroma of its contents filled the air. The steward should have been about, but he was probably taking a nap.

Harry made his way through the wardroom to Bentley's cabin without hesitation. It was a room he had seen before, though occupied by a different premier. It was at the very rear of the wardroom on the starboard side, and the most spacious, as befitted the occupant's rank. And it would have those most precious things in a ship at sea, privacy and daylight. He stood back to let Outhwaite pass him. The surgeon turned the handle and walked in. Harry followed him. No light came through the glass of the stern-light casements. Their two lanterns illuminated the room and the white sheet that covered the body in the cot.

'This ain't right, sir. We should have Mr Craddock's permission for this.' Craddock was now the acting premier.

'I think Mr Craddock will be grateful for his slumbers.'

Harry pulled back the sheet. Bentley lay, his hands folded across his chest, the angry purple face now white and at peace.

'We shall have to put him in spirits in the morning,' said Outhwaite. 'Though I doubt he truly needs it.'

Outhwaite would quite easily acknowledge that Bentley was a drunkard, just as he would vehemently deny that he suffered from the same affliction.

Harry pulled the arms off the chest. Then he pulled the coat open. It was damp, which struck him as odd. Pulling it closed again he examined it thoroughly with his lantern raised. It wasn't blood that had made it damp, for down Bentley's right side was a streak of white. Dust? It had mixed with the damp on his coat to make a chalk-like mark. He opened the coat again. The man's waistcoat was covered in his blood, making observation difficult.

'The wound, Outhwaite. How do I find the wound?'

'By touch, sir. Unless you mean to undress him.'

Harry was not squeamish, but the thought of running his fingers through a long knife cut was more than he could stomach. He started to unbutton the waistcoat.

'Mr Ludlow. I can be no party to this without permission.'

'What can possibly be wrong with a surgeon examining a body?' The waistcoat fell open, and Harry started on the shirt underneath. Once it had been white, but now it was wholly black and sticky. He pulled the shirt open to reveal the white flesh with the angry black gash where Bentley had been skewered. Outhwaite moved his lantern closer.

'Not a stab wound, Outhwaite.'

'No, sir. He has been gutted like a fish.'

'Could you say which way the knife went in?'

'I think so. It seems quite clean down here at the base of the stomach. I would say that the knife went in there.' Outhwaite produced a knife of his own, and gently inserted it in the wound. He eased it out again.

'Seems to have been stabbed this way,' he said, indicating a right-handed thrust. 'It's a very deep cut.'

'And was then pulled upwards and sideways?'

'It must have sliced into the aorta. No wonder there was so much blood.'

'Did you examine him before?'

'Didn't seem no point, Mr Ludlow, seeing as how he was plainly dead.'

'How long would you say that wound was?'

'More than twelve inches, I'd say.'

Neither of them had heard the door open. The voice made them both jump.

'I would be obliged if you could explain what you are about?' They spun round to see Craddock filling the doorway. His grey hair was sticking out sideways from a nightcap and he was wearing nightclothes. He was also aiming a pistol at Harry's chest.

79

VII

Harry, standing between the two marine sentries, recalled the events of the previous night and could not suppress a smile. Hardly surprising, given the element of farce in what had occurred.

He and Outhwaite must have looked like a pair of bodysnatchers as they leant over Bentley's corpse. Craddock, in nightshirt and cap, with the pistol in his hand, his grey whiskers sticking out sideways, looked absolutely ridiculous. It had been entirely in keeping when Harry had calmly replied to his question.

'We are examining the body.'

'At this hour. And you, Mr Outhwaite. What pray are you about?'

In the confused hierarchy of the Navy, a ship's surgeon had a dual loyalty. Outhwaite, no doubt operating on the principle that the best means of defence is attack, replied sharply.

'I am responsible to the Sick and Hurt Board in matters medical, Mr Craddock. I do not have any requirement to explain myself to you.'

Craddock, taken aback, could not quite respond. His mouth moved but no sound emerged. Outhwaite decided to press home his advantage.

'I would be obliged if you'll leave me alone to finish my examination.'

'At this hour?' said Craddock, recovering his composure. 'I will not have you skulking around the wardroom at this hour.'

'Mr Craddock. If I had asked you for permission to examine the body, what would you have done?' asked Harry.

'I would have referred the matter to the Captain.'

'Then I, for one, make no apology for "skulking around" as you call it. I have good grounds to believe that the Captain would have refused me permission.'

'That's as maybe, Mr Ludlow. I cannot see what you hope to gain.'

'My brother stands accused of murder, Mr Craddock. While it may be in order for everyone else aboard ship to presume his guilt, I must presume his innocence. I must therefore gather what information I can to assist his defence.'

'And I am here to ensure that such an examination is carried out on a proper scientific basis,' said Outhwaite in a magisterial tone. It would have been better for him to say nothing, for Craddock had understood what Harry was saying. But such a remark from a man like Outhwaite entirely destroyed the tone.

'This is outrageous,' snapped Craddock. 'Sick and Hurt Board be damned, Mr Outhwaite. Return to your quarters. As for you, Mr Ludlow, I will require you to do the same, but under the escort of a marine guard.'

Outhwaite picked up his bag and walked past the bristling Craddock.

'I would happily return to my quarters, Mr Craddock, unescorted. But our late friend here did not bother to assign me any, and neither, sir, have you.'

Craddock's face fell. This was a shocking breach of good manners, a thing he was very fussy about. It did not seem to occur to him that until two hours ago it had been Bentley's responsibility, not his.

'I beg . . .' he started to say.

'However, I am happy to bed down in the surgeon's quarters for now. You may send a marine to stand watch if you wish.'

With that Harry walked past the crestfallen Craddock and went on his way.

*

81

His escort came to attention, and for all the world like a defaulter marched him into the Captain's cabin. Craddock stood there, looking very grave.

'Well, Ludlow. Explain yourself,' said Carter.

'I dare say Mr Craddock has given you any explanation you require.'

'I require an explanation from you.' Brisk and humourless as usual.

'I wish to gather evidence for my brother's defence.'

'A noble aim, if not a waste of time. You do not feel it would have been prudent to ask first?'

'Time is pressing.' Harry looked at Carter, as if to say: 'What would be the point of asking?'

'I am curious to know on what grounds you feel your brother could be innocent?' Brisk he might be, but Carter was nevertheless relaxed, enjoying himself. 'He has a public quarrel with Bentley, is found a few hours later standing over the body with the knife that killed the man in his hand. And then he refuses to say anything. Your brother has not protested his innocence at all. Yet you choose to presume it?'

'I cannot conceive that James would do such a thing. And I have reason to suppose that he was merely the first to discover the body.'

'What is this?' Carter's eyebrows arched dramatically. 'The first to discover the body? You are saying that when he found the body, Bentley was already dead?' He turned to include Craddock in the conversation. 'I have often read of such a defence being put forward, in fact, I imagine it to be quite a common one in such a circumstance, and usually, as I recall, pure invention. However, let us assume that you are correct. Your brother discovers Bentley. What does he do then? Seek to aid the dying man? Raise the alarm? Perhaps call for the surgeon? No! Your brother does none of these things. Instead, he picks up the knife. And there at his feet a stricken man goes begging for assistance.' Carter almost snarled. 'What noble behaviour!'

'We all do things on the spur of the moment that we wonder at afterwards. What I need to know is, can I count on your good offices to gather any information that may materially affect his defence?'

'Such as?' The Captain sat back in his chair, his hands making a spire in front of his mouth.

'Firstly, I would like to see my brother.'

'And?'

'I would like certain things I have already observed, recorded and witnessed. I would also like to examine the knife that my brother held in his hand.'

Carter stood up, and walking round his desk began to pace up and down in front of it. He did not look at Harry as he spoke.

'What I found strange, Ludlow, is that your brother killed Bentley.'

Harry, surprised at this turn in the conversation, watched to see if Craddock felt the same. The older man looked as bemused as he felt.

'It did not seem right, albeit that they had a quarrel.' Carter had his head bowed as he waited, hands behind his back, a picture of deep thinking. 'I set myself to finding the truth of the matter. You know that it is difficult on a ship to gain privacy. Can two men really have a fight on an open gangway without being observed? You see, Ludlow, your brother threatened to put a bullet in me. In fact to kill me. Knife or bullet, what's the difference? Can you imagine him, seething in his quarters over the loss of your ship? We all observed how uncontrollable his passions are. He sees me as the author of all your woes. Can he really be content to wait for the chance to put a bullet in me?'

Carter stopped pacing and looked directly at Harry. His voice, hitherto level, had taken on a theatrical quality.

'He comes out of his cabin, knife in hand, intent on murder. Who should he chance upon but Mr Bentley, going about his duties. They may well have had high words, but surely that is now forgotten.'

Harry could hardly interject to point out that Carter was mistaken. That would not serve his cause at all. But could Carter really be so self-obsessed as to believe this rubbish?

' "Hold," says Bentley. "What are you about?" ' Just like in a melodrama, Carter held up his hands.

' "Out of my way," says your brother. "It is Captain Carter that I want to see." '

He turned to Craddock. 'A scrub, he called me. Scum of the earth was also mentioned. Did he not threaten me, Mr Craddock?'

'To a duel,' snapped Harry. Craddock said nothing, but he did have the good grace to blush. Carter held up an accusing finger.

'But reflect upon this, Ludlow. I was acting within my duty. Your brother, realizing this, also concludes that he will receive no redress in a court of law. No court can condemn an innocent man. Bentley, seeing the knife, guesses what your brother is about.' That theatrical tone again!

' "Return to your quarters, Mr Ludlow," he says, placing his hand on your brother's chest. "Stand aside," cries Ludlow. Bentley refuses and tries to take the knife off him. They struggle, and in his passion your brother strikes the mortal wound!' Carter, his eyes distant, jerked his arm forward. Craddock was giving him the strangest look, his thick grey eyebrows knitted in concentration, unable to comprehend this man whose moods he found difficult to fathom even under normal circumstances.

'Has my brother told you this?' Harry's face showed the confusion of his thoughts.

'No,' said Carter, his eyes clearing. 'As far as I am aware, your brother still refuses to speak.'

'Then this is pure speculation.'

'I don't think that my witnesses would take kindly to that, Ludlow,' he said with a trace of a smile on his face.

'Witnesses?' The sudden lift of the acting premier's eyebrows matched Harry's disbelief. Craddock's bright blue eyes were wide open. It was the first he had heard of it too.

Carter went behind his desk and sat down again.

'Yes, Ludlow. Witnesses.'

'Who are these witnesses? When can I see them?' Harry's urgency was not matched by Carter, who took a long time to reply.

'It is perfectly in order for you to have an attorney examine them in court. Until then, it is safer for them to remain anonymous.' Carter was looking at the papers on his desk, but he was also smiling.

Harry was fighting to control himself, and the effort showed in his face. Craddock had moved forward a step thinking he was about to attack Carter.

'I demand to see these men.'

'Demand, Ludlow?' Carter looked up. 'Yesterday you required this, that and the other. Today you demand. I must remind you that I command this ship, and no one has the right to demand anything of me.'

'All right. I beg you.' Harry was looking over Carter's head. He did not see the grin of satisfaction on the man's face.

'Begging is better than demanding, I must say. Much more pleasin' to the ear. So let us list the things you are beggin' for. To talk to your brother was one. To have recorded certain facts for his trial. And you want to interview the witnesses.'

Carter rubbed his chin, as if contemplating the requests.

'I think not, Ludlow. I really cannot see that the routine of the ship can be upset just to oblige you. You know how jittery the hands can get.'

'You cannot deny me the right to see my brother.' Harry was almost pleading.

'There was one other thing you asked. You asked to examine the knife that killed Bentley. Just to prove that I am not uncooperative, I think that would be in order.'

He reached into his desk, and pulling out the knife, he laid it on the top. Harry gasped, recognizing it immediately as his own. The knife had a long blade, but you could see how sharp it was. The handle was mother-of-pearl inlaid with gold. The initials HL were wrought in gold on the handle.

'I wondered at the initials,' said Carter. 'You wish to see your brother. See him you can. If you care to stand on the poop you will see him going about his duties.'

Harry tore his eyes away from his knife and looked at Carter without comprehending.

'I cannot justify feeding a man who does not work, Ludlow. I have set your brother to work. I dare say a spell before the mast will temper his arrogance. Perhaps he will also learn some manners.'

The smile was infuriating. Harry's fists were balled tightly.

'You may see him, Ludlow. But,' he turned to include Craddock, 'and this is my express command, you may under no circumstances address and interfere with his going about his duties.'

Harry reached forward slowly and picked up his knife. The dried blood was caked around the blade near the hilt. He ran his fingers over his initials on the hilt. Carter had a wide grin on his face, enjoying the way he had discomfited his enemy.

Suddenly he pulled his hand back, raising the knife in the air. Carter, grabbing tightly at the arms of his chair, pushed himself backwards, his eyes wide with surprise. At the same time he grabbed for the drawer of his desk.

Craddock started to move to intercept, as did the marines standing to attention behind him. Harry, his knees bending, dropped down, and stuck the knife in the deck. Craddock froze, uncomprehending. Carter, sensing that the danger was past, sat forward to see what was going on.

Having pulled the knife out of the deck, Harry inspected the cut with his finger. He looked up at Carter and smiled. Craddock stepped forward sharply, signalling to the marines. He knew if this interview continued that Carter would continue to goad Harry. There was more than a chance that Harry would attack him. In the face of direct orders there was not much he could do. But at least he could prevent Harry from giving his commander grounds to lock him up as well. The marines stood either side of Harry. If Carter was curious about what had just taken place, he hid it well.

'I think this interview is at an end, don't you?'

Craddock dismissed the marines outside Carter's cabin. His face was set, but Harry guessed that the man probably sympathized with his plight. No one could doubt that Carter was doing everything he could to make Harry suffer. Yet within the bounds of naval convention Craddock had few options. His captain could be a raving lunatic, and after that very theatrical performance probably was. Yet there was little an acting first lieutenant, desperately hoping to be confirmed, could do.

86

'I have arranged for you to occupy Mr Bentley's quarters,' he said softly.

'Then I hope you have seen fit to remove Mr Bentley.' Harry immediately regretted the remark. Taking his anger out on Craddock would get him nowhere.

'Of course.' Craddock's gentle reply confirmed Harry's opinion of his sympathy. The older man's face had a kindly concerned look. 'I will arrange to have your dunnage shifted.'

'Which section has my brother been put in?'

'Topmen.' Craddock looked away as he said this, seeking to hide his embarrassment.

'With your permission, I will take a walk on deck.'

Harry walked away without waiting for a reply. He made his way on to the deck and up to the poop. Leaning against the taffrail, he looked aloft at the soaring masts and the great sails they supported.

'Topman,' he said to himself. 'James. You'll be lucky to see Gibraltar.' He closed his eyes to prevent the tears that stung his eyes from showing. Turning, he looked out over the wake, a broad white line stretching back to where this had started. Started with his impetuosity.

His knife! Suddenly he remembered the look that James had given him, standing over Bentley's body. His knife! Lingering doubts, which he had fought but had still persisted, vanished. Now he could understand James' silence.

Harry Ludlow was a man of action. Plans and solutions did not stem from contemplation but from the changing nature of events. The first thing was to keep James alive. Only then could he contemplate the steps necessary to prove him innocent.

'Mr Craddock,' he said walking briskly into the wardroom 'May I see you privately?'

Craddock, sitting at the head of the table, stood up and nodded without speaking. The other officers, still really only faces to Harry, exchanged knowing glances. Craddock made his way into his cabin, a smaller space than Bentley's, but still blessed with daylight. The morning sun blazed through the side windows. Craddock closed the door as Harry came in behind him.

Craddock walked over to the plain deal desk and stood beside the chair. There was a sea-chest beside his cot, which, hanging from the deck-beams, swung gently as the ship rolled, and another behind the door underneath his hanging uniforms. He indicated for Harry to sit if he wished.

'I will not mince my words for the sake of politeness, Mr Craddock. For reasons I cannot fathom, your commanding officer seems bent on a strange form of revenge. You will be aware of the bad blood that exists between him and myself?'

Craddock gave an imperceptible nod. With his face set in a noncommittal way, his sparse grey hair and side whiskers made him look like a stern grandfather.

'No doubt this has prayed on his mind these past years. And while I can see that he would take great pleasure in discomfiting me, I cannot see how this extends to my brother James. Yet it does. Revenge! He is so bent on it that it has entirely warped his judgement. You may tell me that he is behaving as he always does?'

'This is none of my affair, sir,' said Craddock, stiffly.

'With respect, sir, that is pure sophistry.'

Craddock was quite taken aback. 'Respect' might be stated, but it was absent in Harry's voice.

'The Captain has seen fit to place a totally inexperienced man in a position where only the most nimble can survive. My brother is many things, Mr Craddock, but he is no sailor, let alone a topman.'

'I did seek to dissuade Captain Carter from this.'

'Yet you failed?' Craddock said nothing. 'It is my opinion that your captain is mad.'

'Mr Ludlow!' Shock registered on the old man's face. And fear.

'Whether his madness is based on just a desire for revenge, I cannot say, but I would hazard that it is of a more general nature. You would know more of this than me, and I dare say the ship's log could go some way to support my allegations, especially in the section headed punishment.'

'I really cannot allow you to speak like this, sir.' Craddock started forward, putting his hand out to open the door.

88

'Are you saying that you will be a party to murder rather than contemplate the truth?' Harry spoke slowly. He wanted Craddock to fully understand him.

'Murder?'

'If my brother dies in the execution of duties that he is incapable of carrying out, I will hold you responsible.'

'I am obeying orders.' The acting premier was casting around vaguely, trying to digest the import of Harry's attack.

'Mr Craddock. Some orders have to be ignored, or at the very least circumvented. You are the first lieutenant of the *Magnanime*. It is well within your authority to do so.'

'Disobey a direct order?' Craddock put his hand to his head, running the finger through the thinning hair. 'I'll be damned if I do!'

Harry raised his voice. 'I can assure you that you will be eternally damned if you don't, sir. I cannot reach the Captain. If he was capable of listening to reason, I would be the last person to extract it. You have already stated, Mr Craddock, that you have tried to reason with him and failed.'

Craddock nodded, his bright blue eyes eager, seeking to convey how hard he had tried.

'I am a man of wealth and influence, Mr Craddock. My brother stands in mortal danger. Everything I own is of no account compared to his safety. Not wealth, not position, and certainly not pride. Do you really think that I will let anyone get away with such behaviour? If Captain Carter was to stop and think, he would see the foolishness of what he is doing. I can only surmise that he is incapable of doing so. I must therefore ask that you relieve him.'

Craddock looked as though Harry had hit him. 'Relieve him?'

'On the grounds that he is unfit to command.'

'I cannot even contemplate such a course.' Craddock pulled himself up to his full height. 'And I would remind you, sir, that to do such a thing would require the support of a majority of the ship's officers.'

'Will you seek such support?'

'I will not.' Craddock was flushed with a combination of anger and embarrassment.

'Then, Mr Craddock, hear this. I hold you personally responsible for my brother's safety. Should anything happen to him I will hound you until your dying day.'

'I do not take kindly to being threatened, sir.'

'I will also add, Mr Craddock, that should you demonstrate an ability to circumvent the Captain's orders, and thus ensure that no harm comes to James, you will earn my gratitude. I will place at your disposal all the influence that I can muster to aid your advancement. Good day to you!'

Threatening Craddock was a calculated risk. Part of the calculation lay in his obvious reluctance to carry through Carter's order. Such instructions could not be anything but repugnant to a man like him. But the offer of assistance was the more dangerous part of the calculation. Craddock could react badly, feel slighted, at what sounded remarkably like a bribe, and ignore both Harry's threats and promises. But he was old for his position. Like many others, it would seem to him that opportunity had passed him by. He lacked the contacts to effect any change in his circumstances. His greatest desire would be confirmation of his present post. For that he needed Carter's help, not Harry's.

Yet Harry's offer might tempt him. Few officers were promoted through any action of their own. Indeed few, even in war, were given the chance to distinguish themselves. Single-ship actions of the calibre likely to catch the Admiralty's eye and the public imagination were rare. It was even less likely that he would be caught up in a successful fleet action resounding enough in its outcome to mean promotion for anyone.

Prior to Bentley's untimely death, Craddock would have considered himself lucky to have his previous post, and be resigned at his age to retiring from the Navy with the rank of lieutenant. Nothing was certain with Carter. The sudden prospect of someone like Harry Ludlow, acting on his behalf, pressing those in power to consider his advancement, could revive his dreams. That was Harry's main hope. Threats, once stated, rarely carried force for very long. Inducements, once the man on the receiving end had time to calculate their value, and wonder at the benefits they would bring, tended to be of more permanent use.

Harry left Craddock and walked straight through the ward-room, the eyes of the other officers on him, trying, no doubt, to discern from his expression what had taken place. His next stop was Outhwaite.

'Mr Outhwaite, I require your assistance.' The surgeon, who had been lounging on his bed, sat bolt upright.

'If assisting you is likely to expose me to the dressing-down I had this morning, I'd rather not.'

'I do not intend to give you any choice in the matter.'

'Indeed?' The response denoted just a hint of wariness. Outhwaite already knew that he was talking to a potentially dangerous man.

'Captain Carter. What would you say his condition is? His fitness to command?'

'It would be above my duties to venture an opinion.'

'Even a private one?'

'I cannot see that it would do me any good.' He made to turn away from Harry.

'He has put my brother before the mast, and billed him as a topman.'

Outhwaite's head shot back round. 'That's madness.'

'Is that an opinion?'

'No, no.' The surgeon shook his head. 'I only mean that he can't do that.'

'He can and he has.' Harry put his hand on Outhwaite's shoulder, pulling him round so he could look him in the eye. 'I have formally requested Mr Craddock to remove him on the grounds of his unfitness, but he has refused.'

'And quite right to, sir. He would spend the rest of his life on the beach.'

Harry continued to stare at him. 'And I am formally request-ing an opinion from you.'

Outhwaite jerked his head away again. 'I have already said, sir, I cannot venture an opinion in that direction.'

'You will have to, my friend. In a court of law and under oath. But that presupposes that something will happen to my brother. What I require from you is assistance in the way the ship divides.'

'Divides?' Outhwaite bent down and started to search under the cot.

'I don't have time for the luxury of making everyone's acquaintance, of testing their feeling and evaluating their views. I want you to tell me about the people aboard the *Magnanime* and how they stand in their relations with Captain Carter.'

'You are engaging me in a conspiracy.'

'A conspiracy to prevent murder. This is an unhappy ship. A blind beggar could see that. Why? Was it Bentley? Is the Captain hated, and if so, how much and by whom? Bentley treated the man like a lackey. How could that be allowed to happen? You have little regard for Carter. That was plain the first time you mentioned him.'

'I cannot be so used.' The surgeon stood up, bottle in hand. He was shaking his head slowly.

'The reputation of the ship . . .'

'Amongst other things.'

'Like your livelihood,' snapped Harry, barely seeking to disguise how he felt about a man who, practising medicine, put money before people's lives. Outhwaite didn't reply.

'Nothing would give me greater pleasure, Mr Outhwaite, than to leave this ship with an enhanced reputation. But I will add that I have never yet met a ship's surgeon who wouldn't be happier, and wealthier, practising ashore.'

Harry turned on his heel and left. Outhwaite too would need time to make up his mind. To press him now would guarantee a blank refusal. He made his way back to the wardroom to see how he was progressing with his first victim. Craddock was not there.

'Mr Craddock?' he enquired from a young officer. He recognized him as the one who had been dressed down by Bentley on the quarter-deck. The man indicated the closed door of the cabin.

'I believe I am to berth in Mr Bentley's quarters. And I am also aware that I have yet to make your acquaintance, sir. Harry Ludlow.'

'Mangold. Fourth,' said the young lieutenant, half rising. Mangold had a round pink face topped by ginger hair, but you could not doubt that he was blushing slightly. The other members of the wardroom, whom he had yet to meet, did not come forward, busying themselves with their various tasks as Harry turned to look at them. He took some pleasure in the fact that his presence was causing them unease. But that would have to change. If there was a spark of good intentions in any of these men, he must find, and use it. Harry turned back to Mangold. He had not been at the previous day's dinner.

'You had the watch last night?'

'I did.' His eyes flicked to the others, listening but not looking.

'Has Mr Bentley been removed?'

'Yes.'

'Not for burial?'

'No. His body is being stowed in the hold. In spirits.' A half-smile crossed the young man's face. Bentley being in spirits would occasion some mirth.

Harry longed to question Mangold, to ask him if he had observed anything the night before, but there were others present. He turned to address the room.

'Gentlemen. I hope to have the opportunity to make a proper acquaintance later. Now, I beg your indulgence. Mr Mangold, would you know, has my kit been fetched?'

'I am not aware of it having been brought aft.'

Harry opened the door to the cabin. There was no sign of his sea-chest. All Bentley's personal things had obviously been removed.

'I am reluctant to trouble Mr Craddock over so trivial a matter!'

'Allow me, sir,' said Mangold immediately. The young man stood up. He gave the slightest pause as he saw the disapproving looks. Almost in defiance he said, 'It would be a pleasure.'

Harry closed the door. As he did so, the silent room broke into a buzz of conversation. The cabin was now bare. If Bentley had anything that marked it out as his home, it had been removed. The room had been scrubbed in true naval fashion. It was spotless. Like Craddock's across the way, it had a cot and a plain desk with a round armed chair. But there was nothing else. All trace of the previous occupant had been removed with the body. There was a knock at the door. Harry opened it, expecting Mangold. Instead it was Craddock.

'May I?' Craddock indicated that he wanted to come in.

'Of course.' Harry stood back as Craddock entered. He turned and gave a significant look at the still open door. Harry shut it. A short period of silence followed. Craddock was embarrassed.

'Mr Ludlow. You cannot be unaware of the tensions that exist, at present, in the wardroom.'

'I can guess. Just as I can imagine that my being here does not help to allay them.'

'Quite. Yet you are a ship's captain. I cannot, in all decency, accommodate you anywhere else.' Craddock's head dropped a little.

At least not anywhere where you can keep an eye on me, thought Harry.

He lifted his head and looked straight at Harry. 'It falls to me to ask you, on behalf of my fellow officers, not to make matters any more difficult than they are.'

'May I speak freely?' said Harry.

Craddock nodded. He was not enjoying this. He looked old and sad, rather than stern and unbending.

'I have every intention of bringing Captain Carter to book for the sinking of my ship. In the course of doing so, it may be necessary for some of the officers of the *Magnanime* to give testimony. Then there is the question of my opinion of the Captain's mental state. You may fear that I will try to influence the members of the wardroom in the direction of that opinion.'

Craddock nodded again.

'But then there is the matter of my brother. That, Mr Craddock, is my overriding concern. His welfare and survival.' Harry did not mention innocence. 'I will not disguise from you the fact that the other matters are of importance to me. But if you think I will spend my entire time as your guest questioning the ship's officers about the sinking of the *Medusa*, then let me allay that fear. If they are called upon to speak, it will be before a higher authority than me. I must trust to their honour that they will tell the truth.'

'Then can I have your assurance that you will not raise the matter while you are our guest?'

'You can. I will not mention either the *Medusa* or the state of the Captain's health while I am in the wardroom.' If Craddock noticed that Harry made no reference to Bentley's murder he said nothing.

'Thank you, Mr Ludlow.' Craddock made to leave.

'Mr Craddock?' Their eyes made real contact for the first time since Craddock came into the cabin.

'Mr Ludlow. I cannot overtly go against the wishes of my superior officer. Yet I hope that you will observe by my actions, that I will do everything in my power to soften the effects of his orders. I am aware of a higher duty than blind obedience. I do not want anyone's death on my hands.'

Harry, who had been holding his breath, let it go with a sigh of relief. James' chances of reaching shore alive had increased tenfold. Craddock had the running of the ship entirely in his control. It gave him ample scope to evade the letter of any order from a captain, remote in his cabin.

'I will require a servant, Mr Craddock. A personal servant.'

Harry could see Craddock's mind working. Harry should have been content with the ministrations of the wardroom servants. He could only want a man of his own for other reasons. They could only be guessed at, but they would not be to Carter's advantage.

Having already challenged him to relieve Carter, and having had that request denied, Harry was more than pleased with what Craddock had eventually said. This was different. It was requesting an act of commission rather than one of omission.

'We are short of the type of hand who makes a decent servant.'

'I would be happy with a seaman, that is if you can spare me one.'

Craddock stood silently, weighing the question. If he understood what Harry was about, he left that unsaid. 'I think I have just the man.'

'Thank you, Mr Craddock.' Craddock made to leave again.

'One more thing,' said Harry. Craddock swung round angrily, like a man being pushed too far. 'I wonder if I might have some of the brandy that came aboard with my stores.'

95

The angry look faded quickly. 'A pleasure.'

'Oh, and Mr Craddock. I have just realized that I have been remiss. I cannot accept your hospitality without offering something in return. Please inform the wardroom that they are to feel free to draw upon my stores while I am their guest.'

'Most kind, sir,' he exclaimed. Craddock was genuinely pleased at this, as his smile showed. Such a gesture would serve to ease the atmosphere considerably. Harry could not know it, but voices had been raised, advising that Harry be confined to his cabin for his meals. But the prospect of good food and wine would please more than just Craddock.

It was not a wealthy set of officers in the wardroom, and James had already alluded to the fact that their fare tended to be meagre. Harry, in the *Medusa*, had carried the stores of a rich man. Added to that, he had taken a number of well-laden merchant ships on his cruise. Their stores had filled the *Medusa*'s hold as well, not to mention the manger. There were sheep and pigs, a milking goat, plus any number of hams and cheeses and tubs of fresh biscuit and butter.

'Perhaps if I could instruct Cook to use some of them for your first dinner. A good meal would stand as a perfect introduction to the wardroom.'

'A capital idea, Mr Craddock.'

'Would it be in order to serve fresh meat. Fresh mutton, say?' Craddock's eyes glowed slightly. He was clearly a man who liked his food.

'Make it so. And choice wines to wash it down. I leave the choosing of those to you. I wish you to treat my stores as if they were your own. Spare no expense.'

Craddock opened the door. A sailor stood outside, Harry's chest at his feet.

'Ah, your dunnage, Mr Ludlow,' said Craddock, smiling.

Harry bent forward quickly, his hand running over the front of his battered sea-chest.

'Mr Craddock. Would you oblige me for one more minute.'

Harry signalled to the seaman to bring in his chest. The man did so, leaving it in the middle of the cabin. As he left, Harry shut the door again.

'Mr Craddock. Would you look at the front of my sea-chest?'

Craddock hesitated. He had no desire to be further involved.

'Sir. I have kept my word. I did not want to ask the question so that it could be overheard.' Harry's head nodded towards the closed door. 'In return, I really must demand that you give me the benefit of your opinion.'

Craddock, with some effort, squatted down and looked at the chest. He too ran his hand over the deep scratches that covered the front of the hasp.

'Would you agree that someone has tried to force the lock?'

'No, sir,' said Craddock angrily, pushing himself upright.

Harry looked at him quizzically.

'There could be another, entirely innocent, explanation.'

'Really. I would be grateful if you could advance one.'

'Come, Mr Ludlow. Your ship was involved in a heated action. At the end of that your kit was hauled aboard in something of a hurry. These scratches could easily have occurred then.'

'The knife that Captain Carter showed me this morning was in this chest.' That was a guess, but it had been in his desk, in the cabin of the *Medusa*. James had made a point of telling him that he had cleared it out.

Harry bent down, and pulling out his key, he opened the chest. Moving aside the clothes, he came upon a leather purse. A quick feel was enough to establish that it still contained his money. The ship's log was also there, as well as the other valuable things that he had kept in his desk drawers. Suddenly with absolute clarity, Harry knew what had happened. He knew that James was not only innocent, but the wrong victim. The whole charade had been mounted to cast suspicion on Harry, not James.

'You have obviously a deep love of coincidence, Mr Craddock. Mr Bentley was killed with my knife. My brother stands accused of his murder. The implication, and no doubt part of the case against him, will be that only he or I would have access to that knife. Yet there are scratches on the front of my sea-chest, which at least raises the possibility that someone else could have had such access.'

'Mr Ludlow.' The older man's eyes had watered slightly, and he spoke softly. 'Do you think that I do not comprehend your desire to clear your brother? It is only natural. But don't, I beg you, sir, go clutching at straws.'

'Called upon to speak in court, you will witness that these marks were evident upon delivery of my chest?'

'I could do no more, for it is the truth.'

'Thank you, Mr Craddock.' Harry was tempted to add more. To say that if James had not killed Bentley then someone else had. But Craddock would only be alerted by such words, and perhaps impede Harry's chances of finding the evidence that would clear James.

VIII

'Mr Outhwaite, can I tempt you to a drop of this?' Harry held out a bottle of a very superior brandy.

'I think I can be persuaded, Mr Ludlow.' He was not fooled by the invitation to join Harry in a pre-prandial drink. He decided he would accept the drink, but he'd be mighty careful about revealing anything else. He emptied the glass that Harry filled, with a smack of his lips to follow. 'Don't often get to drink such as this.' His eye was firmly on the bottle.

'Feel free, Mr Outhwaite.' The surgeon picked up the bottle and refilled his glass. Habit made him cradle it in his arms, rather than put it back.

'Now, sir. I require the use of your brain.'

Outhwaite immediately assumed a guarded air and emptied his glass.

'We are having dinner with the wardroom in an hour. A dinner I have provided. I have spared no expense since I require the goodwill of these officers more than I require meat and drink.'

Outhwaite refilled his glass and downed the contents again.

'I am willing to give you a general opinion of the Captain and his relations with his officers. But you cannot engage me in any other way.'

'That would be helpful.'

'As far as the commissioned officers are concerned, there is, in the main, a great distance between them and the Captain. Bentley saw to that. And Oliver Carter is not really a sociable man, so he's had few occasions to change their minds. There is one exception, his nephew. He's Oliver too. Oliver Turnbull is the marine lieutenant. He is often closeted with the Captain. He was thick with Bentley too, but that was because they were overfond of the bottle. Nobody likes him because he's the Captain's nephew. Yet I think he's a decent enough lad. We've had the odd tipple together, and away from Bentley and his bad influence, he's a different man. Be interesting to see how he fares with Craddock as premier.'

'Carter?' said Harry, bringing Outhwaite back to the point. The surgeon's round purple face took on a mystified air.

'The real problem is that he is so very changeable. They never know how they stand, all smiles and praise one minute, and then cursing and damning you the next, and for no reason that anyone can see.'

Harry's smile made him pause.

'Moodiness is not madness, Mr Ludlow. As for the warrant officers, they see him as a good seaman, careful with the ship and its rigging. The gunner will like him for he never fires the guns, the carpenter because he never damages a spar, the purser for the care he takes with the ship's stores.'

'The master?'

'Not over-fond, I'd say. Carter is a good seaman, and a better navigator than the master will ever be. They've swapped high words at times, but Carter usually has the right of it, be it the sail plan or our position.'

'The crew don't like him, I'll hazard?'

'Hard to tell. Bentley was the only one they really hated.'

'I heard one of the crew call him a murderer. A name was mentioned.'

'Larkin?' asked Outhwaite.

'That's it. Who was he?'

'He was one of the ship's boys. He died. Lots do, and it's no wonder, the way they go on, dashing about in the riggin'.'

'I haven't observed much of that going on aboard the *Magnanime*.'

Outhwaite turned his face away. It was not a subject he wanted to talk about. 'Tell me more about Carter. Who are his favourites?'

Outhwaite almost sneered. 'He has no favourites that I know of. Why, Bentley even chose his barge crew. The rest he ignores when he is even. They tend to be flogged when he is in a bad humour, though it will be interesting to see how that goes with a new premier.'

The door opened and Harry's new servant came in. He was carrying clothes that had obviously just been pressed.

'Just put them on the cot, Pender. Thank you.' The man obeyed and left.

'Pender is your servant?' asked Outhwaite, surprised.

'He is. Mr Craddock provided him.'

The surgeon poured himself another generous measure. At this rate he would be drunk well before the meal.

'He seems a strange man to be appointing as your servant.'

'Why?'

'Best ask Mr Craddock.'

'That would be impolite. I would much rather you told me.' Harry took the bottle and put a drop in his own glass. He did not pass it back to Outhwaite.

'No harm, I suppose. Pender, "Pious" they call him. Came aboard in the draft at Spithead. How he has never received a floggin' I'll never fathom. Too slippery, I shouldn't wonder. But he's one of those coves who can be insulting without the victim really knowin' it. He's not really a sailor, yet for all that he managed to stay out of harm's way.'

'But he's a volunteer?'

'Aye. But I don't reckon he's at sea for a love of King and Country.'

'Pious?'

'On account of the time he spends on his knees, I suppose, pickin' locks.' Outhwaite put his hand out, and Harry passed him the bottle.

'A thief?' asked Harry, masking his surprise.

Outhwaite nodded. 'And by all accounts, a good one.'

Harry said nothing. Coincidence? If it wasn't, such a fact

certainly put Craddock in a different light. Perhaps the new premier was not as neutral as he seemed.

'A rare treat this. I don't suppose it's the only bottle you brought aboard?' Outhwaite took another generous glassful.

'I think I can guarantee you a drop or two more. Interesting what you say about Pender. Almost as interesting as some of the things he has told me about the ship.'

'He wouldn't know much. As I said, he only came aboard when we were at Spithead.'

'Yet he seems to have picked up a remarkable amount of information.'

'The hands will talk, and exaggerate.'

'Such an unhappy ship. Damn near a shot-rolling ship I've heard?' Harry was bluffing. He had only exchanged a few words with his new servant. But he was implying a crew close to mutiny.

'Stuff and nonsense. As bad as the parson with their superstitions.'

'You'll never cure a tar of that vice,' said Harry. But the word intrigued him. 'Some would say that the whole thing is such a trivial matter. Carter was not always so ready to resort to the cat.'

'That's true.' Outhwaite was being infuriatingly slow. Harry urged him to drink some more brandy.

'I don't suppose you would care to speculate on what brought about the change.'

'No, I would not, sir.' The bottle was now half-pointing at Harry, and the surgeon's face seemed to go a deeper shade of purple. 'An' if you go listening to the hands going on about a young lad goin' overboard, then you are as daft as they.'

'It's not only that, surely?'

'That an' a couple of other unexplained deaths.' Outhwaite was slurring slightly now, and poking the air with his finger. 'But that's common enough at sea, sir, an' you know it. Trouble is, some of the dafter buggers have got hold of it. The fuss they made about that boy.'

'He went overboard?'

'He did.' The bottle waved towards the sea outside the

102

windows. 'An' you know that it happens all the time. Messing about, I shouldn't wonder.'

'A calm night?' Harry knew enough about sailors to speculate that no one would think anything amiss about a disappearance during a storm.

Outhwaite just grunted.

'So what exactly are they saying?'

Outhwaite leant forward, finally prepared to confide something. 'That the Captain feels the curse on himself. That he knows he is going to die, and that he has given up all authority because of it. The boy was well liked.'

'As you say, stuff and nonsense.' Harry reached for another bottle.

The dinner was a success, though not entirely trouble free. Once the wardroom had realized that Harry did not intend raising embarrassing matters, the general reserve of its members had thawed considerably. After a shaky start, and several false sallies by Craddock, the conversation had begun to flow. And Harry made every effort to be pleasant, name-dropping outrageously to leave them in no doubt of his elevated social status. Like all sailors they found they had many mutual friends, as well as the common enemy, a parsimonious government that did not value its naval officers highly enough. Good food and wine did the rest, and it was well set to be a convivial affair.

Turnbull had tried to barb Harry a few times, only to find himself checked by Craddock. The others seemed pleased to see him so treated. Apart from anything else, the officers were having dinner without the overbearing presence of Bentley. From the little that Harry had gleaned the late premier at the head of the table had been less than amusing. Harry did not truly resent Turnbull's remarks. He would naturally be partisan on his uncle's behalf. The rest of the officers avoided Carter's name. That was cause for some hope.

The only one who did not seem to relax was a midshipman called Denbigh. A tall young man of about eighteen, he sat stiffly, hardly drinking anything, and staring at Harry all the time. True he was distracted sometimes, being engaged by one of his neighbours. But he always turned back to look at Harry when they had finished speaking.

For the rest, they were a fairly typical set of men, more concerned with their own worries than anyone else's feud. Naturally they talked of the war and the prospects for advancement and profit. This led to the most unpleasant moment, and the one when Craddock had been particularly severe on poor Turnbull. Heron, the ship's purser, the portly individual he had pointed out to Prentice, had raised the question of prize money. That was a subject dear to every sailor's heart, and would normally have occasioned a lively debate about the value of the *Verite* as a ship, and the members of her crew, who would earn the *Magnanime*'s company head money. Several conversations were started at once to try and cover this potentially embarrassing drift in the purser's conversation, so many that none of them could be sustained. The brief silence allowed the young marine lieutenant a clear run.

Turnbull, whose face was nearly as red as his marine uniform, due to the tight white stock around his neck, had consumed a great quantity of drink. With the stove going, the wardroom was hot. Everyone was perspiring slightly but Turnbull seemed in worse straights. Beads of sweat stood out on his forehead. He was quite a good-looking young man, but his puffy face betrayed his love of the bottle. His eyes were hooded and his head swayed slightly as he put his question to Harry.

'Being a commercial cove, Ludlow, you probably have a better idea of the value of merchandise than we tars,' he shouted down the table. No one looked in his direction, or Harry's.

'How much would you say the "Frenchie" will fetch?'

Craddock glared. 'First she must be brought in, Mr Turnbull. And that is not certain to happen. The Master Attendant may think her worthless.'

'What! A fine frigate like that, practically undamaged.' He stressed the last word.

No one spoke. Turnbull smiled wolfishly, no doubt feeling that he was doing well. Denbigh briefly desisted from his staring to look at the marine. As he turned back, the boy's dislike was plain on his face.

'However much she fetches, Mr Turnbull, it will not be enough to cover any loss of reputation.'

'Damn me, sir. You are a fine one to be prattlin' on about reputation.'

'Mr Turnbull!' snapped Craddock, as the young man leant forward to press home his attack. 'Your manners are not of the standard that I expect at this table. Perhaps your tongue would be less free if your hand was somewhat less liberal with the bottle.'

Turnbull's flushed face reddened even more. He sat back, knowing that he had been formally told to shut up.

'Gentlemen,' said Harry, smiling broadly. 'It would be death to conversation if we were to entirely ignore recent events.' Craddock shot him an alarmed glance. 'But I for one will draw a veil over certain things. Indeed, I have given your premier an undertaking to do so. But let me say this. The *Medusa* had a very successful cruise. And just so that you will appreciate how much I welcome your hospitality, let me say that nearly everything we have consumed at this table was taken from the enemy.'

'Which makes it all the more pleasant, sir,' said Mangold, his round pink face creasing into a grin.

'This wine, Mr Ludlow. How did you come by this?' Craddock was quick off the mark, keen to get conversation moving again.

'I took that one out of a merchantman carrying sugar. And a fine chase he led us, for he had a sound vessel, and the captain was a proper seaman. He spotted us at sun-up and was already running before we smoked him.'

Harry continued his tale of a long and sometimes dangerous chase. For the merchantman had shifted some guns to fire as stern chasers, and had shown a rare ability to use both them and the sailing qualities of his ship. The rest of the table sat forward listening to the story, for this was the stuff that sailors loved. Chasing prizes, and successfully at that! Turnbull and his remarks were quite forgotten and the mood had been restored by the time Harry neared the end of his tale.

'As you know, a merchant captain will usually strike quickly. Not this fellow. He fired his popguns repeatedly and had he been better armed it would have been a hot engagement. As it was, we had to board her and fight our way to the poop. The crew fought like tigers. Most unusual.'

Several heads nodded, agreeing that it was most uncommon.

'Jacobins?' asked Heron.

'Very likely, though I have to admit I didn't enquire as to their politics. But their fighting spirit was soon explained. When we searched the ship, and questioned a few of them, I discovered why the crew had been so tenacious. They had run in with a Spanish ship from the "Main", and engaging in a little piracy, had relieved her of a quantity of gold.'

'Which you, in turn, relieved them of?' asked Parfitt, the Master, an exceedingly thin individual with prominent eyes. As a man without money those eyes gleamed at the thought of gold.

'I most certainly did.' Harry smiled, and observed the wistful looks on all of his companions' faces. Mentally they were all capturing ships full of gold.

'So let's raise our glasses and drink to the damnation of the French,' cried Harry. Great gulps of claret were consumed.

'And to cargoes of gold,' cried the purser.

'Amen to that,' said Craddock, as he drank deeply. Harry looked down the table to where Crevitt sat. Outhwaite had long since fallen asleep on his hands, dead drunk. The parson sipped his wine, his face registering his disapproval. He probably thought that Harry was debauching the officers. Even Turnbull joined in the toasts, his sour look quite disappeared. Indeed, he seemed positively merry. Harry put it down to excessive consumption.

The cloth was drawn, the loyal toast given, and the decanter passed happily and frequently round the table. The general air of mirth increased as the officers related tales of failures rather than successes. Mostly other people's mishaps, of course. Harry hoped the sound of merriment was carrying to the cabin above.

He was walking on the quarter-deck, trying to clear his head, when the parson approached him.

'May I?' He indicated he wished to join Harry in his pacing.

Harry nodded. 'A successful dinner?' Thin and tall, he stooped forward as he walked, making the prominent nose seem even larger than it was.

'You would be as capable of judging that as I, Mr Crevitt.'

'Not so. For I would not be entirely privy to the purpose.' One eyebrow was now raised, giving Crevitt a comical air.

'Purpose?' Harry, stopping, matched the look, before walking on.

'I cannot think that you have any reason to love the *Magnanime* or any of its officers. You could also be said to have other concerns. Yet you choose to throw a dinner. You provide fine wines and food, way above the normal fare, and throughout you behave as though you have not a care in the world.'

'It would hardly have been a pleasant affair if I had aired my problems.'

'You seem to have hit it off with the wardroom. They were very warm in their praise after you came on deck.'

'You sound as though this did not please you.'

'We return to the purpose, Mr Ludlow. For if, as I suspect, the whole thing was arranged to turn the officers against the Captain, then I would indeed be displeased.' Crevitt looked at Harry as though he were a poor sinner.

'Not displeased enough to refuse the offer of good food and wine?' Harry stopped pacing again, and smiled.

'You have a failing, Mr Ludlow, one shared by Outhwaite. And that is an inability to let the opportunity of an insult pass by.'

Harry's smile disappeared. He started his pacing again. Crevitt stayed with him looking towards the sky as if seeking inspiration. 'And I wonder if that was not part of the original cause of your dispute with Oliver Carter.'

'I believe you enquired about this before, Mr Crevitt.' Harry made no attempt to disguise his anger. 'I advised you to seek such information elsewhere.'

'Any man can hate, Mr Ludlow, sin though it is. But it takes two to create such a situation. I am close to the Captain. I count myself lucky to call him a friend. I like to think I have his respect. I would, indeed, wish to speak with him about this continuing feud, and the futility of it.'

'But you dare not?'

'Choose not to, at least for now. But I am also a man of the cloth. What you are engaged in, both of you, is sinful. I see it as my duty to do what I can to bring you together.' Crevitt stopped and moved in front of Harry, forcing him to do the same.

'That's easy, Mr Crevitt. Just find a quiet open field.'

'It would be fair to say that you have tried that and failed.' Crevitt held up his hand to stop Harry's words. 'If I said to you that you misunderstand the Captain, what would you reply?'

'That I understand him only too well.' They both looked at the entrance to the great cabin under the poop.

'Do you, I wonder? I have often thought that one of Oliver's problems was an inability to attract friends.' Harry's surprised look escaped Crevitt. He was looking in the wrong direction.

'I have remarked to him about this, and believe me, I have not laid the fault for this at other people's doors.' His voice became softer, almost warm and they walked.

'I have known him since he was a boy. We were much of an age, and our fathers had neighbouring parishes. Perhaps because of that we were thrown together. He was not an easy person to get to know, even then, but in the similarity of our backgrounds, we had much in common. And I did, at one time, harbour some hopes of marrying his sister.'

'Why are you telling me all this?'

'Because I think what I have to say may have some bearing on why this situation has developed. Since I have known the Captain a long time, I am aware of his reasons for hating you. I knew your name long before I met you. Indeed I have sought to point out to Oliver that you cannot be as bad as he paints you.'

'Spare yourself the trouble, Mr Crevitt.'

The parson was sharp in his response. 'I have a duty, sir. And I require no one's permission to exercise it.' His tone changed as he resumed his tale.

'As children, I observed even then that Oliver invested too greatly in his enthusiasms. He was the type of boy who liked someone too much, and to the exclusion of all others. As a friend I was repeatedly discarded in favour of some new acquaintance, a person who would occupy all of Oliver's time and thoughts. Such a new acquaintance would be invested with such powers!'

If this had hurt the young Crevitt, you could not hear any evidence of it now. There was neither praise nor condemnation for anyone as he continued.

'Needless to say, such worship rarely bears fruit, and in his disappointment that his new-found friend was not perfect, he would often start to goad them, as if testing their friendship to see if it would break. In most cases it did. It is a habit he has not entirely lost, nor have the consequences much changed. It has made him mistrustful. Outside of myself, and of course his sister, whom he worships, he has few friends.'

'All this is leading up to something,' said Harry, trying not to sound bored.

'Of course it is, Mr Ludlow.' Crevitt turned to face him, forcing Harry to stop again. 'Would I not have achieved something, if I could bring you together?'

Harry made to speak, but Crevitt talked eagerly over his attempt.

'Armed not with weapons, Mr Ludlow, but with Christian charity. Enough charity to put an end to the quarrel. I make no pretence when I tell you that Captain Carter is my dearest friend. And while I will naturally tend to take his part against those who seek to harm him, I do feel that what lies between you and he does him no good at all. I would venture to suggest that you have little to gain from it either.'

'Are you going to come to the point?' asked Harry. Crevitt was altogether too prosy for his liking.

'I suggest that something be done to breach the deadlock. A gesture of some sort, one that could be met with another gesture.'

'You are going to ask me to make a gesture?' Harry's disbelief was very evident.

Crevitt's cheekbones twitched, but he did not manage a smile.

'Perhaps, under the circumstances, it would be more appropriate if Oliver were to make the first move.'

Harry really wanted to tell Crevitt to jump overboard, but no advantage could be gained from that. 'Do you have something in mind?'

'Perhaps if he were to allow you to meet with your brother?'

Whistles blew and suddenly the air was full of shouted commands and running men. Craddock had called 'All hands'. Harry took Crevitt's arm and pulled him against the hammock nettings as the men rushed to their stations. Craddock had been joined, on the quarter-deck, by all the officers. Harry had been so engrossed in his conversation with Crevitt that he had not noticed. They were still in their dress uniforms, looking slightly bemused.

Carter came on deck last. He looked down to where Harry and Crevitt stood. A brief smile crossed his face. Without turning he addressed Craddock.

'About time we indulged in a bit of sail drill, Mr Craddock.' He made sure his voice was loud enough to be heard by the whole deck. 'Would you be kind enough to request those not directly engaged to clear the way. After all we don't want anybody to get hurt.'

'Ay, ay, sir,' said Craddock sharply. He looked to where Harry stood and gave a slight nod. Harry made his way to the poop without a word. Crevitt followed him. Turning round Harry could see James. He was dressed in purser's slops and he stood with a group of men on the starboard gangway. They exchanged glances just as the orders came to send the topmen aloft. While his companions rushed for the shrouds, James hesitated, unsure what to do.

'Move your arse, Ludlow.' The command, from a man in a pea-jacket and a round hat, was accompanied by the sound of a rope's end striking his brother's back. Harry gripped the rail, as he saw James do the one thing that he dreaded. He turned to retaliate against his assailant, a natural reaction in anyone but a sailor. The petty officer let fly with the rope's end, beating James back towards the shroud.

'Get aloft, you no-good bastard!' Turnbull, standing beside his uncle, turned to see how Harry was reacting. A sharp command from Carter had him facing forward again.

James was now cowering in the scantlings as the blows continued to rain down on him.

'Belay that!' shouted Craddock. The master-at-arms hesitated, his rope in the air.

'Belay, Mr Craddock?' snapped Carter. 'A man refuses his duty and you cry belay when he is shown the rope's end? I would have had a different response from Mr Bentley.'

Craddock went bright red. James had started up the shrouds, climbing slowly out of harm's way. But Harry knew he was heading for a greater danger. He would have to climb to the upper yards, and having reached them, he would then have to walk out along them, his feet slipped into the roped slings beneath him, and his arms wrapped round the yard to keep him there. If his companions took care of him, he might just survive. If they ignored his inexperience he could well miss his foot or handhold and tumble, either to certain death on the deck, or if he was lucky, to a slim chance of survival over the side.

'With respect, sir, the man does not know his duty,' said Craddock. Harry waited for the explosion, silently blessing Craddock nevertheless. Carter would crucify the acting premier for daring to question his orders.

'I am minded to take heed of what you say, Mr Craddock.' Carter turned with a smile, ostensibly addressing Craddock, but really aiming his remarks at Harry. 'Even if I disapprove of you daring to check me on my own quarter-deck.'

'I meant only . . .'

'I know what you meant, Mr Craddock, just as I know that refusing your duty is an offence that normally brings the culprit a flogging. Call that man down,' he shouted, before turning back to Craddock. 'However, on this occasion we will allow for everyone's inexperience, both yours and our newest recruit. You may send the men about their normal duties.'

Carter turned and headed back to his cabin. He stopped and looked briefly at Harry. Brief it might be, but the look spoke volumes.

Go ahead, it said. Wine and dine my officers and seek to turn them against me. Just remember that I hold your brother's life in my hands. Offend my pride or my person at your peril.

'Mr Crevitt. If you could use your good offices to any effect, I would be most grateful,' said Harry quietly. This was no time for foolish pride.

*

'Come in, Pender,' he said. The man smiled as he came through the door, showing a set of perfect white teeth. Harry, shutting the door behind him, sized up his new servant. The smile was odd. It wasn't servile or obsequious, yet neither did it convey insolence or familiarity. Pender was of medium height, slim enough in his purser's slops, yet the way his shoulders were set implied that he was physically strong. He had a dark complexion, and his face, round, impish, and topped with tight black curls worn short, still held that smile. And there was a look in his eye to go with it. Arrogance, thought Harry, knowing, deep down, it was really just self-assurance.

'I want you to have a look at my chest. I believe it is something you are familiar with, locks and the like,' he said. The smile slowly faded.

'I don't think I know what you mean.' A steady voice, with a soft West Country burr.

'You're too modest, Pender. You have quite a reputation aboard ship, though it probably pales beside your reputation ashore.' Pender said nothing. He stared silently at a point over Harry's left shoulder.

'Please don't be alarmed. I want, indeed I value, your expertise. I would be grateful if you would take a close look at that chest. What would you say has happened?'

Pender bent down and looked at the lock. He ran his fingers over a scratch, then inserted a fingernail into a deeper indentation.

'Well?'

'I think it would be best if I was to be going about my duties.'

'You are going about your duties, Pender. Mr Craddock has appointed you as my servant.' Pender, still squatting, gave him a look of stony indifference. 'Think about it, man. Why would Mr Craddock do a thing like that? You're no more a manservant than you are a sailor.'

Pender stood up and thought for a moment, weighing the odds.

'I would say that someone tried to open this here chest before.'

'You?'

'What?' Pender was genuinely offended. 'Me? Not me, your

honour. If'n it had been me, you worn't of seen no scratches.'

'An amateur then?'

'I'll say.'

'Could you show me how you would open it?' Harry held up a gold coin.

Pender smiled again. He pulled a set of thin metal rods from his pocket. He bent down before the chest, and with practised speed he inserted, one after the other, three of the rods. He fiddled about for a couple of seconds, and the lock sprang open.

'A most impressive display. Thank you, Pender.' Harry had him. Pender had not opened the lock to earn the gold coin, he had done it to show off. And in showing off he had told Harry more than he should. Mistaking the thank you as a dismissal, Pender straightened up and made to leave. Or was it a realization of the fact that he had been a trifle foolish, for he made no attempt to take the gold coin.

'Wait,' said Harry. 'How much would you say that particular skill is worth? Ashore I mean. Somewhat more than a rating's pay?'

They looked at each other silently. Pender's grey eyes were steady. He was not a man to be stared down.

'Beats starvin', your honour. An' that's what you get when times are 'ard.'

'With that skill you would never starve. Yet you take the King's bounty, and opt for a life afloat. Seems strange.'

'That's as maybe. But it's what I chose to do.' There was the unspoken comment, barely disguised, that it was none of Harry's business, in the way he said it.

'I have half a mind to threaten you, Pender,' said Harry quietly, still holding that stare. 'I cannot but feel that there are those ashore who would welcome news of your whereabouts.' Pender didn't react, standing absolutely still. Not even his eyelids flickered.

'But something tells me that would do no good. Something tells me that you would not respond to threats.' Pender looked away, breaking off the contest. He was now gazing over Harry's shoulder again.

'I can't think what you have a mind to threaten me with, sir.'

'I think you have. You're not here because you love the Navy or your country, are you? You're here because it's too hot to be ashore. Too many people around who would like to get their hands on you and perhaps string you up. At the very least you would be down for Botany Bay. However, that is none of my concern. I have more pressing worries. I dare say it is common talk below decks, my situation and that of my brother.'

'That kind of talk is best avoided, your honour.'

'Do you like being a sailor?'

'It suits me well enough,' said Pender. Harry was getting nowhere with the oblique approach. The man's self-contained air was infuriating. If Pender adopted this attitude with his officers he would be accused of mutiny. Yet Harry, from what Outhwaite had told him, knew that he applied something close to it in his dealings with his superiors. The man was very sure of himself. Not cowed, or afraid, and certainly not frightened. But most important, nor was he stupid.

'I apologize, Pender.' No response. 'But you must understand that I do not know you, and another man might well have responded to a threat.'

'Can you claim to know me now then, your honour.' Pender looked him straight in the eye. It was not a question.

'I am forced to make rapid judgements because I do not have time for anything else. My brother is set to hang unless I can prove that he is innocent. In order to do that I require assistance. While I can move about the ship, my movements are naturally circumscribed. This makes it extremely difficult for me to either talk to anyone or question them; in short, to find out the truth. You are aware of this, and so is everyone on the ship with any brains.'

'That leaves out a fair amount of people, your honour.' Pender's snub nose crinkled, and he nearly smiled again.

'I need help, and I want you to help me. In turn I will help you.'

'I don't recall as how I was asking for help.'

'Do you really so enjoy being a sailor? And then it may be that you want something, something that money can buy. I have money.'

'You want to buy my services?'

'You may give them freely if you wish.'

Pender smiled properly this time.

'I am going to the heads now, your honour.'

'And?'

'I shan't be long, your honour.' There was something peculiar in the way he said 'honour'.

Pender pushed past Harry and out of the cabin. Harry could only pray that he did not report their conversation to Craddock. He paced up and down waiting either for the man's return or the knock that would herald Craddock and an embarrassing interview. Pender came back alone and entered the cabin without knocking.

'Name your price,' said Harry.

'I've not said what I think yet.'

'Yes you have,' said Harry. He knew he would be buying the man's services only. Pender could not be bought by anybody.

'I'm not so sure that "price" is the right word.'

'Conditions? That is, if you don't want money.'

'Money is a very useful thing.'

'But not just money?'

'A new identity, a place to live. Somewhere to bring up my nippers without the fear of a hand on my shoulder. And money. But money to use, not to spend. Enough to set me up in a trade. Who knows. Maybe I could set up as a locksmith.' He flashed a genuine smile. It lit up the face. Harry sensed that Pender was a man who loved a joke. He was the type to be popular with his messmates. A man to have a laugh with, perhaps a man you could trust. And this was more like it. Pender wanted to get away from a life of crime. A life that could only end one way if it continued.

'Done,' said Harry.

'Even if your brother hangs?' Pender wasn't smiling now. But neither was he indifferent. It underlined Harry's earlier feeling that the man was clever.

'That would depend. If you have done everything you can to help, and it has been of no avail, then yes. Even if my brother hangs, I will give you the funds you need.'

'I don't want the funds,' said Pender sharply. 'I've had funds before. But never for very long.'

'I understand, Pender. What of the crew? Do they think my brother guilty?'

'It's not something I'd know for sure. And since he says nothin' . . .' Pender paused as he looked at Harry. The eyes were set hard. 'But I would take leave to doubt it. He don't look the type.'

'Captain Carter claims to have two witnesses.'

'I wouldn't want to be the Angel Gabriel in the dock with those two lying bastards Carter's got lined up to witness against your brother.'

'You know them?'

Pender nodded. But he had become reserved suddenly. He wasn't fond of the supposed witnesses, but they were on the lower deck, and Harry most certainly wasn't. Harry sensed an inbuilt reluctance to 'rat' on his own kind.

'Could they have witnessed anything?'

Pender took a long time to answer, his head to one side, thinking carefully. 'I can't see it. That's not where they normally hang out.'

'How much is he paying them?'

'He's not paying them. If'n he was doing that it would be easy. All you'd have to do is outbid him. No, it ain't that. Them two . . .'

'Who are they?'

Again that hesitation. Harry found it reassuring rather than frustrating. It demonstrated a degree of loyalty, which was, to him, a valuable commodity.

'Meehan and Porter. Rated able both of them, though they are useless sods. They help crew the captain's barge.' Having decided to speak, he held nothing back. 'They are a rum set, the barge crew, and they're afraid of somethin'. That's my guess.'

'Would it have anything to do with a missing ship's boy?'

It was wonderful the way Pender didn't react. He had a lively, expressive face, yet he'd managed to keep it blank without effort. He merely shrugged. 'Maybe. There's been so much talk of that, everyone stands condemned.'

'Go on.'

'There ain't no more to go on with.'

'Yet there are people who are convinced that the ship carries a curse.'

'Daft sods, the lot of them.'

'The first thing you must do is speak to my brother.'

Pender held up his hand. 'In time, Mr Ludlow. But I've no mind to get a knife in my ribs, him bein' watched the way he is. I'll talk with your brother, but it will be when the chance presents itself, an' not afore.' He looked around the cabin. 'They've locked you up here, good and proper, right at the back of the wardroom. First thing is to make it so's you can move about.'

Harry offered the gold coin as Pender made to leave.

'You can put that to my account, Mr Ludlow.'

Again that expressive smile.

IX

Harry woke from a troubled sleep, full of dreams in which he or his brother had been repeatedly hanged. He'd spent the rest of the daylight hours on deck. He felt that his mere presence would stop anyone going too far, though this did mean that he had to endure the taunts of the petty officers, who delighted in shouting 'Ludlow', with instructions to 'shift his fuckin' arse'. A rough lot, even by the standards of Navy petty officers, they had no doubt been hand-picked by Bentley for their love of the rope's end. They started men at every opportunity. One in particular, a burly, pock-marked fellow called Howarth, the master-at-arms, seemed to have taken James' naval education upon himself.

James was repeatedly struck, but much as Harry sympathized, he could not intervene. To do so would only make matters worse. He stood there for some time, just abaft the gangway, as Howarth sent James up the shrouds and called him down again. At least he was not letting him go right to the crosstrees. His sport seemed to be in the exhaustion that James would experience through constant climbing.

Carter had come on deck to enjoy the sport. Perhaps it was all he had, since Craddock had yet to present him with any victims for a flogging. Even the man whose brains Bentley had nearly crushed the day before had been saved by the premier's untimely death.

Harry and Carter did not speak. They did not even look at each other. The whole quarter-deck was on tenterhooks as they paced up and down, Carter on the sacred windward side, reserved for the Captain, Harry near the gangway, as far down the ship as he could go without crossing the invisible line that separated the two halves of the ship.

Harry stopped pacing, just staring towards the forecastle, and the shrouds on the foremast that were James' ladder, praying for the watch to change and remove his brother from harm's reach. He cursed softly, as Howarth, with a vicious blow, caught James around the ear. It was too much; he spun round to shout at Carter. Instead he found himself looking into the face of Turnbull, who had come up behind him, unannounced. The young man seemed quite recovered from his earlier debauch, looking pink and healthy in the fading light.

'Would you wish me to intervene?' he asked.

Harry, surprised, looked over Turnbull's shoulder to where Carter stood.

'I am aware that my uncle is on the quarter-deck, Mr Ludlow. Excuse me.' He squeezed past Harry and walked down the gangway. Howarth was standing, his hands on his hips and his head back, looking up at James as he climbed. Turnbull spoke, and the man turned. What he said, Harry did not hear. But Howarth stopped shouting, and James was sent below when he came down.

Turnbull came back towards him. Harry fought the temptation to turn and see what effect his nephew's action had on the Captain. Instead he smiled at Turnbull.

'Thank you,' he said.

'I owe you an apology, Mr Ludlow. I was rude to you at dinner. I admit to being somewhat in my cups, and I hope you will understand that I naturally support my uncle in any quarrel. The proper course would have been for me to decline the invitation.'

'I don't think your uncle will be pleased by your intervention just now.'

'I am old enough to choose my own manner of making amends.' The air was rent with whistles, shouts, and running feet. It was time to change the watch. Harry felt the tension drain out of him. James would be safe for four hours. Turnbull nodded and walked away. Harry saw Carter give the young man a cold look, before he himself turned and left the deck.

He saw Pender. He didn't acknowledge Harry, and the thought flashed through Harry's mind that Pender could easily betray him. Yet he doubted it. Pender struck him as a man who would always keep his mouth shut about the affairs of others. Besides, Craddock's attitude seemed the same, friendly in private, distant but affable in public. He stood on the starboard gangway, half-way between the quarter-deck and the forecastle deck, looking down into the open pit of the waist. Men were going across the upper deck, heading for the stairwells that would lead down to the gun-deck and some rest. Harry felt weary himself. Ignoring everyone, he made straight for his cabin and lay down in his cot. Surely Pender should have given some sign? Harry couldn't help but wonder if, realizing the danger, he had decided to forget the whole thing. It was with that thought that he fell asleep, a troubled slumber. When he awoke, he knew that something unusual had disturbed him.

There was a steady knocking on the sternlight glass, plainly audible over the groaning of the ship's timbers and rigging. Harry, on his walks, had surreptitiously availed himself of a marlinspike. Reaching under his cot, he picked it up, before unlashing and opening the casement. Pender slipped through and into the cabin. He was wearing a pea-jacket several sizes too big for him, and he had the remains of a length of rope round his shoulder. The remainder snaked out of the window.

'Here, your honour,' he said quietly, slipping off the rope. 'You'll be needin' this.'

Harry took the rope and quickly lashed it to the hook that held his cot.

'That'll allow you to come and go as you please, at least at night.' He reached into his pea-jacket and produced a T-shaped piece of metal with a square end.

'I've rigged the after gun-port on the lower deck, nearest I can get to below this one,' said Pender, holding up the metal. 'It's weighted with shot, so it'll open a treat. There's a hole dead centre at the bottom. Use this and you'll be able to lift it from the outside. It's well greased so's it shouldn't make no noise as it opens. My hammock is slung hard by it, and I know my mates will say nowt. But you'll need to have a care all the same. Provided we are on this tack you can practically walk down the tumblehome. If not, then there's the rope. Don't drop the key, for Christ's sake. I had a hellish time getting the armourer to fashion it.'

'I'm going to need some clothes,' said Harry.

Pender slipped off the dark pea-jacket and handed it to Harry.

'That'll do for most, at least at night. I dare say that you've got some pants of your own. Best rip the bottoms off 'em or you'll be spotted for a gent.'

Harry changed quickly, using the sword to cut the bottoms of an old pair of pantaloons. He slipped on the pea-jacket, and gave Pender a look that indicated he was ready.

Pender smiled, looking at Harry's head. 'Well, you'll never make old bones in the thieving game, an' that's for sure. That there is like a rabbit's arse.'

Harry put a hand to his head, having completely forgotten about the white bandage round his head. Quickly he removed it.

Pender flashed another smile. 'I brought you this.' He produced from his waistband a short sword. 'There'll be hell to pay an' no pitch if'n they find this missin' in the mornin'. I got word to your brother that you are concerned for him.' He grabbed Harry's arm tightly, as if to quell his excitement. 'And I mean "a word". The only time he is alone is when he's asleep. Christ, he even has one of his watch with him in the heads.'

Harry followed Pender out of the quarter-gallery casement, the line well secured for the return journey. Being French built, the *Magnanime* had a broader hull than that of an English seventy-four. This width narrowed with each deck, and the heel of the ship meant that the rough painted planking along the side was like a sloping roof. The same breeze which had blown for the past forty-eight hours was carrying the ship along at a steady six knots towards Gibraltar. Feeling it on his back made Harry impatient, a feeling that he had to fight back. Caught in this garb wandering about the lower deck would, at the very least, see him confined to the ward-room for the rest of the voyage.

Pender had already opened the lower gunport and slipped through. Outside sounds were covered by the noise of the wind in the rigging. On the lower deck the groaning of the ship's timbers and the stretching of the various ropes were enough to cover the sound of their bare feet as they made their way between the men sleeping in their hammocks.

Again, Harry thought, not all of them would be sleeping. Illegal activities took place in the darker recesses of all ships. There would be a group of gamblers somewhere, with dice and cards, perhaps more than one. Probably, given the example set so recently by the French, and the conditions of life at sea under a captain like Carter, there would be a group in some corner of the ship indulging in a lot of talk about mutiny. Then there would be the others, men trapped in a ship of the line who could not keep their passions in check.

Sodomy and bestiality were both capital offences, yet they were endemic in a fighting ship. How could it be otherwise, when you took a large group of men, and cooped them up, for months on end, with no female company? They were not even allowed ashore in an English-speaking port, for fear they would desert. Most could keep their passions in check, but there was always a minority who could not. It was a hanging at the yard-arm for those who were caught. Few were, through a combination of natural guile, and a desire by everyone in the Navy to ignore such goings on if they could. The official attitude was stern and unbending, and there was certainly the odd hanging when matters got out of hand. The practical attitude was that it could not really be stopped, and that provided the correct level of discretion was observed, a blind eye could be turned. So theirs would not be the only movement around the ship. But those indulging in nefarious night-time activities would be just as keen to avoid contact. The only real danger came from chancing across someone in authority. Given the low light from the ship's lanterns, they could feel reasonably safe.

Pender led Harry to where James lay asleep in his hammock.

Years as a midshipman, skylarking about and getting into all kinds of mischief, had made Harry a master at the art of dealing with a sleeping man. He pinched his brother's nose between his forefinger and thumb, using the rest of his hand to cover his mouth. James's eyes opened in alarm. Harry tipped his hammock causing him to fall out. His arm caught the weight as he lowered his brother to the floor.

Harry crouched down, and James followed suit. Silently, scurrying underneath the mass of swinging hammocks, Harry led the way to the stairwell and they slipped down on to the orlop-deck. Pender stayed up top to keep a lookout. Silently they crept past the various sleeping quarters of the ship's warrant officers, forward to a point near the pump shaft. Here some bolts of canvas were stacked, just outside the sail room, and Harry slipped in between two of them. In the gloomy light, Harry could not see the true extent of the bruises covering his brother's face. But he could see the swelling and as James spoke, he could tell that he was nursing a swollen lip.

'I knew you would come,' said James.

'Then you knew more than I, brother. You have been in the wars.' Harry put his hand up to touch the swollen face. James pulled back, as if to avoid more pain.

'Howarth, the master-at-arms, has taken upon himself the task of teaching me my duty. I made the mistake of defending myself.'

'I saw.' Harry wanted to tell him to keep his temper in check, but he reasoned that was a lesson James no longer needed. And this was a rougher ship than most.

'That was before, on deck,' whispered James. 'This took place below. He wasn't on his own. Two of his cronies held my arms.' Howarth had obviously enjoyed himself, free from the restraint imposed by an officer's presence.

Harry whispered urgently, 'We have to get you out of this. First of all you must tell me what happened with Bentley.'

'Would it not be more to the point if you were to tell me?'

'You assume I killed him?'

'Didn't you?' James sounded as though doubt on this score was a novel idea. Harry felt a slight flash of annoyance.

'James! Do you really think that if I had killed him, I would allow you to suffer in my place?'

'No. But I needed to hear you say it. I must admit I found it strange.'

'Did that allow you any doubts?' Harry reminded himself of the way his own mind had been working, and felt his slight anger change to guilt.

'Plenty. But what did I have to set against them?'

'My knife.' Harry's resigned tone matched his brother's.

'I recognized it immediately. I took it out of your desk myself, and put it in your sea-chest.'

'And you picked it up?'

'Yes. I heard an argument taking place outside my berth. At first I ignored it. I felt I'd had enough confrontation for one day. It was the drumming that made me get up.'

'I heard that too.'

'Yes. I presume Bentley's death throes. His heels drumming on the deck. So I turned up my lantern and went to investigate.'

'And found Bentley?'

'And found a body. I didn't know who it was until Carter turned him over. But I did see your knife stuck in the deck. I grabbed it.'

'To get rid of it?'

'I suppose so. I wasn't really thinking clearly. Then you came out of the dispensary. I didn't have time to say anything before the others arrived. I suppose I froze.' James sounded a little displeased with himself.

'What a loyal pair of brothers we are. You remain silent because you think I killed him, and I, seeing you stand there with a knife in your hand, was convinced for a while that you had done it.'

'For a while?' There was a note in his brother's voice that Harry recognized. Half mockery, half guilt.

'I couldn't believe it of you. Oh, I had my doubts. You were in such a passion after Bentley insulted Caroline Farrar. And I admit I was shocked when Carter produced my knife. After all, my sea-chest was in your berth. But when I thought about that, and how it had been left to be found . . .' Harry knew that he needed to explain more fully, but there was little time. 'If we had both stayed in bed, I would have been here instead of you.'

'What are you saying, Harry?'

'I am saying that I was the intended victim, not you. Someone forced my sea-chest open and took the knife. They knew where I was asleep, I suppose. Bentley was killed close enough to incriminate me. A neat plan. The knife was left in the deck deliberately.'

'How do you know that?' Was that a trace of doubt again?

'By the mark in the planking. I had a look before they managed to swab the decks. There was a huge pool of Bentley's blood and another smaller one where the blood had run off the knife. And there was a deep cut in the deck. That knife was not dropped. It was deliberately stuck there, and with some force. It was coincidence that you found it before anyone arrived. Strange, that. Why did they come then? Who raised the alarm?'

'The murderer?'

'Yes.' James was silent. 'If you are waiting for me to tell you who that is,' said Harry, 'all I can say is there are enough candidates on board to man our next ship. As you yourself observed, Bentley was much hated.'

'You must have some idea.'

'I have too many ideas.' Harry had more than that, but he didn't want to share his thoughts with James. He justified this to himself on the grounds of uncertainty. 'What I don't have is anything to point me in the right direction. I was hoping you could help out in that.'

'But if you can find out who raised the alarm . . . ?'

'How? I can't ask any questions. It has been made plain to me that your survival is dependent on my good behaviour. The next time you may well have to go aloft.'

'But if you cannot find the murderer, Harry . . .' James was straining to stay calm.

'I know. You are likely to hang. A neat situation for whoever the killer is. And Carter has discovered that having you at his mercy is a very good way to vent his spite on me.'

'We have to do something.' James grabbed Harry's wrist.

Harry covered his brother's hand with his. 'Yes. But the risk will be greater for you than it is for me, James. Someone killed Bentley, and the only way I can see to trap the culprit is to invite them to kill again.'

'Then that is what we must do.' James' grip tightened.

'James,' said Harry, using a slightly pedagogical tone that his brother hated, but silently endured. 'Right now you are threatened by the hangman. You are in even greater danger from Carter's hatred of me. Do you really want to add another threat to the list?'

'I can see no choice. Besides, you will be as much at risk as I.'

'Hardly.'

'Harry. Whoever killed Bentley did so in a place where it must have been possible to be observed. And given the presence of your knife it was planned that way. Don't tell me that my risk is any less than yours.'

'I am not normally one to regret my actions . . .'

'Please, brother. No apologies. For if we were to—'

Harry's hand must have hurt James as he clamped it over his mouth, but the sound he had heard warranted the pain. Some-one was listening to them, someone close by. The muffled cough would have been covered by the noise of the ship, if it had not been followed by a wheezing sound. Harry slipped behind one of the bales, motioning James to stay still.

James, listening hard, could hear the wheezing now. He had no doubt who it was. He crouched back against the bulkhead, his heart pounding in his ears.

Howarth's bulk cut out most of the available light, but he could still see James.

'Ludlow, you bastard. How much does it take to get you to learn, an' you callin' yourself a fuckin' gentleman.'

Silhouetted as he was, James could not see the man's face. But there was pleasure in his voice. The wheezing, as Howarth breathed, was very pronounced now, seeming to fill the small gap between the bales.

'An' you creepin' round the ship at this time of night. What could you be about, eh! Maybe you be plannin' to do somebody else in. Nice cosy spot for a quiet chat. Cosy enough for anythin', I say. Perhaps you've become a sailor quicker than I thought.' Howarth stood back, looking up and down the gangway. 'I heard voices. So who was you havin' a talk to? Lost your tongue?' James' silence was upsetting him, his voice turned angry. 'Well there's only one thing for it. To finish off what I started earlier. Then maybe you'll mind your lesson.'

Howarth stepped forward, raising and swinging a short club as he did so. James cowered down and it caught him on the back, causing him to cry out in pain.

'And then I'll see you flogged, you bastard, when I be finished with ye.' The club was raised again. James, realizing he stood no chance crouching down, lunged forward, grabbing his assailant round the knees. He waited for the second blow on his back that was sure to follow. Howarth, his club raised to deliver it, gave a sudden gasp. James stood up, meaning to grab his throat, but Howarth's body arched as he did so, seeming to gain several inches in height. His eyes were wide open, bulging out of his head. He started to fall forward. Harry stood behind him, a wild look in his eye and his short sword lost in the man's back.

'Grab him,' he hissed impatiently. James reached up to stop the body thudding on to the deck.

'Lower him gently,' said Harry. 'Keep him face down. And leave that sword, or there'll be blood all over the place.'

They lowered Howarth on to the deck. James looked at his brother's face. 'Well, Harry. We are both for the high jump now.'

'There was no choice, James.' Harry's voice was quite calm. 'He was out to kill you, I think. If not today, then before we reached port.'

'What do we do now?'

'Get rid of the body, James. Had you been at sea for any time, brother, you would know that it is not uncommon for a bully to go overboard in the night.'

'Then why has someone not done for this one before?'

'Because he wasn't stupid. A bully picks his victims carefully.

But I think he picked you because he was told to. Can you help me get him upright?'

Pender came running along the gangway. He stopped when he saw Howarth's body.

'Christ Almighty. We have to scarper, Mr Ludlow. Something's up, I don't know what, but the marines are out with orders to search the ship. Supposed to be planning a surprise for someone, but I saw them being raised from their hammocks, quiet like. Anyway they are now getting set to block off the companionways.'

'We can't leave him here,' said James.

'We'll have to,' said Harry. 'It'll be all hands on deck once they have shut off the lower parts of the ship. Then anyone missing is up to no good.'

Harry said no more, heading for the stairs back to the gundeck. He had just started to climb when he stopped suddenly. The light at the head of the steps was increasing as someone approached with a lantern. The sound of footsteps clacking on the deck left him in no doubt who the light belonged to. On board ship, only officers and marines in uniform wore shoes.

He signalled for Pender and James to head back the way they came. James, now in the lead, quite naturally took cover between the bales again. Pender followed him. Harry ran on past with a whispered 'Come on'. They emerged and followed him.

'Thank God one of us is a sailor,' he said, grinning at his companions. And thank God this is a French-built ship, he thought, praying that in some refit the *Magnanime*'s old suction pump had not been replaced. They were doomed if it had.

'We have got to get up on to the gun-deck before they finish posting sentries. Now it's going to be pitch dark, as well as dirty and quite possibly wet. And if it works, we are going to emerge smack in the middle of the gun-deck. Let's hope that it'll be so dark up there that no one will notice. Till then, stay with a crowd and keep away from any lights.'

'What about you?' asked Pender.

'I've got to get out of that gunport without being seen.' He gave his brother a quick explanation.

'A tall order, Harry.'

'One step at a time, James. Besides, I can stay hidden if I wish. I can only hope that whatever they are looking for, it's not me.'

Harry, holding his breath, turned and pulled open a hatch to the pump shaft. He breathed out with relief as he saw that it was still the old suction type, a hollow chamber with a canvas hose, now hanging limp, running down the centre.

'There's a ladder just to the side. Let's hope they haven't posted anyone to guard the hatch by the cistern. You two go first. Go past the next hatch.'

'How will we know we've passed it in the dark?'

'Keep going till I call you to stop. I'll go through first. If I am spotted, stay where you are until all hands are called!'

Harry thought that it was a faint hope that anyone looking into the shaft after catching him would only look down instead of up, but he said nothing about that. Caught, he would be in trouble, for sure. But James and Pender would find themselves rigged to a grating. Then he suddenly realized that he had completely forgotten about Howarth. They would all hang!

James and Pender were through now. Harry followed pulling the hatch to behind him. That would be discovered probably, but by then they hoped to be in the clear.

Harry counted the rungs as he climbed, hoping that his memory would extend to a recollection of the right number. He had not climbed this pump-shaft ladder since he was a boy, making mischief that too often ended in a beating.

The smell from the bilges was strong in this confined space. He could hear a scurrying sound as the rats escaped from this intruder. In the dark he felt for the hatch cover, fighting a slight sense of panic as his search for the wooden latch failed to locate it. A rat nipped his outstretched hand as it felt around the planking. He swiped at it, cursing. Above him he could hear James and Pender breathing heavily. Even in the dark, he shut his eyes to increase his concentration. Putting both hands on the damp rung, and trying desperately to calculate the distance from the ladder to the latch, he reached out. Surely this was where the latch would be if he had got the number of rungs right. He touched the side, running his hand up and down the wood of the shaft.

Nothing! Harry went up one rung, closed his eyes again, and did the same thing. Still nothing. One more step, and the same set of movements. No catch. He went down four rungs and shot his hand out in the dark. Like a man opening the door of his own home, his hand hit the latch dead on. He lifted it and slipped out. The shaft and the cistern were surrounded by hammocks, still full of men. There was a faint glow of the lanterns around the gun-deck, but he was hidden by the mass of bodies. He called quickly to Pender and James, and they slipped through after him.

'Try to get back to your own hammocks,' he whispered. 'If you can't, stay still till the call "all hands".'

James went one way and Pender the other. Harry thought about following Pender, so as to be ready to slip through the gunport as the men made their way on deck. But then he reasoned that he was better off where he was. Being in the centre meant being in the middle of the group. Less exposed.

The slight creak of the hatch behind him nearly made him jump out of his skin. He scurried away, careering into a hammock as he did so. He stood up to silence the man who, rudely awakened, would be asking what was about. No sound, no movement. Harry's hand shot into the hammock, and he knew as he felt that the hammock was occupied by a bundle of some kind, probably someone's dunnage, rather than a human presence.

He moved a bit further on, then stopped to look back. The hatch was open now, and a group of shadowy figures emerged and silently made for the hammocks close to the shaft. Harry counted six of them, each one quickly throwing the bundles over the side of the hammock to swing below it, before climbing in and adopting the position of a sleeping man.

'All hands. Rise and shine,' came the cry. They had been a long time about it. Then he realized that they had probably been looking for Howarth, who, as master-at-arms, had the job of rousing out the men. The cry had men tipping out of their beds quickly. No man would lie still when a captain like Carter had the ship. There were many flogging offences in the Navy, and lying too long in your hammock was one of them.

Harry joined the rush for the gangway that led up to the main deck. He saw as he went that all the lower decks were shut off by marine sentries, fully clothed in their red coats and muskets at the ready.

'What's afoot, mate,' said a man next to him.

'Don't know, mate,' replied Harry in a gruff voice. 'An' I don't intend asking.'

Pender was standing by the gunport. He was taking a risk since he should have made for the deck with all haste. Harry was grateful, since Pender pushing it open allowed him to slip through quickly while there were still enough sailors milling along to hide him. If any of them noticed, no one stopped or raised the alarm. Pender shut the gunport as Harry grabbed the rope and swung away from the opening.

The ship had altered course, and the side was like a sheer cliff. He put his bare feet on the planking and began to walk up the side, his hands pulling his bodyweight up on the line. The trickiest part was getting his casement window open so that he could squeeze through. He took a half turn with one hand on the rope to support himself, and grabbing the frame, he heaved it open. Noise was not a problem since there was an abundance of it on the rapidly filling deck above.

He was stuck. True he had the window slightly open, but he could release neither that nor his hold on the rope. If he did take his hand off the frame, then the casement would slam shut with the force of the wind. Plainly, if he relaxed his grip on the rope, he would end up in the sea. Harry pushed the frame shut slowly. He knew he would just have to wait until the ship changed course again. Then the side would heel over enough to allow him to hold the quarterlight open, without the need to hang on to the rope quite so desperately.

He threw the rope round his back and pulled the end up under his arm, allowing him to lean back slightly and take the strain off the arm he had been using. Thus he waited. Looking over his shoulder he could see the phosphoresence of the ship's wake. The wind, cooling the sweat on his body, made him feel cold. And from time to time, a larger wave would swallow the stern of the *Magnanime*, bringing him perilously close to a severe ducking. But he had been over the side in any number of ships, so his present situation caused him no concern. He knew that the real danger was that someone would look over the side and raise the alarm. Barring that he was safe.

Drills and searches could take place as often as they liked. But the ship still had to reach its destination. That was paramount, and regardless of what was causing the present confusion, when the time came the orders were given that brought the ship back on to her southerly course. The wind took the ship and heeled her bulk over, reducing the cliff, once more, to a gently sloping roof. Harry pulled open the window, jammed his knee in to keep it open, and eased himself through. He released the line and coiled it up, hanging it over a carved *fleur-de-lis*, part of the elaborate decoration that covered the rear of the ship. All the while he was thinking about the events of the night.

Howarth's death might raise problems, but nothing could be done about that. And there had been no choice. The man had singled out James for regular beatings, and no one was going to either stand in his way, or order him to desist. Indeed, Harry was convinced that Howarth had been given the task of ensuring that his brother didn't reach Gibraltar. James didn't understand how his isolation, his lack of lower-deck mates, left him vulnerable to someone like Howarth. Harry had seen it before.

Then his mind turned to the men who had followed him out of the pump shaft. They must have been on a lower deck than him. Thus it had taken them longer to reach the gun-deck. What were they about? He smiled as he thought of the shock they might have had, if in climbing the ladder they had put their hands on his feet.

He looked at his filthy face in the mirror. The *Magnanime* must be a very dry ship, for though he was dirty, it was nothing to what he had been as a lad, when he had used the same route to fool some of his mates or escape from possible punishment.

He'd always emerge from there black from head to foot.

The water in the jug was cold, but it helped to remove the worst of the grime. Harry then undressed and crawled into his cot. Things were no better now than they had been an hour ago. But at least there was movement. Something was, at least, happening.

X

Pender entered the cabin bearing a jug full of hot water. He was bright and cheerful, showing no sign of last night's escapade. Harry, already awake, lay in his cot, his mind turning over again the possibilities for proving his brother's innocence.

'Mornin', your honour,' said Pender, standing in the doorway.

'Seemed to be a bit of a commotion last night, Pender. What was all that about?' Harry's voice fairly boomed out the question. Pender realized that this was for the benefit of the wardroom and held the door open as he replied.

'Terrible doin's last night, Mr Ludlow. Another killing. Hands are beginning to wonder if we aren't double cursed since we sunk your ship. Why, there's even talk of a "Jonah" aboard.' With that he closed the door. Harry suppressed a laugh. The man was marvellous. They could hardly have achieved more if they had rehearsed it.

'That'll get their tongue's waggin', for sure,' said Pender, flashing one of his grins. 'Now if you will take to your chair, Mr Ludlow, we will see if my skills extend to shaving a "nob".'

Harry rose as Pender poured some of the hot water into the basin. Quickly he washed away the last of the grime from the previous night, before sitting down in his chair to be shaved.

'Well?'

'Whatever they was about last night went by the board when they discovered Howarth. God knows what they were after, but they were set to search the whole ship.'

'Has that sort of thing happened before?'

'Not since I've been aboard. I tackled one of the marines, but he couldn't tell me nowt. Seems his Mr Turnbull was as surprised as anyone. But the rumour is that it was Carter's idea. He was after somethin', but the Lord knows what.'

'A nice touch as you came in the door,' said Harry, acknowledging the man's inventiveness. 'Might be worth spreading that one around. There's no telling how far you can get with superstition in a sailor.'

'That might not square with what I've been saying forrard.'

'Which is?'

'That it seems a bit dangerous to go around bullyin' a Ludlow. That perhaps there be those aboard who have served with Master James's brother, and take serious exception to him being mistreated. That Mr Howarth would have been well to realize this before he got a sword in his back, rather than after.'

'I can see no harm in both.' Harry lay back content, and Pender started to lather his face.

'We was a mite lucky last night, your honour.' His dark-skinned face had a worried look.

'Luck? We'll need a damn sight more if we are to get anywhere.'

'I take it that you are in no doubt about your brother now?'

Harry was surprised at the question. It caused him to move suddenly. Just as quickly Pender pulled the razor away.

'Please don't do that, Mr Ludlow. I don't want my saying this ship is double-cursed to come true.'

'Sorry.' Pender had not been privy to the brothers' conversation. Again he was showing his good sense, for it was necessary that there be no doubt on that score.

'Quite convinced,' said Harry, and as Pender shaved him he told him of last night's talk. Yet he did not tell him all he knew or suspected, and he didn't quite know why. There could be little doubt now that Pender was to be trusted. He hadn't really told James either, and not just because of a lack of time. For once in his life he was being very cautious, husbanding the facts to himself. But would that serve his purpose?

'One question, Pender. Who slings their hammocks by the pump shaft?'

'Quite a few. Barge crew for one. They mess by there too.'

'Any others?'

'I'll look into it.' He applied more lather to Harry's face, determined not to ask why. But this was one Harry knew he would have to share.

'Someone came up the shaft behind us. I nearly died of fright. I was standing by the hatch just after you left and it started to open. One of the closest hammocks was empty, as well. I can't be sure, but I think about six men came out of the shaft. It was too dark to see who they were.'

'They must have been right down in the hold,' said Pender.

'That's what I thought.'

'Pardon my asking, Mr Ludlow, but I don't see what bearing this has on your brother's case.'

'Perhaps none. But there are over six hundred and fifty men on this ship. Bentley must have been seen by someone that night. If he was observed then so, possibly, was the killer. And how was the alarm raised and by whom?' And to himself, he wondered what Carter was after, searching the ship. That would be something else to find out. 'There are so many questions that it is difficult to know where to start.'

'You need someone in the wardroom on your side, Mr Ludlow. Sure I can tell you some of what's goin' on below decks . . .'

'Could one of the crew have killed Bentley?' There was an element of testing Pender's loyalty in that question, and the way the man paused meant he knew it. Ingrained habit alone would make the man avoid spilling on his mates.

'He was hated enough. But think on this. Someone broke into your chest and stole your knife. When? We don't know.'

'The banquet?'

'Most likely, but there were lots of other times.'

'But not when all of those in authority were otherwise engaged.'

'Always guessing we are talking of one man.' Pender didn't have to spell out how much that would complicate things with six hundred and fifty suspects. 'Which is why you need a friend in the wardroom. 'Cause I can ask around below decks, cautious like, especially now, with Howarth sewn in canvas. But I can find out nothin' from the officers. And it is more likely to be one of them than one of the crew.'

'What makes you so sure?' Harry felt the same way, but he wanted to hear Pender's reasons.

Pender kept shaving as he talked, for all the world like a professional. 'Sure anyone could have knifed Mr Bentley. But I'd say that one of the crew, or more than one, would have just knifed the bastard. And they would have wanted to sling him overboard after, so it would not have happened below decks. And then, I can't see them goin' to the trouble of setting out to blacken you with the murder. It's too much bother.'

'Go on.' Harry closed his eyes, pleased to hear some of his own thoughts confirmed.

'Well the way I see it, Mr Bentley wasn't knifed for being a drunk or a flogger. He was knifed for a reason. Happens, someone might have wanted to get him for a time. You arriving on board, like you did, gave them a chance to do it, all the while settin' the dogs on the wrong scent.'

'Which argues a powerful motive,' said Harry.

'It does that, your honour. It's well known that the premier was a shade impolite. But it can't just be that. If'n people was goin' to go knifing their fellows for an insult here and there, promotion in the King's Navy would be quick. For officers are forever steppin' on each other's pride.'

'But even so, we cannot eliminate the crew.'

'I wasn't sayin' that, Mr Ludlow. But given that we have little time, where do we look hardest?'

'And given the time we have, other people's *amour propre* is of no account.'

'I'm sure you're right, Mr Ludlow, but I'm buggered if I know what you're sayin'.' He towelled Harry's face dry and retied the bandage round his head.

*

'Good morning, gentlemen,' said Harry, as he emerged, washed and shaved, from his cabin. The officers sitting around the table at various stages of their breakfast seemed tired and subdued.

'I hope I find you in good spirits.' He could tell that his hearty air was not welcome. He leaned over the table, pressing on with his cheerful manner.

'I see that the hens are laying well, Mr Craddock. I trust you have availed yourself of their sterling efforts.'

'I have, thank you.' Craddock gave a tired smile.

'And you, Mr Mangold.' Mangold nodded. His face did not look quite so pink this morning.

'Pender tells me of another fatality, Mr Craddock. You must begin to wonder if there is a homicidal maniac aboard.'

'Coincidence, I'm sure, Mr Ludlow,' said the purser.

'At least my brother is clear on this one I trust.' Harry realized his mistake, even as he spoke. Craddock reddened visibly. A cooler head would have withdrawn. 'I'm sure you will understand my concern, sir,' said Harry sharply, his temper interfering with his plans.

'Just as I understand an undertaking.' The rest were very still.

'Undertaking would seem to be a fitting occupation aboard this ship.' No one laughed. Harry really did not expect them to. 'As for my word, sir. It stands since it applies only to your superior's deplorable behaviour in the sinking of my ship. You will understand that I cannot allow the possibility of a few ruffled feathers to interfere with my attempts to clear my brother's name.'

Craddock opened his mouth to speak, but Harry was in full flow. He had no real time for verbal subterfuge, plain speaking being more in his line.

'For I tell you now, gentlemen, that my brother is innocent, and I have some proof to underpin that assertion. So you will now find it necessary to examine your memories, and your consciences, to see if there is not some fact that you could add which will either support or refute that theory. And while you are about it, you would be as well casting your mind back to previous incidents that have resulted in an unexplained death. Such as that poor ship's boy that everyone goes on about. What was his name, Larkin? Why, I have heard it said that the ship is cursed because of it.'

'Mr Ludlow. This is outrageous behaviour!' snapped Craddock. The faces of the others present were equally tense. 'Why, you are practically accusing the men in this room of taking part in a conspiracy.'

'I am doing no such thing, sir. What I am trying to bring to your attention is this. That my brother is innocent of the crime he stands accused of. But that does not remove the fact of Mr Bentley's death.'

Harry did not have to spell it out.

'How would you have me proceed, Mr Craddock?' He sat down, and spoke more softly. He had made his point in too brutal a manner. Sure it would get them to think. Now he must try to repair the breach he had made in their good opinion of him.

'I really cannot say, sir.' Craddock's anger had not abated. There followed a general avowal of hurt pride from the others.

'I appeal to you, gentlemen, to hear me out.' Harry was speaking very quietly and earnestly now. 'For I must ask you, as honourable men, how you would behave in such a case. Mr Craddock says that I am accusing you of engaging in a conspiracy. I am not, for I do not know whom to accuse. But there has been a conspiracy, for someone stole a knife bearing my initials, and used it to murder your superior officer. I have established to my own satisfaction that my brother is not the culprit. I ask you again, what would you have me do? I am as wedded to good manners as you are. Should I fall back on good manners, letting an innocent man hang, while a guilty one goes free?'

'Perhaps if you were to share your certainties about your brother, rather than your doubts about us, you would get more cooperation,' said Turnbull. He was sitting at his usual place, near the wardroom door.

Harry ignored him. It was a reasonable remark, but not really one he was either willing, or ready, to respond to. He stood up again, and addressed only Craddock.

'I will understand, sir, if you wish me to mess elsewhere. I will understand that the officers of the *Magnanime*, who will all surely lay claim to be honourable men, are not only willing to contrive to cover for the cowardice of their captain . . .'

'That's a lie!' Turnbull again. Harry ignored him.

'. . . but, being honourable, are, for the sake of the reputation of their ship, willing to allow one of their number to escape his just deserts for the murder of Mr Bentley, as well as to ignore other matters which would bear investigation.'

Damn their opinion of me, thought Harry. It was a collective slap in the face, a challenge to all the officers in the room, as well as those not present. He stalked out of the wardroom wishing that he had helped himself to a beaker of coffee before he had started. Behind him he heard the buzz of animated conversation.

Harry made his way to the dispensary. How to handle Outhwaite? Threaten him? Bribe him?

'May I come in,' he said, pulling back the canvas screen. Outhwaite had been leaning back in his chair, in a somnolent position.

'Do,' he said, sitting quickly upright. 'I was going to send for you today. Time to remove your bandages and have a look at your wound.'

'Then my visit is most fortuitous. I have just set a fox amongst the chickens in the wardroom. Given what I have said, I may have need of your services again.'

Outhwaite stood up, indicating that Harry should sit down in his chair. He did so, and Outhwaite started to undo his bandage. He stopped for a moment, and Harry looked up at him.

'I am, of course, agog to hear what you have said.' Outhwaite continued his unwinding. Harry turned away to avoid his breath.

'I have formally, and publicly, accused your captain of cowardice. I have also served notice that my brother is innocent, and that I suspect a member of the ship's company to be the real murderer of Mr Bentley.'

'Well, there's nothing like doin' things by halves, I say.' Outhwaite bent to examine the wound. His neutral air intrigued Harry.

'You don't seem surprised?'

'Was I not there to see you crawling on your hands and knees examinin' the deck? And why would you examine the body, if 'n you didn't have cause to think your brother wrongly charged? Only a matter of time before you upset someone. 'Cause the only way you can truly clear brother James is to nail someone else. And all that buttering up of the wardroom.'

Harry smiled. 'You weren't fooled?'

'Not by a mile, or by a couple of pints of fine brandy neither.'

'I rather thought I had been straightforward with you.'

'Yet you cannot help thinkin' that you can get around me by fillin' me with drink.'

'That's not true.' But the words lacked conviction and they both knew it was true.

'And then,' Outhwaite said quietly, 'I have a particular way of applyin' a bandage.'

Harry stiffened involuntarily.

'Still, you must have found sleep hard to come by last night, what with all the things on your mind.'

'Yes.'

'Taking the bandage off would be just you trying to get comfortable, I suppose? Just as well the wound's healin' up nicely.' Outhwaite's voice was full of irony. 'As you know, I subscribe to a scientific way of thinkin'. Now that rules out divine intervention completely, and it don't hold much with chance neither. The master-at-arms takes to bullying James Ludlow, and that very night he's found with a sword embedded in his back.'

'So Pender told me.' Harry hoped his voice sounded as neutral as the surgeon's.

'I don't know many people that like bein' used, Mr Ludlow.'

Harry turned to face him. 'Given the choice, I would rather not try to.'

Outhwaite's gaze was unusually steady. 'You came here with a purpose. I would be more willin' to listen if you was to come straight to it.'

'I need help.'

'What possible help can I give you?'

'Well. If you have any suspicions of who might have killed Bentley, it would be helpful to hear them.' Now it was Harry's voice that was full of irony.

'I was with you. Nothing you saw the other night was enough

to support such convictions.' Outhwaite sat back on his sea-chest, his rheumy eyes steady on Harry. 'And you are a man of action. Would you want me to pass on such as I'm thinkin' to others?'

'Thoughts prove nothing.'

'True. Yet you are asking me to do the same thing for you. To pass on thoughts that may mean nothing.' Outhwaite tilted his head forward. His chins folded into each other, making him look like an unshaven bulldog.

'The case is different.'

'How so?'

'An innocent man may hang.'

The surgeon lifted his head to look him in the eye. 'While a guilty one goes free?'

Harry was not sure to whom Outhwaite was referring and the man had no intention of enlightening him, merely dropping his head into his chins again.

'I can only trust that you will see a difference. I cannot explain it to you.'

'Ask what you will, Mr Ludlow. But expect little.' Harry waited for Outhwaite to explain his willingness. 'Why? Perhaps I think that you will kill everyone aboard this ship if you have to. And, to tell the truth, I could use a good night's sleep.'

The surgeon lifted his head and smiled, exposing his black teeth.

Harry was still with Outhwaite when the summons from Crevitt came.

'Perhaps I am to be chastised for upsetting the officers,' he said. Prentice, again the unfortunate messenger, looked blank. 'Please inform Mr Crevitt that I will attend upon the Captain presently.' Prentice nodded and left.

'Is there any more?' he asked Outhwaite.

'What do you mean, any more? I've already said that there's likely nothin' in the first place. The boy just fell overboard.' Outhwaite had started drinking again, his friendly air evaporating the more he drank.

'But you've just told me that none of the hands believe that to be the case. They believe he was "done in", as you put it.'

'Well, if they have any grounds for that I've never heard them speak. All I'm telling you is what the talk was.'

'It would be interesting to look at the ship's log,' said Harry.

'Anyway, that's when the floggin' got bad. Bentley had always been keen, but the Captain must have felt it was necessary too, 'cause he stopped interfering, and just confirmed whatever the premier wanted.'

'But it didn't really work, did it?'

'Well it didn't cow the hands if'n that's what they intended. Bentley drank more, then flogged more.'

'And Carter?'

'Ask him, 'cause I'm damned if I know what he was thinkin'.'

'Maybe I will.' Harry stood up and left.

'I have summoned you here . . .'

'I am here at Mr Crevitt's request,' said Harry stiffly.

'I'm aware of that, Ludlow.' Carter could not bring himself to look Harry in the eye. He was plainly having trouble containing himself, since he paused for a considerable time. Harry said nothing to help him. Crevitt, Craddock, and Turnbull also held their tongues.

'You have been asked here because it has been reported to me that I have been less than charitable in my attitude.'

He looked at Harry as if expecting some response. He received nothing but a blank stare.

'I am not the sort of man who refuses to listen to reason, nor am I one to ignore my Christian duty. Mr Crevitt has represented to me that by refusing you permission to speak with your brother, I am in danger of being both unchristian and unreasonable.'

'Sir, if I may . . .' said Turnbull. He was silenced with a look.

'There are, of course, certain conditions attached to this.' He looked towards Crevitt.

'I have suggested, Mr Ludlow, that an interview in my presence might be acceptable.'

Harry did not answer right off. He was left to wonder how much of this change was due to Crevitt's pleading, and how much to the words he had spoken in the wardroom that morning. For if Craddock had not passed them on, then Turnbull would have done so. So would Crevitt. His silence worked to his advantage, for Crevitt, having worked hard to get this far, had no intention of letting things drift. His bony frame was bent forward eagerly.

'Should you find this unacceptable, I have suggested that Mr Craddock should also be present.'

Harry nodded.

'Mr Turnbull,' snapped Carter, 'fetch the prisoner.' Crevitt closed his eyes, pointing his beaked nose towards the deckhand. For it would have been kinder for Carter to have asked him to fetch Mr Ludlow. Turnbull hesitated for a second, but his uncle's look sent him on his way.

'You may have the use of my cabin.' Carter stood up, gave Crevitt a long, cold look, then, jamming his hat on his head, left the cabin.

'I think that some progress has been made,' said Crevitt, attempting a smile. It made him look like a bodysnatcher.

'I'm curious to know what you will require of me in return.'

Craddock looked from one to the other, his ruddy face creased up, obviously mystified by the exchange.

'I don't think the Captain would be angry if we availed ourselves of his seats.' He invited Harry to sit, but he refused, remaining standing. The door opened behind him and he spun round. Turnbull ushered James into the cabin, then closed the door.

'James!' Harry rushed over and put his arms round his brother. He whispered one word in his ear, just the word 'careful', before he stood back to look at him. The things he had only guessed at last night were now plainly apparent. His brother's face was a mass of dark bruises, and both lips had barely healed splits in them. Harry turned on Crevitt.

'What do you say to this, Parson, and you, Mr Craddock? Are you so little in command of your ship that this sort of thing can happen with impunity?'

'I was not aware till this morning,' said Craddock, lamely tugging at one of his whiskers. 'I have given direct orders . . .'

'Which I am sure the Captain will confirm,' said Crevitt hastily.

'I want to know who is responsible.' He turned to his brother. 'James, tell them who did this to you.'

'I'm sure the Captain would welcome the opportunity to chastise them at the grating,' said Crevitt.

'No. That would never do, brother. A member of the lower deck splitting to an officer.'

'You are no more a member of the lower deck than I am, Mr Ludlow,' said Crevitt. 'And if you wish the people who are responsible for this to be punished, you must give us their names.'

'Is not humility a prized virtue in the Church, Mr Crevitt?'

'Most certainly.'

'Then let me consider this as a penance for sins unspecified, for it is my affair, and it will be settled as such.'

Well done, James. The use of the future term implied culprits still living.

'You are sure of this?' asked Harry.

'Quite sure.'

'Then let us move on to more important matters. Please tell us what happened with Mr Bentley.'

'That is not why we are here.' Crevitt waved his arm to include Craddock. The acting premier looked from one to the other, saying nothing.

'It is why I am here, sir,' snapped Harry. 'For as you are no doubt aware I made certain statements to the wardroom this morning. James?'

James, ignoring the frown on Crevitt's face, went through the same tale he had told Harry the night before, omitting the part about Harry's possible guilt. Crevitt, in spite of himself, was intrigued.

'Can I ask you why you remained silent, Mr Ludlow? After all, you were given the opportunity to speak up at the time.'

James reacted angrily. 'Am I to explain myself to all and sundry, sir? To address the mob and appeal for justice? How was I to know that Captain Carter would refuse to allow me to plead my case to him privately, or at least in front of a few people of some station? And to then be put before the mast, without even the opportunity to talk with my own brother. Please do not be deceived by the stoic way in which I have reacted. Captain Carter's behaviour has been monstrous, sir, and I trust that now I have at last been given a chance to express my total innocence of the charge—'

'An expression of innocence is not sufficient to remove all possibility of guilt,' said Crevitt.

'That is for a court of law to decide, Mr Crevitt. But it is a tenet of English justice that you are innocent till proven guilty, and I was not aware that silence impeded that basic right, enshrined in Magna Charta. Do I not have the right to plead? One would be justified in asking why we are set to fight any Frenchman that comes along, if that is not one of the principles we are defending. Or are we to see the Revolution's guillotines set up on the quarter-deck of British ships? For I tell you, sir, that such goings on are no better than the behaviour of those responsible for the present state of poor France. Am I to be denied the opportunity to establish my innocence, and merely condemned? I repeat, sir, the Captain's behaviour is monstrous!'

'It might be better to point out to the Captain that what he has done is not legal,' Craddock said to Crevitt in a quiet voice, his face blank. Harry had the impression that Craddock had already tried that on Carter, to no avail.

'Illegal?' Crevitt's huge nose spun threateningly towards the acting premier.

'On two counts, Mr Crevitt. The first being that you cannot press a man who is not a sailor by trade.'

'Was not Mr Ludlow serving aboard the *Medusa*?'

'Serving!' cried Harry. 'He owned a third of the damned ship.'

'Ill-tempered language will not enhance your case.' Harry felt as though he had just been admonished by a schoolmaster.

'It would be impossible to say he was serving,' said Craddock, seeing Harry about to explode. 'Besides he is a gentleman of means. It would not hold in a court, should it come to that.'

'Which it most certainly will,' said Harry.

'You said on two counts, Mr Craddock?'

'Even if Mr Ludlow here was a sailor, which I take leave to doubt, having been arrested on a capital offence, he cannot then be set about normal duties.'

'If you call being a topman "normal duties".'

Craddock turned to Harry, his face hardening to show determination.

'I took the precaution of moving your brother to the "waisters".'

Without consulting Carter, thought Harry. Craddock turned back to Crevitt.

'By rights, young Mr Ludlow should be confined on his own, exercised twice a day under guard, and allowed such visitors as the Captain finds appropriate.'

Crevitt looked at Harry, brow furrowed, before turning his head back to Craddock. He gave the lieutenant a stern look that promised possible damnation.

'And I for one,' continued Craddock, refusing to be cowed, 'can see no reason why that should not include his brother.'

'I was appraised of your threats, the ones you made to the ward-room this morning,' said Crevitt without taking his eyes off Craddock.

'Hardly threats.'

'Perhaps they gained something in the telling, for they sounded like threats to me.'

'I intend to find out who killed Bentley.'

'It is right to believe in your own flesh and blood.' He took both the brothers in at a glance. 'Understandable and commendable. But the evidence, Mr Ludlow . . .'

'What evidence?' said James quietly.

'You standing over the body, a knife covered in the man's blood in your hand.'

'I have explained that.'

'At some point, perhaps soon, you are going to meet your maker, Mr Ludlow. It would be better for you to confess than put your brother through this torture.'

'Confess to something I did not do?'

'You were seen, Mr Ludlow.' Crevitt's voice was quiet,

147

sacerdotal. Craddock was now looking at his feet. 'You have concocted a fine tale, but to no avail. The prosecutor will produce sworn statements from two witnesses who saw you plunge the knife into Mr Bentley's heart.'

'Witnesses?' James gasped, looking at Harry. The unspoken question was there.

'Men I have yet to question,' said Harry.

'It is not your place to question them, sir. That is the job of the prosecuting counsel. You will then be furnished with a transcript of what they say. That is the proper form.'

James made to speak. Harry held up his hand, letting the parson speak.

'You asked what the Captain wanted in return for allowing this interview. Merely this: that you accept that there is a process of law, which will be adhered to, and that you stop going around threatening to expose a non-existent murderer. For Captain Carter has already pointed out to you that such actions are bad for discipline.'

'And if I refuse?'

'I am not in command here. That would be for Captain Carter to decide.'

'And how to react to the points raised by Mr Craddock.'

'I will pass them on. But surely they are academic.'

'Academic?' said James.

'It may be that some of the Captain's actions border on illegality. But I cannot see how a condemned or even executed man can bring a case against him.'

Craddock sniffed loudly. He was angry as he walked over and opened the door. The marine sentry stood to attention as Turnbull entered.

'Mr Turnbull. Take Mr Ludlow to the forepeak. Hold him under guard there till you receive further orders.'

'The forepeak?' protested Turnbull, looking at Crevitt.

'Carry out your orders, sir,' snapped Craddock. 'And do so without consulting anyone on the way.'

James was led out. Crevitt looked long and hard at Craddock. The older man was not about to be chastised by a mere parson, and his look said so.

'Well?' asked Crevitt, turning to Harry.

'I will do nothing that interferes with the running of the ship. Nor will I take any action that is likely to undermine discipline.'

'With respect, Mr Ludlow, that is rather an equivocal response.'

'You may rest assured, sir, that it is the only one you are likely to receive. I must ask you, Mr Craddock, am I still a guest of the ward-room?'

'You are, sir. Most assuredly so,' said Craddock. At least the man was nailing his colours to the mast. Harry nodded his thanks, turned and walked out.

Craddock came into the ward-room, his face white and set.

'Mr Ludlow, a word if you please.'

Harry followed him into his cabin, shutting the door behind him. Craddock sat down rather wearily, inviting Harry to do the same.

'All your life you long to progress, to rise in the service.' He was almost talking to himself. He pulled himself up to address Harry.

'I have just informed the Captain that I will not stand by and allow him to flout both convention and the law. Your brother will not be returned to serve before the mast. As is proper he will be confined as I outlined.'

'Will I be allowed to visit him?'

'I have made it plain that I will force a court martial if he takes any action I deem prejudicial. I have included that in the list of my demands.'

Harry could only wonder at the words that had been used in such an interview with a man like Carter. They would need to be strong on both sides as Craddock was well within his rights. He, along with the other officers, did have the right to challenge the captain and to force him to have their case adjudicated over by senior officers. Indeed, a great deal of senior captains' and admirals' time was taken up sorting out the squabbles that occurred between captains and their officers.

'Thank you, Mr Craddock.'

149

'I did it because it was the proper thing, Mr Ludlow. I require nothing from you in return.'

'That is surely for me to decide, sir,' said Harry, aware of what Craddock had risked. 'I dare say you will not be confirmed in your present post?'

'A mite unlikely.' A small trace of a smile accompanied this. Craddock rubbed his face wearily. 'I would not like to confirm that I will be employed at all.'

Harry could ensure that, but this was not the moment to say anything.

'Mr Craddock. I do not know where you stand on the question of my brother's guilt.'

'I stand on the side of the law, sir.' A trifle bombastic, Harry thought.

'As indeed you have already proved. But what do you think? I beg you to speak plain.'

His face took on a sorrowful look. 'Why then, I'd have to say it looks bad, Mr Ludlow. Very bad.'

'Does my conviction carry any weight with you?'

'A very natural way to behave. But that doesn't alter the facts.'

'Are they facts? Two witnesses that I have not had an opportunity to question. Have you?'

'Not my place to, sir.' He smoothed his hands over the grey whiskers, trying, and failing, to get them to stay in place.

'Let us examine what will happen when we reach Gibraltar. My brother will be marched off to prison. What then?'

Craddock tilted his head to one side, thinking before speaking. He tweaked his broad nose between forefinger and thumb.

'Questions will be asked. Statements will be taken. A case will be put together and your brother will stand trial.'

'And where will you be by then?' Harry strived to sound patient, trying to give the older man time to catch up with his train of thought.

'Only God knows that, Mr Ludlow. Wind and tide . . .'

'And witnesses who will swear that they saw my brother kill Mr Bentley. Where will they be?'

'On board ship.' The old man looked at him, wondering if he

was foolish. Harry continued with a relaxed air, almost light-hearted.

'So they will make a statement to the prosecuting authority. They will then sail away. That testimony will then be used in court, without any chance for a defence counsel to examine the witnesses.'

'Their statements will be taken under oath.'

'Let me put this to you, Mr Craddock. There is someone aboard this ship, probably an officer, although we cannot exclude the crew, who has deliberately used my presence on board to rid himself of Mr Bentley. My brother finding the knife was true. I was supposed to stand accused, not him. And given Captain Carter's attitude to me, the outcome could be pretty certain.'

'Is that not a mite far-fetched?' said Craddock, whose face had shown increasing incredulity as Harry talked. 'I mean no disrespect, sir.'

Harry leant forward to make his points. 'James will tell you that he pulled that knife out of the deck. I can show you a gouge at the scene of the crime, so deep that it could only have been stuck in there deliberately. It will match exactly the one you saw me make in the great cabin. Mr Outhwaite will confirm both that, and the fact that we found traces of wig powder at the scene of the murder.'

'You must forgive me, Mr Ludlow, for I cannot see where this is leading you.' He did look genuinely mystified, or was that disbelief warring with good manners?

'Don't you? Can you not see that this points to certain things . . . Mr Outhwaite will also confirm that there were white dust marks on Mr Bentley's coat. Wig powder, Mr Craddock? And it was just after the Captain's banquet. You will recall that there were very few people at the banquet who were without wigs. Myself, my brother, and Mr Bentley. Oh yes, and Mr Turnbull. You yourself have already seen the scratches on my sea-chest.'

'None of this is very remarkable. There could be any number of explanations.'

'Or one. Surely it is enough to create some doubt. Enough

to lead you to enquire further. And you are in a position to do one thing that I cannot do.'

Craddock had caught the 'you', and it was plain that he was made uncomfortable by it. His countenance closed. Harry could not blame him; he had every right to tread carefully. But curiosity outweighed caution.

'And what would that be?' The question was asked in a wary voice, and Craddock made no attempt to mask his displeasure at being dragged into matters which, he felt, were none of his concern. His face had the look of a man offered stinking fish.

'If the two men who claimed to be witnesses were truly there, what would be their first action on seeing the crime?'

Craddock shrugged. His mental processes were too slow for the speed that Harry was making.

He pressed home his point. 'Perhaps to apprehend the killer?'

'Who's going to go for a man with a knife, Mr Ludlow?'

'So what else would they do?'

'Raise the alarm. Call for help?'

'Yes. They could, of course, just ignore the whole affair and say nothing.'

'But then why come forward later?' If Craddock realized that he had made Harry's point for him, it didn't show.

'Quite. So we are agreed that they should have raised the alarm.'

A shrug. 'Yes.'

'Well, I am willing to wager that they did not. And if they did not raise the alarm, then that puts the whole question of their testimony in doubt, does it not?'

'Well . . .' Craddock was not convinced.

'In doubt, I say, Mr Craddock. I have not yet said that their story has been concocted.'

'But that is what you want to say!' A flash of anger crossed his face.

'What I want to do is this. Simply to create in your mind some room to consider that my brother is innocent. That I can only do by casting doubt on what is said to exist already. I want you to find out who raised the alarm.'

'You are very sure that it wasn't them.' The first shred of doubt showed on his face.

'As sure as I can be.'

'May I be permitted to ask why?'

'Because they were not there when my brother was arrested. I asked Pender to point them out to me. Believe me, Mr Craddock, the face of everyone there is etched on my brain. They were not, and I find it hard to believe that having called for help, they were not there to see the culprit apprehended. Imagine, Mr Craddock, witnessing such a deed, and not there to claim the credit?'

Craddock was still looking at Harry, trying to get the import of what he was being told, when the loud knock at the door disturbed them.

'Come in.'

The door opened. The midshipman called Denbigh was there. Surprised to see Harry, he just stared at him, then seemed to recall why he had come.

'Mr Platt's compliments, sir, but he fears that the weather is set to worsen and he would request your presence on deck.'

'Inform Mr Platt that I shall be with him shortly.'

'Ay, ay, sir.'

Denbigh shut the door behind him. Harry cursed the interruption, feeling that he had been as close as he was likely to get to enlisting Craddock's help. Now the man's mind would be on other things.

'The glass has been falling steadily all morning,' said Craddock.

'I noticed,' said Harry.

'Mr Ludlow,' said Craddock, standing up and putting on his hat. 'I need time to consider what you have told me. First I must attend to the needs of the ship. I'm sure you understand.'

The interview was over. Harry walked out into the deserted ward-room followed by Craddock.

'Dear me.' Craddock looked around the empty room. 'I shall be last on deck, I fear.'

'A privilege of rank, sir,' said Harry. 'Long may you enjoy it.'

XI

The weather was changing rapidly. Dark clouds covered the western sky and the remaining sunlight had a brassy quality. The sea was getting up as the wind increased. Harry swayed easily on the poop as he watched the crew reducing the area of canvas on the masts.

'Looks like we are in for a blow, Mr Prentice!' shouted Harry cheerfully to the young mid.

Prentice looked rather alarmed for a moment, but Harry's apparent calm seemed to reassure him.

How many storms at sea had Prentice seen? Harry had rather taken to the boy. Carter, it transpired, did have a down on him, since he had been forced to accept the youngster aboard ship after much pleading by Prentice's parents. Not that the wishes of parents would have moved a captain like Carter. But they had enlisted the aid of Admiral Hood, through a relative, to plead their son's case. That was too powerful an appeal to be ignored. Prentice had come aboard practically in the wake of Hood's letter, and to a frosty reception.

In conversation Harry had learned how keen the boy had been to get to sea. Like a lot of his fellows he was enchanted by the tales of heroism and wealth that sailors tended to spread while ashore. As they had already discussed, the lad was less impressed with the reality. And there was worse to come. Now, just a week out of port, the water and biscuit were fresh. How would he cope with water covered in green slime, knowing that he must drink it to wash down the tasteless hard tack? The other mids would tell him horror stories about the size of the weevils he would have to tap out of his biscuit, but even they would not be able to exaggerate the taste of rancid butter, and the odour of cheese so high that the bilges smelled like a boudoir in comparison.

But just as Harry remembered his own shock, he knew that Prentice would become accustomed to all of it. Three months from now he would be trapping and fattening rats with the best of them, and if he was skilful in that department he would be selling them to his messmates at a shilling on the barrel. Squalor, smells, and rotten food diminished with familiarity. There were other dangers but Prentice looked sharp enough to avoid any familiarity with the older midshipmen. It was to be hoped his father had seen to his education in that department, for he was a handsome boy, and he would not want for undesirable offers.

In a happier ship, Prentice would be skylarking in the rigging with the other young gentlemen, and well on the way to enjoying his life at sea. He struck Harry as just the kind of youngster he would have wanted aboard, if he'd ever commanded a man-of-war. The boy had certainly adopted the eating habits of his messmates, which was to consume everything put before them as quickly as possible, before looking around to see if there were any scraps left on another plate. Harry himself had one abiding image of his life as a midshipman. He could remember always being hungry.

'Mr Prentice,' said Harry, with a slight twinge of guilt.

'Sir.'

'I cannot help noticing how the mids do not lark about. When I was a lad we were forever in hot water for the noise we made.'

'It is discouraged,' said Prentice.

'By the Captain?'

'In our berth, sir. Both the gunner and the senior mids have made it plain, though I noticed at Spithead it seems common enough in other vessels.'

'Certainly in every ship I've sailed in. Did they say why?'

'Most emphatically, sir. I was informed not to draw attention to myself in any way. And it was represented to me that there was no quicker method than that.'

'Does the name Larkin signify?'

Prentice looked slightly alarmed. He opened his mouth to speak, but before he could, Denbigh's voice cut in.

'Have you no duties to attend to, Mr Prentice?'

Without another word, Prentice dashed off. Denbigh gave Harry that cold stare again, before turning away.

Craddock was now on deck, doing what he had done hundreds of times in many seas: making the ship secure. The topgallants were being struck down. Extra ropes were bowsed tight over the ship's boats, slung above the waist. Men were checking the lashings on the great guns. One of those guns (two tons in weight if you included the carriage) loose on deck in a storm could wreak havoc. The guns below were even heavier, rising to nearly three tons on the gun-deck. Harry looked out over the windward side, the freshening breeze whipping his hair. He heard the orders given that brought the *Magnanime* round to sail as close as possible into the approaching storm. With a lee shore to larboard, Craddock was gaining as much sea room as possible. Perhaps it was just a squall that would pass over quickly. But at this time of year, and in these waters, it was just as likely to be a full south-westerly gale which could last for several days. To the east lay the rocky shoreline of northern Spain and Portugal, the graveyard for many an unprepared ship.

The pumps were clanking away, sending spurts of water over the side. The *Magnanime* was dry and weatherly but in a storm she could ship a great deal of water over her decks, some of which would find its way into the bilges. And in a heaving, pitching ship, some water was bound to make its way through the seams. Harry could see the men on deck and in the rigging going about their duties quietly and efficiently. Carter was lucky. Unhappy ship she might be, but the *Magnanime* had been in commission at the outbreak of war. All the hands were volunteers. He had at least been able to man his ship with proper seamen. Those coming after him would not be so fortunate, and a fair proportion of their crews would be landsmen.

Not that Carter was a bad seaman himself. He was a fine navigator and Harry guessed that in his disputes with the master, the grumbles of which were loudly proclaimed in the ward-room, Carter was as likely to have got the course and position correct, while the master had been some way off in his reckoning. And Carter trusted Craddock to do his job too. His absence from the deck proved that.

Craddock had everything in hand, with men working efficiently all over the deck, when the cry from the mast-head froze them in a dumb show. Two sails, fine on the starboard bow, as yet unidentified. The news brought Carter out of his cabin, telescope in hand, though it was far too soon to see them clearly from near sea level.

Harry, itching to go aloft himself, looked with envy as Mangold was sent to see what he could make of them. Men returned to their assigned duties on deck, but with a detached quality to their work. All eyes were pulled to look over the starboard bulwarks, to where the storm clouds gathered. Harry could imagine their thoughts. They would be praying for a pair of fat merchantmen, laden with wealth and only too keen to surrender without a fight to a ship the size of theirs.

'Seventy-fours,' shouted Mangold from the tops. 'Can't see their colours, sir.'

Craddock looked to Carter for an order. Carter said nothing, merely walking to the windward side and raising his glass to look out over the side. He stood for a while doing nothing then turned and spoke. 'I think we best wait until we have identified them,' he said at last.

If Craddock was disappointed, he showed no sign of it. Harry could see the logic in Carter's thinking. In these waters, given their course, it was a fair chance that they were hostile. In calmer seas, without the possibility of an approaching storm, Carter would probably have cleared for an action right away. But to undo all the precautions that had been undertaken to secure the ship for a rough sea would be foolish, and possibly dangerous, if the seventy-fours turned out to be friendly.

'French, sir,' screamed Mangold. 'They're hoisting more sail.'

Carter still paced up and down. He did have a difficult choice to make. How long before the storm was upon them? He had to assume that the French would fight if they could, just as no one aboard expected him to turn away from a superior force. Harry did not envy him, for the safety of the ship was paramount. Few captains would choose to face a storm cleared for action, with guns cast off and the multitude of things necessary for a battle at sea lying around the deck. And the French had the weather gauge, giving them the right to accept or decline battle in their own time.

'They're coming on, sir.' Mangold must have been, like everybody, in an agony of suspense, lest they turn away. At least he was in a position to influence the debate.

'Can you see their decks yet, Mr Mangold?' shouted Carter.

'No, sir.'

'Then let me know the minute you can. The very minute, you hear!'

'Ay, ay, sir.'

With that Carter tucked his telescope under his arm and, again, he began to pace up and down the quarter-deck. You had to approve of the display of calm. For most men's minds would have turned from the prospect of wealth and comfort. Now, with odds of two to one, they would be thinking of survival and possible glory. Mangold called down to the deck, identifying the enemy as the *Achille* and the *Jemmapes*.

The *Magnanime* ploughed on, her bowsprit now dipping into the rising seas as the swell increased, all the time her course converging with the enemy, bringing them closer. All the excuses were there for Carter to decline immediate battle. The odds, the weather, the direction of the wind, now moving round into the west, and the possibility that if he turned tail, he might well lead them towards a superior force. And even as a superior force, the French might in the end decline battle. The choice would be theirs right to the point where the ships engaged.

Carter would not decline battle. Harry instinctively knew that there would be no room in the Captain's mind for such a thought. The man was no coward, and all his life he could wait for a chance like this, and it would never come again.

He would fight them if they showed a desire to engage,

weather permitting. He would seek to stay with them if it did not, ready to take them on when the weather moderated. The odds meant glory and honours if he was successful. Possible death or capture if he failed. But still glory, in a battle it would be no shame to lose. Harry would have done the same in Carter's place.

'They're clearing for action, sir.' Mangold could now see their decks.

'Then we shall do likewise. Beat to quarters, Mr Craddock. Note the time, Mr Denbigh.'

The marine drummer, who had been standing with his sticks raised, immediately started to beat the tattoo on his drum that sent men racing to their various duties. Bulkheads would come down, furniture would be shifted. Breakables would be packed and sent down into the hold. Guns would be cast off and powder bags filled in the magazines. More shot was being fetched from below, to be stacked alongside the guns. Netting would be rigged to catch falling blocks and spars.

The ward-room would soon cease to exist. From Harry's cabin right to the front of the upper deck would be a clear space. Home most of the time, it would become a fighting platform, painted red so that spilt blood would not show. Two decks below, in the cockpit, Outhwaite would be putting the midshipmen's sea-chests together to form a table and laying out his instruments, ready to go to work on men whose blood had stained that red-painted deck. A swig of neat rum, a leather strap in the mouth, and lashings to hold you still. Then the surgeon would go to work, ignoring the curses and screams from his patients. Harry shuddered at the thought. He'd seen a cockpit during a battle. It was as close to a living hell as any man was likely to witness.

'Mr Ludlow, sir,' said Pender, who had come up unnoticed. 'I took the liberty of fetching these.' His servant held out a pair of pistols.

'Thank you. But I shan't need those for some time yet.' This would be Pender's first battle. The man showed no fear, still prepared to smile. They walked off the poop and down to where Craddock stood. On another ship he would have addressed the captain, but he could not bring himself to address Carter.

He steadied himself on the pitching deck. 'I am at your service, Mr Craddock. Please feel free to employ me in any capacity you wish.'

Craddock lifted his hat to acknowledge the offer.

'You may remain on deck, Mr Ludlow,' said Carter, without turning round. 'And you may employ yourself where you see fit.'

There was no way to say anything to the man's back. 'Have I your permission to go aloft?' he asked Craddock.

'Most certainly, sir. And please take a glass with you.'

'I have them now,' said Carter, acknowledging that the two Frenchmen were visible from the deck. The sun had a cover of wispy cloud now, and just to the west light-grey clouds merged, behind the French ships, into a rapidly blackening horizon. The barometer in the wardroom was still falling, presaging very foul weather. Which would engage them first: the enemy or the storm?

Harry ran for the shrouds. He reached the cap and started up towards the crosstrees. Up here the pitching of the deck became a wild gyration as the mast exaggerated the movement of the ship. He slipped his leg across one of the upper yards, and found a line with which to lash himself on.

Keeping his glass steady was difficult, since he was travelling thirty feet in either direction. And up here the roll was as pronounced as the pitch. Still, he had them in his glass now.

A whole host of questions come calculations were subconsciously going through his mind. How do they handle? How well are they manned? This could indicate whether they intended to try boarding, or to stand off and use gunnery to subdue the *Magnanime*. How long had they been at sea, these two? Was their rigging worn and sparse, or could they, fresh out of port, risk losing spars in a close engagement? Where had they come from? The West Indies, where their crew would have been exposed to yellow fever and thus weakened, and their rate of sailing affected by the weed covering their bottoms? The East? Or from a French port, which would see them with clean bottoms and a full complement, albeit inexperienced?

His mind turned to the coming battle. They would seek to engage with both ships at once. Carter would be best to try to avoid that, and attempt to fight them one at a time. And how much time would there be? The weather was worsening, and the wind was singing through the rigging. This, and a heaving sea, would make manoeuvre difficult. That counted against the inferior force, especially as Carter would have to keep his lower gun ports closed. In this sea, opening ports so close to the waterline was to invite disaster.

On the other hand the same weather would likewise induce a degree of caution in the enemy. They would not wish to sustain serious damage with a gale in the offing. Closer now, and much closer in his telescope, Harry watched the crew going about their duties. A mite slow, he reckoned. And much shouting of orders and the need to push men to their duty. More importantly, neither ship had nettings rigged to deter boarders. The lead ship, *Achille*, was shortening sail, allowing the *Jemmapes*, her consort, to come up. Harry watched intently, noting how long this activity went on. And having gained her purpose, it took some time for her to set those sails again. Those sails? They seemed in very good order, with none of the patches of a ship that had spent a long time at sea. What about the captains, now sailing neck and neck with less than a cable's length between them? What would they make of the *Magnanime*? She too looked like a ship just out, but if they had properly observed the way she handled, they would smoke that she had been at sea for a long time.

Harry, having seen everything he needed to know, made his way quickly back to the deck. Their aim was now plain to him. They intended to engage on both sides, firing several broadsides into the *Magnanime*, then attempting to board in the smoke and confusion. A quick affair, with capture rather than destruction the aim. No doubt they were relishing the prospect of taking a French ship that had, for so long, been in the possession of their ancient enemy.

Harry reported his observations and conclusions to Craddock.

'Fresh out of port with an un-worked-up crew. Sail handling and gunnery likely to be poor. Numerous however, and well fed. Their intention is to board as soon as practical, having attacked both sides.'

The acting premier acknowledged the information, looking slightly bemused at the certainty in Harry's face. He then passed it on to Carter. If that caused him to adjust his intentions, there was no sign of it. The *Magnanime*, now cleared for action, ploughed on towards the approaching enemy. Harry waited for further orders, but Carter gave none.

Again Harry felt the frustration. He knew what he would do. Perhaps Carter intended the same, but his silence gave no clue. The Frenchmen were not going to engage in any fancy seamanship, which was probably just as well. Without being fully worked up as a crew, it would endanger them more than their enemy. So it made sense for the French to rely on weight of metal and manpower, rather than sailing qualities to defeat the *Magnanime*.

By the same set of calculations, Carter had an experienced crew, who could be relied upon to outsail the enemy. Harry, well aware that the French had telescopes trained on the *Magnanime*, could have deliberately slowed the preparations to make the hands appear inexperienced. Carter, if it had occurred to him, decided against any such subterfuge. But surely he must see that being the lesser force he must seek to redress the balance by splitting the enemy, driving them apart, and away from their plan, so that he could exploit their weaknesses.

Time was rapidly running out. Carter should have already got his topgallant masts re-rigged, and some men aloft ready to increase sail. True, the storm was approaching, and he'd likely have to get them down again in difficult circumstances. But the French were going to fight, and beating them was the first task. Those telescopes, seeing the British sailors rigging masts to carry more sail, might presume that the *Magnanime* intended to flee, causing the subsequent actions to come as even more of a surprise.

By staying on this course, with perhaps a touch more southing, suddenly increasing his speed would produce a definite gain, since the French would take much longer to achieve a similar result. If he could achieve sufficient speed, their courses would converge at a moment more of Carter's choosing, the aim being to force the French into line ahead, to be fought one at a time. If not that, he still held an even stronger card simply because of the nature of his crew and officers. By letting fly his sheets and bearing up at the right moment, he could cause them to overshoot enough on their converging course to nullify the advantage they now held with the wind in their favour. If he could get windward of the *Jemmapes*, it was only a short step to getting athwart her stern. A modicum of luck would see such a weight of shot pour through her rear as to render the ship useless.

And if all that failed Carter could wear, turning away from his enemy and forcing them into a stern chase. Not glorious perhaps, but that at least would be a situation pregnant with possibilities for splitting the enemy, given that he could manoeuvre so swiftly. To Harry, taking the initiative was vital. For if Carter did not negate that numerical advantage, and tried to fight both the *Achille* and the *Jemmapes*, then he was courting almost certain defeat.

The minutes ticked away. Still Carter did nothing, simply standing staring at the approaching enemy. Not even a rousing speech to the men, silent beside their guns. Harry looked at Craddock and the other officers to see if they too had any doubts about their captain's behaviour. All he saw were set jaws and an air of keen anticipation.

'Captain Carter,' said Harry, walking over to where he stood. 'Would it be in order for me to suggest a course of action?'

'It would not, Mr Ludlow. Making yourself useful does not extend to interfering in the running of the ship.'

'Then might I ask what your intentions are?'

'Intentions?' Carter turned and looked at Harry without comprehension. 'Why, I intend to fight these two Frenchmen.'

'I was more curious about the method you will employ.'

'Method? I shall put myself alongside the enemy and engage them.' There was a note of exasperation in his voice, as though the question was stupid.

'Yard-arm to yard-arm?'

'Precisely!'

'Mr Craddock passed on to you my observations?' It was a great temptation, this desire to tell the Captain the foolishness of this course of action. Harry fought to keep the strain out of his voice, but time was rapidly slipping away.

'I have received a lot of information, most of it with my own eyes, Mr Ludlow.'

'Then you will be aware that the enemy will probably attempt to engage you on both sides?'

'I am.' Carter's shoulders tensed.

'You have the ability to outsail them, even in a rising sea. Could I not suggest to you, as a more profitable course of action . . .'

Carter spun round, his face suffused with anger. 'Damn you, Ludlow. Will you never cease to carry a superior air. It is insufferable to be addressed so at such a time.'

Harry was aware that he was incurring the disapproval of everyone on the quarter-deck, not just Carter. He was indulging in a shocking breach of manners.

'I would wish you to be successful, sir, for my country's sake, if no other.' This was said in a loud voice to carry to all of them.

Carter, turning away again, replied through clenched teeth. 'Then, sir, please leave the running of the ship, and the conduct of this action, to the person your country has seen fit to put in command!'

There were many more things he could have said. Like Carter's aversion to exercising his guns meant that his crew would have a slow rate of fire. Faster than the French perhaps, but too slow to make up for the effect of shot coming from both sides.

Harry was tempted to spell out to Carter precisely what he would do, but how could he address Carter's back? And what would he achieve? The man's jaw was as set as his tactics, which were of the pounding variety. He was going to rely on the bulldog quality of his crew, and a tradition of victory, to make good the deficiency in guns and men. Perhaps he was right. All Harry knew was that to speak would be useless. He walked over to Craddock.

'Mr Craddock. The enemy will try to board us. May I suggest

that I put myself with a party for the purpose of repelling them.'

'Mr Turnbull has charge of that duty, sir.'

'I am aware of a Marine officer's place in action. But I would like to gather those hands who will become superfluous when we engage to form an extra group with which to counter-attack.'

'Carry on, Mr Ludlow.' Harry looked towards Carter's back.

'Please take the Captain's approval as read,' said Craddock, looking over Harry's shoulder. The other officers likewise avoided his eye. He had become a nuisance.

Harry, given young Prentice to assist, gathered the spare hands as they completed their duties. They tended to be the less nimble members of the crew, mentally and physically, and they would normally have been set to carrying the wounded below. He could see Turnbull with half of his marines lined up as if on a parade ground. They had taken station at the rear of the quarter-deck. The other half of his men were in the tops, acting as sharpshooters, their presence wasted in Harry's view. They would be needed on the deck. A steady discipline in a close fight more than compensated for any lack of numbers. Besides, he disagreed with too much firing of muskets from the rigging. It was as likely to set fire to the ship as cause discomfort to the enemy.

Harry's party was pitifully small, some twenty hands. For what was coming he needed more men and he racked his brain to think where to find them. Looking down the deck, he could see that all the hands were fully occupied, the problem being compounded by Carter's decision to fight both sides and man the gun-deck, even though the ports were tight shut. On the gun-deck, quarter-deck, and forecastle, the guns had been loaded and run out, and the crews stood like horses before a race, in a high state of tension.

'Mr Prentice. I suggest that we take station by the beak,' said Harry. Prentice looked at him without replying. Pender, standing behind the boy, smiled.

'You, young man, are in command. After all, I cannot give orders to the crew.' It was amusing to watch the child digest this information. He was totally unused to real authority. But he would find that, young as he was, in the Navy, one could suddenly find oneself pitched into the most difficult situations with no one to rely on. Giving some orders would boost his confidence.

'Yes,' he stammered nervously. He took off his hat, and wiped his forearm across his fair hair. His thin face was set in a concentrated way, as he tried to work out what to say. Then his face cleared as he had a thought.

'But I would welcome any advice, sir.'

Harry laughed and patted him on the shoulder. Prentice smiled, and led his party along the gangway towards the bows.

'Might I also suggest that the hands take cover behind the bulwarks, Mr Prentice. No point in presenting the enemy with easy targets.'

Prentice started to say, 'Ay, ay, sir.' But he checked himself and passed on the necessary orders.

'They're getting close now, Mr Ludlow,' said Pender, who had remained standing.

Harry looked out past the bowsprit at the French ships. They had head-reached the *Magnanime* and altered course to bring themselves round into her path, the *Jemmapes* slightly ahead of the *Achille* to avoid taking the wind out of her consort's sails. And they were edging closer together, reducing sail, so that when they engaged, they would hardly have any way on them.

The sea was making life difficult, pitching them about. That and the wind, which was still steadily increasing in force. But that same wind stood to benefit the French as they came alongside. Simple, to make the *Magnanime* spin a few points. The wind would check her, and bring her to a halt. She would be at their mercy. They could then lash themselves to the British ship and, at the right moment, after several telling broadsides, seek to board.

Harry's plan, if he could call such a desperate throw a plan, envisaged waiting until one section of the *Magnanime*'s crew seemed to falter. Then he would endeavour to take the attackers in the flank and check their progress. But he had pitifully few men to effect any change in the outcome, and he fully expected to be the guest of a French commodore at dinner that evening. Either that or he would be dead.

I pray that I am not wounded, he thought, his imagination picturing the coming scenes in the cockpit. I would face anything rather than Outhwaite's knife. That vision proved a wonderful aid to his concentration.

'Mr Prentice,' he cried, completely putting aside his earlier reservations about the proper chain of command. 'Go below and tell the officer in command of the party manning the relieving tackles to send his men to the forecastle forthwith. Say it is the Captain's express wish that he do so.'

Prentice hesitated, looking at Harry with fear in his eyes.

'Go on, boy. I will take the responsibility.'

'But the Captain's express wish?' said Prentice.

Harry looked back over the bowsprit. Prentice followed his gaze. The French ship loomed very large now.

'You must say "wish". Do not, under any circumstances, say it is an order. We need those men, Mr Prentice, for they are useless where they are.'

The relieving tackles were ropes connected to the rudder. Should it become impossible, through damage sustained, to con the *Magnanime* from the quarter-deck, then these men on the ropes would be employed to haul on their lines to steer the ship.

'We will be engaging in no manoeuvres, Mr Prentice. Once we are alongside, those gentlemen will bring us to.' He did not add that the men below were very likely the most useless in the crew, picked for muscle. Hands whose only skill was to haul on a rope when told. But they would be brawny men, and that was what he needed.

'Ay, ay, sir,' said Prentice, running off. Harry wondered what persuaded him, for the boy could be in serious trouble if the truth came out. He put the thought out of his mind as he set Pender and the others to gathering weapons for another forty fighters. Prentice arrived back with Denbigh, who had commanded the party. He was leading his hands behind him. Prentice was well in front.

'Did anyone ask you what you were about?' said Harry quietly.

'Several people. But I told them what you suggested.' The boy indicated that his fellow midshipman was one of them. Prentice then turned to Denbigh. 'Mr Craddock has put us both under Mr Ludlow's instructions.'

Harry smiled at the boy's cheek. Having burnt his boats, Prentice probably thought he had nothing to lose by telling another lie. And it showed good sense, him saying Craddock. No one would have believed that Carter would have given Harry such powers. Denbigh stared coldly at Harry, then half turned, as if to go and check the veracity of Prentice's words.

'There is no time, Denbigh,' said Prentice. The boy swung his arm in a heroic gesture. 'The enemy will soon be upon us.'

Harry bade the new arrivals to join their fellows behind the bulwarks. He looked out again. Now the faces of the enemy were clearly visible. They too had men in the tops with muskets, but very few. They would be husbanding the rest, keeping them to swell the ranks of the boarders. He could see the French officers on the quarter-deck, silent and still, like those aboard the *Magnanime*.

The forward guns on both sides could have been brought to bear, but both Carter and the French were saving all for the first rolling broadside. Given the pitching of the ships it would be a barrage which would either clear the rigging or the lower gun-decks. Carter was down to fighting topsails now, and given his course he had very little forward movement, even with his yards braced hard round. His ship slowed even more as the bulk of the lead French vessel took the wind out of his sails. But it also took some of the swell out of the sea, and Harry, hearing a creaking sound, looked over to see the lower gunports opening. Carter was taking a risk, but if he was right, he would double his firepower with that one stroke. He hoped to God that Carter had given standard instructions to fire on the up-roll, for if the French had not manned theirs likewise, those great guns would be firing into an empty enemy gun-deck.

'Fire as you bear,' came the command from the quarter-deck. Even with the noise of the wind, Harry was sure he could hear similar instructions from the French officers. The *Jemmapes* came alongside on the starboard quarter. Both sets of guns opened fire simultaneously, and suddenly the air was full of sound. It was gunnery at point-blank range. Carter had the luck with the pitch, his lower-deck guns firing straight into the Frenchmen's upper deck, and his upper-deck and quarter-deck guns swept the rigging, slicing rope and cracking wood, causing blocks, sails, and spars to fall on the crowded deck. The *Jemmapes*'s guns seemed aimed at a point below the gun-deck as they went off. The *Magnanime* shuddered as their shots struck her, then the pitch of the sea reversed itself and Harry was staring through the Frenchman's gunport at the eager faces of the men manning the upper-deck guns.

The *Achille* was now coming alongside on the larboard quarter and again the guns opened fire simultaneously. The Frenchmen had both backed their topsails and spun their wheels to trap the *Magnanime* and turn her into the wind. Carter was in no mind to avoid this manoeuvre, and the ship seemed stationary as all three of them exchanged incessant fire.

The *Magnanime*'s guns were being reloaded and run out, but with little discipline or co-ordination. It was every man for himself, and the results were immediately apparent. The lack of firing practice would now cost Carter dear. Nothing is so telling as a rolling broadside delivered from each gun in turn. The fire is continuous, allowing the enemy no time to gather himself to resist. But although Carter's guns were achieving a better rate than the French, they were firing piecemeal, so that a great deal of the effect was lost.

The French ships were edging closer. Men stood ready to cast grappling irons into the *Magnanime*'s rigging. If the Frenchmen could get close enough there was a fair chance that one of them would foul the *Magnanime*'s shrouds, and they would really be locked together. The guns were more stable now as the proximity of the three great ships created a calmer sea between them. A steadier platform meant a steadier aim, and damage was being sustained on the decks on both sides. Harry could see that one of the *Magnanime*'s quarter-deck cannons was dismounted. It was hard to detect through the billowing smoke what effect the fire of the remaining guns was having on the enemy, but from the screams that came across the intervening water, they were suffering as much damage, if not more, than the British.

Harry could see Carter, obvious in his best uniform, calmly directing operations. Craddock stood beside him, a speaking trumpet in his hand. Men were now being carried below, some dead, some badly wounded. A midshipman lay at Carter's feet, his blood staining the deck. All down the sides of the ship men sweated and cursed, as they strained to reload the cannons, working the guns, pushing wads or shot down the barrels, or hauling on ropes to pull the charged guns up for firing. Powder monkeys ran from the after hatch carrying gunpowder and shot, as a cascade of wood, ropes, and the occasional body fell amongst them. And all the while the whistles of bullets cut through the surrounding air.

A great clanging sound, and Harry saw that a huge gap had been torn in the side of the ship, hard by the forrard forecastle gun on the larboard side. Men had been blasted aside like dolls. One headless body twitched as a fountain of blood spurted from the neck. More men were wounded as great splinters of wood flew through the air, embedding themselves in soft, pliant flesh. The shot had hit one of the twelve-pounders square on, severing its breachings and tipping it on to its side. The *Magnanime* pitched suddenly as a heavy wave rocked the three ships, and the gun and carriage, two tons of wood and metal, started to slither across the deck, gouging the planking as it went. Harry shouted a warning to the crew opposite, but to no avail. The noise of guns going off, of men shouting and screaming in pain, was too great. Concentrating on reloading, they were too busy to notice the danger. Too late, one of the gun crew saw the monster nearly on them and yelled a warning, himself jumping over his gun to escape. His mates were too slow. Men were crushed by its great weight, as one cannon careered into the other. The sound of crushing bones and the cries of men in agony were plain, even above the crash of the other guns.

'Follow me,' shouted Harry to those near him. Pender, Denbigh, and half a dozen hands rushed forward, Harry grabbed a line as they did so. They were not alone. Others had seen the danger of this huge gun slithering around the deck. They too rushed forward and threw ropes round the first protruding piece

170

of the gun and carriage that presented itself. They would have to pin it where it lay. Men were still trapped between the two guns, but their fate was second to that of the ship. They would have to remain there, to die if need be. Harry got his rope round the upturned carriage wheel and quickly lashed it to a cleat on the side. More lines were lashed to the tompion and the carriage wheels to secure it to the side. Bullets whistled around them as the French sharpshooters tried to disrupt their efforts. A sailor beside Harry spun round suddenly and collapsed at his feet, blood spurting from his chest. Tying the last half-hitch, Harry and Pender bent and lifted him, calling for help from some of his party who had followed them.

'Get him below!' he yelled to his servant. 'Then back as quick as you can.' Harry, followed by Denbigh, ran back to where Prentice stood. The boy was pale and frightened, as he stood trying to comprehend the death and destruction taking place around him. Harry put his hands on the boy's shoulder, and turned him so that he could see him smile.

'Grapeshot soon, Mr Prentice. Please get down. You too, Mr Denbigh.'

'Down,' said Denbigh, either uncomprehending, or aghast at the suggestion.

'You're no use dead, boy. Get down!' he snapped. Denbigh obeyed, throwing Harry a sour look. Still holding Prentice, he shook him slightly, and the youngster forced a smile. 'As long as you do your duty, boy. That is all that can be asked. Now down behind the bulwark.'

Harry stayed upright. Pender came back, his trousers drenched with blood, to stand beside him. The fire from the *Magnanime* was slackening, but more on the larboard side than to starboard. The *Jemmapes*, having been subjected to the first British broadside, had probably suffered the most. The *Achille* had fared better, and the British guns aimed at her were in disarray. The enemy would use grape soon, he had no doubt of that. They would have decided before the action commenced which crew would board first, for it was from the *Jemmapes* that the first indications of an impending attack became apparent. Through the smoke he could see men being gathered. The firing from the quarter-deck of the French ship stopped as the whole of the top layer of guns were loaded with grape, and the muzzles trained enough to make sure that the shot swept the British deck. The danger of some shot damaging their consort was obviously a risk they were prepared to run. The *Magnanime* still shook from the shots pounding her side from the French twenty-four pounders on the *Jemmapes*'s upper deck. And the crash of the guns beneath Harry's feet was continuous. It would be hell below, on both ships.

'Grapeshot!' Craddock bellowed through a trumpet, his voice carrying over the din. Just in time most of the men ducked as the small shot whistled over their heads. Some, deafened by the sounds of the guns and still upright, did not hear and paid the price.

'Stand by to repel boarders!' shouted Craddock. Harry could see the messengers running to tell the officers on the upper deck to load with grape. The men on the guns rushed to their task, furiously loading the remaining guns as the French ship crunched into the side of the *Magnanime*. Lines snaked out, thrown to lash the rigging together. Men crowded on to the side of the *Jemmapes* armed with cutlasses, clubs and pikes. Harry could see the French officers exhorting their men as their opposite numbers on the *Magnanime* struggled to elevate their guns.

'Fire!' shouted Craddock. It was not a clean affair. Some of the guns were not ready, and some were still loaded with round-shot. But it did great damage, tearing gaping holes in the ranks of their attackers. One French officer, standing on the *Jemmapes*'s bulwark, waving his sword, was literally blown in two by round-shot. The top half of his trunk disappeared, his blood and flesh spraying out to cover those around him. Others fell back amongst their companions, either wounded or dead. The French had reloaded their guns with proper shot, and they fired at point-blank range, seeking to smash more holes in the *Magnanime*'s side, once more filling the air with deadly splinters. Great billowing clouds of smoke obscured the men on both sides. The noise of the guns and the roars of half-crazed men all mixed together in an endless wall of deafening sound.

The smoke cleared enough to show the *Jemmapes*'s bulwarks

full of sailors, some covered in blood already, waiting to jump the last few feet between the ships. Pikes were already being jabbed across the gap, to be parried with a variety of weapons. The French were pressing forward, shouting imprecations at the British defenders. Some lost their footing, to fall to almost certain death between the two ships. The *Achille*, still firing on the larboard side, let off some of her guns at the wrong moment. The shot swept across the deck and cut into her own compatriots on the *Jemmapes*.

The noise seemed to die suddenly, as though by a pre-arranged signal. With a great cheer the boarders leapt from their ship on to the side of the *Magnanime*. Turnbull had already brought forward his marines and they formed two ranks, one kneeling, the other standing. Carefully, picking their targets, the marines poured fire into the men seeking to board, quickly cutting down their numbers. The gun crews were now engaged in hand to hand fighting, using clubs, swords, pikes, axes and knives. Harry could see one of the *Magnanime*'s crew with a huge lump of wood in his hands, which he was using to fell as many Frenchmen as he could. Guns were going off singly with a loud crash, drowning out the noise of screaming and shouting, of cursing and dying.

'Sir?' said Prentice. His thin face was still anxious, but he also looked determined to get at the enemy.

'Not yet, Mr Prentice,' shouted Harry. 'This is not the main assault.'

Harry pointed one of his pistols to where the whole process was being repeated on the larboard side. Grape was fired into the back of the defenders, catching some of the attackers as well. Men fell and were trampled on in the mêlée. Not warned through the speaking trumpet this time, it took a greater toll, especially amongst the file of standing marines. Turnbull was looking wildly from one side to another, not sure which way to face his men. His hat was whipped off as sharpshooter's bullet took it on the brim. Blood from dozens of bodies was running across the deck, to fill the scuppers and trickle over the side.

Great yells were emanating from the throats of the *Achille*'s boarders. But the quarter-deck had seen their move. They suffered too as Craddock's orders sent a fusillade of grapeshot into them. Carter was directing as much musket fire as he could into the seething mass. But undeterred, full of the lust for battle, they were soon jumping aboard, using the billowing smoke to camouflage their attack. Again French guns smashed the side of the British ship, trying to create gaps for the second wave of attackers to pour through.

Harry had his pistols cocked now. He knew, even though the smoke made it hard to see, that the crisis was approaching. If the French could gain enough of a foothold on the *Magnanime*'s deck there would be no getting rid of them. Sheer weight of numbers would tell in the end.

The second wave of *Achille*'s attackers leapt over the gap between the two ships, slipping on the blood and tripping over the bodies of their fellows. The starboard attack was being contained, but this new assault faced a less organized defence, and try as they might, the *Magnanime*'s gun crews, still firing, could not prevent the French from getting aboard in numbers.

'Ready, men!' shouted Harry above the screaming, gunshot, and wind. 'Steady until I give the command. And when we attack, I want to hear you!' Harry's party stood up, crowding towards the larboard gangway. Pender was right beside him, sword in hand. Prentice pressed forward gamely. He bent to give his orders to the two pale midshipmen. Looking back at the deck, he could see one of them had been sick. Harry did not ask who.

'We will concentrate on the larboard side. Our aim is to break up their attack, and if possible push them back over the side. Sweep the gangway forward to the quarter-deck. And gentlemen, kill if you can, maim if you can't. Accept no offers to surrender. Once we have dealt with the *Achille*'s boarders, we support the starboard. Keep an eye on me.'

Both nodded. Harry looked overhead. The storm was on them now. The sky was full of black rushing clouds and the sea had ceased to be an even swell. The water was now full of spume and waves of differing heights, as well as bodies and parts of all three ships. The seventy-four's sides were grinding together and the waves lifted them in turn. God help those who fell between them. There would be no rescue in this sea.

'Good-luck' Harry was calm, for the situation was developing just as he had predicted. What he intended might not work, but he hoped that the sudden appearance of a disciplined body of attackers, at the height of the crisis, would turn the tide. The right moment? That would be a guess. Too soon, and the French would repulse them. Too late, and their number would be insufficient to affect the outcome.

Ignoring the continual difference in height caused by the two ships being tossed in the rising waves, the enemy was pushing aboard in great numbers on the larboard side, their weight causing the defenders to fall back. It was an inch by inch affair, each width of planking fiercely contested. Swords slashed, pikes jabbed, but worst of all, the axes, in the hands of strong and battle-crazed men, hacked limbs and cleaved heads. It was hard to keep upright with the slippery blood and flesh that covered the deck. Guns were still being fired into the *Magnanime*. That was another factor in the timing of Harry's attack. When the French commander was sure of the outcome, he would cease firing, and order every available man on his ship to cross to the other deck. Harry must strike before that happened.

Turnbull, foolishly, had split his marines. Harry saw them fix bayonets, present, and attack in both directions. They made little difference to the state of either battle, being thrown in piecemeal. Turnbull should have withdrawn to the quarter-deck, regrouped, then attacked. Now the starboard crew, sensing rather than seeing the weakness at their back, began to falter too.

'Now!' shouted Harry. And his party, sixty men yelling like banshees, swept down the larboard gangway. It was hard to keep together on the pitching slippery deck, and the narrowing gangway pushed them into a tight mass which caused their attack to lose some of its impetus. But the defenders took heart at the sight, and brought the enemy's progress to a halt. Harry's men careered into their backs, clubbing, stabbing, and cleaving. Harry stood back, firing his pistols, before cutting off the last section of his party. He set them to fighting the Frenchmen still trying to board.

Those attackers who had got on to the *Magnanime*'s deck were now between two forces, and had no immediate prospect of support. What Harry had prayed for came to pass very quickly. Their frenzy slackened. They started to think as endangered individuals, rather than a cohesive attacking group. He spotted a French officer, a tricolour wrapped around his waist, trying to rally his men. Grabbing a sword from a dead man at his feet, he charged into the mêlée with Pender at his back. Cutting his way through, using his sword and his pistol butt as a club, he got on to the quarter-deck and went straight for the boarding party's commander. As if by magic a space cleared as the defenders fell back. The man turned, warned by one of his men, just in time to parry the thrust that would have cut him through. But Harry's knee followed, catching the officer in the groin. As he jerked forward, Harry struck the back of his neck with the hilt of the sword and the officer crumpled on the deck.

Was this decisive? Or was it the sudden torrential downpour that cascaded down on attackers and defenders alike? Harry could not tell. Water engulfed him till he could hardly see, as the gap closed and the fighting intensified. But the French pressure was slackening as some of them tried to get back aboard their own ship. It only took a few to break the spirit of the attack. They had lost all cohesion now, and that made them vulnerable. Some were even trying to surrender to avoid injury.

'Mr Prentice, Mr Denbigh! To starboard!' shouted Harry, glad of the water that filled his mouth as he did so. He was almost pitched into the scantlings as the *Magnanime* lurched suddenly, taken by a freak wave. He prayed that Carter had closed the lower ports. If ever water got through them the ship would sink like a stone. One quick look confirmed that the French ships were in the same unstable condition. The sea was worsening further, and the wind was now drowning out the sound of the ragged gunfire.

That pitch of the sea added extra momentum to his party's charge across the deck. They practically bundled the French back into the *Jemmapes*. Carter was still yelling commands. Even fighting hard, slashing and stabbing, Harry could hear the orders to cut the ropes that were binding the ships together. Perhaps the French would regroup, but if that could be delayed then the *Magnanime* might get free.

Suddenly he realized that the French were trying to cut free as well. Shouts rang out, ordering their men back aboard. With the state of the weather, all three ships were now in grave danger: for if one ship foundered then, lashed together, they would all go down.

Sporadic gunfire was being exchanged again. The discipline and greater experience of the British sailors told here, and very soon the *Magnanime* was inflicting damage on the enemy. Their actions kept the French at bay while men in the rigging, using axes and swords, cut the last of the bindings. With a great wrenching sound, the wind tore the *Achille* away from the *Magnanime*. The Frenchman's mizzen topmast, still attached, went by the board. The *Achille*'s captain must have realized his peril, for he ordered his men to cut his ship free from the wreckage and make sail. In this sea and with this wind, with a mast trailing over the side, to have no way on the ship was to invite almost certain doom.

The *Jemmapes* was still stuck to the *Magnanime*, the pressure of the wind and sea pushing her into her enemy's side, grinding up and down with a horrible rending sound. But with her consort no longer pinning the opposite side the two seventy-fours started to spin slowly, pushed by the wind.

It was now an even contest. As the wind came between them, they started to drift apart. Then they both jerked horribly, before coming together again with a resounding crunch. Again they drifted apart. Ropes held them, stretching out taut, ready to be cut. Axes flashed on both ships. The crew of the *Magnanime* cheered as the gap opened further. The shots from the remaining British guns went into the water. Craddock yelled loud orders through the speaking trumpet.

'Cease firing. All hands to make sail!' The cheering died as men rushed to their duty. Harry suddenly found himself in the way.

*

The three ships drifted further apart, each one more intent on survival than any immediate renewal of the battle. Scraps of canvas were hurriedly rigged, storm canvas that would allow the seventy-fours to run before the wind, with enough speed to stop them broaching in the heavy seas. There was precious little daylight left, and given the state of the sky, it was already so dark that it was becoming difficult to spot their enemies through the driving squalls of rain. Craddock was bellowing orders through his trumpet to the teams of hands who were busy trying to repair the damage caused by the recent action.

The two enemy ships, eager to board and capture the *Magnanime*, had not, as was customary with that nation, fired almost exclusively at their opponent's rigging. No one would want to take possession of a dismasted hulk with a storm in the offing. But the *Magnanime*'s top hamper had not completely escaped the effects of the French bombardment. The pitch of the sea had sent several heavy broadsides into the air. The foretopmast, smashed by more than one heavy ball, was severely wounded above the cap, and frantic efforts were being made to repair it. If the storm grew any worse, there was a general feeling that it could go by the board.

Again a difficult set of choices for Carter. Should he strip it of rigging and canvas, thus reducing pressure on the mast? Proper repair was impossible in this sea. But it was because of that same sea, and the wind that was whipping it up, that he needed the foremast to keep the ship's head pointed in the right direction.

All that could be done was well in hand. Men were fishing the mast with capstan bars seeking to strengthen it where it was damaged, affixing the lengths of timber and then binding them tightly with a stout cable. Extra stays were being rigged to ease the pressure. That was the most important problem but there were many others, not least the shortage of officers and men, casualties in the recent fight. Harry did not know how high the toll was, but a brief visit to the cockpit had shown the crowded gangways and the blood-soaked Outhwaite, operating desperately to try and save lives and limbs. It had been a shock to see James there, also heavily bloodstained. Craddock had ordered him to be released into the surgeon's custody at the start of the action. Harry tried to speak with his brother but he was waved away. James was far too busy.

The carpenter kept sending his mate up to report a rising level of water in the well, as the pumps were unable to keep up with the amount of water the ship was making. Parties were slaving down below, shifting stores, bales, and water casks, to come at the places where the *Magnanime* had been holed, so that they could be plugged.

The damage to the decks would have to wait, although one of the carpenter's mates was repairing the damage to the ship's boats, hauled back on board as soon as was practicable. A team was manning the capstan and lines were running through the rigging attached to the dismounted guns so that they could be righted and bowsed tight against the side. The only alternative would be to cast them overboard. You could not strike them down into the hold on a deck that was angled like a roof, and pitching like a crazed horse.

XII

Harry pulled himself along on the man-ropes to where Carter stood. He was wearing a borrowed oilskin coat and the water from the rain and the flying spray was running off it by the gallon. Carter, similarly dressed, was standing head back looking at the foremast, his face lined with worry. The *Magnanime* was normally a dry, weatherly ship. Given that the damage below was not too great, she should have been capable of riding out this storm. But if that mast was toppled, then all his calculations would go with it, with a consequent increase in danger to everyone aboard.

It was full night now, which seemed to increase the sound and fury of the wind. The only light was that given off by the ship's lanterns. Harry would have liked to ask their position, but he doubted that anyone really knew within ten miles. More important was their position when the action started. They had drifted some way to leeward during the fight, and the wind was now pushing them further in the same direction. With the sea as it was the best course was to run before it. But how far away was the Portuguese coast?

'I must run, Ludlow. I have no choice.' Harry was surprised that Carter had spoken to him, if you could call his shouted words speaking. He must badly need someone to talk to. 'That foremast is badly damaged. I fear to put any strain on it.'

'How long can we run?'

'By my reckoning, not for too long. The master maintains that we have ample sea room, but he's a fool.'

'Well, if you are right, you are going to have to try that mast some time. Would it not be better to do so in deep water?'

'A fine set of choices.'

Harry knew that Carter was not asking his advice. Perhaps he was weighing up the possibilities with the only man on board who knew something about ships yet did not expect a captain to be omniscient. Perhaps, with everyone in danger, it was no time to indulge in personal animosity.

The *Magnanime* ploughed on, her bowsprit diving deep into the angry waters before dragging itself out and up high into the air, sending a great cascade of water scudding aft. At least the spray was being blown forwards, giving them a clear view of the ship from the quarter-deck. Harry stood silently with Carter, his ears tuned to the sounds of the ship. Various officers and warrant officers came aft to report. The carpenter seemed to think that he had come upon the last of the holes, and he was busy plugging it now. Craddock reported that the pumps seemed to be gaining. Harry realized that Carter was waiting for the information to be generally favourable. As soon as it was, he would try that mast. Once again, Harry had to admit that the man was a good seaman.

His mind ran back over the recent battle. Carter could have beaten those Frenchmen. Perhaps he could not have taken both of them, but he could certainly have disabled one, and as this storm had turned out, he would have effectively sunk her. A successful action against odds of two to one! He would have been the hero of the nation, possibly knighted, and certainly voted a goodly sum by the Patriotic League. And his officers: Craddock would have gained his step, becoming at least a master and commander, with commensurate rises for the others. A good seaman, yes, but what an unimaginative fighter.

Craddock came aft to report that the pumps were now definitely gaining. Carter gave orders for all hands to come on deck to make sail. The men were weary. They had fought a hard battle, first against the French, and then against the damage and the elements. Harry would have tried to give them something hot before trying what Carter intended, something to revive their spirits, at the very least a tot of rum. But he dare not interfere. Unheard by Harry, Craddock must have suggested something similar.

'Again, Mr Craddock, you expose yourself again!' shouted Carter angrily. His voice was clearly audible above the wind. 'I really cannot contend with a premier who so wants to coddle the hands. Now oblige me by giving the orders as I have outlined them.'

Craddock, his whiskers plastered to the side of his face, turned and raised his speaking trumpet. The orders roared out, men ran up the foremast shrouds, ready to drop the forecourse, reefed for the state of the weather. Some went further, above the wound in the foretopmast, now fished with the capstan bars. Others ran to bend on the spritsail course and the flying jib, yet more to man the falls, ready to raise them to run between the bowsprit and the foremast. Everything was happening at once, for all the world as though the sea was calm and the mast intact. Again Harry felt those reservations that made him a different man from Carter. He would have taken things one at a time, exposing as few men as possible to danger. Perhaps that was what Craddock had suggested. To raise the triangular sails would give better steerage, but it would also put differing pressures on the mast. That might cause it to snap. If it did the men up there waiting to set some scraps of canvas from the foretopsail yard would be likely to go overboard with it.

The men started to haul on the lines and the spritsail creaked up towards the foremast. The hands on deck sheeted it home. Harry realized that he was holding his breath. The mast held. Craddock ordered the forecastle cleared before shouting the orders for the topmen to let go. The hands let out one reef in the topsail, just enough to take the wind. Again everyone waited for the tearing sound of breaking wood. Again it held, and the progress of the ship was now smoother through the water, as the foretopsails took some of the strain off the ship, driving her head forward as she emerged from the troughs in the waves and took the wind. Craddock called the hands down and issued instructions for all to be made secure.

Finally men were being sent below to get some rest. Pender again appeared silently, seeming to spring up from nowhere, this time with a mug of hot wine spiced with brandy. Harry drank it gratefully. He should go below. There was no reason for him to be on deck, let alone stay. This was not his ship. But he was apprehensive. He felt the presence of land, an instinct which many would deride. It was one common enough to seamen. Was that why Carter was still on deck. Could he feel it too?

'I dare say the rest of the officers would like a tot of this, Pender.'

Pender looked meaningfully in the direction of Carter. Harry nodded. He had no intention of putting aside the differences between them. Although he could not have defined it, if asked, Harry knew the *Magnanime* still to be in danger. It would do no harm to behave as human beings until the weather cleared.

Pender returned with the steaming mugs. No one asked him how he had contrived hot drinks. The cook had insisted that it was too dangerous to relight the galley stove, extinguished before the battle, because of the motion of the ship. They just took the drinks carefully and gratefully, thanking whatever deity they worshipped for the warmth it spread through their bones.

Abruptly the man set to watch in the beak shouted a warning. Carter ran forward, followed by Craddock and Harry. It was hard to hear above the noise of the wind, and the thudding of the ship into the heavy waves. But it was there. The sound of water crashing against rocks. A lee shore.

'All hands, Mr Craddock,' shouted Carter, as the premier approached. 'We must try to go about and claw off. If we cannot do that, we must try and anchor. Anchors on the cathead, and the hawsers bent on.'

'Ay, ay, sir,' said Craddock, moving away. Carter called after him.

'Mr Craddock. Put a marine guard on the spirit room. And arm the officers.'

A guard on the spirit room was a reasonable precaution, since in a situation like this, when sailors could get into their heads that all was lost, they would raid the spirit room determined that if they were going to die, they would do so drunk. The effect that drinking had on their efficiency virtually guaranteed that this wish was fulfilled. But Harry could not understand the idea of arming the officers. With what? Pistols that would be too damp to fire in this weather? It said more about Carter, and the type of captain that he was, than it did about the reliability of the crew.

Weary men were roused out from their hammocks. Word spread quickly of the danger to the ship. With much shouting and cursing, the hands were pushed and shoved to their stations. Was it weariness that made them so listless, or a hint of despair? After everything that had happened today, did they feel that this was one problem too many? It was at such moments that trust between officers and men counted.

Harry, making his way aft, was suddenly aware that he had become the object of much attention from some of the crew. Men were pointing at him, and he heard the odd curse. Before they had been openly curious. But the looks he saw now were anything but neutral. That seemed to have been replaced by something altogether more unfriendly. He caught the word 'Jonah' as he passed by a group of the waisters. And the looks that accompanied that word left him in no doubt that the remark was aimed at him.

'Pender,' he called, entering the wardroom. 'What's afoot?'

'In what respect, your honour?' Pender came out of his cabin. He had a rope in his hand, which he had been using to fashion a sling for Harry's sea-chest.

'That humorous remark you made yesterday about some of the hands thinking that there was a "Jonah" aboard. Was that pure invention?'

'It was.' Pender seemed defensive, as though his honesty was being challenged. Harry looked at the rope. He was too sharp not to be aware of the danger to the ship.

'Well, I fear we may have succeeded too well. Get on deck and find out what the hands are saying. I got some very queer looks just now.'

'Your dunnage is secure. I took the liberty of putting my bits and pieces in with yours.' He looked directly at Harry. Then he smiled suddenly, as though he knew what his master was thinking. 'Just looking after my own.'

'That reminds me,' said Harry, opening his oilskin and reaching into his coat. 'I wrote this earlier.' He passed Pender a sealed letter. 'It is instructions to my brother-in-law that you are to be afforded all the protection you need, and quite specifically entreats him to grant you that which you asked me for. I should find an oilskin package and put it about your person.'

'Are we really in that much danger, your honour?' Pender was not an experienced sailor. But he, for certain, would have asked someone who was.

'I won't lie to you,' Harry said. 'Our situation is one that sailors dread. We have a strong wind which we may not be able to sail into. That is blowing us towards a rocky shore. Mr Carter will attempt to put the ship about. If the foremast holds we can claw off.' Harry did not want to emphasize how difficult this would be, how the crew would be up all night shifting scraps of sail as the *Magnanime* sailed tack upon tack out of danger.

'And if it doesn't hold?'

'Let's hope it creaks a bit and stays where it is. But if it doesn't, then we must run in with the tide and wind, and try to anchor the ship. That depends on the ground. If we can do that we are safe.'

'Well, if it don't, I can't swim.' Pender seemed calm, despite this revelation, in contrast to some of the more experienced hands.

'If we do have to abandon ship the crew will panic. Stay away from them and the boats, because that will be bedlam. If you can, stay with me. Failing that, you want to cling to something that floats. A spar.' Harry smiled suddenly. 'Or an empty sea-chest. With luck that will carry you ashore. Now please be so good as to find out what the crew are about with their murmurings and black looks. Then fetch my brother on deck. Brook no argument. Just tell him that it is vital that he do so.'

Harry left the cabin and went back up to the quarter-deck. He fought his way out into the howling wind just as Craddock gave the orders to let fly the sheets. The deck and rigging were full of men. It took an intricate set of calculations to try this manoeuvre in a heaving sea. But it had to be done quickly before the shoal water started to increase the size and power of the waves. If they tried this any further in, they would be bound to broach to, and be smashed ashore sideways on. The sails flapped noisily as they were released from the strain of the ropes. The wheel spun and the *Magnanime* came up into the wind. Carter dare not wait for her to come round all the way. He signalled to Craddock. Men hauled on the sodden, protesting ropes, dragging the yards round to take the wind. Others fought to sheet home, lifting the bottom corners of the sails to increase their angle to the wind.

From being at a dead stop, the ship started to move slowly forward, breasting the waves. Not at any speed, but at least she wasn't being driven backwards. Tense faces relaxed as they realized that the manoeuvre had worked. They wouldn't make much progress, and they would have to work like Trojans just to keep this up, but just heading away from the shore, however slowly, was speed enough.

The crack of the foretopmast giving way drowned out all the other sounds. It was like a magnified pistol shot. There were still hands up there and Harry could plainly hear their screams of terror as the mast slowly parted and leant to one side. It seemed to stop there for a few seconds, a time which gave Craddock the space he needed to put the ship back on to its previous course. Again they were heading for the shore, with parties of sailors rushing to free the anchors. Then, with a final wrenching sound, the mast went overboard.

Carter ran forward calling for men and axes. Craddock, showing great presence of mind, issued the orders that would rig some sails on the remaining masts, putting the *Magnanime* back under some form of control. Harry knew he was useless on the quarter-deck. He raced after Carter. The mast was over the larboard side of the bowsprit, a mass of tangled rigging holding it to the ship and making all efforts to steer useless. It would have to be cut free or it would drag the ship sideways on to the swiftly running sea.

Harry grabbed a boarding axe from a stunned, stationary sailor, diving into the tangled skein of ropes, hacking at them as he did so. He could see sailors entangled in the rigging being ducked under the water, then hauled out again, flailing and gasping. If they could not free themselves they were dead men, but there was nothing he could do about that. It was imperative that the foremast be cut free. If they stayed entangled they would go to the bottom with it.

Carter was ahead of him. He had thrown off his oilskin and uniform coat. His sodden white shirt showed clearly, illuminated by the phosphorescence of the crashing water around the bows. He too was hacking away, cutting every rope before him, not knowing which ones were holding the fallen mast. He had made his way out on to the bowsprit. Harry followed him. Behind him men were hacking at the ropes they had missed. Out of the corner of his eye Harry could see that some of the topmen had got free and were crawling up the loose and dangerous rigging to get back aboard.

Suddenly Carter, standing to hack at a heavy cable, slipped and fell off the bowsprit. His foot caught in a rope and he was dangling upside down as the *Magnanime* dipped into the waves. He went under, with the ship, for what seemed like an age. The bows lifted and Carter came out of the water again. He still had his sword in his hand, but to slash at the rope round his foot was to invite certain death, since that was the only thing holding him to the ship.

Harry looked back at the hands still cutting away. There seemed to be very few lines still holding the foremast. They were nearly clear. He edged out as the bows went under again, clinging desperately as the freezing water came up around his chest. Up again, and Carter was there, still held by the foot. Harry lunged forward and grabbed the rope. His head was now lying on the furled-up canvas of one of the bowsprit sails. He clamped his mouth shut as the *Magnanime* dipped again and he was plunged into the foaming sea. As he felt the ship begin to lift itself out of the water he hauled with all his strength on the line.

By the time the *Magnanime* was at the height of its travel he had Carter's foot in his hand. Then it started to dip again and Harry just held on, as best he could, while they both received another icy ducking. This time, as the ship breasted itself out of the water, he reached down and grabbed the front of Carter's

187

shirt, hauling furiously to bring him upright. He felt the man searching for some part of him to hold on to. Eventually their hands met and Harry had him. Under they went again, but as they resurfaced Carter was ready to throw his leg over the bowsprit and haul himself up. Harry swung his axe and cut the line that held the man's foot.

There was a loud snapping sound as a line further up parted. A cable whistled past Harry's head like a bullet. The mast went slowly over the side and spun clear. That danger was past. But the crashing of the waves was loud now and the water before the bows was disturbed by more than the *Magnanime*'s progress. Harry inched backwards off the bowsprit followed by Carter. As soon as he reached the deck, Carter staggered back towards the quarter-deck. Harry was bent double, trying to retch the water he had swallowed at the same time as he gasped for breath. He staggered as the *Magnanime* spun in its own length, vaguely aware that all the sails were flapping wildly. She was now stern-on to the shore, the roar of the sea outdoing the noise of the howling wind. Men fell over as the movement of the ship was checked. The anchor was over the side and, at this moment, it was holding. He could hear the shouted commands at the capstan, exhorting the hands to haul away and, by shortening the cable, pull the ship back from danger.

Short of air as he was, Harry stopped breathing now. This was the last throw. If the anchor would not hold, or the cable snapped, they were done for. The motion of the ship steadied as the strain was taken on the huge hawser. He sensed the ship moving. The cable, a twenty-three-inch diameter rope, was holding, as was the anchor. No one would want to spend the night here held by a single anchor. But if it held long enough they could pay out another cable somehow, and put down another anchor. With two they stood a real chance.

The wind was freezing for a man soaked to the skin. Harry, holding the man-ropes for support, clawed his way towards the quarter-deck.

'Mr Ludlow, quick!' It was Pender, shouting above the howling gale. Harry, exhausted after his efforts, was slow to respond.

'You must come now, sir,' said Pender. Harry felt a sword pressed into his hand. 'Some of the hands are talking about slinging your brother overboard.'

'What?'

'Someone has fired them up with tales of a Jonah aboard.'

Harry was being pulled bodily towards the gangway, his mind still trying to grapple with what Pender was trying to tell him.

'Jonah?'

'Stupid bastards. Believe any old tale.'

Pender had got Harry down the first few steps. Being out of the screaming wind seemed to help clear his brain. They ran across the gun-deck and down the companionway, with Pender explaining breathlessly.

'Some of the men shirked their duty, thinkin' that the ship was done for.'

'The spirit room?'

'Drunk as lords they are. And claimin' that it's all James Ludlow's doin'.'

'Carter put a guard on there.'

'Well, God knows where he is, for the door's wide open. There's a party of the worst cases heading for the cable tier.'

They shot down the stairwell on to the orlop-deck. The sound of voices, raised in anger, came up towards them. As Pender reached the bottom he stopped. Harry fell on his back trying to do likewise, nearly knocking his servant over.

Half-way along the passage was a group of sailors. Two of them were holding James by the arms, pushing him along. He had the blood of fresh wounds on his face where he had tried to fight them off. They stopped as they saw Harry and Pender. Harry rushed past Pender who was still on his knees, yelling as if possessed, and waving his sword as much as he could in such a confined space. He knew that if he gave these men time to think, there would be a knife under his brother's throat, and no chance of rescue. Pender, hauling himself up, followed on.

The sailors on either side of James, surprised at the sudden assault, halted and fell back slightly. James immediately tried to get away from his captors. His efforts distracted them long enough for Harry to get close. The temptation was to run one of them through, but angry as he was, Harry had the sense to see the dangers in such a course. Instead he aimed to wound, choosing the man that was holding his brother's left arm. His sword took him in the shoulder, and the man swung round screaming in pain. Harry followed through by just barging the other sailor aside. Trying to ward Harry off, he had released James, who grabbed at his elder brother, arresting his forward movement before he fell into the mass of the mutinous party.

The rest of the sailors started to crowd forward, after the few seconds they needed to recover their senses. Hemmed in by the lack of space, they could not all come at the Ludlows at once, but there were still too many of them to fight. Harry, pushing James behind him, held out his sword and backed towards the stairwell. The sailors came on, emboldened by the retreat, growling and cursing, ignoring their wounded companion, and stepping on, rather than over, his prostrate form.

'James, up the stairs, while Pender and I hold them off. See if you can find an officer.'

'And leave you to the mercy of this lot?'

The sound of the gun going off beside his ear nearly deafened Harry. He ducked away from the sound, and Pender pushed past him, the other pistol held out.

'Now which one of you buggers wants a bullet in the guts, instead of over your head?'

The noise had halted the forward progress of the sailors. They stood looking at Pender, trying to decide what to do.

'The ship's at single anchor and safe. If you lot don't want a rope at the yard-arm for mutiny, you'd better get to where you are supposed to be, and damned quick.'

'He can only shoot one of us,' said the sailor at the front.

'You're right, Smithy. You take the bullet and I promise that you won't go unavenged.'

Drunken crowds are strange, being able to turn from humour to a fatal form of anger in a flash. But they can go the other way just as quickly. One of their number laughed at the absurdity of the remark made by the man urging Smithy to sacrifice himself. Another joined in. Suddenly they were all laughing, repeating the line, some of them jokingly pushing Smithy forward.

'Take my advice, lads,' said Pender. 'The officers ain't going to be busy much longer.'

The ugly mood had gone out of them, as they each began to consider their position. Harry touched James and Pender, and they moved away up the stairwell, leaving the crowd to figure out how they could get back to their proper stations without being observed.

Harry led James towards the wardroom.The acrid smell of gunpowder still permeated everything. The wardroom itself was in total disarray, as the hands who had been erecting the bulkheads, and replacing the furnishings, had been called away to attend to the more pressing duty of saving the ship. Harry righted a set of chairs.

'Water, Pender,' he said, pushing James down into a chair.

'What has been happening?' asked James. 'First I am dragged from tending the wounded, and slung back in the cable tier, by one set of men. Then I am hauled out by another lot, this time as drunk as lords.'

'They were going to sling you overboard,' said Harry grimly. He had grabbed the first piece of cloth he could find and was dabbing the blood off James' face. 'I noticed some right odd looks before the mast went by the board.'

'The mast?'

'We have had an interesting time of it today, first a battle, then a full gale, the foremast threatening to broach us, and a near run thing with a lee shore. O for the life of a sailor!'

Pender came in with a jug of water. 'Cold, I'm afraid, your honour.'

'I would appreciate it if you would tell me what has been happening,' said James. Harry looked at Pender.

'They've secured another anchor, Mr Ludlow. We should, according to them in the know, be safe enough now.'

'You saved his life?' The tone in James' question left little doubt that he felt such an action bordered on madness.

'I wouldn't go that far,' said Harry. 'He would probably have got himself out of difficulties without my help.'

'Unless you are exaggerating, brother, I cannot see how.'

'All I did was help him. One sailor to another, James. It all happened very quickly.'

'And if you can persuade him to meet you on a cold morning you will just as quickly put a bullet in him.'

'That's different.'

'I suppose it is. Perhaps that's why you did it.'

'We shall have to rough it tonight,' said Harry, looking about the wardroom. 'We'll take turns asleep, an hour each.'

'Is that necessary?' asked James.

Harry did not want to explain. 'Let's just say that I would hate to wake up in hell and find out that it was something I should not have omitted to do.'

'Then I shall go first,' said James, 'since I was asleep when that mob came to get me.'

'Right,' said Harry gratefully. He lay down on the deck, put a bundle of cloths behind his head, and was asleep in seconds.

'You too, Pender,' said James, noticing the man's hesitation. It was not for the likes of him to bed down here. 'Just give me the pistol.' Pender handed him the loaded gun. 'Do we have the wherewithal to load the other one?'

Pender reached inside his jacket and produced a pouch containing powder, wads, and shot.

'Fine. Now do as you are told, man, and get some sleep.'

Pender lay down beside Harry. He stared at the ceiling for a while, but he too was exhausted by the day's events and he was soon fast asleep.

Harry awoke to the strong sunlight streaming through the stern windows. Sailors were busy removing the heavy wooden deadlights that they had rigged before the battle. Others were starting to put the rest of the wardroom to rights, their efforts hampered by the bodies that lay everywhere, as the officers tried, in any way possible, to get some sleep.

'James. You didn't wake me?' he croaked. The taste of salt was still strong in his mouth.

'No need. I was content just to sit here and observe the comings and goings of human beings for a while. They are not dissimilar to the to-ings and fro-ings of rats.'

'Did anyone ask what you were doing?'

'Most were too exhausted to care. Those who might have asked must have been deterred by these.' He indicated the pistols on the deck. 'There is something to be said for a homicidal reputation in that respect.'

'Breakfast, your honour,' said Pender, rubbing the sleep from his eyes. He had been awakened by a discreet, possibly jealous, kick from one of the carpenter's mates.

'I could eat a horse,' said Harry.

'One horse, Pender. Lightly broiled.' All James' insouciance seemed to have returned. 'I will settle for a large cup of coffee.'

'I'll go and see if the stove is lit.'

'I wonder if we should put those out of sight now?'

James handed Harry the pistols. 'They'll need to be wormed. They're both loaded.'

'It would be quicker to fire them off.'

'No shortage of targets.' James looked above his head to Carter's cabin.

'As soon as my berth is up, we'd best get you in there. I would say we could all use a change of clothes.'

James' coat and breeches were a dark brown colour from the bloody work he had been doing in the sickbay, but somehow Harry seemed a more shocking sight, his white shirt streaked with grease, his face filthy, and his hair matted on his head.

'No doubt I shall soon be back observing my colony of rats.'

'Not if I can help it. There was supposed to be a guard on that spirit store last night. I want to know why there wasn't. And I want to know who was getting the hands all excited about your being a Jonah.'

'You don't think they came by this suspicion naturally, given the number of dead bodies around?'

'Think, James. It's you again. Not me!'

'Perhaps they think that you are a more difficult proposition.'

'Let's find out who "they" are. In here.' The bulkheads were all in place now, the slumbering incumbents being roused so that the room could be made shipshape. 'You must need some sleep now,' said Harry. 'You'll have to use the floor if you do. It will be a while before they fetch up my cot and sea-chest. I'll have yours brought here as well. Then you can change.'

'Extremely comfortable, especially compared to the other accommodation I have had aboard this ship.'

Harry went out leaving James to fend for himself. Pender came into the wardroom bearing two cups of coffee.

'Mr James is going to get some sleep, Pender. If you can find anything to make him more comfortable, I would be obliged.' Harry took the coffee and sipped gratefully. 'I shall go on deck and see what's going on.'

Grabbing an oilskin, Harry went up on deck. The wind was still blowing hard, straining the cables holding the *Magnanime*, but nothing like the night before. The sun, occasionally obscured by scudding clouds, was shining brightly. All around, great cliffs surrounded the rocky bay. At the very head of the bay the waves, having spent their force, were running up a white sandy beach. A few fishermen's cottages sat at the base of the deep tree-lined valley cut out of the surrounding hills, yet there was no other sign of human life. There was an angry reef off the starboard side, the seas still pounding against it. The ship sat in the middle of the bay, lifting and falling as the waves swept by to crash noisily on the nearby rocks. Harry knew that they had been very lucky, for they had entered this bay with little ability to steer. That they had managed to avoid any rocks, that they had managed to find good holding ground for the anchors, was near miraculous.

Craddock was on deck. From his face, caked with salt, and his eyes, red from the wind, it was plain that he had been there all night. Yet when Harry looked around he could see little evidence of the damage the storm must have done. The battle damage was still plain, and the missing foremast was obvious. But the decks had been tidied and any loose rigging had been either cut away or re-rove.

'Mr Ludlow,' croaked Craddock. 'I am heartily glad to see you well.'

'And you, Mr Craddock.' Harry handed him the remains of his coffee. Craddock drank gratefully. 'A busy night, I see.'

'The Captain has just retired.'

'I should suggest that you follow his example.'

'Soon, Mr Ludlow. Soon. I would say that we are safe enough here.'

'No point in trying to rig a jury foretopmast while the wind is so strong.'

'Ay.' Craddock looked about him. 'Mr Denbigh.'

The midshipman, curled up against the bulwarks, was sound asleep. Harry walked over and shook him awake. He crawled out from under his oilskin, and got unsteadily to his feet. Craddock had looked the other way, not wishing to have to reprimand the boy.

'Sir,' said Denbigh, still half-asleep.

'Please be so good as to rouse Mr Collins to take over the watch.'

'Mr Craddock. If I may make a suggestion?'

Craddock looked at him with a frown. Tired, he saw any delay in his reaching his cot as an unwarranted intrusion. Yet his manners covered his exhaustion and his anger.

'While you and your officers have secured the ship, I have, for my shame, been sound asleep. Since I hazard that you intend to undertake no arduous tasks until the weather moderates, might I suggest that I take the watch, and give both you, and your officers, some opportunity to rest.'

'Most gallant, Mr Ludlow. Most gallant, sir. I am sure that all the officers will be grateful.' Then the frown returned.

'I shall rouse you at the first sign of any danger. And I am well qualified, Mr Craddock. I have had the watch on bigger ships than this.'

'Carry on, sir. Only essentials, Mr Ludlow. The hands are in as bad a way as the officers.'

XIII

The weather was clearing, the wind dropping noticeably. But the sea was still rough from the previous night, great waves turning to angry spume on the reef to starboard. Pender appeared bearing a plate of hot food. Harry reflected on the nature of someone who had only been his servant for a few days, yet who took such care of his comfort and safety. It was almost as though the younger man had adopted him.

'Like the morning after the night before downstairs, Mr Ludlow.'

'Has anyone mentioned Mr James?'

'No. They're more concerned with sleep than anything else. Seems we have the ship to ourselves.' Pender smiled at the possibilities that presented.

'It would be interesting to be able to use that time. However, I can't. I have told Mr Craddock I will stand watch, and I must fulfil that promise.'

'Strikes me that if anyone deserves a promise honoured, it'll be Mr Craddock.'

'Odd, that spirit room being unguarded,' said Harry.

'Just as odd the drunken sods sorting your brother out as a Jonah. It don't make sense. I know they get rattled about the boy that went overboard, 'cause some of the hands had sort of adopted him as a kind of mascot. He was a cheeky little bugger by all accounts. But how they can put that down to someone who wasn't even aboard at the time, I can't see.'

'Sailors are a superstitious lot, Pender. You haven't spent enough time at sea to know just how stupid they can be.'

'I might not have seen much evidence of superstition, your honour. But I've seen enough stupidity to last me a lifetime. And as for them sorting out your brother, it just seems to me that it happened mighty quick. From what I've heard, that sort of thing takes months to get goin'.'

'True. And it usually takes more than one storm to make everybody feel that way. Mind, we have had the odd unexplained body laying about.'

'There's not a jot of sympathy for either of them. That I can vouch for. No one has been flogged since Mr Bentley got his.' Pender dropped his voice to a whisper. 'And as for Howarth, he was such an arse-licker that no one was sad to see the back of him.'

'Odd then, as you say. It all seems to come back to that boy. Outhwaite said as much, though he hates to let on that superstition exists, let alone good grounds for it. Things changed after his death, especially the amount of punishment. Carter and Bentley, hitherto friendly . . .' Harry looked around the rigging as though doing so would enlighten him. He heard the words that the sailor had spat at Bentley. 'Murderous' the man had called him, mentioning Larkin. But if the boy had fallen overboard? And Prentice had been alarmed by his name. He might have said something if Denbigh hadn't interrupted him. But Prentice wasn't aboard at the time. The person to talk to was Denbigh himself.

Bentley was killed for a reason. That reason is aboard this ship. If it is, then others must know about it, or at least, know something that will point in the right direction. Harry's thoughts turned to the secret life of the ship. People who breached the rules knew what was going on. They had to if they wanted to survive. Those too, he must speak to. The only alternative was to question the whole crew, and that would not be allowed, even if it were possible. 'Did you find out anything about the barge crew?'

'Mess by the pump shaft, lazy buggers.' Crewing the captain's barge was considered to be a privileged position. Not only did they do less work, but they were allowed to run ashore every time the captain did so.

'Who's Carter's coxswain?'

'Marchant. Swarthy bugger. You might have noticed him. Tall. Wears gaudy clothes. Always sewing coloured threads into his jacket.'

'Doesn't sound the type for Carter. If ever there was a man who liked things plain . . . I wonder what they get up to when they go down the pump shaft?'

'Any number of things, your honour.'

'Surely the crew talk about it?'

'Best not to, I was told. First thing I found out when I came on board was that the barge crew was best avoided. Law unto themselves, I was informed. They keep themselves separate, and they make it plain that they will warrant no enquiries into their doings.'

'But does it not make you curious?'

Pender's face took a pious look. 'I learned when I was a lad that curiosity is a mortal sin, best avoided. So I don't enquire if'n a thing don't concern me.'

'Remarkable, Pender. It almost flies in the face of human nature.' Harry was trying hard to keep the smile from showing on his face.

'Well, it don't interfere with staying alive,' Pender nearly snapped at him. 'And I'd best be getting your belongings sorted out.'

'Pender. I can well understand your reluctance to rat on your mates. It must be hard for you to understand that I don't represent authority, at least not on this ship. I only represent myself, and of course, James. My only reason for enquiring about anything bears directly on that matter. And please understand, I know ships and sailors better than you. The rules are broken all the time in the Navy, but nobody minds so long as they are not flouted. And if there is something going on, it may be kept a secret from the officers, but it is in no way a secret from everybody. Is it?'

Pender's face closed up, so unusual in a man with such an

open countenance. 'I told you, Mr Ludlow. I don't enquire.'

'And I am telling you that I don't believe you. You may have a way of finding things out that avoids the direct question. But you are the type who needs to know what is happening. You wouldn't feel safe otherwise.'

Pender said nothing, just looking at the deck.

'I owe you a great deal already, and I will not use pressure to get you to talk. But if you don't tell me, then I must find out for myself.'

Pender looked up slowly, his tongue running over his teeth. Harry admired the way the man could look him straight in the eye, without a trace of fear.

'It probably has no bearing on who killed Bentley. But I must enquire in case it does. There could be endless reasons for his death. They could be something that has its origins ashore. I don't know. All I know, is that the killer is on board ship, and I must look at every possibility, and eliminate them if I can as the motive. Only by doing that can I narrow things down to the point where I will be able to come at the truth. And I would remind you that I don't have any time for subtlety.'

'What you're saying, Mr Ludlow, is that if I let on to you what I know, then I will be, more'n likely, protecting my shipmates, rather than dropping 'em in it.'

'That is what I am saying.'

'Well, if'n you'll forgive me, I don't feel much like sayin' anythin' here.' Pender looked about at the exposed quarterdeck. There was only an anchor watch set, a few men to keep an eye on the cables holding the *Magnanime* in position. But it was still a place where you could be overheard.

Harry soaked himself, and the cabin, luxuriating in hot water. Pender sat on top of the desk. With the canvas bath in the cabin there was little room for anything else. He had enjoyed an hour with James before someone had realized that he was missing. Turnbull, having bedded down in his uncle's cabin, was not aware that James had spent the night in the wardroom.

The ship was searched, and no sign was found. There were a

number of hands missing after the storm. It could only be con-cluded that James Ludlow had joined them. It was a doleful Turnbull who had come to inform Harry that his charge was missing. The unhappy look soon turned to an angry one as Harry stood aside to reveal his brother standing behind him. The ship rang with Turnbull's angry shouts, as he ordered the marines to come and take him back under restraint again.

In the hour they'd had together, it had been possible, for the first time, to properly examine the case for and against James. Harry still held back, not entirely willing to trust James with the conclusions he had drawn. Asked to say why, he could not have answered. But whatever was left unsaid, it did not look good, and it was only their natural optimism, plus their mutual refusal to depress each other, that kept them from being downhearted.

The ship had come alive again. A few hours' sleep had restored everyone to a semblance of health, and the whole ship resounded with hammering and crashing as things were put right. Craddock had the deck holystoned and swabbed to remove the bloodstains, evidence of the cost of the recent fight.

Most important, they were beginning to rig a jury foretop-mast, and preparations were well in hand to get under way. The wind was still foul, though moderate. If it died away any more, they would have the boats out, and use the falling tide to tow her out of the bay.

Harry, having considered, and rejected, the idea of trying to get James ashore here, was as keen as anyone to get the ship to sea. Only when the *Magnanime* had returned to a normal routine would he be able to get on with his investigation. He dare not distract Craddock to ask if he had found out who had raised the alarm on the night of Bentley's murder, because the man was far too busy. Nor could he investigate the various things that Pender had told him because both watches were working flat out to repair the ship. Everyone was busy except him, so busy that he had got first use of the canvas bath, an item which had apparently been the property of Bentley.

Pender had laid out some fresh clothes on the cot, and was making a pig's ear of trying to repair the shirt that Harry had taken off. If anything revealed that Pender was not a sailor, it was this. The needle he was using spent more time embedded in his skin than it did in the cloth of the shirt. Sharp intakes of breath accompanied the sewing, and the unspoken curses constantly formed on his lips.

'For God's sake leave it alone, man,' said Harry eventually. 'I will do it myself.'

Pender looked quite shocked at such a suggestion. After all, he was supposed to be the servant.

'All right,' said Harry, recognizing the injured look. 'But give it to someone who can do it. I don't want you expiring from loss of blood.'

Pender's face showed all the resentment of a man who was convinced that he could do anything well, given proper instructions and a chance to practise. Harry stood up, ignoring the water that cascaded over the side. Pender threw him a towel. There was a little more force in the throw than was truly necessary.

'The spirit room?' he asked.

'According to the "bullock" I talked to, no one got any orders to guard the spirit room,' said Pender.

'Is this man reliable?'

'Can't be sure. The only way to be sure is to question the lot of them.'

'It's enough to sustain a complaint.'

'Poor Mr Craddock. He gets it all.' The slightly anxious look Pender flushed at Harry was a silent plea to seek another course. When it was discovered that the spirit room had been left unguarded, despite Carter's express instructions, Craddock would carry the blame. It was part of the unenviable task of being first lieutenant, in that you took responsibility for everything. Put plainly, you took all the blame for the inability of others, while the captain took any credit for your efficiency.

'Can't be helped, Pender. Those men would have slung James overboard. Can you find out who got them into such a state?'

'Even if they'll talk to me, they wouldn't let on, me being a new boy. And then they would be wanting to know why I was asking. What do I tell them?'

'A bribe?' asked Harry.

'Might work. But a threat would be better.' Pender had a gleam in his eye, and his smile had returned. He looked like a man who had just had a good idea.

'Go on.'

'Well. If'n I start asking questions, they are goin' to see me as some kind of spy. But if I was to say that I'm havin' the devil's own job in stoppin' you havin' them all lined up on deck so's you can identify the suspects, that might open them up a little, especially that Smithy character. 'Cause if you was to go ahead and do that, then they might be for the high jump. The best they could hope for is a floggin' round the fleet.'

'And they might tell you to avoid blame?'

'That's it. If they are afraid, they will blame anyone to save their own skin. So we might be able to come at the name of whoever started it.'

'Should I make a complaint?'

'No. But you should behave as if you can't wait to do so.'

'It might be an idea to demand an interview with the Captain.'

A knock at the door. Pender opened it, and Crevitt took a step in.

'Mr Ludlow.' The parson looked at Pender.

'Carry on, Pender,' said Harry.

Pender grabbed the end of the canvas bath, and bade Crevitt, still in the doorway, to stand aside. You could not say it was deliberate, but the way Pender jerked the bath as he passed the preacher, causing the water to shift out all over the bottom of his breeches, soaking his stockings and his shoes, gave an air of insincerity to his apologetic protest.

'Shall I fetch a towel, sir?' asked Pender, his face concerned.

'No need,' said Crevitt, showing Christian forbearance. 'It is not a novelty to be wet at sea.'

'God knows that's right, sir,' said Pender, in such a way that no one could be sure that the 'God knows' was an affirmation of faith, or a curse. Harry had to turn his back to avoid Crevitt seeing his face. Pender pulled the bath out from the doorway, and Crevitt, with a squelching sound that added to Harry's suppressed mirth, came into the cabin. Fighting to control his face muscles, Harry turned to hear what the parson had to say.

'I come from the Captain, Mr Ludlow.' He clasped his hands before him.

Harry merely raised an eyebrow. 'And?'

'He wishes me to convey to you, that he is grateful for your efforts over the last twenty-four hours, on behalf of this ship and your country.' Crevitt was nodding slightly as he spoke, as if he was trying to convince himself of the correctness of his words. 'He is of course far too preoccupied to convey these thoughts to you himself.'

'Please inform the Captain that no thanks are required,' said Harry coldly. The absence of a personal thank you was very telling. Crevitt frowned.

'He also asked me to ensure that you had every comfort, and to see if there is anything that you require that is in his power to grant.'

'That seems like a superfluous statement. Mr Craddock has made me very comfortable, and what I require has already been laid before him.'

The frown deepened. 'He did stress that it must be in his power to grant it.'

'Fine. I would wish for my brother to be housed in more comfortable quarters.'

'Thank you, Mr Ludlow. I will convey that wish to the Captain.' Harry realized that Crevitt was a little embarrassed, realizing that Carter should have offered more, and that Harry could certainly have asked for more.

'Please convey to the Captain that I have no wish to risk being snubbed again.'

The clasped hands came up, his index fingers together on his bent chin. 'I think I would rather say that you have been commendably modest in your requests.'

'I presume, Mr Crevitt, that you have accurately delivered the message that Captain Carter gave you. I would be obliged if you could carry out precisely the same service for me.'

'As you wish, Mr Ludlow,' he said sadly. 'I had hoped for a more charitable response.'

'What?' snapped Harry, his eyes flashing angrily.

'Not from you, Mr Ludlow. Not from you.' Crevitt put one

hand to his head, and the other out to steady himself. Harry had last seen him hard at work, in the cockpit, tending the wounded. That task would not have ended with the ship safely anchored. 'Now if you will forgive me, I have to prepare for the burials.'

'How many?' asked Harry quietly.

'There will be forty-four when we get under way. There are at least ten more whom Mr Outhwaite assures me will be over the side before the day is out. Others are in a bad way. They are in God's hands. A terrible bill, Mr Ludlow.'

And an unnecessary one, thought Harry, recalling the options that had been open to Carter. 'I am just about to go on deck,' he said, opening the door. Crevitt, whose mind had wandered, jerked himself back to reality.

'Of course. Forgive me. I was thinking of those poor men. Boys, some of them. It is a harsh service in wartime, the Navy. But God is on our side, I am sure.'

Perhaps it was because he was tired, but he sounded anything but sure.

Harry made his way on to the quarter-deck. Carter was there, for once dressed in a short jacket instead of his uniform coat. He turned away as Harry came on deck, not wishing to catch the eye of the man who had undoubtedly saved his life. Harry strode past him, ignoring him completely. Craddock was standing on the gangway, supervising the installation of a stay to support the jury foretopmast.

'Mr Craddock,' said Harry formally.

'Mr Ludlow.' Craddock was smiling. He had quite missed Harry's tone.

'I wish to formally request an interview with Captain Carter.' The smile disappeared. 'I wish to lodge a complaint.'

'Is it a repeat of one that you have lodged already, Mr Ludlow?'

'No, sir, it is not. But it is a serious one. Enough to warrant the Captain's full attention. And I presume that you too will have an interest in what amounts to mutinous behaviour.'

The only sounds were the ship's sounds. Apart from that, you could have heard a pin drop.

*

Harry paced the empty gun-deck for well over an hour. He was back in the wardroom when the command was issued for the ship's company to assemble by divisions. The officers hurried into their cabins to don uniform coats, before running out and yelling the orders that would assemble their men. Harry thought it a curious thing to do under the circumstances, and at the time of day. Surely they would leave the burials till they were out at sea? He was even more surprised when Prentice came into the wardroom to request his presence on the quarter-deck.

Harry put on his coat and followed him. All the officers were assembled at the head of their divisions. Craddock stood beside Carter in silence. Carter whispered something to him before turning away. He came over to Harry, his face worried. He did not look at Harry as he spoke.

'Mr Ludlow. The Captain has been apprised of some of the events of last night, things that should have been reported earlier than this.'

'Never mind the preamble, Mr Craddock,' snapped Carter without looking in their direction. 'Proceed with the business at hand.'

'Some of the hands broke into the spirit room last night.'

Harry kept his gaze steady.

'They overcame the guard that was posted there to stop that very thing. They then proceeded to free your brother from the cable tier. It has been represented to the Captain that they may have done so hoping that he would lead them in their aim of taking over the ship.'

It was so absurd that Harry actually laughed. Craddock finally looked at him, his face anxious. 'Mutiny is no laughing matter, Mr Ludlow.'

'There was no mutiny, Mr Craddock. Just as there was no guard on the spirit room. The sailors you mention had been told that all their troubles stemmed from the presence on board of a murderer. They were encouraged to believe that my brother was a Jonah and that the way to ensure their survival was to chuck him overboard. They were in the act of doing this when I stopped them.'

'You would agree, Mr Ludlow, that to break into the spirit

room, given the dire straits that the ship was in, is a very serious offence?' asked Carter, turning to face him.

'Since I am not a naval officer, I do not feel competent to judge.'

'No one is asking you to judge, Mr Ludlow. Merely to witness. How many hands would you say were involved in this affray?'

'About a dozen,' said Harry, deliberately dropping the actual number.

'Then be so kind as to look over the crew and identify them.'

How had this come about? It was only a couple of hours since he and Pender had talked about this. Yet here he was on deck with the entire ship's company. And where was Pender?'

'I would be delighted to do so,' said Harry enthusiastically. He felt, rather than saw, the entire crew stiffen. 'But in the light, I'm not sure that I could, with certainty, identify anyone. It was very dim.'

'Look, Mr Ludlow, if you please!' said Carter.

'I'll do my best.' Harry stepped forward. The men were lined up on the gangways and in the forecastle in untidy ranks. The marines, in their bright red coats, were lined up with their muskets on the poop, rigid and smart, in stark contrast to the sailors.

He walked slowly down the starboard gangway, carefully looking at each face. They all stared back at him without blinking. He passed Smithy on the forecastle, and he thought he recognized another one of the men who had been with him in the same mess. Come to think of it, the drunks had all probably been from the one section.

He continued down the larboard gangway, occasionally stopping and pretending to look closely at some seaman, before coming back to the quarter-deck.

'I fear I was correct in my earlier observation, Mr Craddock. I cannot be sure. The light was poor.'

Craddock turned to report to Carter.

'What a confusing situation we have, Mr Ludlow.' He had his back to Harry again. 'I am told that some hands released your brother for the purpose of taking over the ship. You tell me an entirely different tale, yet you are unable to identify the culprits. Which am I to believe?'

'I could see no purpose in freeing my brother to take over the ship. My brother is an artist, not a sailor.'

'Quite,' said Carter. 'That thought had occurred to me.' The Captain turned and looked at him. Seeing the smile on his face, Harry realized that he had just walked into a trap. 'And you cannot identify the people you claim to have fought last night. Do you see how it looks, Mr Ludlow? For, as you say, your brother is no sailor. But you are.'

'This is preposterous,' said Harry.

'I agree,' said Carter, the cold smile still there. 'So we cannot have people wandering around the ship, stirring up the hands, and frightening people with tales of how you intend to exact revenge. Bring forward the prisoner.'

Two bos'n's mates came up the stairwell. They had Pender between them, holding his arms pinned to his side. His face showed the signs of a fierce struggle.

'Mr Turnbull?' snapped Carter.

'Sir. It has been brought to my notice that this man was heard indulging in behaviour prejudicial to good order and discipline.'

'You hear that, Mr Ludlow?'

'I hear it.'

'Do you have anything to say?' It was not clear if this remark was addressed to Pender or Harry. Neither spoke.

'Nothing. Do you wish to plead for him, Mr Ludlow?'

'I most certainly do,' said Harry. He had to stick to the proper form. 'This man is most attentive to his duty, and if he has done any wrong, it will have been at my behest. It follows that all blame is attached to me personally. He is therefore someone I would most heartily plead to be excused punishment.'

Carter walked over to Harry. He stood so close, and spoke so low, that no one else could hear.

'I asked you to mind yourself. To stay in your cabin and leave things alone. But you would not abide my request. You carry on with your games. I will not have my ship used so. And I know you. The thought of someone else suffering in your place will cause you more grief than if I were to flog you myself.'

'Let him off, Carter. If for no other reason than I saved your life last night.' The man didn't even blink.

'I have spent the whole morning asking myself what I would

207

have done if the positions had been reversed.' Carter turned and walked back to the centre of the deck. 'Bos'n, rig the grating. Ten of the cat. All hands aft to witness punishment.'

The grating was lifted forward and lashed to the quarter-deck rail. The two men holding Pender dragged him forward and tied him, arms stretched upwards, to the metal grille. The bos'n stepped forward. He had a red baize bag in his hand. The hands, called upon to witness, shuffled aft, spilling on to the quarter-deck. The shirt was ripped off Pender's back, exposing the bare flesh, and a piece of leather was pushed into his mouth.

The cat was out of the bag. The bos'n swung the vicious whip several times, as if warming up his stroke. The nine tails swished noisily. Harry had watched this so many times, but still he never got used to it. The bos'n stood square on to Pender's back, ready to proceed.

'Carry on, bos'n,' said Carter.

The whip cracked across Pender's back. Angry red weals appeared. The bos'n's arm came back and he struck again. The skin split where the whip struck the same spot as before. Pender's eyes were shut tight, his teeth clenched to the leather strap. Again the whip struck. His knees started to give way, but he hauled himself upright. The bos'n grinned as he lashed Pender again. The cry of pain was muffled by the leather, but it was there. His back was now covered in long red streaks. Another stroke and Pender's knees gave way, leaving him hanging on the ropes holding his arms. The next stroke saw his head drop in despair, and the cry from his throat was clearly audible. Again the whip struck, the bos'n sweating now. Seven. Had Pender passed out? There was no sound.

The last three strokes were delivered in silence. The bos'n stood back, his chest heaving, as he coiled the whip and put it back in the red bag, so coloured to stop the blood showing. Pender's back was a mess. A sailor stepped forward with a bucket of sea water and threw it over the victim's back. Then he was cut down. Outhwaite, who had been standing in the background, stepped forward to examine Pender. He felt his heart-beat, nodded to Carter, and ordered the prostrate servant carried below.

Crevitt, who had been standing with his eyes shut, silently praying, opened them again. Harry caught his eye, but Crevitt looked away.

'Mr Ludlow,' said Carter. 'I hope you will admonish your man, and tell him to be more careful next time.' He started towards his cabin, then pretended to have an afterthought. 'Oh, by the way. I am releasing your brother into Mr Crevitt's care. At his request. Dismiss the hands, Mr Craddock.'

Harry went below to the sick bay. He found Pender lying awake on his front. His back was covered in a salve that had been applied by Outhwaite. Harry knelt down beside the cot.

'I'm sorry.'

'Weren't your fault, Mr Ludlow.' Pender raised himself painfully on to his elbows. 'It was my fault. Turns out it was one of the marines that had been getting them worked up about your brother. Trouble was the bastard must have heard me talking to Smithy and his mates. Sore heads the lot of them, and sorry for the trouble, if you please. I was coming to see you when they grabbed me. Couldn't fight them off.' Pender gently let himself down again. 'Nothing you said would have stopped them flogging me.'

'Mr Outhwaite.'

'Sir.'

'How long will his back take to heal?'

'He'll be up and about, but stiff, mind, by tomorrow. He won't be fit for much for mor'n a week.'

'I want you in my cabin, Pender. Can you arrange that, Mr Outhwaite?'

'Are you saying to stay aft?'

'I am.'

'Don't see as there are many of the officers will appreciate that.'

'I shall probably kill the first one that says anything.' Quiet spoken he might be, but there was no doubting Harry's intensity.

'Harry! What happened?' James was standing in the doorway,

Crevitt behind him. Harry looked at the parson. Crevitt walked a little way off. Harry pulled James into the sick bay.

'Another warning to me, James. They flogged Pender to warn me to stop asking questions.'

James looked at Pender's raw back. He blenched slightly and turned away.

'Every turn we take, James, someone is there to cross us, or stand in our way. We are not dealing with one man aboard this ship. We seem to be up against half the crew.'

'Not half,' said Pender, face down.

'A turn of phrase. But since we don't know how many there are . . .'

'You mean more than one person killed Bentley?'

'No. I think it was one person. But it is a person who has others to do his bidding.' Harry looked away, not wishing James to see his face.

'Then do as Carter asks, Harry. Stop asking questions.'

'I can't.' He wanted to tell James that if he could find the motive, he would have proof. But that would lead to an explanation he wanted to avoid.

'You'll end up with a knife in your back.'

'And you'll hang.'

'Brother, if it comes to the point where they knife you, I won't survive you for very long.'

'I can't stop now.' Still he would not look at James.

'You think it's Carter, don't you?'

Pender turned sharply, and gasped with pain. Outhwaite's jaw dropped. Harry just stood still, finally looking at his brother.

'Don't you?'

'Yes. I do.'

'So, are you pursuing this to save me, or to get him?' Harry was silent again. 'I'm willing to take my chances in a court.'

'No.' Soft but very definite. 'Mr Outhwaite. Please arrange to have Pender taken to my cabin. There is room for another cot.'

'What are you plotting, Harry?'

'Your release, James. And the conviction of a murderer. When did you guess?'

'This morning. I had a feeling that you weren't telling me everything.'

Harry smiled. 'Then perhaps that is the first thing I should do. But I don't know everything, so I can't. I intend to know by tonight.'

'Or be dead?'

'Dead. Rest assured, James, that if it comes to that, it won't be me who is dead.'

'I cannot dissuade you?'

'No. And as for you taking your chances with a court, James: why, the way things have developed here, I would not give you odds. Someone is determined that you should hang, for no other reason than to clear themselves. Once you are convicted no further questions will be asked. If I am right, then the personal satisfaction of seeing me suffer is just a bonus.'

'Mr Outhwaite,' said James, trying to enlist the surgeon's aid.

'I'm not sure that this is right, Mr Ludlow . . .' Harry's look stopped him from saying any more.

'I should stay away from the brandy tonight, Mr Outhwaite. You may develop a loose tongue and that could lead to great danger.' No one was sure if Harry was directly threatening the surgeon. 'No drink, d'ye hear?'

'Clearly, Mr Ludlow. Clearly.'

'Good. Because people who are prepared to kill to keep a secret generally aren't too fussy about who turns out to be the victim. Just so long as the secret's safe.' Outhwaite left quickly, looking very worried.

'I'll get a couple of hands to help Pender.'

Harry turned back to his brother. 'James. Stay with Crevitt tonight. Don't let him out of your sight. You are safe as long as you are with him.'

James just nodded.

'James. I mean it. No heroics. You will do more harm than good. I need to make Carter think that I have heeded his warning. If you start trying to help me, you will ruin everything.'

'Not a very heroic role.'

'You may castigate me for it for the next fifty years. But you will abide by my wish?'

James nodded and turned his head away. Pender had raised himself from the cot and was trying to get up.

'That's it then,' said Harry. He looked at the serious faces. 'Come along, don't be so glum. Don't you know, I've the devil's own luck?' He gave James a mighty slap on the back. Pender shrank back lest he be tempted to do the same with him.

'You'll need it, brother. I think even Old Nick would blench at the thought of taking on over six hundred souls in their own backyard.'

'My backyard too, James. I was born to this.'

It was a long day for Harry, though his brother, confined to the conversational pleasures of Crevitt, was to claim later that he had suffered most. James had very little in common with the parson, whom he found unctuous, rather than pious, and parochial in the extreme. Not that James was one to sneer at provincial life. At home in town, he still had a great regard for the open country where he had been raised, and for the people who inhabited that land.

It was just that Crevitt's experience seemed so narrow. James knew many people whose horizon was limited to the next village. He found it strange that Crevitt, who had taken holy orders at Oxford, and had since spent time in other parts of the world, seemed to concentrate on the pleasures to be derived from life in a hamlet on the windswept fens. Was it all just a thinly disguised attempt to make James more charitably disposed towards his friend Carter? Certainly the Captain, and his family, cropped up repeatedly in the conversation. He was told repeatedly how much Carter cared for his sister and his nephew. The lady's husband, however, was not included in this rosy remembrance, having apparently disappeared not long after siring young Oliver Turnbull.

The parson could not hide his own feelings for Turnbull's mother. Even when talking about Carter's young wife, who had died in childbirth, having already miscarried twice, that lady was held up as an example of all that was wise, good, and admirable. James listened, summoning all his innate politeness, to this dreary tale, reflecting none the less on the potential benefits of death by hanging.

The ship edged out of the bay on the falling tide, and once clear of the surrounding cliffs turned due south, setting courses and topsails on the main and mizzen, bracing her yards round to take advantage of the westerly wind. The sun shone and the clement weather had returned. The hands, once the ship was under way, were set to making and mending again, although they were called away continually to trim the sails, since the absence of a proper foremast was making the *Magnanime* sail a bit crank.

Pender slept face down in Harry's cabin. Outhwaite had administered a sizeable dose of laudanum so that he was in no pain. Outhwaite himself was shaking visibly from his lack of a drink, but he was too frightened of Harry's strictures to even contemplate assuaging his needs. Harry himself sat in the wardroom, waiting for Craddock. Strange that it was only yesterday that he had challenged the man to find out what he knew. So much had happened in the meantime.

Few of the other officers were present. Those on watch were on deck, and those who were not had decided to catch up on their sleep. The exception was Turnbull, who sat at the other end of the wardroom, by the door, sorting out shot and powder for the two pistols on the table before him. Occasionally he would look up at Harry, gazing at him, as if trying to make out what he was thinking. The object of his curiosity sat there, going over in his mind what he knew, what he suspected, and how he intended to go about proving it.

He was nagged by the continuing suspicion that he might be wrong. That the cause of the whole affair had originated on shore, and that the actual murder of Bentley was not, in any way, connected with the ship. But the events of the last two days kept dragging him back to his original conclusions. Why excite the more gullible sections of the crew with tales of Jonahs? Why then attack Pender for having asked questions about it? The motive, whatever it was, had to be something that had happened, and could therefore be unearthed, on board ship.

And then there was the possibility, more apparent to James than to him, that he might be looking in the wrong place. One by one, Harry ran through the warrant officers and commissioned officers, trying to find reasons why they should be included in the list of suspects. One by one, he dismissed them from his calculations. It was nothing to do with motive, since they had all disliked the man. It was a matter of power. The power to make things happen.

He was left with Carter. The Captain had massive authority. And he did not have to rule through loyalty, with the potent weapon of fear so readily to hand. There was one other point to clarify, one that could again point to Carter, but that would have to be confirmed by Craddock.

'Find the motive.' The words rattled around in his brain. What would make Carter murder Bentley? The late first lieutenant had shown him scant respect, but that was reason for court martial, rather than a knife in the ribs. Another question. Why had Carter tolerated such an open display of arrogant disregard for the normal conventions of the service? What advantage did Bentley have that so allowed him to flout the chain of command? The little that Harry had seen, and all that he had heard, gave the impression that Bentley was in a position to break Carter, instead of the other way round.

That was the only thing Carter cared about, his position. Harry knew the man well enough to recognize his obsession with rank. He was still relatively poor, even as a post captain, and given his lack of patronage, still financially and professionally insecure. So the answer must relate to that. Like all men, Carter had a vision of the future. If Bentley had threatened that vision, then he would have to die. And if the late premier's behaviour was anything to go by, then he had certainly done just that. He tried to recall every word that Outhwaite had said, seeking, in the surgeon's tale, for a possible clue.

'Bentley had been like that for some time, though it has to be admitted he did not behave in such a cavalier fashion right at the start of the commission. Anyway, he and Carter were close. The premier was allowed many liberties denied to others of his rank. Carter let Bentley run the ship, and appeared happy with the way things were.

'There had been a couple of deaths that could not quite be explained. But that happened in ships, what with bullying and gambling debts not being paid. But the boy, Larkin, had upset the hands, and no one, apart from the fact that the lad was well liked, could quite say why the crew were so rattled.

'Carter and Bentley responded to this discontent with a massive increase in punishments, and they were in agreement on that. You had to admit it worked, for whatever set the hands to grumbling was successfully quashed by the cat. Things seemed to return to normal, if you can call a crew cowed by the lash "normal".'

'No one,' he had said, 'could quite recall the date at which all that changed, the date at which the Captain started to question the premier's decisions, and Bentley to behave the way he did, because it grew slowly. The man had always been a heavy drinker, but it had got progressively worse, at the same time as his attitude to the Captain's authority had deteriorated. It centred on the punishments, which Carter wanted to reduce. Bentley was dead against this. From the odd frosty exchange, it turned to thinly disguised insults. The Captain tried to rope him in, but after a while, he seemed just to give up.'

It had come as no shock to the wardroom. From what Harry had gathered, Bentley had always treated the officers in an even more disdainful manner, insulting them all freely, and making the dinners in the ward-room, which he insisted they attend, an absolute hell. The experience was generally made tolerable by the fact that Bentley regularly passed out before the meal ended. As James had said, he was not sorely missed, and had things stopped with his death, Harry would have been left with any number of suspects, including the crew, most of whom had at one time or another been flogged for some trivial offence at Bentley's behest. After all, in truth, anyone aboard could have filched his knife.

But things had not ceased. Not satisfied with catching his brother, knife in hand over the body, two witnesses had appeared, as if by magic. Men whom he was sure had not been near the scene of the crime. On the surface, Carter had such a watertight case against James that there was no reason for him to do anything. But he had, making plain that Harry was not to question the officers or the crew. And that chance remark of Pender's about a Jonah had been taken up and turned against them. The lack of a guard on the spirit room, and the fact that those men had been allowed to plunder it, stood out starkly for attention. The accusations of mutiny, which were universally held to be absurd! But the final indication was the unnecessary flogging of Pender.

If Carter did not want Harry to ask questions, then he must have something to hide. It had to be something to do with the ship. Between them, perhaps because of their growing animosity, Bentley and Carter had turned the seventy-four into a floating hell. Outhwaite had been adamant that it had not always been so. Though never a truly happy ship, the *Magnanime* had been a deal better than many he had sailed on. All the information pointed to a sudden breach between the two senior officers.

An event? The death of that boy, Larkin? Again more questions than answers. But there had to be an answer, and if it was to be found aboard the *Magnanime*, then tonight, when some of the ship slept, he must find it. Given this wind they could well raise the Rock in the morning, James would be carted off to the gaol, Carter's witnesses would swear their testimony. And Carter? He would chase the dockyard to replace his mast, and badger the Port Admiral, saying how keen he was to join the growing fleet in the Mediterranean. As soon as was humanly possible he would be on his way, leaving Harry to defend the indefensible.

'Mr Craddock,' said Harry, standing up as the acting premier entered.

'My cabin, Mr Ludlow, if you please.' Not a glance at Turnbull.

Harry followed him into the cabin. Craddock, still red-eyed, flung himself into a chair.

'How is your man?' asked Craddock.

'As well as can be expected,' said Harry. 'You know why I am here?'

'I do. I did as you requested, although given the events of the last twenty-four hours, it has been far from easy.'

'If time was not so vital, I would not be pressing you.'

'All I can tell you is that no one can recall precisely who

raised the alarm on the night of Mr Bentley's death. The news was shouted to the quarter-deck. A voice calling out to come quick, and that Mr Bentley had been murdered.' Craddock dropped his head.

'Murdered?' It wasn't significant to Craddock. 'That's all?'

'No. Mr Mangold, who had the watch, was very vague. But the quartermaster says it was a voice used to command. Not a sailor's voice. When I put this to Mr Mangold he thought for a bit, then agreed, though he could not place who the voice belonged to. But he did recall the sound of running footsteps.'

'Shoes?'

'That's right. Denbigh must have been asleep as usual, for he remembers nowt. But what does that signify, Mr Ludlow? An officer's voice, not that of one of the hands? And shoes?'

Harry did not wish to explain how much it meant to him.

'Quartermaster was quite sure. He said no hand would dare to shout to the quarter-deck in that manner.'

'Meehan and Porter?'

'None of the officers remembers seeing them, but that don't mean much, Mr Ludlow, since they weren't looking.'

'An officer's voice?'

'Or a gentleman's,' said Craddock with a steady look. 'Anyway, everyone rushed to the scene. The rest you know.'

'Tell me, Mr Craddock. How long did that dinner go on after my brother and I left?'

'Well into the evening, Mr Ludlow. The Captain was determined to remove any memory of what happened. Mr Bentley passed out, of course. The Captain had him removed. After that the atmosphere eased a lot. I would not say it was entirely convivial, but when it broke up, it was a contented set of officers who left the cabin. We'd all had a lot to drink.'

'And Bentley?'

'Woke up in a foul temper, demanding claret. We were in the wardroom, in a benign frame of mind for once, when he came out of his cabin. The steward offered him some of our ward-room claret, but he pushed it away, saying that it was "blackstrap" and not fit for human consumption. He demanded some of the choice wine we had taken out of the Frenchman. I

217

reminded him that the Captain had taken charge of that, and so he stood up and said that if the Captain had it, then the Captain would damn well just have to part with some of it.'

'What happened then?'

'With that he left, cursing us all for no-good swabs.'

'And where did he go?'

'Why, to the Captain's cabin, of course. We could hear them yellin' at each other, though we had no idea of the words they was saying. Now that was unusual, because I tell you no secret when I say that Mr Bentley did not show proper respect to the Captain. How a man like Oliver Carter bore it I don't know.'

'So what was unusual?'

'Why, the Captain shouting. Normally he didn't really respond to Mr Bentley. Not that I haven't seen him struggling to do so.'

'What did you do then, you and the others?'

'We had been sitting talking the way sailors do. Mr Heron, the purser, had even sung us some very nice songs, I recall. The master accompanied him on the German flute. But Bentley acting like that had spoiled the mood. The party broke up more or less immediately, everyone goin' their separate ways.'

'Being?'

'That I don't know. Some would have gone for a breath of air, others to their cabins. But I can't recall who went where, an' I don't suppose anyone else would either.'

'How long was it before the alarm was raised?'

'A good thirty minutes. Mr Mangold remembers Mr Bentley storming out of the Captain's cabin, saying he knew what was stowed in the hold, and it was high time it saw the light of day.' Craddock saw the question on Harry's face. 'The drink I imagine, since he was hard by the spirit room hatch when he was stabbed. Seems the Captain followed 'im out lookin' very black. But he stopped when he saw Mr Mangold, and went a-walking on the windward side of the the quarter-deck.'

'Could he say who was where, among the officers?'

'Not for sure. You don't pay much attention if you don't have to.'

'The officers. Were they still in full dress?'

'Full dress?' Craddock's face creased, trying to get the drift of the question. 'For the dinner, you mean?'

Harry nodded.

'Some were, others not. First thing I did was to get out of my best uniform. Can't be too careful with that.'

'And wigs?'

'I can't recall properly. But I think most would get rid of their wigs, don't you? Stands to reason if you get out of your best rig. As I say, I don't recall very much because I wasn't lookin'.'

'So you wouldn't be able to tell me who was still wearing theirs?'

Craddock shook his head. 'Some were, others not, same as the uniform.'

'Thank you, Mr Craddock,' said Harry. It would have been more reassuring to be certain, but that would require questioning all the officers. One thing was sure, being bald, Carter always wore a wig.

'Thank you!' The irony was plain. 'I don't know if I've done the right thing, Mr Ludlow. You know, when you're a youngster, you think as you get older things will become simpler. Clearer. That with knowledge you'll be able to see things right. Make the right decision. Truth is, as you get older, you realize that men don't stop being what they were as children, only worse. The arguments they have are more serious, and their ability to forget them evaporates.' Craddock shrugged, unable to continue in this vein. He looked at Harry in an avuncular way. 'You know what I mean, Mr Ludlow. Only I would hate to think that you are as blind as some others I know.'

'I'll try not to be, Mr Craddock,' said Harry, going out of the door. The older man smiled, but Harry meant something very different from the drift of Craddock's philosophizing.

Harry crossed the wardroom. Turnbull was still cleaning his pistols. He raised one of them and aimed along it. Harry sensed it was trained on him. He turned, and the young man dropped the pistol, with an apologetic look.

Pender was still asleep. Harry sat on his sea-chest and ran over in his mind what Craddock had said. It tallied with what Pender had gleaned from the wardroom stewards, though they had paid no attention to the state of the officers' dress, being too busy consuming the left-overs from the dinner.

It looked as though Bentley had gone to Carter's cabin,

roundly abused the man, and then headed for the hold. Carter, intending to follow him, had stopped when he realized Mangold was there. Instead he had started to walk. The question was, how far had he walked?

Had he stayed on the quarter-deck? Or had he walked on, along the gangway, then slipped down on to the upper deck without being seen. No one, even if they saw Carter, would question his right to be there. He could go anywhere in the ship he pleased. And if he knew where Bentley was going, he would know his avenue of return. A simple thing to wait for him, and then pounce.

Harry's blood was racing. He stood up and paced up and down the small cabin. He was both angry and excited. Angry that Carter should seek to fasten the murder on him, and excited that he had deduced how it was carried out. Could he prove it? Was there some evidence aboard the ship that would either damn Carter or force him into the position in which he might confess to the crime? Harry looked out of the stern windows. The light was fading fast.

He dropped in on James for the last time. There was one more thing to do. If everything else failed, they must resort to bluff. Crevitt was trying to get his brother to play another hand of whist, but James complained that he would be bankrupt if they continued. He looked so relieved to see Harry.

'Mr Crevitt, I wonder if it would be in order for my brother to have his drawing materials?' Harry asked.

'I see no objection, Mr Ludlow.'

'And may I have a private word?' Crevitt merely nodded this time. Harry took James out into the gangway.

'You've often told me that you can draw anything from memory, James.'

'Imagination tends to supply what memory doesn't.'

'When you were apprehended, with the knife in your hand. Does your memory run to that?'

'Etched here.' James tapped his head. 'Every detail.'

'Then kindly etch it on paper, more than one drawing if you have to. Can you do that?'

'Yes.'

'And I want one more drawing. I want a drawing of Bentley being knifed.'

'And who do you want as the murderer?'

'Don't be obtuse, brother.'

'Just as long as you are not allowing a personal animosity to warp your judgement, Harry. Because if you are, you are no better than Carter.'

'I don't deserve that from you, James.'

'You have no idea how much I hope that you are right.'

'It's the only way, James. I have told you. The only way to prove you are innocent is to put the guilty party in the dock.'

'Good luck, Harry. And please have a care.' Harry would have liked to embrace his brother, but they were still in Crevitt's view. It would not do to alert him.

'Perhaps you can persuade my brother to do a portrait of you, Mr Crevitt,' said Harry, walking back into the narrow screened-off cabin. 'Do you see yourself in an heroic pose? Nimrod, perhaps. I'm sure he can do whatever you wish. Myself, I am off to invite the surgeon to partake of some of my brandy. If he is in my cabin, he can tend one of his patients and slake his thirst at the same time.'

'Just as long as he does not ignore his other charges,' said Crevitt.

'Those that are to die, will die. Those that will recover, do not need the ministrations of Mr Outhwaite to slow their recovery.'

Outhwaite was uncomfortable with the role assigned to him, although the prospect of being left to drink as much of Harry's brandy as he saw fit, especially after a whole day of abstinence, was an enticing one. But, much against his will, he was now part of Harry's conspiracy, without being quite sure how he had got there. He had left his two surgeon's mates to tend to those recovering from wounds sustained in the battle, and having been at his work almost continuously since that event, he felt entitled to finally relax.

But he was a bag of nerves, and several sips of brandy had done nothing to calm him. He watched as Harry changed out of his clothes, and donned the garb of a seaman. He took the knife that he had borrowed from Outhwaite and tucked it in his waistband. He had also fashioned a garrotte by attaching some fishing line to a couple of wooden pegs. Then his pistols. Lastly he took a small canvas bag, heavy with sand, tying the loop on it to his belt.

He opened the gunport, and lashed the line to the eyebolt holding his cot, the rest snaking out into the dark night. Another line, holding a shaded lantern, was gently lowered out until a knot tied in it rested on the edge of the frame.

'Now, Mr Outhwaite. If anyone comes a-calling, tell them to bugger off, as you and I are in the process of getting drunk.'

Outhwaite didn't even nod. Harry gave Pender, now awake, a slight wave, before he squeezed out of the casement, and into the night.

XIV

Harry made his way quietly along the gun-deck through the rows of swinging hammocks. He walked on tiptoe heading for the very front of the deck by the bows of the ship, blessing the fact that his geese had been eaten long ago, since his approach to the manger would have been heralded with their squawking. Stopping outside he laid down his lantern and the garrotte. He checked his knife and took out his pistol before entering.

The animals did not stir as he went by, proof that they were used to the passage of human beings through their part of the ship. The smell was strong even by shipboard standards. One of the pigs got up and started rooting about in his straw. The chickens stirred slightly, but he hoped not enough to disturb the men he had come to see.

He could just hear the clicking of the dice over the noise of the ship. There was a regular thud as the bows, just forward of the manger, hit the swell. Harry sat still, getting the rhythm of the sounds, before moving forward slowly as the thuds covered the noise his feet made in the loose straw.

The glimmer of a lantern came from the last stall. They really should have posted a guard, but no doubt the lure of the game had enticed the man who should be watching to look at the roll of the dice. Harry waited listening to the quiet bets being placed, the suppressed grunts of joy and disappointment. This was just one of the groups that Pender had directed him to. Other games would take place during the daylight hours, but this was where the inveterate gamblers gathered, those who played at every opportunity.

They were engaging in a serious breach of the regulations, and a keen officer could have easily put a stop to it. But here were few superiors who did not gamble themselves, so they tended to turn a blind eye to these activities. Some ships were cursed with evangelical types, who saw it as their duty to persuade the men away from gambling and strong drink, an uphill task for men who loved risk, and who consumed, as their rations, a gallon of beer or two pints of diluted rum a day. The *Magnanime* was free from such problems. Bentley would certainly not have objected to gambling, and Craddock would be indifferent, as long as it did not interfere with the running of the ship. So these men had become lax, allowing him to get close enough to hear their voices.

'Good evening, gentlemen,' said Harry, blocking off the entrance to the stall. The gamblers spun round, and froze as they saw the barrel of the pistol glinting in the faint light. 'Forgive me for disturbing you.'

They did not respond, keeping their eyes on the pistol. Harry was curious about their escape route. There had to be one. No point in risking a flogging, in a place from which you could not disappear at the first hint of trouble. Harry waited quietly. He saw one of them glance above his head.

'The hawse hole,' he said, smiling. 'Which, in an emergency, would put you on the beak. Where do you go from there? Do you sit it out, or do you clamber on to the forecastle?' Simple but effective. Harry had wondered if they had cut a trapdoor somewhere for an escape route.

'You know who I am?'

'We do, Mr Ludlow,' said a voice from the back of the group. Harry could not see his face, which was in shadow.

'Good. For I have to persuade you that you are in no danger from me.'

'Then put up your gun,' said the voice.

'I shall, in a moment. Perhaps you would come into the light where I can see you?'

'I think not, Mr Ludlow. Whatever it is you want, seein' my face ain't going to alter it. I don't think you are here to partake of the game.'

'True. And nothing would give me greater pleasure than to leave you in peace to continue yours.'

Again silence. Harry heard a slight scratching sound. It could have been anything, but it could also be someone searching for a weapon.

'You must all be thinking that the best thing to do would be to rush me. After all, if I were to let on about this, you would all be in for a fair number of lashes. What really worries me is that this gun will go off regardless. That will make it very difficult for all of us.'

'Belay, Jeff, for fuck's sake. That pistol's pointin' at me.' The scratching sound stopped. 'Your bein' here would require explainin' too.'

'Yes. But not to the bos'un.' Harry paused to let his words have some effect. 'But I am not here to threaten you. I am here to ask you to help me.'

'An' if we choose not to?' It was infuriating not being able to see the man's eyes. Harry found it hard to try and judge his intent, just by the tone of his voice.

'Nothing will happen.' He raised the pistol slightly. 'This was merely to get you to think, to stay still long enough to let me explain my case.'

'As well as to keep you alive.'

'That too.'

'So you are sayin' that regardless of what we do, you're not goin' to split on us.'

'No. And for several reasons. One, it is none of my business, and two, if it is as easy as this to sneak up on you, I doubt if any of your officers want the trouble.'

'And just what is it that you want from us?'

'Information, freely given, about the night Mr Bentley was murdered.'

'And if we was to give you information, what would you do with it?'

'If it was what I seek, I would use it to help clear my brother.'

'Information would be no use unless it is sworn.'

'Let's start with the information. Were you here on the night of Mr Bentley's death?'

'Mr Ludlow. There is not a man here who knows anything about that. Because we was here, and when the alarm was raised, we scarpered back to our hammocks fuckin' quick.'

'Not just you?'

A long pause, then that same steady voice. 'Likely that's true.'

'Is this the only gambling school?'

'Ay.' That was quick and definite, and probably a lie.

'But there are other people who are about at night?'

'We keep ourselves to ourselves. An' they do the same.'

'On your way back to your bunks did you see anyone else?'

'Mr Ludlow. Supposing that I was to tell you that one of our number saw something, and that that somethin' would be of help to you. Would you then undertake not to ask the man's name, nor press for anythin' to be sworn?'

'Would you trust me if I said yes?'

'I can only speak for myself. But I saw you on deck this mornin'. And I know that there were quite a number of men who, had you choose to finger them, would be facing a floggin' round the fleet, if not a rope round their necks. You knew who they were, didn't you?'

'Not all of them.'

'One would have been enough within those buggers. He would have named his mates just to save his own skin.'

'So?'

'So I'm sayin' that if you will give me your word, then I am inclined to accept it.'

'Then you have it.'

'I'd be obliged if you would say it out loud. Make me feel safer.'

'Should you give me information that will help my brother, I will not say where it came from, or ask you to swear.' The faces he could see relaxed a bit. 'Without coming back to ask you first.'

'That's fair,' said the voice, quieting the murmur of protest from his mates. 'No one would want to see your brother hang, Mr Ludlow. Not for somethin' he didn't do.'

'You seem very sure.'

'Not sure, your honour. But one of our number, an' I'm not sayin' who, exceptin' it weren't me, saw somethin' that throws a bit of a question on what is bein' said.'

'Which is?'

'Which is, if those two no-good bastards, Meehan and Porter, were supposed to be on hand to see Bentley sliced, how come one of our number saw them scurrying to their bunks, and coming from the other direction at that?'

Harry tried to keep the excitement out of his voice. If he had needed proof that his suspicions of Carter were not just based on personal prejudice, then here it was.

'I leave you with a question, gentlemen. I will keep my word. But if those two swear to what they saw, perjuring themselves in the process, it will be scant comfort to me, or my brother, to have such unattested knowledge.'

'People die, Mr Ludlow. More poor bastards die on the lower deck than abaft the mizzen. There's plenty that's gone on aboard this ship that needs investigatin'. Trouble is, it's too late to save the person wronged.'

'Larkin?'

'Him, for one. A proper scamp that boy.'

'But well liked?'

'He had a way with him. Even Mr Bentley used to laugh at his antics.'

'So what happened to him?'

'They say he fell overboard.' The voice cast no opinion, maintaining that steady, almost monotonous tone.

'What do you say?'

'Christ. It's not what I say. It's what we all say.' There was some emotion in the voice at last. 'That boy knew no fear. He would go anywhere and do anything. As long as it could be said to be a bleedin' laugh. And he was like a monkey in the riggin'. Lad like that is not goin' to fall overboard on a dead calm night, with no cunt to see him going. No scream, no crying out. It don't add up.'

'But he did go overboard.'

'Some say in a sack.'

'Who?'

'You're in the wrong part of the ship for that question.'

Harry realized that he'd been sidetracked. Sad as the death of the ship's boy was, his reasons for being here were more pressing.

'I return to the question. If I can find no other way to clear my brother, can I count on you, whoever you are?'

It was chilling, the way no one but the speaker responded.

'One thing at a time, Mr Ludlow. You can't expect people who you have come on sudden with a gun in your hand to leap into somethin' without considerin' it. But I say you can come back an' ask.'

'Enjoy your game, gentlemen.' Much as Harry would have liked to stay and try and persuade whoever it was to reveal publicly what he had seen, it was better to leave the man who had spoken to use his influence. That he intended to seemed plain from what he had said. No good would be served by Harry trying to aid his efforts. He backed out of the manger, still careful not to disturb the animals. Once out on the gun-deck again, he tucked the pistol in his belt, picked up his lantern, and headed for the nearest companionway.

Down on the orlop-deck he walked silently past the various screened-off quarters of the ship's warrant officers. No one was about, and he made his way quickly aft, ignoring the carpenter's walk, a narrow space on both sides of the ship for the carpenter to come at the hull, and a likely spot for nefarious activity. Below the waterline, damp air and the smell of the bilge water were very strong. He went right aft till he was under the gun-room.

He unshaded the lantern a fraction, just enough to remind him of his direction, for he had not been in this part of a seventy-four-gun ship for years. He made his way along the walkway, until he was outside the bread-room. He stood at the door, in the dark, listening. The room was lined in tin to keep out the rats, and no sound came from within. But a sound came from behind him, and Harry quickly dropped to his knees.

There was a loud thud above his head, followed by a curse. Harry put his lantern on the deck and flicked the shutter fully

228

open. The light revealed a man standing over him, club in hand, uncertain of which direction to aim it. Harry grabbed both the man's ankles as he looked down at the light. He pulled hard. On the damp walkway the feet came easily, and his assailant crashed to the ground.

The bread-room door flew open, knocking Harry over on to his adversary. He rolled on, pulling his pistol from his belt as he did so. There was enough light from his lantern to see several figures crowded in the doorway. The light was on the wrong side of the door, leaving them in shadow. Harry slid forward and pressed his pistol into the neck of the man struggling to rise from the deck.

'Hold there, my friend,' he said, pushing hard, causing the man to yell in pain, 'and the rest of you stay, or I'll bring the whole ship down around your ears.' When they made to move towards him, Harry pressed the gun into the man's neck again. Again he yelled, this time trying to suppress it.

'Stay,' croaked the man lying on his back.

'We're damned if we stay,' said one of the men from the bread-room door.

'I'll see you damned if you go,' snapped Harry. 'If not you all, then this one.' Again he pressed hard with the gun. 'Now back off!'

'Christ, lads,' croaked Harry's victim. 'Didn't you hear him? Back off!'

'Fuck you,' said one, and he started to run down the gangway. As though a spring had been released, he was followed by the others, their bare feet making little sound, as they disappeared up the companionway.

'Loyal friends you have,' said Harry, easing the pressure of the gun a bit. He pushed the bread-room door shut with his free hand, and leaning over he pulled the light towards them. The man made to move as the lantern was lifted, but Harry hit him in the jaw with the pistol butt, before pressing it back into his throat.

'Now, what would your friends have been talking about in the bread-room, at this time of night?'

He didn't respond. Harry knew. Pender had told him that he

would be likely to find the malcontents gathered here. They had tried to recruit Pender when he first came aboard. It had been a subtle approach, as befitted recruitment to a group who could only pray for a hanging if caught. Pender, having turned them down, had then made it his business to find out where they met, and who made up their numbers. As Harry had surmised, Pender was a man who would not feel safe if he did not know what was going on, and where.

'They'll be back in their hammocks by now. What do you suggest I do with you?'

'Do what you will. But I'll say nothing.'

Privately, Harry was sympathetic to the many grievances that sailors in the King's Navy had. Their pay had not been raised since the time of the second Charles, and it was always in arrears. Due to the endemic corruption in the administration of the fleet, their food was often rotten, their water foul, while the discipline which their officers administered could be sadistically harsh. Given a man like Bentley as premier, and a captain like Carter to do his bidding, it was not surprising that some of the crew gathered to discuss mutiny. And he could understand why the others had run and left this man at his mercy. That would be the first rule that they would all swear to obey. That and the rule of silence if they were caught.

'Sit up,' said Harry, crouching back on his haunches, his gun aimed at the man's head. The sailor obeyed, and Harry could now see his face clearly.

'I want some information.'

A firm shake of the head.

'Not about your mates.' Harry turned the lantern so that it shone on his face as well. 'How do you think it would look if I was found in the company of a group of seditious mutineers?'

He knew that he had been recognized. The man tried not to respond, but it was plain in his eyes that he knew whom he was addressing.

'I don't know what you're on about.'

'I think you do. And I think you will also realize that while I am in a position to personally harm you, I am not likely to do anything that will ease the mind of your commander. So, think a little. Then I am going to ask you some questions. Failure to answer could be painful.'

The man started to say something, but the sudden proximity of the pistol to his cheek stopped him.

'Think first.' Harry stayed silent for some moments. 'Did you have a meeting the night Mr Bentley was murdered?'

The man said nothing. 'You will answer me,' Harry pulled his knife out of his waistband, 'because I'll truly hurt you if you don't.'

'Do your damnedest. I'll say nothin'.'

'My damnedest? I wonder if you really appreciate what my damnedest could be. You have recognized me, I know that. My brother is set to hang unless I can find out who killed Bentley. There are no lengths I won't go to, in order to gain such information.'

The man's laugh took Harry totally by surprise.

'Happen your brother didn't do it. But let him fuckin' hang anyway. You can all hang, all you folks with your money, your power and your heel ground in the face of ordinary folk. Let him hang I say. Then let them find the real killer, another of your ilk, I dare say. And then hang that bastard too.'

The man was spitting as he spoke. Something in Harry's eye must have told him he was in no real danger. He started to pull himself away, slithering along the deck on his bottom.

'Do you really think I care? I'd do what the Frenchies have done. They've got the right idea. String the lot of you up. Or put some of them there guillotines in front of Westminster Abbey.'

He was enough of a distance from Harry now to stand up. Harry still had the pistol aimed at him, but to no effect.

'An' you can turn me in if you want. But I'll say nothin' to no one. Not about my mates, or anythin' else.'

'You know who killed Bentley?'

'I do not. But I knows this. That if'n you're lookin' for another candidate for the rope, you'll make up some story against one of the hands, most likely. It won't be the first time one of our number has paid a price on this fuckin' barky to save a gent.

'Larkin.' He kept coming back to that boy.

'Please a gent, was more his problem. But the price was the same. Over the side in a bloody sack, and no questions asked.'

'I must save my brother.'

'I can't help you, no more'n I could help that lad. Those in power will do as they pleases, and flog any poor bastard if he dares protest.' Talking about Larkin had blunted some of the man's anger. 'But times'll change, and different folks will hold the power. So be sure: if you put some poor sod in your brother's place, make certain you have the right of it. For your day will come, the fuckin' lot of you, an' I hope I am there to see you and all your kind swing.'

The man turned and walked away, disdaining the need to run. Harry knew that he had wasted his time. He was down to his last chance. The men playing dice had helped, but he could not be sure how far that would extend. One more place to look, with no idea of what he'd find at the end of it.

Harry approached the pump shaft slowly, looking as he passed into the hammocks, to see if they were occupied. His first task: to find out if there were people missing, and if possible how many. He shivered. Narrow spaces were not to his liking, and he knew that if certain people were out of their beds, he was going to have to go down the pump shaft and look for them.

He came to the hammocks slung round the cistern. They swung with the motion of the ship, but unlike the others he had examined on the way, no sleeping face looked up at him. He counted eight empty berths, all of them the ones closest to the shaft. An entire mess. Men who would eat together, drink together, and, in this case, crew the barge together. They should be the most trusted hands on the ship, men who could form the backbone of a press gang.

Desertion was rife in the Navy, especially in wartime, and ships in commission when they touched an English-speaking port refused their hands permission to go ashore. But that could not apply to everyone, especially not the commander, and the barge crew were particularly favoured in this respect. It was held to be a great privilege to be part of that mess. For one, they were excused a lot of the normal duties undertaken by the other hands. They were encouraged to dress well, some captains providing them with a special rig. They withstood the cat-calls of their shipmates. It was worth it for the perquisites.

Harry checked his rig before opening the hatch. Pistol, knife. Then a sudden feeling of being watched made the hairs on the back of his neck rise. He turned suddenly but could see no one in the dim light.

Nerves, he thought. The lantern was a problem. Did he need it? He did not know where he was headed, nor what he would find when he got there. But it was an awkward thing to carry whilst climbing a ladder. He took the garrotte and made a sling out of it, looping the two wooden ends around the handle, and slinging the line over his shoulders. Again he had that feeling of being watched, of unseen eyes boring into his back. This time he turned slowly, but the effect was the same. Nothing stirred.

He opened the hatch and slipped through, his foot finding the ladder. The pumps had been used that day, and the air was damp and foul smelling from the bilge water. This had passed through holes in the canvas hose which ran up the centre of the shaft.

Not very well maintained, he thought.

There would be precious little room in the shaft if the pumps were in use, but now the canvas hung loose and empty. Harry opened his lantern a little, just enough to see, and enough to send the rats scurrying for a dark place. Then he closed the hatch to the gun-deck and started down the ladder.

Half-way down to the orlop-deck he remembered his previous journey up this same ladder and climbed back up to the gun-deck hatchway, before descending again, counting the rungs as he went. Twenty brought him to the next hatch down, the orlop. He made a mental note, before continuing down to the hatch that would open into the hold.

There was an easier way to do this. Just go down into the hold and search it from end to end without using this shaft. But the men he had seen used this very exit in an emergency. Pender had no idea of any secret openings down there, just as he could

233

not tell Harry what the barge crew were about in their nefarious night-time journeys. So this shaft might lead directly to the point at which they met.

Another twenty rungs. He was abreast of the opening to the walkways just above the various holds. Gingerly he opened it and climbed out. The compartments below, sectioned off, contained the mass of the ship's stores, plus a fair amount of ballast. Walking up and down, he could see nothing that indicated where a party of eight men might gather.

Reluctantly he climbed back into the shaft. There should be another hatch lower down. But that could only be got at by shifting the ship's powder barrels, a laborious task at any time. It was only used if the pumps fouled and the hose needed to be cleared. He clambered down. The ladder was very wet now. His foot slipped and he had some difficulty regaining some purchase, as his fingers clutched a wet rung above his head.

He came to the lower hatch. Sometimes, in ships that tended to make a lot of water, there was a gap left by the hatch, an access space, so that it could be got at without shifting all the powder. He pushed and it opened, a sure sign that this was the case. Strange in such a dry ship? He heard a low moan, then the sound of muffled laughter. Where was it coming from? He pushed the hatch open a bit further, shutting off his lantern for a moment to see if there was light coming from anywhere else. Nothing, just stygian blackness.

A laugh, very faint. Harry pushed both the hatch and his lantern full open, before climbing through. There was a ladder on the other side, set in a narrow gap between the roped-off powder barrels and the side of the hold. Getting his bearings he shut off his lantern again, and swiftly climbed to the top of the hold. His head bumped painfully against the walkway. Again he opened the shutter and saw that he was above the barrels of powder, in the open hold, with the walkway just a few feet away.

He stood still and listened for a full minute. No sound. Leaving the lantern open he set off back down to the pump shaft hatch. He climbed back on to the dripping ladder and opened his lantern fully, trying to see if there was anything below him.

Again a voice. One word, sounding like a command. In the circular shaft, there was no way of telling where it had come from, since the sound seemed to be coming from all round him. He shut his lantern again, turning his head in the blackness. A thin white line, forming a rectangle, was plain on the other side of the shaft.

Another hatch, one that should not be there. Harry pressed his ear to the wood, hearing muffled voices. Unshading his lantern he looked for the footholds that must be there. Now that he was looking in the right place, he saw that there was a special sliding section fitted to the shaft, no doubt to shut off the secret place beyond. And just below it was a strake that held the circular planking of the shaft together. But this strake was a lot wider than any of the others, and it formed a perfect place to stand while the hatch was opened.

Harry let himself down on to it. He shut his lantern again and felt for the mechanism that would open the other hatch. Nothing! It must push open. A moment's hesitation, his hands poised against the wood. Would making an entrance now be the right thing to do, or would it be better to wait and come back when the place was empty? He knew, as these thoughts flashed through his mind, that there was little time, and if he did not look now, he could never be certain who was in there. He leant on the hatch. It shot open with surprising speed, and Harry was momentarily blinded by the bright light coming from the room.

A second's glance took in the walls lined with drapes, the fancy brass lanterns, the floor covered in multi-coloured velvet cushions, and the men lying around in various stages of undress. Harry grabbed the top of the opening to stop himself from falling in. The men inside were frozen, as if in a tableau. Harry, reaching behind himself, whipped out his pistol and levelled it at the nearest member of the barge crew, Marchant, the coxswain. They had all started to make for him and the hatch, but froze at the sight of the pistol.

Marchant, wearing a silk robe which had been held closed by his hands, had started to reach for the intruder. Now it had fallen open to reveal that he was naked underneath. Harry took them all in in one sweeping glance, counting to eight as he went.

He could see bottles and glasses around the place, and a hookah sat on a small table. Meehan, completely naked, stood with his hands covering his genitals. Another member of the group was trussed like a bird, his skin showing the signs of a recent beating. It seemed like an age, but only seconds passed before Harry spoke. He could not keep the shock out of his voice.

'Don't move, any of you!' His mind racing, he could not believe what he saw before him. It wasn't what these men had been about, though the trussed sailor was strange. Harry had never served on a ship that had been entirely without it. Indeed he had been approached so many times by pederasts, as a midshipman, that he had become very early in life, like the rest of the service, blasé about sodomy. It happened. Most did not indulge, but those who did tended to be discreet, and no one was really harmed by it.

But the room. He was shocked by the room. It was so elaborate. It must be tin-lined behind those drapes to keep out the rats. The velvet cushions would not last a week if rats got at them. And you could feel how dry it was, and that in a damp part of the ship. He reasoned that it was the section of the hold set aside for holding shot. And that meant that with this space taken up, the ship was deficient in that article. There was no way that a room like this could exist without the knowledge of a higher authority. Yet Carter was not of that inclination, at least he had not been when Harry had served with him.

Men change, he thought. He turned the pistol on to the naked Meehan.

'This is where you were when Bentley was murdered.' The man's eyes did not move. No one moved. The sense of danger struck Harry just as the decanter smashed into his gun. There were nine men in the room, not eight, and one of them was behind the open hatch.

The gun flew out of his hand and glass sprayed everywhere. The hatch was slammed shut, jamming Harry's hand in the join. He yelled an oath as the pain took over from the shock. With all his strength he threw himself at the opening. He must have caught whoever was on the other side off his guard, because the hatch opened a little. Not much, but enough for Harry to pull his hand out.

He knew he was in great danger. Having discovered this secret room, these men would have to kill him. There could be no promises of silence this time. The two men who claimed to be witnesses were in there. Harry raised his injured hand and tried to get it round a rung above his head. It was nearly useless. He could not close it to get a grip. He pulled his hand down, jamming his elbow in between a lower rung and the side of the shaft. That held him while he reached up with his good hand. He jammed his elbow in again to repeat the manoeuvre, when the hatch flew open and a head popped out. Harry kneed the face, and the man shot backwards into the room.

That gave Harry enough time to get up three more rungs, before another, cleverer than the last, put both of his hands on the top of the hatch, and came through feet first. Harry tried a kick to stop him, and he did connect, but the man was moving too fast to be stopped and, scrambling and cursing, he grabbed one of the rungs well below Harry.

Elbow and hand, elbow and hand. Harry was up two more rungs before the man recovered. He looked up. The light from the hatchway showed Marchant's face. He'd thrown on a shirt and breeches and, having recovered, he started up the ladder after Harry. A kick aimed at his head achieved nothing. Marchant just ducked away from it. He tried to catch the swinging foot with his free hand, but failed. Harry moved his elbow up another rung, struggling to get a grip. The action of his arm opened the lantern still tied round his neck. The shaft was flooded with light. Looking down he saw Marchant grin. The light had revealed that Harry had only one good hand.

'Everybody out,' he cried. 'The bastard's done for!'

Marchant reached inside the open hatch. His hand came out with Harry's pistol. Slowly he lifted it, to aim at the man above him. Harry put his good hand on the lowest rung he could reach and just dropped. His foot connected with the gun as it went off, and his still dropping body carried on until it hit Marchant square in the face. His upper arm was wrenched as it took the full weight of his body, but he had dislodged Marchant, who fell backwards, desperate to maintain his hand and foot holds. Harry reached up and, despite the pain, pulled himself up with his injured hand. Marchant, recovering quickly, came after him.

The coxswain was much faster, having two good hands. Leaping up, he grabbed Harry's foot.

'Go!' shouted Marchant, desperately hanging on, his weight pulling Harry down. Harry hooked his bad arm round a rung. He pulled the knife from his belt, and swung it down to try and wound his adversary. He saw a figure dive through from the secret hatch, straight across to the powder-room hatch. He swung again, but the knife could not reach Marchant's head. The man seemed content to hang on to Harry's leg, taking no other action to either hurt or stop him. Another figure shot through from one hatch to the other. Then another. They were taking their second escape route whilst Marchant occupied Harry. He kicked violently. Marchant gasped as the foot drove down into his ribs. He lost his hand hold on the ladder, but he still did not let go of Harry's leg, merely swinging out into the centre of the shaft and back again.

More figures shot through the two hatches. Something flashed. Blood on a white shirt. He hoped he'd been the cause, perhaps the man he'd kneed in the face. But he could not see. He must have been the last, for his voice echoed, as he shouted an order up the shaft. Marchant let go of Harry's foot and scrambled down the ladder. He went straight through the powder-room hatch. It slammed shut behind him, and Harry was alone.

He eased himself down till he was level with the two hatches. The one to the powder room was shut tight. He tried to open it. It would not budge, obviously secured on the other side. He turned to the open hatch, and the blaze of light that came from the secret room. He had no hope of catching them now. They would all be racing up the stairways and making for their hammocks. Stupid. For the cat was out of the bag for them. They could pretend to be asleep. But when Harry brought this before a prosecutor, and anybody else who cared to listen about this room, then the case against James would alter. Not collapse, perhaps, not right away. But a thorough investigation would take place, and no captain having allowed and perhaps condoned this sort of thing on his ship could hope to remain in command.

Harry slipped through the open hatch, determined to have a proper look. The first impression of luxury was somewhat less

238

obvious on closer inspection. The drapes were worn, as was the velvet on the cushions. Erotic drawings lined the walls, depicting ancient Greek males in various sexual acts.

There was a cabinet in one corner, open, and showing rows of wine bottles. Harry recognized some of his own. There were still various pieces of clothing lying about, including the robe that Marchant had been wearing. One wall was covered in an array of whips and manacles, plus a selection of chains, showing that whatever they got up to in the privacy of this room, it included a certain amount of inflicting pain.

Pain! The throbbing in his wounded hand was a constant reminder of reality, in this place dedicated to fantasy. He must get back to his quarters, and the thought of that, of climbing that rope with his hand in this condition, caused him to pause. Then he saw that he was being foolish. There was no need for subterfuge now. He must get hold of Craddock as soon as he got on deck, and bring him down here to show him this room. The man knew nothing of it, he was convinced, and he would be just as shocked as Harry. Shocked that such a complex arrangement could exist on his ship, without his knowledge.

One last look around, to see if there was anything that might positively aid James. He started to move the cushions, and in doing so, noticed that they all seemed to carry dark stains. Blood. He rubbed his fingers over the stain on one cushion, while inspecting the rest. He kicked them aside. He had been right in one of his first impressions. The room was tin-lined. Nothing could get in or out, including the blood which covered the underside of the faded velvet cushions. Harry turned to look at the instruments covering the walls. They were there for someone's pleasure. But they screamed of the pain that such pleasure brought. A scamp. A daredevil, fearless, like a monkey in the rigging. No wonder the ship's boys were quiet. Subdued. Was this what happened to young Larkin? A game perhaps? One that went too far?

Painfully he eased himself out of the hatch and made his way slowly, elbow and hand, up the ladder. He came abreast of the hatch to the hold walkway and tried to push it open. It didn't move. A slight feeling of panic seized him, and he made his way as quickly as he could up the rungs to the orlop. He pushed. That too had been secured. He hung, gasping from his efforts, trying to examine his situation. They had shut off the exits. There was only one more. If that was secured, it would mean that they were coming back to get him. If it was open, they were waiting for him. They would seize him as he climbed through. Seize him for what? Not to talk. More likely to cart him to an open gunport and sling him through.

Harry considered staying where he was, but they would not wait for him all night. If he did not appear they would come after him, and there was no way he could deal with eight or nine men in this confined space, especially with an injured hand. Could he hack his way out with a knife? He tried the blade in the jamb of the hatch. No effect, and a glance at the stout planking told him he would be wasting his time trying to cut his way through. Better to be out in the open, even if it was what they wanted. There at least he could make a noise. If he stayed in this shaft he would die, and he could yell his lungs off. No one would hear him.

Elbow and hand, elbow and hand, he made his way up to the gun-deck hatch. He deliberately went on past it and carefully checked his position. With some difficulty he lifted the lantern off his shoulders. Again using his crooked arm to hold him, he untied the garrotte. Jamming the lantern between the ladder and the side of the shaft, he looped one end of the garrotte round his injured hand, leaving about six inches of line dangling. He tried the knife, then put it back in his waistband. He only had one good hand, but could not cope with knife and ladder. The light was not good, but it was enough for what he had in mind. The last thing. He pulled out the canvas bag full of sand, and using his teeth, he tore it open. A last chance to think, then he knew he was ready.

Pulling back his boot, he aimed a kick at the hatch. If it was secured he would merely have announced his presence. But he had to believe that it was off the latch. It was the only thing that made any sense. The hatch flew open. He waited, crouched on the ladder. It seemed like an age before a head came through. He flung the sand into the searching eyes, and followed it up with a well-aimed kick to the head, a kick which hurt his bare foot as much as it did the exposed head. The man shot back through the hatch, coughing, spluttering, and cursing. Both hands above his head, propelling himself with all his might, the pain in his swollen hand now excruciating, he dived, feet first, through the hatchway, hoping that his momentum would carry him on.

He nearly succeeded. He could feel them trying to grab his damp shirt, and failing. But one caught hold of his clothing, then another. He opened his mouth to yell and a hand was clamped over his entire jaw. More hands secured him, despite his frantic attempts to escape. Whispered commands, and the hand over his mouth was pulled away, to be replaced by a cloth which stifled the cry in his throat. He was held by a number of men, some sitting on his feet and lower body to contain the wild jerks he was attempting. Another cloth, or a rope, was lashed round his legs, and Harry knew that he was lost. He was going to die. They grabbed hold of his trussed legs, then his arms, and lifted him up. Surely someone had heard. But then sailors were well accustomed to turning a blind eye.

As he was being carried towards the side, his earlier thoughts of an open gunport becoming horribly real, all hell broke loose. He hit the deck with a thump and all around him men seemed to be fighting. He was stood on, and kicked repeatedly, as they battled over his prostrate form. Men were stepping over him wielding clubs. Suddenly there was no one. The fight had moved on. Then a face, a crooked smile, and he felt the bonds holding his feet cut.

'There you go, Mr Ludlow.' The man undid the cloth from his mouth. 'You're clear now. We've seen those buggers off.'

Harry turned to see the face of his rescuer.

'Smithy!'

'Ay, your honour. Never let it be said that old Smithy doesn't repay a favour. You held our lives in your hand this mornin' and you held your tongue. So did Pender. I never thought that such a smooth bastard had it in him. But we are square now, your honour.'

'How long have you been here?' asked Harry.

'Why, we watched you go down that hatch half a glass ago.'

His feeling that someone was watching him was right.

'What in damnation is going on here!' An officer's voice, loud and angry. As if by magic, Smithy and his rescue party melted away. Harry pulled himself to his feet, as Mangold came forward with a lantern raised. His jaw dropped when he saw Harry.

'Mr Ludlow!'

'I dare say I look a sight, Mr Mangold.'

Mangold looked him up and down, as if to confirm his worst suspicions of the state he was in.

XV

'Mr Mangold, this is no time to be wondering what to do. Every minute is vital.'

Disbelief was writ large across the face of the young lieutenant, who could not accept that someone like Harry should be in this state, on the gun-deck, and on his watch. On top of that, Harry's persistent demand that he rouse out Craddock forthwith, without explanation, was coming it mighty high. And that wasn't all he was demanding.

'And I want a pistol and a couple of reliable men. Every hatch on the pump shaft to have a guard, and a party of seamen down in the hold.'

'Mr Ludlow, what is all this about?' Mangold demanded, his hands held up as if to quieten the irate specimen before him. The situation was becoming increasingly difficult, and the young man cast about as if seeking a solution from elsewhere.

'Mr Mangold!' shouted Harry. 'If you do not do as I ask, you will probably spend the rest of your life on the beach.'

Heads appeared out of hammocks. Given what had just happened, Harry found it impossible to believe that they had been asleep. They would have stayed abed at the noise of a fight. But this was different. They saw an officer, who seemed to be involved in a furious argument with a common seaman. Harry realized Mangold's predicament, but there was no way he could explain himself in the middle of the gun-deck, with half the ship's crew eavesdropping.

'Please do as I ask.' Harry dropped his voice low, but the urgent tone remained. 'If I tell you that every officer aboard this ship is in danger of court-martial, I would not be exaggerating. Only by acting quickly can any of you save yourselves.'

Mangold's mouth opened and shut but no words came out.

'And I want men who are now on watch. Sailors.' His enemies were close by. He would feel safe with the men on watch. They were in the clear. 'The ship is in grave danger.'

He had chosen the right words. A danger to the ship was easy to comprehend. The young man seemed to snap out of his daze.

'Follow me.' They ran up the companionway, along the upper-deck, and up to the quarter-deck.

'Mr Prentice, rouse out the premier, if you please . . .' Mangold looked at Harry. 'Ask him to come to the powder store.'

'Quartermaster, hold the ship steady on the present course. Mr Prentice, you come back here and take over the watch.' Mangold ran along the gangway calling out names.

'The men in my division,' he explained to Harry. Mangold had the upper-deck gunners in his division. A sizeable party of hands gathered. 'It would be best if you instruct them, Mr Ludlow.'

Harry barked out orders that sent pairs with marlin spikes to guard all the hatches. He ordered the rest to follow him, and they ran back down, through the ship, to the hold. If any of the rest of the crew was curious, they did not trouble to follow them, content to wait and see.

They came to the walkway above the powder store. Harry bade the seaman to wait, while he and Mangold went down into the hold. Harry reached the hatch, and undid the lashing which held it shut. He pulled it open. Mangold looked past him, seeing nothing.

'Mr Ludlow.' There was a great deal of doubt in his voice.

'Never fear, Mr Mangold. But let us wait for Mr Craddock.'

'Do I warrant an explanation in the mean time?'

'Best wait.'

They heard the pounding of several shoes on the gangway. Harry, not sure exactly who was approaching, eased his knife into his hand. Mangold, seeing him do this, raised a quizzical eyebrow. Then they heard Craddock's voice, loud and clear.

'Damn you, sir, where have you been!' he shouted. 'Am I to do your duty, as well.' Someone could be heard mumbling an explanation.

'Well it's time to find out what this is all about. Mr Mangold, where the devil are you?'

'Down here sir, in the hold, by the pump shaft hatch.'

'Well get your arse up here, sir, and provide me with an explanation.' Craddock was obviously in a high temper. The language was unusual for him, and besides, that was no way for one officer to address another.

'I think it best if you join us down here, Mr Craddock,' shouted Harry.

'Who's that?'

'Mr Ludlow, sir. He insisted that I rouse you out.'

'Insisted! Damn his insistence.' But they could hear Craddock coming down the ladder. He joined the other two outside the open hatch. 'What is the meaning of this, sir?' he demanded, almost shouting.

Harry met fire, with fire, shouting even louder. 'Mr Craddock. What lies on the other side of this shaft?'

Harry's angry tone only stopped Craddock for a moment.

'Damn me, sir. Have I been roused out to tell you the anatomy of a seventy-four?'

'What should be there?'

'Should be? Is, sir. That is where the shot is stored.'

'Then kindly follow me, Mr Craddock.' Harry climbed through the hatch, leant across, and flung open the hatch opposite. The room was still fully lit, the drapes and velvet cushions the same. Harry climbed into the room looking about him feverishly. Craddock followed him in, his mouth wide open.

'Damn me,' he said. Harry felt like saying the same.

He was kicking the cushion, looking underneath, but there was nothing. The pictures, the instruments that had lined the walls, had gone.

'Damn me,' said Craddock again, turning slowly to take in what his eyes could not believe. He reached out to touch the drapes in an effort to reassure himself.

'The Captain,' he said, half to himself. 'I must fetch the Captain.'

'No,' said Harry. Craddock turned to look at him, mystified by his interruption. As he did so, Harry realized that Craddock had no choice. Even if this was all Carter's doing, by rights, Craddock could do nothing other than inform his superior.

'I'm sorry. You must, of course. The Captain.'

'Mr Mangold. My compliments to Captain Carter. Would he please oblige by joining me in the hold.'

'Ay, ay, sir.' Mangold would have seen a little of the room from the other side of the shaft. He must be afire with curiosity.

'And Mr Mangold.'

'Sir.'

'Resume your duties once you have done that, and get the hands in your division back to their proper stations.'

'Ay, ay, sir.' A very dispirited response this time.

Harry looked about him ruefully, trying to gauge just how much the loss of the pictures meant. With those, he would have had scant difficulty in proving the purpose of this room. Without them, there was an area of doubt, especially since the person doing the doubting would be Carter. In the same way, the bloodstains lost a lot of their meaning without the presence of the manacles, whips, and chains.

On the plus side, he had enough to expand the inquiry into Bentley's death. Harry would not let Carter hide this from his superiors. He must show it to them. A full report would be called for, as to how such valuable space, in one of His Majesty's ships, could be so used, without the apparent knowledge of those in authority. And that was the nub. It could not be. The actions and motives of everyone aboard would come under close scrutiny. But most of all the man with the ultimate power, and the final responsibility. The Captain. Evidence and witnesses be damned. Suspicion would shift from James, and the man who was truly guilty would stand trial for the murder of Bentley.

'Mr Ludlow. I must ask you how you came upon this?'

Craddock, for the first time since they entered the room, was really looking at Harry. His eye took in the dishevelled, dirty clothes, the bruises around his face, and the badly swollen left hand.

'I fear I have abused your trust, Mr Craddock. But I have done so in a good cause. I think an explanation can wait, don't you?'

'No, sir, I do not.' His weather-beaten face was even redder. Part effort, part embarrassment, part anger. 'Was this room in use?' Harry did not reply. 'Mr Ludlow, judging by your appearance, you have been in some kind of fight. That means this room was not empty when you discovered it. Would you be able to recognize the men who were in here?'

There was just a touch of irony in the question. Craddock had not been fooled by his performance that morning, when he refused to pick out the miscreants from the night before.

'All of them are members of the barge crew, bar one.'

Craddock blinked. 'Then I think the sooner that these men are taken up the better.'

'I would be interested to hear the Captain order that, Mr Craddock.'

The import of what Harry was saying, added to the way he said it, struck Craddock like a physical blow. He shook his head slowly.

'I cannot . . .'

Raised voices stopped him. Carter was coming through the hatch, cursing. The oaths died on his lips, as his head poked through the hatch. He looked around him with utter amazement.

Is he such a good actor, thought Harry, for it was a wonderful performance, enough to convince Craddock at any rate. He gave Harry a very old-fashioned look, before proceeding to report.

'Mr Ludlow came upon this, sir, then had Mr Mangold rouse me out. He has yet to reveal to me the circumstances, or to tell me what he was doing, wandering about the ship in the garb of a common seaman.'

Carter's eyes came round, first on to Craddock, then to Harry. Stepping through the hatch into the room, he pulled back the drapes to reveal the tin sheets hammered on to the planking. Carter tapped it with his knuckle, as if to convince himself. Then with a sudden burst of anger, he pulled hard on the curtain, tearing it from the wall. Carter held the loose cloth in his hands for a moment, his head down. Then he let it drop slowly to the ground.

'Mr Ludlow tells me that he will be able to name the men he found in this room.'

'Will he indeed,' said Carter without turning.

'Perfectly simple, Captain,' said Harry, using Carter's title voluntarily for the first time. 'This room was occupied by your barge crew. Marchant, Meehan, Porter, and the rest. They were in a state of some undress when I first came upon them.' Carter did not respond, but Craddock, who had been looking at his captain, swung sharply round to look at Harry.

'There were also drawings on the wall, drawings of an erotic nature. And whips, as well as other instruments. I would also bring your attention to the bloodstains, on both the drapes, and the cushions. If you look down here,' he pointed to the spot where the stain was greatest, 'you will observe, that at some time, there has been copious bleeding.'

'Instruments?' asked Carter quietly.

'The kind used to inflict pain. Whips. Manacles. They have all been removed, as have the drawings. In the time it took me to raise the alarm, someone came back here and removed them.'

Harry waited for Carter to refute his statement. But he just stood still. He sighed, raised his head to look at the ceiling and said, 'I dare say.'

'These pictures, Mr Ludlow. Erotic you say?' asked Craddock.

'Every ship has its sodomites, Mr Craddock. Only on board the *Magnanime* they seemed to enjoy a rare degree of latitude.' Carter still did not turn, yet it was obvious what Harry was implying.

'You will oblige me, Mr Ludlow, if you will return to your quarters,' he said. 'And if Mr Outhwaite is not drunk, I would suggest that you get him to tend that hand. Mr Craddock and I will, of course, wish to see you when you're back to rights again.'

Carter turned and looked at Harry. It was as though he was seeing him for the first time. There was a great sadness in his eyes, but little of the hate that had been there previously.

'That is my express wish, Mr Ludlow.'

Harry left, for if he had not done so, he was in no doubt that he would have suffered the indignity of being forcibly removed by a file of marines.

He climbed the ladder. Marines lined the walkway, with Turnbull pacing up and down just aft. He turned and looked expectantly at Harry as he emerged from the hold. Had Mangold told him what had been found? He thought that it was not his place to enlighten him, though the look on the young man's face was inviting him to do so. Harry merely nodded in reply, and headed back to the wardroom.

The whole ship was awake now, abuzz with rumour and conjecture. Harry walked across the gun-deck and the upper-deck, all eyes upon him. Silence reigned while he walked by, but as soon as he entered the wardroom, he heard the loud buzz of conversation begin. It was similar in the wardroom itself. Everyone was awake. They looked expectantly at him as he crossed to his cabin. The door was locked. He knocked sharply.

'Bugger off,' came Outhwaite's voice, loud through the door. 'We're getting drunk in here.' Potentially humorous, but no one behind Harry laughed, as he identified himself, and the door was slowly opened.

At least Outhwaite was not lying. The man could barely stand. He looked at Harry bleary-eyed and tried to speak. But no words came, and he just waved his hands in the general direction of the casements. Pender was up on his elbows, equally curious, but silent and sober.

'Later, Pender,' he said. His servant continued to look at him. Harry nodded, and the man lay down, satisfied that the night's work had been attended by some success.

'Mr Outhwaite. You will have to oblige me with some assist-ance, for I doubt if I can change my clothes on my own.'

'Delighted, sir,' slurred the surgeon, and staggered forward to help Harry off with his shirt. Harry remembered seeing a dumb show once, in which a drunken servant had to help dress his master. If the actors who had undertaken the roles had seen Outhwaite, they would have quit the stage immediately, on the grounds that their performance could be so bettered.

'Your hand,' Outhwaite tried to say. It came out as 'Y' han'.

'I will have one of your mates attend it, Mr Outhwaite. Now please try and hold my jacket still so that I may put it on.'

This was a relatively simple affair, taking only two minutes, which compared favourably with the time it had taken for Harry to get into his breeches.

'You stay here, Mr Outhwaite. I must call upon my brother.'

Harry left. Outhwaite, trying to bow, fell to his knees. Again the expectant looks, as he crossed the wardroom and the decks. He looked neither left nor right as he made his way to the parson's quarters. James was sitting on a stool drawing Crevitt, when he pulled back the screen.

'Well, brother,' said James, without looking up. 'What have you been about? The whole ship seems to be awake.'

'I think that you will find yourself released from Mr Crevitt's parole very shortly.'

James was a study in sang-froid, disdaining to respond in any obvious way. Not Crevitt. He stood suddenly, forgetting his height, and bumped his head painfully on the deck beams above. Another man would have cursed heartily. Crevitt merely pursed his lips.

'Please do not ask me to explain the events of tonight to you, Mr Crevitt. Suffice to say, that I have entirely discredited the testimony of the two supposed witnesses to Bentley's murder.'

Crevitt would find out soon enough the degree of his friend's troubles. Even without a charge of murder, Carter could not survive the fact that he had condoned sodomitical practices, let alone flagellation and the like. It was a strict breach of the Articles of War.

The parson rubbed his head silently.

'And I am also in a fair way to naming the culprit,' said Harry.

'It really is very difficult to draw someone who will not stay still, Harry. Please stop exciting my subject.'

With his good hand Harry pushed James off his stool.

'I have taken the precaution of confining my barge crew, until this matter is cleared up,' said Carter.

'Cleared up?' asked Harry. The way Carter said it dented his confidence. He and James were in the great cabin, seated on one side of the table. They faced Crevitt and Carter. Craddock stood off to the side, stony faced, for all the world like an umpire at a cricket match.

'It would be helpful if you could explain the events of last night, Mr Ludlow,' said Crevitt, leaning forward, his hands clasped together.

'I would have thought I might be called upon to describe, sir; but to explain?' Harry enjoyed that play with words. It was the kind of thing Carter indulged in.

'Explain, describe. What difference does it make?' snapped Carter, slapping the table. 'Just tell us how you came across this place.'

Harry started to speak, to say how and when he had observed people coming out of the pump shaft, but he checked himself just in time. Called upon to say when this had happened, he would incriminate himself in the death of Howarth.

'You and I have both been at sea long enough to know what goes on aboard ship. And since there is no one here to record what we are saying, and the meeting is therefore unofficial, I will speak freely.'

'Just as long as you speak truthfully, Ludlow.' Carter seemed to have recovered from last night. Both his composure, and his loathing, were intact. Harry ignored the insult. After all, he could afford to play with the man.

'On any ship, there are always things going on which are forbidden by the Articles of War. We all know this, and we all, officers and men, turn a blind eye, as long as a certain level of decency, and discretion, is observed.'

Carter sniffed loudly. 'Please do not allude to yourself as a King's officer, Ludlow, except in the past tense.'

Harry ignored this, maintaining the level voice. 'I have never subscribed to the theory of my brother's guilt. So I set out to find everything that was going on aboard this ship, in the hope of unmasking the true culprit.'

'In direct contravention of your word, Mr Craddock informs me.'

Even Crevitt was irritated by Carter's constant interruptions, but he could not speak. But the sideways glance and the slight roll of his eyes did.

'You go skulking about the ship, despite my warnings, and despite giving your word to Mr Craddock.' Carter looked angrily at James. 'It is to be hoped that the word "honour" is not going to crop up in this tale.'

'If you would rather I desist, Carter, and keep what I have to say for a Court of Inquiry, please say so.' Harry had the satisfaction of seeing Carter's mouth shut like a trap. The man was going to deny any involvement, that was obvious. But it would do him no good. Harry had enough to put him in the witness box, as a stepping stone to the dock.

'My intention was to bring what evidence I could to bear to establish my brother's innocence. By discreet questioning, I came to have grave doubts about the presence of your two witnesses at the scene of the crime. Indeed I had information that those very men were totally unreliable, and had been observed, that night, scurrying for their bunks at the time the alarm was raised.'

'So?' Carter made no attempt to disguise his impatience.

'So they were not where they should have been,' said Harry, with some asperity.

'That does not mean that they did not witness the crime. They came forward with their testimony the following day.'

'I will contend that they were on their way back to their bunks from the room at the bottom of the pump shaft. That is where they were last night, and given what they were about, I would wager they were in the same place the night Bentley was murdered.'

'Which still does not prove your brother's innocence.'

Harry sat forward. 'Someone raised the alarm, called the officer of the watch. It was not Meehan or Porter?'

Carter shook his head. The question seemed to mystify him. He looked at Crevitt, who shrugged. 'I don't know,' said Carter.

'Have they said that they raised the alarm?' asked Harry.

Carter shook his head again.

'Do you know who raised the alarm?' Another shake.

'But someone did, and I have satisfied myself that it was not one of them. And yet that someone, who called for assistance, has not identified himself. If that person, whom I am assured spoke like an officer, saw Bentley's body, and if my brother was guilty, then that person would surely come forward to witness seeing the murder take place. I'm sure that no one here would suggest that my brother himself raised the alarm, and then returned to the scene of the crime, and stood over the body, knife in hand.'

No one spoke. Carter seemed to have retreated into a private world. Crevitt stared fixedly ahead, his face blank. But it was obvious that he had drawn the right conclusion. Carter's face conveyed nothing. Turning, Harry saw that Craddock was looking confused, still trying to work out the implications of what he had heard.

'So we are left with the conclusion that Meehan and Porter are lying. That they did not witness the act of murder. It then follows, that the person who alerted the quarter-deck to the presence of Bentley's body is in fact the killer.'

'We,' said Carter, coming out of his reverie. 'You have drawn this conclusion, and drawn it on the grounds that Meehan and Porter are lying.'

'Surely after last night there can be no doubt.'

'Just because I have put my barge crew under restraint, does not mean that I have accused them of anything. If you want to know, they have denied your allegations to a man. And you claim that sodomitical practices were taking place in the hold, but there is not a shred of evidence to support that either.'

Denying it was one thing, but to accuse Harry of lying was too much. Harry longed to accuse Carter, but he checked himself. Why nail the man for one crime, when, with a little patience, he could get him for two.

'Again I draw your attention to the bloodstains in that room. We are not merely dealing in sodomy here, but in a much more terrible vice. I maintain that someone died in that room, or was so seriously hurt that it makes no odds. And I think that everyone aboard ship knows who that is likely to be.'

'Larkin,' said Craddock, surprised. Carter looked at him angrily.

'You may wish to say that is another matter. I say that the two deaths may well be connected. I cannot yet prove that, but you must agree, with the things that have been allowed to go on here, there is enough doubt to require the presence of your officers and crew at a trial, if my brother is to stand accused.'

Carter said nothing for a moment, then nodded.

'I would like to hear you say it out loud, Captain, so that others present can be in no doubt.'

'Yes.' The word was spat out.

'Thank you. And now I must ask for your permission to pursue the other matters I have just mentioned. Those, too, require a thorough investigation.'

'The other matters do not concern you.'

'They do, Carter, and they bear directly, I think, on the murder of Mr Bentley.' Harry smiled. 'You may wish to continue this conversation in private.'

Harry was excited. His moment had come. He was determined to accuse Carter to his face. He didn't want anyone else there, either interrupting him, or seeking to persuade him he was incorrect. And Carter would guess what was coming, because he must know that Harry had found the solution. Here was the explanation for Bentley's behaviour, plus the motive for his murder. He had discovered Carter's secret, and was thus in a position to break him, any time he chose. Carter could twist and turn, he could try all his tricks, but he would eventually stand trial for the murder of his first lieutenant.

'Private? With you? I would want no private conversation with you, sir. I would want everything said between us attested to. In fact, Mr Ludlow, you may now consider this meeting to be official. You have taken some advantage of my good offices to speculate wildly. Mr Crevitt, oblige me by taking notes of everything that is said.'

Harry was thrown for a moment. This was not what he had expected.

'Harry. Consider carefully before you speak.' James, who had sat silent throughout, spoke for the first time.

'James.' Harry turned to his brother, feeling slightly betrayed. 'Surely you do not believe him?' He pointed to Carter.

'Believe me? Damn you, sir, what do you mean!' he demanded.

'Are you going to pretend that you knew nothing of the presence of that room, nor the purposes it was put to?'

Carter looked as though he had been slapped. He sat back in his chair, for the moment unable to respond to Harry's accusation.

'Mr Ludlow. That remark is unwarranted,' said Crevitt, half standing.

'Unwarranted,' croaked Carter.

'Mr Crevitt. You are not a sailor. You have little experience of the sea. But if you ask any of the officers, they will tell you that a tin-lined room, stuck in the bowels of the ship, occupying space that should be preserved for the shot the ship needs to fight, could not be created, and maintained, without the knowledge of the captain of the ship.' Harry stood up, his finger pointing. 'The paintings that hung on the walls may have disappeared, and the men who used that room may have denied both being there and indulging themselves. But I saw it all with my own eyes. If a captain allows that sort of practice to proceed, without interference, it can only be for one reason.'

Crevitt was now fully out of his chair, scattering papers on the floor, his face suffused with anger.

'How dare you!' he yelled in a voice that could be heard at the crosstrees. 'How dare you, sir, accuse my friend so.'

'Damn you, Ludlow,' said Carter, in a quiet, hurt voice. Such an accusation, even half-believed, at a Court of Inquiry, and he was finished in the service.

'Harry!' said James, touching his brother's arm.

His brother could not respond. He was looking at the cabin floor, at the papers which had dropped off the desk. There was still a mark in the planking where he had stuck his knife. And that clearly did not make sense. The events of the past days raced through his mind. Yes, Carter hated him, and would take whatever chance he got, fair or foul, to damage him. But he

255

had become the same. Getting even with this man sitting opposite him had become an obsession. He had become just like his adversary. Yet he had given the man ample warning. If Carter had killed Bentley, he would have understood immediately why Harry stuck his knife in the deck. He would have known, in that instant, the danger that he was in. Harry's life would not have been worth a bent farthing. A man who had contrived to kill Bentley, who knew of, and had used, that room, and with the barge crew at his beck and call, and such a secret as the death of Larkin to protect, would have rid himself of both Ludlow brothers in a trice.

'Mr Ludlow,' said Craddock, stepping forward, his bulk coming between Harry and the table. 'If I may speak. You are quite right that it would take a degree of authority to create that room. But if I may venture to suggest another possibility. . . .'

'Bentley,' said Harry, not looking at anyone.

'Harry. I think an apology is in order.' James' quiet request merely produced a nod. He stood up and walked out of the cabin. James followed him. No one sought to restrain him.

'Well, I made a proper ass of myself there, brother.'

'It does however beg the question. If I didn't kill Bentley, and Carter didn't kill Bentley, then who did? What I am saying, Harry, is that we are really no further forward.'

'Bentley must have been of that persuasion himself.'

'One would think so, if he was indeed responsible. But from what you say, it was the flagellation more than anything else that so excited him. I can hardly see him going to all the trouble of providing such a facility, if he was not going to indulge.'

'It is incredible. How did they manage to keep it so secret? Pender swears that the rest of the crew didn't know.'

'That aspect of it is academic to me. I shan't feel entirely safe until we have found the real culprit.'

'One of the barge crew I'll bet. But we would have the devil of a job to prove it. I can't even prove that they were in that room when I found it. And it may well be someone else. You are right, James. We are back where we started.'

'Come in,' Harry said, in response to a knock on the door.

Craddock did just that, his hat under his arm. He had obviously just come from the great cabin.

'Mr Ludlow.'

'Please, Mr Craddock. If you have come to berate me, then I am here to tell you *mea culpa*. I confess to being more than a touch myopic.'

'Hardly your fault, sir. Only being part of the ship's company, part of the wardroom, I had hold of certain facts that you didn't.'

'Such as?'

'Like the fact that Captain Carter did not choose the crew for his barge.' Harry did not let on that he had been told. 'He left that to Mr Bentley, as he did most things. I include the stowing of the hold when we took on stores. Mr Bentley was always sober for that, come to think of it, and he took pains to supervise it personally. Not that we need take on much powder and shot. He was dead against what he called "the useless expenditure of powder and shot", never mind the mess it made of the decks. Add all that up, and it is plain to see who's at the bottom of it. As I say, you weren't to know.'

'It would have been wiser to find out before speaking.'

'I can't tell you enough of how Mr Bentley ran the ship. At first with the Captain's blessing, seeing how close they were. I think Mr Carter even wrote to their lordships recommending him for promotion.'

'Anything to get rid of him, I shouldn't wonder.'

'No, sir. This goes back always, to when they were like two peas in a pod. It ain't common for captains and premiers to see eye to eye, but they did, in all manner of things.'

'But it didn't last.' Harry had a vision of his own dealings with Carter.

'They had a row one day over the floggin'. After that boy died, the crew were very sullen and the punishments increased. But that had passed by, and the Captain hinted, not said mind, just hinted, that perhaps Mr Bentley was a mite too keen on it. Well, Mr Bentley went white. I had the watch. He reminded the Captain in the stiffest way, of the consequences of lax discipline, and in front of everyone.' Craddock sounded and looked suitably shocked at this breach of manners.

'No superior could stand for that, and Captain Carter, quite calmly, alluded to the quantity of drink he was used to consumin', clouding his otherwise sound judgement. I must say that under the circumstances it was a mild rebuke.'

'But things deteriorated from then on?' There was more than a touch of irony in the question.

'Why yes, sir,' said Craddock, amazed. 'You are quick, Mr Ludlow.'

'Let us say that some of my experience pre-dates yours.' He did not add that he had all this from Outhwaite.

'Things went on like that for a bit, but it couldn't last.' Craddock had the air of a man who'd found betrayed everything in which he believed. 'Well, there was an almighty row, behind closed doors, but you could hear it through the skylight. They became cold to each other, quite like normal in fact, except that Bentley still laid on the candidates for the cat. The Captain commuted as many of them as he dared, but he didn't have a great deal of leeway, if the charge was pressed by a first lieutenant. It was a situation that could not go on, an' we all waited for the Captain to formally rebuke the premier. He had words one day, but not with Mr Bentley. It was his nephew who got the blast. The lad is not beyond a touch of insolence with his uncle, and he had been drinking. The Captain was angry with him for seeming to side with Bentley against his own flesh and blood. Mr Turnbull refused to plead for one of his men, which made it impossible for the Captain to let him off. I've often wondered if Mr Turnbull was just trying to bring matters to a head. The Captain offered again, with some choice words about the responsibilities an officer had to both his commission and his family. Mr Turnbull took the hint and begged his man off. Bentley was incensed at this. And right there in front of the whole crew, he requested an interview. God only knows what they said to each other, for there was no yelling this time. After that things went to the dogs.'

'Why didn't Carter relieve him?'

'Why, I guess that it would look mighty odd to go relieving a man you had so recently recommended to their lordships as deserving promotion.'

A point, thought Harry, but barely enough of one.

'The atmosphere in the ward-room was never very pleasant, but it got worse as the Captain took to checking him more and more, and his replies became very intemperate.'

'He didn't seem in any position to check him recently,' said James.

'That's right,' said Craddock, turning to address James. 'Some of us thought that he had just given up the ghost. Bentley drank even more, and upped the punishment as well. Things went from bad to worse for the whole ship, officers and men. I have to say that Mr Bentley was not much loved.'

'Nor sorely missed,' said Harry.

Craddock didn't reply to that, probably considering it too disloyal.

'Anyway, I wanted you to know some of these things, because the Captain is in enough of a stew as it is, with that kind of accusation floating about.'

'Mr Craddock. Did you know that Bentley was a sodomite?'

'Can't say that I did, sir. But I've been a sailor long enough not to pay it much heed. It happens, and where's the harm I say, as long as it's held in check. There are worse things that one man can do to another.'

'You show a commendable understanding of your fellow men, Craddock,' said James.

'Maybe. Or maybe I'm just accustomed. I find the way he flogged more disturbing. It's my impression he loved it.'

Harry thought of the blood in that room.

'Can I ask you, Mr Craddock, who do you think killed Mr Bentley?' asked James.

Craddock looked at him. James added quickly, 'Always assuming you think I am innocent.'

The older man's face took on a determined look. 'If I may speak freely, I must say I don't rightly know. But I will say this. There has been the odd time, when the man was full of drink, and a bit free with his insults, that I could have skewered him myself.'

Harry threw up his hands in despair. 'Well, if you feel the need to kill him, that means there is no one on the ship we can leave unquestioned. Mr Craddock, I am going to have to talk

259

to all the officers. It is the only way to get to the bottom of this.'

Another knock at the door. Harry opened it. Crevitt stood there with James' scratch pad under his arm.

'I brought you these, Mr Ludlow,' he said to James. All present knew that was an excuse. He turned to Harry, his gaunt face lined with worry. 'And I wonder if I might have a word with you.'

'I'll be on my way.'

'No,' said Crevitt quickly. 'Stay, Mr Craddock. I would want someone independent to hear what I have to say.' The inference was plain. James, taking the sketch pad, raised his eyebrows, and looked at Harry.

Harry smiled. 'I have already narrowly avoided a keel-hauling from Mr Craddock, Parson. I rather suspect that you will want me to go down on my knees.'

'You may see this as an occasion for jocularity, sir, but I do not. My friend stands in grave danger of severe censure by his superiors. Had this been discovered in the normal run of events, it could have been hushed up. Mr Bentley's murder makes that impossible.'

'Then the man will have served some purpose.'

'Your continued animosity is unbecoming, sir.'

'Is it, indeed,' snapped Harry in reply. 'Well let me tell you something, since you are such a nautical ignoramus, Mr Crevitt. Your friend is a weak commander. He is inclined to hand over executive authority to an officer just because he likes him. In Mr Bentley's case, he seemed competent in everything else but his manner of drinking, so this ship still floats.'

'Captain Carter is a brave and competent officer, sir.' Crevitt was blazingly angry, fighting not to raise his voice.

'Gentlemen,' said Craddock, both hands raised.

'Brave, oh yes, he is brave. He doesn't care how many men he kills with his bravery! The other day we fought two French ships yard-arm to yard-arm. You spent half a day burying the results.'

'A most commendable affair.'

'Commendable!' Harry laughed. 'Stick to prayers, Parson. A

junior midshipman could have done better than your much-vaunted friend. Those two Frenchmen were not long out of port. This ship has been in commission for three years. Carter chooses to fight them exactly on their terms, and it was only by luck, and the state of the weather, that we survived the engagement.'

Crevitt tried to recover his composure. 'I dare say the great Harry Ludlow would have done better.'

'You are a fool, Crevitt, as blinded by your friendship, as I was by my hate. We could have out-sailed those two. Nearly every man on this ship can hand, reef, and steer. We could have run rings round them. Instead, with that pigheadedness for which your friend is famous, we came to a halt in between them, and let them practically pound us to pieces.'

James intervened. 'Harry. You are shouting at the wrong person.'

'You're right,' said Harry, suddenly deflated. 'Please do not come defending him to me, Mr Crevitt. The man is a dangerous fool.'

'Do you intend to repeat the allegations you so nearly made in his cabin?'

'No, Mr Crevitt. But I would ask you to examine your conscience, and when you are telling people how good a commander Captain Carter is, ask yourself how many men in charge of a ship would have let such a thing happen. Then go to any officer, and explain truthfully what happened with the *Verite* and the *Medusa*. Not the officers on this ship, because they see loyalty to their captain, and their careers, to be above anything else.'

'Harry.' Again James failed to stop his brother, as did the blush on Craddock's face.

'Perhaps you will hear the truth from other lips. That your hero behaved like the worst kind of scrub. And you will observe, that should you mention that occasion, every officer aboard this ship will blush, and rightly so.'

'I think that we have done all we came for Mr Crevitt.' It was obvious that Craddock felt sorry for the parson, by the way he took his arm and led him out. All the officers were standing in the wardroom facing Harry's cabin. He had not held his voice

261

in check, and it had carried through the door. They were stony faced, for he had finally said to them what he had wanted to say for days.

'Well damn me, Harry,' said James in a languid voice, 'just when I need their good offices, you have to go and tell them the truth.' Somehow, what James said was a bigger slap in the face than the words Harry had used. His air was so insulting.

Harry shut the door.

XVI

'Perhaps we are not entirely back where we started,' said Harry. 'I can't think the testimony of the two witnesses will stand up in court. And the whole nature of the prosecution will be thrown into doubt by the things that have been allowed to go on aboard the *Magnanime*.'

'Intensive examination of the barge crew might produce a result.' James had picked up the folder that Crevitt had delivered.

'Not just them, James. Everyone. Carter can't interfere now. There are the officers, and the midshipmen, in fact, the entire crew.'

'You realize that we are probably not terribly popular.'

'Damn popularity. What I want is the truth. The truth about that boy, and the name of whoever killed Bentley. If I have to offend every officer in the Navy, I don't give a fig. I'm aware that you think me a ruffian, James, but that is the way I am and I will not change . . .'

James sat silently touching up his drawings. His silence seemed a form of reproach, and Harry felt it keenly.

'You think I went too far?' he asked.

'Perhaps. In one breath you say to Craddock that the only way to clear this matter up is to question all the officers. Then you go and tell them all that they are little better than scoundrels. In truth, brother, I sometimes wonder if you should be let out alone.' James' smile took the sting out of the remark.

'Perhaps it needed to be said, to clear the air.'

'I cannot see that venting your spleen at this juncture will materially help our cause, putting aside the fact that I am still under suspicion of murder.'

'Materially? Have no fear in that respect,' Harry said gaily. 'Why, we will probably even be compensated for the *Medusa* now.'

'I can't see what has changed so drastically to make you say that.'

'Can't you? It doesn't occur to you that Carter is probably finished?'

James smiled. 'You always were of a sanguine nature, Harry.'

'It has got me out of many a scrape.'

'Cruel of me I know, but I feel the need to remind you that it got you into this one.' Again the disarming smile.

Harry paced up and down the cabin. 'At the same time it rather depresses me,' he said.

'What does?' James still flicked at his drawing.

'The way that everyone on this ship will now seek to assure us of their support, should we call for an inquiry into Carter's conduct.'

That made him look up from his pad. 'Are they such a pusillanimous crew?'

'I told you before, did I not? Lord, it was only a couple of days ago, yet it seems an age away. They care about their careers. A few days ago Carter was a successful commander. He had taken a prize, and if the circumstances were questionable, it at least looked good in a dispatch.'

'And all that is altered?'

'Come, James, even you must see that. You have no idea how the Admiralty frowns upon sodomy, though I should think half the Board has been guilty of indulgence at some time in their careers. Crevitt was correct. Without Bentley's murder it would have been hushed up, and all the officers would have entered into the conspiracy. Not now, and all those men out there, in the wardroom, are thinking that it might not be a bad idea to distance themselves from a captain who is so clearly headed for the professional rocks.'

James frowned. 'I find it hard to believe that Craddock will behave like that.'

'He has no choice. For if he does not, he could well sink with Carter. He will be called upon to tell the truth, and in his case, I think that is all he will do. But others will gild the truth, to show themselves in a better light. And it will only take one of them to hint that the action with the *Verite* was open to misinterpretation, for them all to be clamouring to tell the court how they tried to dissuade him from letting us down.'

Harry looked at his brother, who had gone back to his sketching. For some reason it irritated him.

'James, will you stop fiddling with those drawings!'

'I am fiddling with them at your request,' said James, surprised. He put aside the colour he was using and turned the drawing towards Harry. It showed Bentley arched backwards, having just been stabbed. Blood was spurting out of his chest. His assailant, dressed like Bentley, in an officer's coat, was correct in every detail, except there was no face. James had drawn the surrounding detail from memory.

'What about the other one?' asked Harry.

'I finished that last night,' said James, producing another drawing from his folder. Harry took it, spreading his arms wide to look at it. The first thing he noticed was himself, with the bandage still around his head, both hands gripping the doorframe. Was his expression at the time really so shocked?

'Is that the look I had on my face?' he queried.

'To the life,' replied James, with an assurance that defied discussion.

'You've got Carter well. He almost looks pleased.'

'With a chap like Bentley, I'm not surprised. I must say I shared your feelings about him to start with.'

'What made you doubt it?'

'I don't know. It just seemed so unlikely. Would a man who had faced you over a barrel stoop to such a thing? Hard to explain. It became clearer as I drew him. His face had a very singular expression, but not that of a murderer, more of a man who has just been acquitted. When did you first suspect him?'

'I can't be sure. I suppose I always wanted it to be him. So neat a revenge. He had everything in his control, a captain usually does. But mainly, it was the wig powder. Bentley had a great streak of it on his coat. And I found some on the deck before the hands had a chance to swab it clean. I taxed Craddock about it. He wasn't much help, not knowing who had their wigs on, and who didn't. That is one of my key questions we have to put to them. But Carter, being bald, was never without his. It looked as though Bentley had knocked the wig off in the struggle.'

James was incredulous, his eyebrows arched in surprise. 'You based your whole case against him on that?'

'The knife being stuck in the deck started me off. But yes, I began my case against him on that,' said Harry, defensively.

'Tenuous, Harry. Very tenuous.'

'There wasn't much else, short of an actual witness.' Harry's voice took on a querulous note. 'Why do you think I went scurrying about the ship? If I'd had any proof to go on, I wouldn't have bothered. What we needed was a motive.'

'With Bentley, his mere existence seemed to be motive enough.'

'Think about it, James. It was quite an elaborate affair. I don't say the whole thing was worked out to the last detail, but my knife was stolen in advance. Stolen to be used on Bentley, to be left to incriminate me. Why me? Who hated me enough?' Harry opened his hands to plead. 'The answer is obvious.'

'But wrong?'

'I admit to an obsession. Thinking calmly, Carter would want to kill me himself, rather than leave it to a hangman.'

'So you are back where you started, and so am I.'

'Not entirely, James. I believe I've narrowed it down to two possibilities. One of the ship's officers, aided by the barge crew . . .'

'And the other?'

'One of the midshipmen. Everyone says how popular that boy was. Was he liked by some of the senior mids? I remember my days in the midshipmen's berth. What a hotbed of passion that can be. I particularly want to talk to Denbigh.'

'Why him?'

'I was talking to Prentice one day. I mentioned Larkin. The boy was about to say something when Denbigh interrupted and sent him about his duties. And he has the most unnerving way of staring at me, as though he is trying to read my mind. And remember that the mids wear wigs on dress occasions. They are too junior to plead fashion. That room, and what happened there, opens up a whole host of possible motives.'

Harry noticed that his brother was looking glum. 'I know the case against you still stands. But with all this evidence to present, it gives us a chance.'

Laying the drawing on the desk, Harry pointed to the wig on Carter's head. 'What we need in this drawing is another one of these.'

'I certainly don't recall any other people wearing wigs.'

'Damn.' Harry was staring hard at the picture.

'Sorry,' said James, 'to have upset your pet theory.'

'Shhh! Let me think.' Harry's mind was off racing through the possibilities. He started pacing the cabin.

'Am I to be included . . .' Harry held up his hand, silencing his brother. He strode up and down, his mind running over the events of the last few days. A vision of his fight in the pump shaft came into his mind. The last one out. The man in command. The blood he thought he had seen. That same person had probably cleared the room of the incriminating evidence. And who had Craddock told off for being missing, once the alarm had been raised? Finally he stopped and looked at his brother.

'The other drawing, the one showing Bentley's death.'

'Yes.' James picked it up.

'I want you to do me another one of those. But with some important differences. And then there is another one I will need.'

'Am I to be told anything?' asked James querulously.

'Why yes, brother. I was wrong about the wig powder.'

'Is that all?'

Harry laughed, in a way that he had not done since they had first sighted the *Verite*. He outlined his requirements to James. He then went to talk to Craddock.

*

267

'You say that Meehan and Porter maintain that they are telling the truth. I say that they are lying, both about being witnesses, and being in that room. All I am asking is the right to examine them. Time is pressing.'

The lookout had sighted the Rock of Gibraltar while Harry was waiting to see Carter. They had been getting closer to the land for some while. The southern coast of Spain was clearly visible to the naked eye.

'And I have told you that it is not your place to do so.'

'Captain Carter. I have but one aim, and that is to clear my brother's name, to remove any possibility that he can be tried for a murder he did not commit. If you let me question these men, I will undertake to stay silent on the uses to which that room was put.'

'The uses that you allege, Ludlow.'

'A moment, Oliver,' said Crevitt. 'Think about what Mr Ludlow is saying.' Crevitt was quicker than Carter. Without that allegation, the importance of the tin-lined room was quite diminished. Once made, even if they were refuted, those allegations would never go away. It said a great deal about Carter's state that Crevitt was speaking. The parson would never have dared to interrupt him before.

'And I will not seek to persuade them to tell me their whereabouts on that night. I only want them to withdraw their testimony against James.'

'I could be present,' said Crevitt.

'No,' snapped Harry too quickly. Carter looked suspicious. Harry added quickly, 'But Mr Craddock can be.'

Crevitt leaned over his friend. 'He is an honest fellow, Oliver. I say it can do no harm.'

Carter said nothing. Crevitt took his silence for acquiescence. He straightened up and walked over to Harry.

'I cannot be sure that you are a Christian, Mr Ludlow, but I shall ask you to swear on this anyway.' He held out his Bible.

'Willingly,' said Harry, putting his hand on the book. 'I will ask only questions that pertain to the murder of Mr Bentley.'

'Do you wish the use of this cabin?' asked Crevitt. Carter

stiffened. The parson was taking liberties. But Crevitt ignored him. Harry reflected that if Carter lost his post, Crevitt too would become unemployed.

'No. I will use mine. All I ask is that you do not forewarn them. Tell no one else what I am about. I would want them brought to me without knowing their destination. If you will be so good to allow me Mr Prentice to assist.'

Silence. Carter thinking, and Crevitt willing him to concede the point. After all, it was the parson's future as well.

'Carry on, Ludlow,' said Carter, by way of dismissal. But there was an air of resignation in his voice, as though he was giving up something quite important.

'Come in.' The little cabin was crowded. Harry, James, Pender, and Craddock, and now these two, small men with trim bodies, not the sort normally picked for a barge crew. Men who would be a liability in a press gang. They hesitated, but Prentice gently pushed them into the cabin. Behind them Harry could see the wardroom was crowded. Everyone who had a right to be there, was in attendance. Crevitt gave him a curious glance. Harry smiled at him, displaying a confidence that he did not entirely feel.

'Thank you, Mr Prentice.' The two sailors looked round at the closing door with alarm.

'Sit down,' said Harry, indicating his sea-chest. 'You are here because the Captain has given me permission to question you. We have met before, but we will avoid that subject, and concentrate on the murder of Mr Bentley. You claim to have witnessed that murder.'

'That's right,' said Meehan without a pause.

'Where were you standing?'

There was silence for a moment. They looked at each other, uncertain what to say. 'Can't rightly say. We was sort of passin' through,' said the other one, Porter. The man had a strange nasal twang, making what he said hard to comprehend. He grinned at Meehan, to indicate the cleverness of his answer.

'And you saw what?'

'We saw your brother,' Meehan pointed at James dramatically, 'knife the premier.'

'Horrible it was.' Porter rolled his eyes. He had not only relaxed, but he seemed in a fair way to enjoying himself.

'And what did you do then?'

'Then?'

'After you saw what happened. What did you do?'

They were both silent.

'Did you raise the alarm, call for help? What did you do?'

'Scarpered,' said Porter quickly.

'Back to your berths?'

They both nodded. Harry sat on his cot. Everyone just stared at the two of them. They began to fidget.

'James,' said Harry, standing up. The two men looking up at him seemed to shrink visibly. James edged past and opened the door to the wardroom. He walked across to the large central table where he had left his drawing materials, the large folder and pens. The room was still full, all the officers there, excepting those on watch, all apparently engaged in some important task, all eager to see or hear what they could. Only Crevitt did not disguise his interest. Meehan and Porter were in plain view, with Harry leaning forward questioningly. James picked up his folder, and started back towards the cabin. He nodded to Harry.

'Now you are sure that's the truth,' said Harry plainly, so that everyone could hear. James came in, and just as he shut the door, Harry said loudly. 'Good. We want no more lies.' The listeners were then excluded as the door shut.

'Right,' said Harry. 'I want you to describe what you saw to my brother. He is an artist, and he will draw what you tell him to.'

Meehan looked at Porter with a worried expression. They had given their statements. No one had yet mentioned that they might have to elaborate them. This was unrehearsed. Nor did it seem to occur to them that if their story was true, the last person who needed a description was James.

'Come along, men,' said Craddock. 'Speak plain. You have nothing to fear, if you are telling the truth.'

They mumbled out their story, less confident under

Craddock's disbelieving stare, picking up from each other, cutting out each other's words, sometimes flatly contradicting what they should be saying. And it was impossible to say where they had stood, without saying how they got there. This led to even more confusion. James sketched away as they spoke. Harry kept asking them questions, making them go back over parts of their tale, telling them to take their time. He did not want them to go too fast. They looked relieved at this, but the effect was soon spoiled, when Harry asked them to go over their story again.

Craddock was looking deeply dissatisfied. But if he knew that these men were unconvincing, he did not say so, contenting himself with the kind of facial expressions which speak volumes.

'A third time, gentlemen, please?' said Harry.

'Leave off, your honour,' squealed Meehan.

'Do as you're told,' said Craddock coldly.

They started again. Repetition was not making things easier. Events were becoming increasingly confused. In trying to embellish their tale, to maintain interest, they spoiled it further. James drew quietly. Craddock tried to crane his neck to see, but a sharp glance from the artist made him step back. At one point Pender laughed, the tale was becoming so outrageous. He got a similar look from Harry.

'Fine,' said Harry, when they stumbled to the end of their third try. He knew that called upon to repeat what they had said in a court, they would rehearse their story, and it would sound much better than this. But Craddock would be called, and he would tell the court of the pathetic performance these two liars had managed originally.

'Finished, James?'

'Oh, yes. Quite finished.' James folded the drawing into his case and pulled out the one he had done before. It was the same in every detail except that the figure stabbing Bentley was wearing a buff coat. James had drawn his own features in.

'Then let me see it,' said Harry. James walked forward with the drawing. Harry opened the door, walked out, and called to young Prentice, leaving it open behind him.

'Mr Prentice, please be so kind as to ask the Captain to spare us a moment. If he says that he is busy, tell him it's a matter that will concern him greatly. We must see him before we dock.'

'Ay, ay, Mr Ludlow.'

Harry looked around the wardroom. Everyone again avoided his eye, except Crevitt. He walked back into his cabin leaving the door ajar. Meehan and Porter were leaning over the picture that James had given them.

'You are quite sure about this, both of you,' said Harry. Meehan and Porter nodded vehemently.

'These are serious allegations. You do understand that?'

'Ay,' they said in unison. If Harry had ordered it, they could not have performed better. They both turned to the open door and smiled. If it was meant to reassure anyone, it had the opposite effect. Almost all the officers recoiled.

'Now take a look at this and tell me what you think.' Harry showed them the drawing of themselves that James had done while they had been speaking. Their faces lit up in amazement.

'A good likeness, wouldn't you say.'

'Amazing,' said Porter. 'Don't you think, Ben?'

Harry, pretending to realize that the door was open, shut it quickly. He saw all the wardroom occupants, who had been intent on the exchange, snap their heads away. He breathed a deep sigh. So far so good. They stood around in silence, waiting. A loud knock at the door.

'Mr Ludlow, sir,' said Prentice as Harry opened it a fraction. 'The Captain says he is very busy.'

'Tell him he must examine these men himself about Mr Bentley's murder, Prentice. And say that we have uncovered another crime as well.' This was whispered, but loud enough for anyone really listening to hear. He shut the door on a whole host of straining ears.

'Well, Mr Craddock. What do you think of this pair?'

'They are as much use at telling lies as they are rowing a boat, and that's no good at all.' Meehan and Porter flinched, as Craddock moved forward and looked down on them.

'Could I ask you to keep them here, while my brother and I go and see the Captain. I did say that I would inform him of the results of my interrogation.'

'Why, yes,' said Craddock, surprised by the request. Meehan

and Porter brightened considerably, sensing their ordeal was over. Craddock stood back. 'But surely a couple of marines . . .' He stopped when he saw the look in Harry's eye. 'As you wish, Mr Ludlow.'

'All set, Pender?'

'Ay, ay, sir.'

Come one, Prentice, said Harry to himself. He was keyed up like a watch-spring. A full minute passed. Too much time, and the tension he had so carefully built up would begin to slip. A knock at the door. Prentice. He spoke loudly through the wood.

'Captain Carter will see you right away, sir. This very minute.'

That boy has talent, thought Harry. The last sentence wasn't in the script, but it sounded just like Carter.

Harry opened the door. James picked up his folder. Craddock looked questioningly at him, noticing that James had left the drawings he had shown the two seamen. James smiled, and Craddock shrugged. Harry walked out into the ward-room, followed by his brother. They made their way down the room. The mass of the occupants edged forward, Crevitt in the forefront. As they came to the end of the table, by the door, James dropped his folder. Two drawings spilled out on to the floor. In a rush, everyone craned forward to look at them.

The figures of Bentley and his murderer were plain. Bentley hadn't changed from the drawing that James had done before. But the other figure had. He was young, and bareheaded. Bentley was spewing blood from his chest, but the bright red of the blood was made plain by the even brighter red coat of the murderer.

The people looking at the picture gasped. Turnbull, the Marine lieutenant, was frozen to his chair. James bent down, and lifted the picture, revealing to them all, the one underneath. Turnbull tried to follow the first picture, but with a horrified look on his face, he was drawn to the second. The same two people in the drawing, Bentley and Turnbull, and between them a small blood-stained sack. It obviously contained a body, the body of a ship's boy, which they were heaving over the side.

Pender slipped up beside Harry, and passed a pistol into his open hand.

'You of all people should never have underestimated the power of fear, Mr Turnbull,' he said quietly. 'A man of Bentley's persuasion, quite prepared to challenge the Captain, would not have forgone the pleasure of baiting you. How many times did he threaten to expose you? A drunk, becoming more and more unstable. How convenient my presence must have seemed. A chance to evade the gallows, and lay to rest a family quarrel. You could count on your uncle to look no further than me. Do you really think it would have all ended with Bentley's death? No. There are too many people involved. And by their silence they became as guilty as you. There are some games Meehan and Porter were happy to engage in, but hanging isn't one of them.'

Everyone was looking at Turnbull. He looked past Harry at Meehan and Porter. Harry turned as well. Again they smiled, to reassure Turnbull. But it read like smug betrayal.

'Rats,' screamed Turnbull, trying to get past Harry. 'I told you to keep your mouths shut!'

'Oliver!' said a shocked Crevitt, putting his hand out.

Harry raised the pistol that Pender had given him. Was it just the speed at which the man moved, or was Harry relaxing because his bluff, a very long shot indeed, had worked? Whatever, Turnbull knocked the pistol out of his hand. James made a grab, trying to restrain him, but with the strength of fear, the marine pushed him aside. He was out of the door before anyone could stop him, grabbing the musket out of the sentry's hand. The man was too shocked to stop him. Harry followed him out of the wardroom at a rush, the rest tumbling along behind.

Turnbull was running for the companionway that led to the quarter-deck. He turned and taking a swift aim, fired the musket. The ball caught Crevitt, who was following behind Harry, in the shoulder, and spun him round. Turnbull dropped the musket and set off up the stairs. Outside his uncle's cabin, another sentry, another musket. Harry felt his pistol pressed into his hand again. Pender was being more level-headed than anyone.

'Keep back,' said Harry, as Craddock joined the throng on the upper deck. 'He's got nowhere to run. No point in getting killed.'

Harry walked to the companionway, and got up on to the quarter-deck. Turnbull stood facing his uncle. Neither of them spoke, but the pain was obvious on Carter's face. Turnbull looked around for some means of escape. Finally his uncle spoke.

'I tried, God knows I tried, Oliver.'

Turnbull pulled a sword out of the rack by the cabin door. The sentry raised his gun, then dropped it again, not sure what to do.

'It's no use, boy. You should have left Bentley to me. I would have dealt with him in time.'

'You!' spat Turnbull. 'I would have waited till eternity for you.'

Carter looked over his nephew's shoulder to where Harry stood, pistol in hand. Harry raised the gun.

'No, Ludlow.' This was said quietly. 'I will deal with this. It is my responsibility, my shame.' He looked back to his nephew, and held out his hand. 'The sword?'

'I'll not hang, Uncle,' sobbed Turnbull.

'You knew,' said Harry. 'All along you knew.'

'No, Ludlow. I did not know.' The emphasis was heavy on the last word. 'The sword?' he said, his hand still out.

Turnbull swung round and went for Harry.

'I can do you one good turn before I go!' he shouted. Harry ducked aside, raising the pistol again. He heard the scrape of metal as another sword was pulled from the rack.

'Hold!' shouted Carter, rushing forward, sword in his hand. Turnbull spun round and almost as a reflex, he struck out at Carter. The thrust was parried.

'Oliver!' It was half a shout, half a plea.

Turnbull pulled the sword down and tried to stab at his uncle's groin. The boy's face was a mask of terror. Swiftly Carter cut to the side and the thrust was deflected. Carter swung his arm and the sword came swinging round, aimed at his nephew's head. This time it was the youngster's turn to quickly parry the cut.

'Carter!' shouted Harry, but the man was listening to no one. His entire concentration was taken up on fighting his nephew. Turnbull backed on to the gangway, cutting right and left to keep the older man's thrusts at bay.

'Damn you,' said Carter. 'Damn you!' Did the boy realize how deadly serious his uncle had become?

The quarter-deck was full of officers now, watching the fight. Turnbull had the fury of a desperate man to aid him, but Carter had experience. He drove his nephew back. A quick cut, a feint to the left, and he was inside the boy's guard. Almost with ease he put one foot behind his nephew's leg and tripped him up. Turnbull fell backwards. Carter stepped in and put his sword on the boy's throat.

'Damn you, Oliver,' he said. He could have been talking to himself. Carter stood there as if trying to decide whether to finish his nephew off. He shook his head, and pulled his sword away. As he did so, Turnbull thrust upwards and ran his uncle through. Carter stood for a moment, no expression, no cry, then he fell backwards, the sword coming out as he did so. Turnbull, a wild look in his eye, jumped up and made to stab his uncle again. Harry's bullet, from less than six feet away, took him between the eyes, and he dropped like a stone.

Carter fell back on the deck as everyone rushed to his side.

'Get back, damn you!' shouted Outhwaite, pushing his way through the crowd. He knelt beside Carter and lifted him up, cradling his head on his knee. Carter's wig had fallen off. Blood stained the front of his white waistcoat. He grimaced in pain, as Outhwaite started to undo the buttons to examine the wound. A trickle of blood oozed out of his mouth. In the background Crevitt was praying, his arms limp, and his head bowed.

'Port Admiral signalling, sir,' came a voice from the masthead.

Faintly they heard the sound of the signal gun. The midshipman on watch tore his eyes away from the scene, and leafed through the signal book till he came to the right flags.

'Captain report to Flag, sir.'

'Acknowledge, Mr Craddock,' said Carter. A great gush of blood came out of his mouth, and covered the deck as he died.

Harry and James were sitting opposite Craddock in the great cabin. Carter's body was in the coach, and his nephew's in his sleeping cabin. Crevitt, his arm in a sling, was poring over two chests, one Bentley's, and the other Carter's, going through various papers.

'You provided the final piece of evidence,' Harry told Craddock.

'Then I did so unknowingly.'

'I asked you which officer you had reprimanded for being late when you came down to the hold. He had been clearing out the evidence in that room. That is why he was not in his cabin, and you had to rouse out the marines yourself.'

'But you suspected him before that,' said Craddock. He fiddled with the papers on the table. He was ill at ease in Carter's chair.

'Yes. But I had been wrong once.'

'Really, it was my drawing that pointed to Turnbull,' said James. 'Also quite unknowingly.'

'I found wig powder near the scene of the murder. All my subsequent thoughts were coloured by that, and when I saw the great white mark on Bentley's coat, which was damp, I assumed that to be wig powder as well. The late Captain being the only one who habitually wore a wig, that led me to suspect him.'

Crevitt raised his head and looked at the bulkhead through which lay Carter's body, as if by doing so he would include personal spite in Harry's motives.

'So now you're saying that it wasn't wig powder?' asked Craddock.

'On the floor, yes. On the jacket, no.'

'You've lost me.' Craddock scratched his grey whiskers.

'When I looked at my brother's drawing, the answer just seemed to leap out. In that dim light, two white objects were very starkly portrayed. One was indeed the Captain's wig.'

'And the other?'

'Pipeclay. White pipeclay on Turnbull's shoulder strap. And then I remembered, in the pump shaft, a flash of red, which I mistook for blood, as the last man left that room. It wasn't blood, it was him trailing his coat. I had maintained all along that the culprit was an officer. No common sailor would go to so much trouble, yet everyone else in that room was just that, a member of the barge crew. So if there was an officer, did he wear a red coat, not a blue one? Then I asked you my question.'

'Hardly proof, Mr Ludlow.'

'No proof at all. And none attainable. Hence the charade.'

'But this drawing.' Craddock picked up the picture of Bentley, Turnbull and the bloody sack.

'Motive. Don't you see, Mr Craddock, that is where it all started? Young Turnbull was included in Bentley's games. No doubt that poor boy Larkin craved excitement too. But Bentley went too far. Perhaps a surfeit of drink, or merely an excess of his natural cruelty. Whatever, it cost Larkin his life, and ensnared Turnbull in a conspiracy from which he could not escape. Bentley probably assured him that it would never be discovered anyway. But he had miscalculated.'

'The hands were upset. Why? Because they knew, or suspected, that Larkin had not just fallen overboard. Those who thought they knew, tried to gather a collective protest. That looked suspiciously like mutiny, at least in the way Bentley portrayed it. Carter resorted to the cat to maintain discipline. But once the hands were cowed, Bentley, with his love of blood, did not wish to desist. Everyone knows that the relationship between Carter and Bentley started to go wrong at that time. But it moved from the odd insolent remark to outright insubordination as Carter tried to stop him. We will never know the words Bentley used, but he must have alluded to the missing boy, and at least have hinted at Turnbull's involvement. Carter couldn't arrest Bentley without implicating his nephew.'

'I cannot believe that the Captain would have knowingly condoned a murder,' said Craddock.

'Perhaps he hoped that time itself would provide a solution,' said James, diplomatically.

'No, Mr Ludlow,' said Craddock, looking at the desk and shaking his head. 'Not even for his nephew. I might not have seen eye to eye with him, but the Captain was as upright a man as you'll ever meet.'

The old lieutenant did not catch the look of disagreement on Harry's face.

'Mr Craddock. We know Bentley and the Captain had an almighty row, yet the premier continued in his duties. Everything following that argument was an attempt by Captain Carter to protect his family.'

'His sister,' said Crevitt. He was sitting over one of the chests, reading a letter, his arm in a sling. They all turned to look at him. His eyes were damp as he looked up. 'That was his family. Not him.' He gestured with his head to indicate the body in the sleeping cabin.

Harry followed the parson's gaze. 'Imagine the fear, Mr Crevitt. Do you think that Bentley would have denied himself the pleasure of turning the screw on young Turnbull, telling him how he could break his Uncle Oliver any time he chose, with a hanging in the family if Carter dared to lay charges against him? And what about the increase in his drinking?'

Harry turned back to Craddock.

'It was plain that he was becoming more unstable through excessive consumption. What with that, his relationship with Carter, and the way he baited Turnbull, it could only have seemed a matter of time before Bentley, in a drunken apoplexy, blurted out the truth on the quarter-deck. Turnbull couldn't wait for his uncle to provide a solution. He must have been racking his brain already to think of a way of saving himself. Then I arrived on board, his uncle's sworn enemy. The opportunity to rid himself of Bentley and point the blame in another direction was too good to miss.'

'He could never have hoped to get away with it,' said Craddock with genuine sincerity.

'Damn me, Mr Craddock,' snapped Harry, 'he very nearly did. And if you can explain how my brother could have cleared me, the intended victim of this plot, I'd be obliged, for it is only by the devil's own luck that I have managed to clear him.'

Craddock held up his hands to calm Harry. 'Mr Ludlow, I . . .'

'And furthermore, as to your upright Captain, he seemed mighty keen to go along with what he must have known was a conspiracy.'

'I cannot think that he knew for certain,' said Crevitt gravely. 'Although he must have suspected. I have found something that might interest you, Mr Ludlow, or rather both of you.'

He reached inside the chest and his hand came out bearing two packages, both opened letters.

'I wonder if you would care to read these?' he asked.

'Why not,' said Harry reaching out.

'This one first,' said Crevitt. 'You will observe that it is undated.'

Harry opened the letter and read it. His face registered no emotion as he did so. He passed it to James.

'From Carter,' said James, to the curious Craddock. 'To the Port Admiral.' James turned to Crevitt. 'Do I have your permission to read this out loud?' Crevitt nodded.

'His Britannic Majesty's Ship *Magnanime*, at sea. There's a gap for the date.

'Sir, Abiding by my instructions I am required to proceed with all dispatch to join Rear-Admiral Gell off Toulon. This is my primary duty, and I can in no way delay my voyage, as I would answer at my peril. You have in custody, with certain information laid against him by me, Mr James Ludlow. He stands accused of the murder of Lieutenant Bentley, late of this ship. Information has come to light, which not only throws serious doubt upon Mr Ludlow's guilt, but may entirely exonerate him of all complicity in the murder. Time and tide do not permit of me to turn my ship back to Gibraltar, but I feel the matter important enough to dispatch the bearer of this letter, in my pinnace, to deliver it into your own hand. A more detailed dispatch will follow upon this, once I have reached Admiral Gell's squadron. Until that time, I would most humbly suggest that Mr Ludlow be released from custody, and allowed all the freedom vouchsafed to an innocent man. I have taken this action to prevent a possible miscarriage of justice. I am yours, etc., Oliver Carter. Captain, His Britannic Majesty's Ship *Magnanime*.'

'The other one,' said Harry stiffly.

'The other one is his last will and testament. He added a codicil two days ago, just before we engaged the Frenchmen,' said Crevitt.

Harry took the will. He leafed through the pages, until he came to the last one. This time he read it aloud.

'I wish to state that being of sound mind and health, I have no desire to meet my maker with another death on my hands. We are about to go into action against a superior force. I shall not decline battle, and I entrust the outcome of what follows to God. Should anything happen to me, I wish to lay before the authorities my dying statement, which has the force of law. I, Oliver Carter, Post Captain, and commander of His Britannic Majesty's Ship the *Magnanime*, am wholly and individually guilty of the murder of Lieutenant Bentley of this ship.'

'Signed?' asked James. Harry nodded.
The voice from the deck came clearly through the skylight.
'All hands on deck to anchor.'

They came ashore just as they started to tow the *Magnanime* into the dockyard. Soon the sheer hulk would be alongside her, laying in a new foremast, and she'd once again be the elegant flier they had first spotted five days before.

As the boat ground against the quay, Pender jumped out first, released by Craddock into Harry's charge as a small recompense for the hands he had lost. He helped James out, and smiled as he swayed slightly on the unfamiliar land, so unmoving after weeks at sea. Harry leapt up on to the quay without assistance.

'Pender,' he said. 'Our dunnage to the Royal George, if you please, and bespeak us a couple of rooms. Come, James. After weeks at sea, you need to walk to get your balance back. I shall show you the Rock, and then we can have a "wet".' He turned back to Pender. 'See yonder tavern, Pender, half-way up the Gut. That is where we'll be in an hour. Be so good as to join us there.'

It was a dusty pair who sat there an hour later, slaking their thirst with a mixture of ale and lemonade. They had talked very little as they walked, each harbouring his own thoughts.

'Where do we go now, Harry?' asked James, waving down the road as he spotted Pender.

'We could go home. Or we could go on. Perhaps to Leghorn.' He looked keenly at his brother. 'In some ways it depends on you.'

'Ah yes,' replied James, not seeking to avoid his brother's drift.

'I have to say,' continued Harry, 'that you are in better shape than when we set out from the Downs.'

'Did you ever read Boswell's *Life of Johnson*? I remember writing to you, and recommending that you do, when it came out in '91.'

Harry shook his head. He motioned to the serving girl to fetch more drinks, pointing to Pender as well. His servant sat on a low wall a few feet away, gazing around him at the unfamiliar surroundings.

'The old man was a great wit. You said that I seem in better spirits, and it is true I am. I think Johnson hit it on the head, when he said that "the prospect of hanging concentrates the mind wonderfully". So, Harry, you decide.'

'What about you, Pender? Do you want to go home?'

'I'd rather not, your honour.'

'Why not?' said Harry, teasing him.

'Why, your honour,' he said, his eyes and teeth flashing. 'In case there be somebody like you after me at home. I wouldn't fancy that at all.'